THE HOUSE OF LIES

HEATHER ATKINSON

B
Boldwood

First published in Great Britain in 2026 by Boldwood Books Ltd.

Cover Design by JD Smith Design Ltd

Cover Images: Alamy and Shutterstock

A CIP catalogue record for this book is available from the British Library.

Paperback ISBN 978-1-83703-573-1

Large Print ISBN 978-1-83703-572-4

Hardback ISBN 978-1-83703-571-7

Trade Paperback ISBN 978-1-80656-238-1

Ebook ISBN 978-1-83703-574-8

Kindle ISBN 978-1-83703-575-5

Audio CD ISBN 978-1-83703-566-3

MP3 CD ISBN 978-1-83703-567-0

Digital audio download ISBN 978-1-83703-569-4

This book is printed on certified sustainable paper. Boldwood Books is dedicated to putting sustainability at the heart of our business. For more information please visit https://www.boldwoodbooks.com/about-us/sustainability/

Boldwood Books Ltd, 23 Bowerdean Street, London, SW6 3TN

www.boldwoodbooks.com

1

Kate Alardyce stared up at Alardyce House, her ancestral home and the place that had haunted her since she was a small child. It was two o'clock in the afternoon and the weak February sun poured onto the old grey stone, transforming the large manor house into a welcoming beacon, the light glinting off the myriad windows making it shimmer. Trees lined the driveway, their aged branches hanging over it like old, stooped men. These sentinels had sheltered the house from view of the road for almost one hundred and sixty years, cutting it off from the rest of civilisation, protecting its special magic.

Every single second in Kate's thirty-two years had been building towards this moment. Finally, she'd reclaimed her family's home which had been lost to them in the 1970s by a particularly reckless and stupid relative. Since then, it had belonged to a millionaire businessman, an idiotic lottery winner and a reclusive writer. Now, thanks to Kate's very lucrative film career, it was back in the hands of the Alardyces. In fact, she was the sole owner. This house and the many memories it cradled within its steadfast walls were finally all hers.

Kate's large blue eyes sparkled with satisfaction. She'd been obsessed with her family's notorious history ever since her grandmother had told her all the juicy stories about her scandalous Victorian ancestors. As the house had always belonged to someone else during her lifetime, she'd never been allowed to visit it before. So much love, drama and death had occurred here and since her gran had died six years ago, Kate had been keeper of the

Alardyce family's collective memory. She had every letter and diary dating from 1878, when her great-great-grandmother Amy Alardyce, nee Osbourne, had come to live here. The originals were now safely stored in a vault at Kate's bank while she obsessively read the copies she'd had made.

The breeze tousled her long chestnut-coloured hair. Kate tilted back her head and smiled as the sun's rays caressed her skin, feeling as though for the first time in her life she was home.

Alardyce was no longer the enormous estate it had once been with lots of livestock and tenant farmers. The land had gradually been sold off during the course of the twentieth century. The family fortune, including the house, had been lost entirely when some moron had inherited it at just twenty-one years of age and squandered the lot in four years. By that time all the land had already been parcelled off and only the gardens remained. The reclusive writer Kate had bought the house from had restored the gardens to their former glory, so it now sat in a colourful haven. An expanse of luscious green lawn ran all around the house, and encircling this were myriad flowerbeds that would burst with colour when summer arrived. The landscapers she'd hired had wanted to cut back the trees, but Kate had refused, knowing they were the only living witnesses to the relatives she'd always felt so close to but who had been dead for over a century. Last night, she'd dreamed the trees had whispered their secrets to her while she slept.

Kate slowly walked up the drive to the front door, the gravel crunching beneath her feet, leaving her car parked at the gates. Part of her was desperate to rush inside the house and finally see the place for herself. When she'd come to view it before buying, it had been hard to grasp the atmosphere with the owner still in residence. Part of her wanted to delay the moment. What if the house was a disappointment? What if she couldn't feel the presence of the ancestors she so longed to know better? Such a crushing disappointment would be unbearable. All the money, fame and celebrity she enjoyed were nothing to her; they'd merely been a means to an end. All that mattered was this moment and this magical place.

Before entering, Kate gazed up at the house, as though seeking permission to enter. After hesitating for a few seconds, she ascended the three stone steps up to the front door. Taking a deep breath, she slid the key into the lock, turned it and pushed open the heavy oak door.

The hall was broad and bright, and black and white tiles covered the floor.

A huge chandelier hung from the ceiling, but it was elegant rather than gaudy. The light that seeped through the front door struck it, the glass sending out bright particles of light that danced around the entryway. Kate smiled. The house was welcoming her, as though it knew here was a member of the Alardyce family at last.

The writer had repaired a lot of the damage that had been done by the previous owners. As a historical fiction author, he'd had a deep respect for the house's past and had restored many of the original features while ensuring the house had all the modern conveniences. Kate intended to put her own stamp on the place and had workmen on standby, but she'd wanted to make this initial visit alone. It was a heady feeling knowing she was in sole charge here, that no one could tell her what to do.

She took the door to her left and entered the enormous drawing room. Thanks to the detailed and extremely meticulous records left by Jane Alardyce, Amy's daughter-in-law, she knew this room had been the scene of so many dramas and tragedies. Amy Alardyce had favoured the chair by the window so she could use the light to read or embroider with her damaged, misshapen hands. Amy's husband Henry had liked to sit by the fire. In Kate's possession were several paintings and *carte de visites* of her ancestors, so she knew what they had looked like and she could imagine them gathered here with their children and feel the deep love they'd shared.

The room was devoid of furniture, the floor covered in a plush, expensive cream carpet. Unfortunately, the original wooden floor was gone, torn up and disposed of by the idiotic lottery winner. Back in the Victorian era that wooden floor would have been covered in rugs for warmth. Kate intended to replace the carpet with a replica of that floor. Thankfully the original grand fireplace had survived and sat opposite the windows in stately dignity.

The room felt to be alive, as though the past was only divided from the present by a veil so fragile she could tear it down with her bare hands and finally meet the people she'd dreamed about her entire life. Kate had never worked out why she found her long-dead relatives so much more interesting than the living ones, but she had always felt closer to them. It was such a shame that she'd been born too late.

She wandered into the small room opposite the hall from the drawing room, which was the parlour Amy had favoured, trailing her fingers across the walls as she went. To her astonishment, there was an armchair beside the original fireplace. Best of all, the chair looked old. Could it have been the chair Amy herself had used before this room had been taken over by Jane after her death? From Jane's diary, Kate knew that she had kept Amy's chair and sat in it every day as it had made her feel closer to her beloved mother-in-law.

Reverently, she moved behind the chair and rested her hands on the back of it. She had a friend who was an antiques expert, so she would get him to look it over. It would be wonderful to have something that her ancestors had used regularly. Kate was tempted to sit in the chair and enjoy the atmosphere but there was still so much to explore.

Next was the dining room, which was once again bare, but Kate could imagine the family gathered here together, enjoying a lavish meal. The echoes of their chatter and happy laughter were almost audible. Back then, they dressed for dinner, the women in elegant gowns, the men in smart suits. The food would be fresh and served over several courses, not like today with people eating slumped before the television in jeans and jumpers. It pained her how much standards had slipped.

An adjoining door took Kate into the billiard room where a modern table stood, then there was the study where first Henry and then his son John had worked, running the estate. Beyond this was another room that had been used for entertaining and hosting soirées, something the family rarely did as they'd been rather insular. It had been converted into an enormous kitchen containing top-of-the-range appliances and Italian marble worktops. Most people would have been delighted to have such an impressive kitchen, but Kate found the modernity rather jarring. She would never find her ancestors in this room, but she also recognised that having an up-to-date kitchen was a necessity.

There was also the grand conservatory where Amy had liked to read, enjoying the sound of the raindrops hitting the roof. Once it had been bursting with plants and life, but now it was bare and empty. Kate wrapped her arms around herself and shivered. Thanks to Jane's account, she knew that a man had been murdered in here. The room felt cold and hostile, so she hastily left. This was the first part of Alardyce House that had felt unwelcoming.

Upstairs there were eight bedrooms. The master bedroom had been occupied by Amy and Henry, the same room where they'd both died within a few weeks of each other. Once again, the room felt to be alive, the energies and imprints left behind by the previous occupants still making themselves known. The house was waking from the slumber it had slipped into since it had fallen out of the hands of the Alardyce family, as though it had always known that it would once again end up where it belonged. Now it was back in possession of an Alardyce, it was slowly releasing all the mysteries its thick walls still held. Soon Kate would leave an imprint of her own on the old building which would mingle with that of her ancestors', connecting her to them.

She explored the rest of the bedrooms, some feeling more alive than others. The ones that had been guest bedrooms rather than family rooms were quiet and still. One room in particular felt to be rather awake, but not in a good way. In fact, it was extremely unwelcoming. Although it was a bright day, the light failed to penetrate here and the shadows hung heavy, especially in the corners. The room was also significantly cooler than the rest of the house.

Revulsion filled Kate and she hastily left, pulling the door closed behind her. Why should that bedroom feel so different to the others? She would have to reread Jane's journals and hopefully find the answer to the mystery.

She returned to the master bedroom and decided to make this her own room. It had a beautiful view of the garden and trees. Once there had been nothing but fields visible from here, rolling out as far as the eye could see, but that was now gone. The village of Alardyce had once been small and populated by people whose families had dwelt there for decades. As the land had gradually been sold off, the once insular village had grown and expanded, new housing estates and businesses springing up, catering to those wanting to live close to Edinburgh. Perth, Stirling and Glasgow were all within easy reach too, so it was a wonderful location. The world had become so much smaller, journeys that would once have taken hours or even days reduced to nothing thanks to the ugly network of roads that now scarred what had once been open countryside. The last Alardyce to own the house before herself had hated the road that had been gouged into what had once been her family's land while the village had expanded, slowly creeping closer towards the house, so he'd had a regiment of pines planted to block out the sight. That had been the only sensible move he'd made because it meant the house had complete privacy. This was extremely important to Kate because she was very much in the public eye, fans and journalists constantly wanting a piece of her. Although she loved to act, she loathed all the attention that came with it. She'd never understood why she couldn't be left alone to get on with her job. Still, it had been worth it just to be able to buy this house at last.

The top level was next, which consisted of small chambers that had once been the servants' bedrooms but were now all completely bare.

Kate inspected the lower level last, which consisted of the wine cellar and what had once been the kitchens and storerooms. These rooms were empty and dusty and simply used for storage. She intended to turn one of these rooms into a modern gym. The renovations would begin tomorrow and would take a few months to complete, after which she intended to catch-up with the present-day Alardyces. She had only invited her four second cousins though. They'd been so close as children, the best of friends. Then a rift had occurred among their parents and they hadn't seen each other in sixteen years. Kate missed them all and she was curious to see who they were now.

This family reunion was a long time coming.

2

SIX MONTHS LATER

The silver Ford Fiesta rolled to a halt outside Alardyce House, tyres crunching on the gravel. A woman with fly-away auburn hair that just brushed her shoulders jumped out of the car with great energy amid a tangle of scarves. She pushed her tortoiseshell-framed glasses up her little snub nose, which was sprinkled with freckles, and blinked up at the house with her large blue eyes.

'Wow,' she murmured. 'It's a lot prettier than I imagined.'

The front door opened and Kate stepped out looking impossibly glamorous in a blue silk dress and matching high heels. Her hair was the same colour as the newcomer's, only longer and it streamed down her back in elegant waves.

'Lucy?' smiled Kate. 'Is that you?'

'It is. Look at you, Kate, you're so glamorous.'

'Thanks. You look nice too,' she replied sweetly, taking in Lucy's crumpled waist-length brown jacket, the belt clinging on by a single loop and dragging on the ground. Lucy's blue jeans were faded and not in the fashionable way, her white trainers scuffed.

'It's been years,' enthused Lucy. 'I remember the last time I saw you I was fourteen years old. You and Aunty June visited Mum's house in Dumfries. You were so shy and awkward with your plaits. Now you're a gorgeous, big time film star.'

'Life has been very kind to me,' smiled Kate, tossing back her hair.

Lucy wondered if she should hug her cousin but thought it might be awkward as they hadn't seen each other in years. Kate solved the quandary for her by embracing her and Lucy hugged her back heartily. She'd missed her cousin.

'I can't believe you own Alardyce House,' said Lucy, releasing her. 'It must have cost a fortune.'

'Not as much as you'd think. The previous owner was keen for a quick sale.'

'Oh aye, the writer. I read in the paper that he'd passed away after a long illness. Did he die here?' said Lucy rather ghoulishly.

'No, he died in a hospice, but he was keen on selling all his assets first.'

'Oh, I see. The vultures were circling?'

'Something like that.'

'I can't wait to see it. Just let me grab my bags.'

'No need. Marcus will do that.'

'Marcus?' frowned Lucy.

Kate nodded at something over her shoulder. Lucy turned and jumped when she saw a tall, staid man with a sallow face and neatly gelled dark hair standing right behind her.

'Oh, hello,' she said breezily to hide her surprise.

'He's the acting butler while you're staying here,' said Kate. 'He came highly recommended.'

By who, the Addams family? Lucy thought but didn't say.

'Come in, take a look around,' added Kate. 'I can't wait for you to see the place.'

Lucy glanced up at the front of the house once more before mounting the steps to the door. This was a surreal moment in her life. She too had been raised on all the stories of their notorious ancestors, but she wasn't obsessed with them like Kate was. Interested, yes, but she'd never had the burning urge to own Alardyce House as her cousin had. No one had taken seriously Kate's many announcements as she was growing up that one day she would be mistress of it, so it was difficult for Lucy to wrap her head around the fact that her cousin had achieved her ambition.

Kate gave her a tour, all the while talking excitedly. Lucy had always considered herself to be an academic – logical, stilted firmly in reality with very little imagination – so it unnerved her that as they toured the bedrooms, she felt sure someone was following them around, curious as to their purpose here.

'This is your room,' said Kate, opening the door into a pleasant, sophisticated bedroom with a wonderful view of the rear gardens.

'It's very nice,' smiled Lucy.

'All the furniture is brand new. Unfortunately, nothing of the original stuff was left here, apart from an armchair in the parlour. An expert confirmed it's Victorian. I'm positive it was the chair Amy used,' said Kate, eyes lighting up at the mention of her revered ancestor.

'Awesome,' smiled Lucy, who did share her cousin's passion for history and even worked in the field.

'This used to be Stephen's room, Henry and Amy's younger son, but he died fighting in the First World War at the Somme. The poor man was only twenty-one. It's so sad to think he left and never returned. They never even got his body back. He's the only Alardyce from that period not buried in the family crypt or the plot at the church. Anyway, I'll leave you to get settled in. Come down when you're ready.'

With that, Kate swept from the room, closing the door behind her, leaving Lucy alone with the thought that this room had once belonged to a dead man.

* * *

The next guests arrived an hour later.

'Jenna,' beamed Kate, once again slinking out of the front door in her dress and high heels to greet the newcomers as they got out of their dusty black SUV. 'How wonderful to see you again.'

'Aye, you too,' replied Jenna, patting her cousin on the back when she embraced her. 'Bloody hell, that was a sod of a drive down from Caithness.'

'How long did it take you?'

'It should have taken just over five hours but, thanks to roadworks and a traffic jam, it was nearer seven. We also got stuck on the A9 behind the slowest prick in the whole of Scotland. Why can no one put their foot down any more? It drives Simon mad,' she added, nodding at her tall, lanky string bean of a husband who didn't look in the least bit ruffled.

Simon merely nodded in agreement. His lazy, heavy-lidded eyes and dreamy smile made it appear as though he'd never once been angry in his life. Jenna in contrast was a small, round ball of fire. She too had the auburn hair that the majority of the Alardyce females had inherited from Amy. Whereas Kate and Lucy's blue eyes were large and soft, hers were smaller and narrower and burned like sapphires when she was angry.

'You look to be doing well,' said Kate, nodding at their flash Audi 4×4.

'Thanks,' smiled Jenna. 'We can't complain. Business has been pretty good. We've expanded into a holiday park with caravans and we're currently building a couple of lodges too, complete with hot tubs. Our own wee slice of heaven, eh, Simon?'

He just nodded again with a shy smile. Jenna frowned when she realised that her husband hadn't yet taken his eyes off Kate. Rather than be offended, she laughed.

'Poor Simon. He can't believe Kate Alardyce is standing before him. He's a big fan.'

'Thank you, Simon,' smiled Kate. 'And it's lovely to finally meet you.'

'He's watched all your films,' continued Jenna. 'He didn't believe me at first when I told him I was your cousin. It took me ages to convince him, even though my maiden name was Alardyce.'

'Haven't you brought the children?' Kate asked them.

Jenna's smile faltered. It hadn't gone unnoticed that Kate talked a lot posher these days, her strong Scottish accent barely audible. Anyone who didn't know her would assume she was English. 'No, we left them with my maw,' she replied, strengthening her own accent in response. 'Olivia's had the flu. She's over it now but she's still feeling pretty weak and wasn't up to the journey. Megan won't go anywhere without her; she adores her big sister.'

'Aww, that's lovely to hear. They must be about seven and five years old now?'

'Ten and eight, actually.'

'Oh, sorry. It's amazing how time flies.'

'Still, it means we get a break. We haven't had a holiday just the two of us in years, have we, Simon?' She was annoyed when he obediently shook his head without taking his eyes off Kate. Jenna turned to study the house. 'So, you've finally done it. It's all yours.'

'I'm still pinching myself,' replied Kate, gazing up at it proudly.

'Quite right. I think it's wonderful that you've fulfilled such a burning ambition.'

'Come on in and take a look. Leave the bags, Marcus will get them for you.'

Simon was similarly sneaked up on by the stealthy butler and he jumped when the man himself appeared at his shoulder. He blushed when Kate giggled.

'Has anyone else arrived?' Jenna asked as she and Simon followed her up the steps.

'Just Lucy so far.'

'Great, I haven't seen her in donkey's years.'

'She's resting in her room.'

Simon and Jenna were also given the same dizzying tour. Kate gave them the room that had belonged to Robert, Amy's son.

'Oh, it's beautiful,' breathed Jenna. 'And what a fabulous view of the maze.'

'I've had it all trimmed,' replied Kate. 'It was badly overgrown but it's ready to walk through again.'

'What's the deal with Marcus?' Jenna asked Kate. 'He seems a wee bit creepy.'

'He's very efficient and don't worry, he has no psychopathic tendencies. At least, they weren't on his CV.'

'Very funny.'

'I'll let you get settled in.'

'Settled in? You must be joking. I'm finally here after hearing about it my entire life. I want to explore. Simon will probably want a lie down though after the long drive.'

Her husband once again obediently nodded, remaining in the room while the two women left.

'He's a quiet one, isn't he?' said Kate as they made their way towards the stairs.

'The poor man doesn't have an easy time being married to me but that seems to be the way he likes it. He'd get bored with a meek wife.'

Kate wasn't so sure about that, but she didn't comment.

'So, who else is coming?' Jenna asked her.

'Well, there's Cameron and his girlfriend, Shannon. Harry said he's coming and he might or might not be bringing his wife with him,' said Kate as they descended the stairs.

'I always liked Harry. I had such a crush on him when I was younger.'

'We all did. From what he said on the phone, it sounds like he's a bit of a player.'

'I'm not surprised if he's still as tall, dark and handsome as he used to be. Poor Cameron could never compete; he looked like a beachball.' Jenna smiled and looked down at herself. 'Not that I can call out anyone's weight. I wonder if Harry's as wild and naughty as he used to be, coming up with mad schemes to get us all into trouble.'

'Like the time he convinced us to go swimming in that dangerous reservoir.'

'God, aye. My maw tore right into him for that one.' Her smile faltered. 'It's so sad that we grew apart after being so close.'

'It is. The five of us were the best of friends. We spent some brilliant summers together. Then everyone found out about my dad's affair with his colleague at work and... well. It split the family...'

'And those long, lazy summer days stopped,' said Jenna sadly.

'I never understood why everyone got so upset. I mean, it happened sixteen years before anyone knew about it. Why couldn't they just let it go?'

'I don't know but it caused so much trouble. I remember all the arguments.'

'I lost my whole family when my parents got divorced.'

Jenna bit her lip and nodded. That childhood sadness still existed deep in her bones. 'Hopefully our time here will help us rebuild, and what better place to do it than in the home of our ancestors.'

'That's just what I was thinking,' said Kate, her smile returning.

'Jenna?' said a voice.

They both turned to see Lucy standing at the top of the stairs.

'Lucy,' she exclaimed as her cousin flew down the stairs towards her. 'It's great to see you again.'

The two women embraced with happy smiles at the bottom of the stairs.

'Can you believe we're here?' beamed Lucy, releasing her. 'It's so surreal.'

The eager gleam returned to Kate's eyes. 'I've had everything refurbished to what it was in Henry and Amy's day as much as possible. This is as close as we can get to the past.'

Lucy and Jenna glanced at each other when Kate gazed around the entryway with what could only be described as zeal in her eyes.

'Yes,' said Jenna slowly. 'But neither should we forget about the present.'

'Oh, that,' said Kate with a hint of scorn. 'Yes.'

'You sound like you'd rather be in the past, which is crazy given how you're a hugely successful actress with millions in the bank.' Jenna said this in a light-hearted way but inwardly she felt a little sad for her cousin. Kate had everything anyone could ever want yet happiness still seemed to elude her.

There was the sound of tyres on the gravel outside and the breezy smile returned to Kate's face, dispelling the shadow, ever the consummate actress.

'That sounds like another arrival,' she said.

The three women rushed to the door, which was flung open by Kate before Marcus could even reach it, and they hurried outside, watching as the gaudy red Porsche screeched to a halt, sending up a spray of gravel.

'Speak of the devil and he appears,' smiled Jenna.

'Harry!' exclaimed Lucy.

The man who struggled to get out of the small, low-slung car was two stone heavier than the athletic teenager they remembered. The sun reflected off the bald spot on the crown of his head and his hair was no longer a deep, lustrous natural black but was obviously the result of a bottle of hair dye. However, he still had the same mischievous gleam in his black eyes and a roguish smile.

'Hello, ladies,' he twinkled at them. 'Come and give your big cousin a hug.'

When he opened his arms, the women rushed to him.

Kate did a good job of hiding her disappointment as they embraced, her acting skills once again coming to the fore. Harry had been so handsome in his younger days and he still was attractive, but he was far from what he had once been. Recently she'd enjoyed indulging in a fantasy of finally seducing him after he'd rejected her so many times when they'd been younger. Now she was confronted by the reality of the older Harry, she found herself lacking in enthusiasm. Maybe it was for the best; it wouldn't be very good for her career if the press ever found out she'd slept with her own cousin, although he was only her second cousin, their fathers being first cousins.

The hug ended and Harry stepped back to appraise the three women.

'What beauties you've all become,' he said.

'Don't lie, Harry,' replied Lucy. 'I look like the geek I am.'

'And I've put on so much weight,' said Jenna.

'So have I. It's called getting older.'

'Kate's the only one who's beautiful,' said Lucy.

'There's no denying that she is,' replied Harry, looking Kate up and down appreciatively. He jumped at movement behind him and whirled around to be confronted by a grim Marcus.

'Who are you, the resident ghost?' he demanded.

'This is my butler, Marcus,' said Kate.

'A butler? That's a bit posh, isn't it?' He looked back at Marcus. 'You should wear tapdancing shoes so we can hear you coming.'

'He'll take your luggage in for you.'

'Back to the good old days of servitude, eh?' He smiled at his cousin while handing the car keys to Marcus. Harry looked up at the house. 'I never thought you'd do it, Kate. I always reckoned you were deluding yourself and that our family's days as lords of the manor were long gone, but that was before I knew you were going to be a famous actress. I got a sneaking feeling though when you got your first role in that blockbuster, you know, the one with the hats?'

'Do you mean the adaptation of *The Age of Innocence*, the very famous book by Edith Wharton?' she said wryly.

'Aye, that. You put on a great American accent, by the way. Not my sort of thing though. I prefer sci-fi films with spaceships flying about and aliens. Are you ever going to do something like that?'

'No, I don't get at all inspired by that genre. I've signed up to a film next year about a nineteenth-century mill-owning family in the north of England.'

'Sounds riveting,' he said flatly. 'Anyway, where was I? I was trying to make a point. Oh aye, that was it – when I saw that film, only then did I think that you were in with a chance of getting the house back. When I got the invitation to come here, there was no way I could pass it up.'

'And we're so glad you made it,' smiled Kate. 'Where's your wife, Kathleen, is it?'

'She used to be, until I met Veronica. I divorced Kathleen and married her.'

'Oh. So where's Veronica?'

'In Hawaii with her Zumba instructor. I suppose I deserved it after cheating on my last three wives.'

'Veronica was your fourth?' exclaimed Lucy.

'Aye,' he shrugged. 'I get bored easily.'

'I'm sorry to hear about Veronica,' said Jenna while secretly thinking he was right and did deserve it.

'Not to worry. Her snoring was hideous anyway. My girlfriend's on her way up though.'

'You have a girlfriend?' spluttered Lucy.

'What can I say? I love women,' he smiled. 'You'll like Harmony, she's a sweet girl.'

'Harmony?' said Jenna doubtfully.

'I know, ridiculous isn't it, but her parents are the hippy types, all pan pipes and crystals. She's a bit of a hippy herself. A word of warning – she comes out with some bizarre things, but she means well and has a good heart. She should be here this evening; she couldn't get out of work early.'

'We'll look forward to meeting her,' said Kate, who was eager to give another tour of her home. The small talk could wait until later. She linked her arm through Harry's. 'We're going to spend a lovely few days together and have a good catch-up.'

'Just what the doctor ordered,' he replied with a hearty beam.

'But first, you must see the house.'

'I can't wait. Lead on.'

While Kate escorted Harry around the house, talking excitedly, Lucy and Jenna retreated into the drawing room to talk.

'This is all very strange,' said Jenna, her gaze wandering around the room. 'And I'm not sure I'm going to like it.'

'Why not?' replied Lucy. 'I think it's great us all being back together after sixteen years apart.'

'Don't get me wrong, that's wonderful. I mean this place. So many terrible things happened here. People were murdered. We had a couple of genuine lunatics in the family. Three if you count Matthew Bettany, which we must given that his blood runs through all our veins, even if he wasn't an Alardyce. His son was just as bad as he was.'

'Don't let Kate hear you call Robert a lunatic. She's always had a thing for him.'

'Which is bizarre given that he's her great-grandfather. It makes me really uncomfortable. Between you and me, I almost didn't come but I did want to see you all again, I've missed you so much. Even though I think it's weird, I was itching to see the house too. I had to after hearing so much about it when I was a bairn.'

'I find it fascinating but more from a professional point of view. Kate's restored the house beautifully.'

'You mean she's spent God knows how long digging up the past. I tell you, it'll lead to no good. Did you notice how she studied each of us, looking for any resemblance to the dead? I reckon she's been disappointed so far. All her hopes were no doubt pinned on Harry, but he certainly doesn't look like Robert any more, not with that fat neck and bald spot.'

'She only needs to look at herself to find the past. She really looks like Amy.'

'You've got the same hair and eyes.'

'So have you, as well as Amy's fiery personality.'

'True but I don't have her figure, sadly.'

'Me neither. I'm like an ironing board,' said Lucy, looking down at her flat chest with a self-deprecating smile.

'We must watch Kate very carefully. She's obsessed and obsession can be dangerous.'

'I think you're worrying a wee bit too much.'

'I don't think so. Are your parents still keeping up that stupid feud that destroyed our family?'

'Yes, they didn't want me to come.'

'Mine too and I know Kate's are.'

'Don't you think it was weird how over the top their reaction was all because Kate's da' had an affair with someone at work? I think there was more to it. The Alardyce family has always had dark secrets.'

'I'd never thought of it like that before, but it did make them all take sides. It could be as simple as that.'

'I asked my mum about it five years after it happened, but she told me never to mention it again. There's more to it, I'm sure.'

They lapsed into contemplative silence. Consequently, when Kate and Harry strode in arm-in-arm and laughing together, they both jumped.

'What's wrong with you two?' Harry asked. Mischief filled his black eyes. 'Have you seen a ghost?'

'No, you just startled us with all your noise,' snapped back Jenna.

'Looks like I touched a sore spot there,' he grinned. 'Anyway, where's this husband of yours?'

'Upstairs resting. It was a long drive.'

'I'm looking forward to meeting him. Kate says he's adorable.'

'She did, did she?' said Jenna, jealousy spiking inside her when she looked to her beautiful cousin, who was smiling benignly.

'And what about you?' Harry asked Lucy. 'Are you seeing anyone?'

'No,' she replied.

'Really? Not found the right man yet?'

'Yes, I mean no. I mean...' She sighed. 'There is no right man for me and there never will be because I'm gay.'

They stared at her in surprise.

'I always knew but I didn't come out until I was twenty-five,' continued Lucy. 'You're not going to freak out, are you?' she added, addressing this last comment particularly to Harry.

'Course not,' he replied. 'I'm not some relic from the stone age.' His trademark grin returned. 'Now I know why you didn't try to kiss me behind the oak tree like Jenna and Kate did.'

Jenna's cheeks turned crimson. 'We were just bairns,' she told him. 'It didn't mean anything.'

'You sure about that? I remember the begging very clearly.'

Kate playfully slapped his arm. 'Don't wind her up, we're here to have a good time and reconnect. I don't want this reunion to end with Jenna beating you to a pulp.'

'Neither do I.' Harry looked back at Lucy. 'So, any girlfriend on the horizon?'

'Not at the moment. I dated a nice woman called Emma for a while. She worked in the café at the university.'

'You're studying again?'

'No, I'm a research associate at Edinburgh University in the School of History, Classics and Archaeology.'

'Wow, impressive. Mind you, you were always interested in dusty old fossils.'

'Which makes it strange that she wasn't attracted to you,' muttered Jenna, folding her arms across her chest. She was irritated when Harry just grinned at her.

'Me and Emma broke up because she said my job would always be my first love and she was right,' continued Lucy. 'That's why I can understand Kate's fascination with this place, because I share it too. People can seem to be just as alive as us, even if they've been dead for years or even centuries.' Lucy smiled bashfully. 'Sorry, that sounded a wee bit crazy, didn't it?'

'No, it didn't,' replied Kate. 'I understand perfectly, Lucy. I'm a little obsessed myself.'

'No,' said Harry sarcastically, gesturing around him.

Kate took no offence and slapped his arm again. 'It's Gran's fault. She told us all the old tales repeatedly, even though they were too strong for children to hear.'

'My maw hit the roof when she heard she'd told me about the time Amy was tortured by her mad cousin and had her fingernails torn out,' said Jenna. 'I was only nine and I had nightmares for weeks. I would only go to sleep with gloves on because I was afraid I'd wake up with no fingernails.'

'Gran was trying to work out who would be most receptive to carrying the torch,' replied Kate. 'She didn't want our family's history to be forgotten.'

'It doesn't mean she was right though. Our family was infamous and did some terrible things. Maybe it's best if it is all forgotten?'

'It's still our history, it's where we came from. None of us would even be here if it wasn't for those people.'

'And Gran chose you to be the keeper of the history,' smiled Harry.

'Something like that,' she smiled back.

'So, History Keeper,' Harry said to Kate. 'What's next now you've bought this place?'

'I have an idea,' she replied. 'But I want to wait until Cameron's arrived.'

'So the wee beach ball's coming, is he? God, he's such a downer. He was always trying to spoil my fun when we were wee, telling me not to do something because our parents wouldn't like it.'

'That was years ago,' said Lucy. 'Give him a chance. He might not be like that any more.'

'I suppose,' he sighed. 'Let's face it, he can't be any worse.'

3

Dinner that evening was served at seven o'clock in the dining room. The guests were surprised to find Marcus on guard duty at the door into the room, which was closed.

'Can't we go in?' said Jenna when she and Simon found Harry and Lucy already waiting to enter.

'The Admirable Crichton here won't let us in,' said an irritable Harry, waving his hand at Marcus.

'I do apologise for the delay,' replied Marcus politely, although he didn't look in the least bit sorry. 'It's Ms Alardyce's orders. No one is to enter until she arrives.'

'How long is that going to take? I'm bloody starving.'

'Don't worry, Harry,' said a voice. 'Your stomach will soon be filled.'

They all turned to see Kate standing on the stairs looking glorious in a pale lilac dress that revealed her long, elegant neck and the graceful sweep of her shoulders, as well as a significant amount of cleavage. Her hair had been left to stream down her back. Harry, Lucy and Simon gaped at her while Jenna glared at her goggle-eyed husband.

'Sorry about the delay,' Kate told them as she descended the last few steps. 'But I have a surprise for you all.'

'I hope that surprise is roast chicken with all the trimmings,' said Harry, snapping himself out of it.

'Don't worry, there's plenty of food for everyone. Marcus, open the doors.'

The butler nodded and pushed open the double doors leading into the dining room before stepping aside and standing like a soldier on sentry duty as they entered.

They all spotted Kate's surprise immediately. As they'd been shown this room earlier in the day, they knew the four portraits hanging on the walls hadn't been there previously. All were very large and took up the majority of wall space, the smaller pictures that had occupied this space earlier having been removed to make way for them. Two were portraits of women, the other two of men. The older couple occupied the wall to the left of the doors and the younger couple on the right.

'Is that...' began Jenna.

'Yes,' replied Kate, smiling up at the portraits. She pointed to the pictures on the left. 'Amy and Henry Alardyce.' She then pointed to the opposing portraits. 'Jane and Robert Alardyce.'

She pronounced Robert's name in a breathy whisper that had the others glancing uncertainly at each other.

'They're very lifelike,' said Lucy. 'It feels like they could step out of the frames.'

'I know. Aren't they divine? They're by an up-and-coming artist I discovered. I'm promoting her work and when I showcase these beauties on social media, I anticipate she'll be inundated with commissions. I wanted you to see them before anyone else. It only seemed right.'

'Amy was a buxom wench, wasn't she?' grinned Harry.

'Wench?' frowned Kate. 'She was a lady.'

'That's not what I heard,' he said, smile broadening while Kate's scowl increased. 'I remember all those dull Victorian photos Gran showed us and they were always so severe. She looked all matronly and proper when in truth she was a right wee raver,' he continued, oblivious to Kate's darkening mood. 'She had a fling when she was a teenager with the footman and got pregnant with Robert.'

'That was years before she married Henry,' retorted Kate. 'She was in a committed, loving relationship with her husband for the majority of her life.'

'How can we be so sure of that? What if another footman took her fancy?'

Kate tilted back her head, eyes flashing. 'Because of the family records.

Jane went into a huge amount of detail about the love Amy and Henry shared.'

'She might have been making it up to protect their memory.' He turned to the portraits of the younger couple. 'Jane looks as much of a raver as Amy.'

'How can you insult your own blood? Amy was so brave and strong and she was pilloried enough during her life for having an illegitimate baby, something women today do all the time. It seems you've inherited all the chauvinism and ignorance of the period.'

'All right,' he said, holding up his hands, although he was smiling. 'I surrender. I won't speak a word against Lady Amy ever again.'

'Good,' sniffed Kate. 'And she was called Lady Alardyce, not Lady Amy.'

'As always, I acquiesce to your superior knowledge,' he said, placing his hand on his heart and bowing to her. 'Lady Alardyce.'

'I suppose I am now, aren't I?' said Kate, the smile returning. 'Even though the title died out decades ago.'

'And if you own land in Scotland,' chimed in Lucy, 'you automatically become a laird or a lady.'

'That's great,' said Harry. 'Now can we please eat?'

'Fine.' Kate gestured to the table. 'Take a seat.'

'The name cards will inform you which seat is yours,' said Marcus.

Jenna hadn't joined in the conversation. She was too busy studying the portrait of Robert Alardyce.

Kate came up beside her. 'Gorgeous, wasn't he?' she said.

'Yes,' Jenna replied, keeping her gaze on the picture. 'The artist has really managed to capture his essence. There's something magnetic about him,' she murmured as she felt herself being drawn in by those deep black eyes, the same colour as his hair. 'It feels like he's watching us. And judging us.'

Jenna surprised herself. The words coming out of her mouth sounded alien even to her, but this portrait felt to be alive, which wasn't good as the man's heart had been as black as his eyes. He had been very gifted in business and had built an enormous fortune, mainly from the sweat and blood of the South African diamond mines. That handsome, chiselled face had hidden a personality that was cruel and ruthless. She looked to the portrait of Jane on the right. It was beautiful; she'd been a lovely woman with gentle blue eyes and blonde curls, but it was what it appeared to be – a picture, nothing more. So were Henry and Amy's pictures. Only Robert's was imbued with a potent energy. Her eyes flicked to his large, pale hands that had committed so many atrocities, and she shivered as she experienced a presentiment of dread. This house had seen so much love, but it had also known pure evil. What if that evil hadn't truly gone?

* * *

Harmony arrived during dinner. She was a whirlwind of smiles, energy and enthusiasm.

'What a gorgeous house,' she said as she was escorted into the dining room by Marcus. 'So pretty but grand at the same time. It was a lovely drive too, the weather's been so wonderful, hasn't it?'

Harmony continued to rabbit on, so Harry got to his feet to interrupt. 'Why don't you sit down and eat,' he told her. 'You must be starving.'

'I am. I skipped lunch because I had so much work to do. My boss is a proper bastard. I tell you, karma's coming his way, and soon. You can't go around putting that much negative energy into the world without some of it being slung right back at you.'

Harmony was a lovely-looking woman. Tall and lithe with waist-length light-brown hair. Her hazel eyes were wide and shone with a naïve optimism. She wore black leggings and a baggy white shirt. A clear quartz pendant dangled around her neck from a black cord.

As she continued to talk, Marcus swiftly placed a plate of food before her. They were all relieved when she tucked in and silence reigned.

'What do you do, Harmony?' Lucy asked her.

She paused shovelling peas into her mouth. 'I work in an insurance call centre. I hate it but it's only temporary. I'm saving up to open my own holistic centre.'

'What's that?'

'I'll do reiki healings, group meditations, massage, yoga, angel therapy and reflexology. I also hope to have a wee shop attached where I'll sell crystals and candles and...'

'What's wrong?' said Jenna when Harmony's eyes widened and she trailed off.

'Who is that?' she replied, nodding at the opposite wall.

She turned in her seat to look. 'Robert Alardyce, Harry's great-grandfather.'

'Really? He looks so powerful, so masterful,' she breathed.

Everyone glanced at each other when she gazed at the picture with her wide, honest eyes. Only Kate appeared pleased with her reaction.

'I take after him, don't I?' said a pleased Harry.

Harmony gave him a withering smile that made his own grin drop.

* * *

After everyone had finished eating, they all retired to the drawing room. It was eight thirty in the evening and still bright outside.

'I wish it was winter,' said Harmony as Marcus handed around the coffees. 'I bet this room would be really cosy with the fire going.'

'I find it so exciting that generations of our family have done in this very room what we're doing right now,' said Kate.

'I wonder if their dinners were as good as the one we've just had,' said a contented Harry, who sat beside Harmony on the couch. 'I've had to loosen my trousers.'

'Thanks for sharing,' said Simon disdainfully.

'Oh, so you do speak then?' retorted Harry.

'The menu was based on a meal recorded in the housekeeper's book for Henry's fortieth birthday,' said Kate.

'That is fascinating,' said Lucy, pushing her glasses up her nose when they slipped down again. 'I would love to look through those records.'

'You want to read about the contents of the larder?' said Harry with a raised eyebrow.

'Records like that can tell us so much. They're like a window into the past.' Lucy took no offence to his scepticism. Harry had always been a bit of a sarcastic git. As a child, he'd got too used to getting away with things others wouldn't because of his good looks; however, without them, the ugly side of his personality was more obvious.

'Into the dull part of the past.' Harry looked to Marcus and held out his coffee cup. 'Slip some brandy in that, will you? It needs livening up.'

Marcus nodded, fetched the brandy bottle from the drinks trolley and poured in a splash.

Harry sipped his coffee and brandy and jumped when the doorbell rang, slopping some of the liquid down himself. 'Bugger,' he sighed. 'My best shirt too.'

'That must be Cameron,' said Kate. 'He's made it at last.'

They all put down their drinks and hurried into the hallway, eager to greet the new arrival.

Marcus opened the door with stately dignity to a tall woman with long dark curly hair, green eyes and very long legs. A light summer rain had started to fall earlier that evening and the woman's hair and cheeks were damp with it.

'Hello,' she smiled coyly when confronted by a group of people all staring at her. 'My name's Shannon. I'm Cameron's girlfriend. Cameron's just getting the bags out of the car.' She glanced over her shoulder. 'Here he comes now.'

Shannon stepped aside and in walked a lofty, broad-shouldered figure. His features were obscured by the hood of his coat, which he'd put up against the rain. He dumped the two small suitcases on the floor and threw back the hood.

They all stared at him in amazement. Standing before them was Robert Alardyce.

'Oh God,' said Simon. 'I knew I shouldn't have had the extra glass of wine. I'm seeing things now. The man from the picture has come alive. I knew he would,' he cried.

'Don't worry, Simon,' said Jenna. 'We see it too.'

'See what?' replied Cameron in a deep, powerful voice.

Kate stepped up to greet him, eyes wide with wonder. 'You look exactly like the portrait of Robert Alardyce in the dining room.' Her gaze flicked over him, taking in every detail – here was the same sulky mouth, the sharp cheekbones, pitch-black eyes and large white hands. 'It's uncanny.'

'Robert Alardyce?' said Shannon. 'That's your great-grandfather, isn't it, Cam?'

'Yes,' replied Kate without taking her eyes off Cameron.

'I suppose it's only natural there's a resemblance,' she said with a forced smile, not liking the way everyone was staring at her boyfriend in amazement.

'It's more than a resemblance,' said Lucy. 'He's absolutely identical.'

Her voice roused Kate from her thoughts. 'How rude of me keeping you standing here in the hallway,' she smiled.

She made the introductions, which were more for Shannon's benefit than Cameron's. Kate had to keep her gaze off her cousin, but it was an effort. She was utterly bewitched. The man was identical to someone she'd been fascinated with her entire life.

After much hugging and handshaking, they all wandered into the drawing room where Marcus served the new arrivals with dinner, a disapproving frown on his face. He had suggested they eat in the dining room, but Kate had immediately vetoed that suggestion by saying it would be rude to shove them into that room all alone when they could be with the rest of the family. The truth was, it would have made more sense for them to eat in the dining room, but she couldn't bear to lose sight of Cameron just yet. It was as though the past she longed to be a part of had suddenly burst into the present. Excitement filled her. This was what she'd been waiting for. The house on its own hadn't been enough; she'd needed something to make her feel that her ancestors were still alive, and then in walked Cameron to make everything perfect. Her enthusiasm was such she could barely sit still and she wrung her hands together.

'What happened to you, Cam?' said Harry in his usual blasé way. 'You're actually a fine figure of a man. Not quite as fine as myself, but very few are,' he added, causing all the women to raise their eyebrows doubtfully. 'You might not know this, Shannon, but he used to be a wee round pudding of a boy.'

'Actually, I do,' she replied. 'He showed me photos of himself when he was a wean and he was adorable.'

'Puberty happened,' said Cameron. 'And I stopped eating crap and started playing football and going to the gym.'

'Good for you,' said Harry, raising his freshly refilled coffee mug in a toast.

'So you can't call me all those names you used to call me when we were boys, like fat arse, dumpling and thunder thighs.'

There was a jocular tone to Cameron's voice but something in those black eyes of his made Harry uneasy. However, he couldn't be sure it wasn't his imagination caused by the alcohol and the shock of his resemblance to that unnerving portrait in the dining room. It occurred to Harry that when younger he'd relentlessly teased a man who was now identical in appearance to a murderer. He just hoped the similarity was only skin deep.

When playfulness entered Cameron's eyes, Harry laughed a little nervously and took a swig of his coffee and brandy.

'What do you think about finally being in Alardyce House?' Lucy asked Cameron.

'It's pretty awesome,' he replied. 'And a little weird.'

'Weird in a good or bad way?'

'I'm not sure yet. We all heard about this place through our childhoods, so it's almost become a living thing in my mind.'

'Don't say that,' said Jenna, a shiver running down her spine for the second time that evening.

'I know I sound like a daftie but Gran was an amazing storyteller and everything she talked about sounded so alive. She made me believe in selkies, will-o'-the-wisps and the caoineag.'

'What's a caoineag?' said Simon, pronouncing it badly.

'The Scottish equivalent of the Irish banshee,' replied Kate.

'Me too,' Lucy told Jenna. 'I was so afraid that one night I'd hear the caonieag's scream and then someone I loved would die. I used to have nightmares about it. My mum went mad at Gran for filling my head with her stories.'

'With our history I'm amazed our family doesn't have its very own caoineag,' said Jenna.

'I hate to say it about our grandmother,' said Harry, 'but the woman was deranged.' He held up a hand when they all scowled at him, particularly Kate. 'Oh, come on, you have to admit it was weird her telling us what our ancestors got up to when we were all so young. I was only seven when she told me Edward Alardyce murdered all those servant girls. She went into all the gory details too. I didn't sleep for a week after that.'

'His body's buried in the crypt at the edge of the garden,' said Kate. 'I must show you all.'

'So many times I considered coming here and asking the owner if I could have a look around. The writer owned it at the time and I decided against it when I heard he was a bad-tempered recluse,' Lucy replied.

'You should have gone for it,' said Kate. 'He was fascinated by our family's history and would have loved to talk to a living Alardyce.'

'Harry has a point though,' said Jenna. 'Gran used to tell us the most age-inappropriate stories.'

'Age inappropriate?' replied Harry, arching an eyebrow. 'Don't tell me you're one of those ridiculous woke people?'

'Do you even know what woke means?'

'I just know that it's made everyone afraid to speak in case they offend some weak wee snowflake.'

'Gran loved going into detail about the passion between certain couples,' said Lucy with a naughty grin.

'I remember that,' replied Jenna. 'It made me really uncomfortable.'

'She was just enthusiastic about the subject,' said Kate. 'Gran only talked to us about it because our parents refused to discuss it. She was proud while they were ashamed and she was so scared it would all be forgotten. There's nothing wrong with that.'

'You're right,' said Lucy. 'It should be preserved and we're the ones to do it.'

'I think it's really interesting too,' said Shannon. 'Cam told me all about it.'

'Our ancestors could be watching us right now,' said Kate.

'What are you talking about?' demanded Jenna.

'Don't you believe in ghosts?' she replied.

'You mean vengeful wraiths draped in white sheets? No, I do not. What a load of shite.'

Kate could tell the subject made Jenna uneasy, and her lips curled into an impish smile. 'This house has such a colourful history. Violent acts have been committed here and all that fear and emotion has been absorbed by the building, which means we can still feel the essence of those events and the people involved in them.'

Jenna couldn't help but glance around uneasily. The sun was finally beginning to set, scattering vague shadows about the room. She wished someone would switch on a light.

'So you're saying it's not actually ghosts,' Lucy asked Kate. 'Just their emotions?'

'It's both,' said Harmony, speaking with authority on the subject. 'Often the spirit moves on, leaving behind echoes of themselves that can be sensed by sensitive people. Or the spirit gets stuck and remains to haunt a place, either because they've got unfinished business or because they loved it so much they can't bear to leave it. I'm sensitive and, in my opinion, both types of hauntings are here.'

Everyone looked around uneasily. The only light came from the fire.

Harry switched on the lamp on the table beside him and smiled with satisfaction when the shadows that had felt to be closing in retreated.

'I don't believe in ghosts either,' said Shannon. 'No offence, but I've never experienced anything that makes me think they do exist.'

'Just because you haven't experienced them doesn't mean they don't exist,' said Harmony.

'You've spent time alone here, Kate,' said Lucy. 'Have you noticed any spooky occupants?'

'No, but one of the bedrooms is really creepy,' she replied. 'I can only stand it for a few seconds before I have to get out, which is weird because all the other rooms feel so welcoming, apart from the conservatory. That's spooky too, but I think that's only because I know a man was murdered in there.'

'Really?' said Harmony. 'What happened?'

'An intruder had his head bashed in with a rock.'

Her eyes lit up. 'Ooh, interesting.'

'You're a ghoul,' Harry told his girlfriend. Personally, he wasn't that interested in the family history. He was a man who constantly looked to the future, to the next opportunity. That was what he told himself anyway so he could ignore the unease that rippled up and down his spine at this talk.

'Do you know that a violent or traumatic death leaves a lot of energy behind that can be tapped into by the living as well as the dead?' said Harmony.

'What is wrong with you all?' demanded Jenna. 'This is supposed to be a nice family reunion and you're turning it into *The Sixth Sense*.' Dread had her in its grip. She didn't like to think of her family's very bloody past. She'd hoped this reunion would be about reconnecting and discovering each other again, not revelling in the evil that had occurred in this house.

'Someone's getting scared,' chuckled Simon, his speech slightly slurred.

As they talked, Cameron realised Kate was staring at him with a disturbing intensity. He'd always thought she was a bit strange when they were kids, especially with regard to her obsession with this house and the people who'd lived in it. Yes, she was beautiful, she always had been, but the strangeness for him negated that. It was why he'd never got jealous when she'd cosied up to Harry when they were children and not him.

Instead, he looked to Shannon, who in his opinion eclipsed Kate entirely. She smiled back at him and took his hand. When he glanced back at Kate, he saw she was still staring at him.

What the hell was her problem?

4

Cameron got a good idea of why Kate had been staring at him so intently when he entered the dining room for breakfast the following morning. Always an early riser, he was up before the rest of the family.

Marcus was placing a large silver dish filled with pastries in the centre of the huge table.

'Help yourself, sir,' the butler told him, gesturing to the large amount of food spread out not only on the table but on the sideboard too.

'Please call me Cameron,' he replied. '*Sir* makes me uncomfortable.'

'I'm sorry but I've had my instructions.'

'Surely my cousin didn't order you to call me sir?'

'Yes, sir. Not just you but all the men. And I've to call the women *madam*.'

'Because that's how it was done back in the day?'

'Yes, sir,' he replied to Cameron's consternation.

Deciding he was fighting a losing battle, Cameron turned to the dishes lined up on the sideboard. 'What's this?' he frowned when he removed the silver cloche.

'Kedgeree, sir,' replied Marcus.

'What's that?'

'Basmati rice, flaked haddock, boiled eggs, cream, lemon and curry powder.'

Cameron hastily replaced the cloche. 'No thanks. Does anyone even eat kedgeree any more?'

'Madam insisted on the same food being served for each meal as was served in the late Victorian period.'

'Seriously?'

Marcus nodded. 'But not to worry, we have porridge, eggs, bacon and kippers,' he said, lifting another cloche, Cameron grimacing at the fishy smell.

'I'll stick with porridge, thanks.' He wasn't really surprised by all this. Kate had always had a fascination with the Victorian era, so why shouldn't she live her dream to its fullest? She'd certainly earned that right.

'Take a seat, sir, and I'll get you a bowl. Tea or coffee?'

'Tea, please.'

While Marcus began arranging his breakfast, Cameron turned and caught sight of the pictures on the opposite wall. At first, he thought it was a mirror until he realised his reflection wore period clothing. This had to be the portrait the others had mentioned the previous night. No wonder his appearance had startled them so much.

He read the name on the copper plate at the bottom of the picture frame – Robert Alardyce.

'A very striking portrait, sir,' said Marcus as he placed a bowl of porridge on the table.

'Very,' murmured Cameron. 'Is it my imagination or…'

'No, sir. He's the very image of you.'

Despite his shock, Cameron thought Marcus had an odd way of talking. He sounded like something from the Victorian era himself. Was that why Kate had hired him or had he been instructed to act like that? Cameron turned his attention back to the portrait. It had been uncomfortable knowing that a murderer's blood flowed through his veins but seeing the resemblance to said murderer was rather disconcerting. At least he could be secure in the knowledge that the resemblance was only skin-deep. He'd never once had the urge to hurt anyone in his life. Well, except for the boys who had bullied him all through school. Cameron's large white hands clenched into fists. He'd wanted to hurt them badly.

Shannon entered the dining room next and found Cameron standing by the table gaping at something.

'Morning, gorgeous,' she smiled. 'What's wrong?' She frowned when he failed to respond.

Shannon followed his gaze and her eyes widened. 'I didn't know you'd had your portrait painted,' she said.

'I didn't,' he replied. 'It's Robert Alardyce.'

'Wow, that's more than a resemblance. He's your doppelganger, or I suppose you're his, given how he was born first. Sorry, I'm not helping, am I?'

'Not really.'

Shannon noticed that his already ivory-coloured skin had turned even paler and realised the resemblance was freaking out her boyfriend. 'Marcus, could you take the picture down, please?'

'I'm sorry, madam, I couldn't possibly do such a thing without Ms Alardyce's express permission.'

'I'll do it then,' she said, walking over to the portrait.

'It's extremely heavy, it took three workmen to hang it.'

'Leave it there, it's fine,' said Cameron, finally managing to turn his attention to his breakfast. He took a seat at the table and picked up his spoon, staring at the porridge while making no move to eat it.

'Cam,' said Shannon, gently. 'You okay?'

'Aye,' he replied, shaking himself out of it. 'Fine.'

Cameron tucked into his porridge while Shannon had the breakfast spread explained to her by Marcus. He tried to concentrate on his food, but the portrait was a constant lurking presence, his ancestor staring down at him disapprovingly. Instead, he turned his attention to the picture beside it of the beautiful blonde, the name plate announcing it was Robert's wife, Jane. Irresistibly his attention was soon drawn back to the portrait of Robert, its commanding presence demanding attention. He couldn't deny that it held a special power. It was unsettling but Cameron also felt there was something in it to be admired. He was willing to bet that no one had ever dared try to bully Robert Alardyce.

The rest of the family came downstairs in quick succession and, rather than provide a distraction from the severe image, each one of them pointed out the resemblance, as though he could miss it.

Harry finally made an appearance looking pale and unwell, his eyes bloodshot. As he entered the dining room, Marcus just happened to place some cutlery on a tray with a rattle.

'Are you trying to kill me?' groaned Harry, pressing a hand to his aching head.

'Coffee, sir?' replied Marcus.

'Please,' sighed Harry, slumping into a chair between Simon and Harmony.

'Feeling delicate this morning, are we?' said Jenna with a knowing smile.

'Aye. I shouldn't have had that brandy, it always takes me this way, but I can't resist it. A strong cup of coffee and I'll be fine. So, where's our hostess? Don't tell me she's still lounging about in bed after I dragged my carcass down here?'

'Madam never descends before nine,' said Marcus.

'It's all right for some,' muttered Harry.

Ten minutes later, Kate floated into the room in a long light-blue robe with very wide sleeves, little white slippers on her dainty feet.

'How did everyone sleep?' she asked while elegantly slipping into the chair at the head of the table.

'I passed out and that was it until Harmony dug her elbow in my ribs and said it would be rude if we didn't come down,' replied Harry.

'I slept very well,' said Lucy. 'My bed's so comfy and it's really peaceful out here. I didn't even hear a car, which is so relaxing after living in the centre of Edinburgh for the last seven years.'

'Wonderful,' purred Kate as Marcus placed a cup of lemon tea before her. 'How would you all like to take a tour of the grounds today?'

'Sounds good,' said Lucy. 'I really want to learn about the history of agriculture in the area.'

'If that's going to be the height of today's excitement then I'm going back to bed,' said Harry.

'Oh no you don't,' replied Kate. 'It's been ages since we spent any time together as a family, so you're coming with us. I promise you'll find it entertaining.'

'Well, that sounds intriguing. I accept.'

'I'm honoured,' she said wryly before taking a sip of tea. Her eyes flicked to Cameron over the rim of the cup.

Cameron didn't like the smile she gave him.

* * *

After everyone had finished eating, they dressed, pulled on their shoes and tramped outside into the sunshine together, Kate leading the way.

'We'll start with the rear gardens first,' she cheerfully called over her shoulder, striding on ahead.

'Why does she have to walk so fast?' moaned Harry, who trailed behind the others.

Jenna and Simon walked directly behind Kate. When Jenna saw her husband's eyes were locked on her cousin's backside, she smacked him hard on the arm, causing him to hastily avert his gaze.

'The maze,' said Lucy when it rose up before them. 'I remember Gran saying something bad happened here once, something evil, but I can't remember what it was,' she murmured more to herself than anyone else.

'It's smaller than I thought it would be,' replied Harry.

'I bet you've heard that plenty of times,' Simon called back to him.

'For someone who's supposed to be quiet you aren't half mouthy.'

'Is it made from yew hedges?' Lucy asked Kate as they came to a halt before the entrance to the maze.

'Well spotted,' she replied. 'Yes, it is.'

'It's a good hedge for a maze – low maintenance, dense and it can be easily cut into different shapes.' Lucy frowned at Harry when he yawned.

'I love mazes,' said Harmony before rushing inside.

'Someone go after her, for God's sake, or we might never see her again,' said Harry.

'Why don't you go?' replied Simon. 'She's your girlfriend.'

'We'll all go in,' said Kate before stepping into the maze followed by Shannon, Cameron and Lucy.

'You'd better go too,' Jenna told her husband. 'Before you lose sight of Kate's arse.'

He just shrugged before following the others.

'I take it everything's not harmonious?' Harry asked Jenna when she sighed and sank onto a bench that sat beside the entrance to the maze.

'I don't know what's come over Simon. He's normally so sweet and loyal but he can't stop talking about Kate.'

'Really? The only time I've ever heard him speak is to insult me.'

'Kate's so beautiful and glamorous and I'm... not. I've tried losing weight, but it didn't work. I don't have the willpower.'

'To be fair, he's no oil painting. He looks like a male version of Olive Oyl.'

Jenna sniggered. 'You always could make me smile, Harry.'

'At least I'm still some use even though I'm no longer the heart-throb of the family.'

'Don't do yourself down, you're still a very attractive man. You've not lost your charm.'

'Kate could never love or care about anyone more than she does this place. She won't even notice Simon's attention and he'll soon get bored.'

'I suppose. It's insulting the way he's blatantly ogling her in front of me though. I'd never do the same to him.'

'You've got a solid marriage with children, a business and a home. That counts for much more than beauty, which is only skin deep.'

'As well as talent and millions in the bank.'

'My point is, what you already have means far more to him than all that.'

'I'm not so sure but I appreciate you trying to cheer me up.'

'I wouldn't object if you pinched my arse a few times and complimented me on my devastatingly good looks if you wanted to make him jealous?'

'That's not a bad idea but I wouldn't want to upset Harmony.'

'You won't. She doesn't get jealous. She doesn't believe anyone can have a claim over another person like that.'

'That sounds convenient.'

'It is,' he smiled. 'So, do you want to go into the maze?'

Jenna was tempted to go after her husband, but she had her dignity. 'No. Hopefully Simon will get lost in it.'

'That's the spirit.'

'Listen to you being sensitive and caring.'

'I know but don't tell anyone, will you? I'd hate to ruin my reputation as a devil-may-care playboy who leaves broken hearts in his wake.'

Jenna smiled. This reunion wasn't all bad. If her husband wanted to embarrass himself that was up to him, but she'd missed her cousins and she refused to allow Simon to spoil them getting to know each other again. She just hoped the darkness that slumbered in Alardyce House didn't come alive once again and hurt their generation as it had their ancestors.

* * *

'Shannon, where are you?' called Cameron. He sighed when no one replied. Stopping, he turned and looked behind him but all he saw were those damn hedges rising up either side of him. Everyone had taken different turnings in the maze and he'd quickly ended up alone. From the outside, the maze didn't look that big but inside it was huge. The sound was also muted, the high hedges blocking everything out, making him feel even more isolated.

'Shannon?' he repeated. 'Lucy?'

Cameron sighed. Nothing. What if they'd all made it out and he was the only one stuck inside, wandering about like an idiot? He'd never had a very good sense of direction.

He took another couple of turns and suddenly found himself in the centre of the maze. The ground was paved, some of the flags cracked and uneven. There was a fountain surrounded by a low circular wall. In the middle of the fountain was a great big gruesome stone fish, water spurting from its mouth. On the wall was perched, to his dismay, Kate.

'I'm glad someone finally made it,' she said.

'You've not seen the others?' he replied.

'No, but they're close. I've heard them a few times.'

'How can you hear anything in here? The sound is so deadened.'

'I know. It's weird, isn't it? I've always had very sharp hearing though.'

Cameron wasn't sure what to do when Kate got to her feet and stalked towards him. He took a couple of steps back and was tempted to delve back into the maze, but his innate sense of politeness wouldn't let him. She was looking at him in that odd, predatory way again.

'Do you know that someone died in here?' she said, coming to a halt right before him.

'It seems someone's died everywhere around here,' he replied.

'For once, it wasn't by our family's hand. The police shot a woman who'd abducted Robert and Jane's daughter.'

'That's terrible.'

Kate shrugged. 'If you ask me, the bitch got what she deserved.' She studied his reaction to this statement, hoping to see the same fascination for the subject in his eyes, but she failed to find it. Kate wasn't disheartened though; she was certain she could provoke his interest. 'The woman died right there, on the ground beside the fountain, a bullet in her head,' she added, gesturing to the area.

'Really?' said Cameron. A shiver ran down his spine. The noise the wind made as it rushed through the hedges made it sound as though they were whispering.

'Yes, really,' she replied, staring at him steadily. 'Robert was an extremely capable man. He got things done. In my experience, they're a rare breed these days.'

'He also did horrible things.'

She shrugged as though all the attacks on women and the murders he'd committed meant nothing. 'That was when he was younger. He grew up to be in absolute control of himself, which is to be admired. Are you in control of yourself, Cam?'

'Sometimes,' he slowly replied, thinking the question a weird one.

'You're just like him,' she said, gazing at him wistfully. 'Physically anyway.' She tilted her head to one side. 'I wonder if you're like him in other ways?'

'No, I'm bloody not. I don't hurt women or murder people.'

'You might feel different if you were a father whose child was threatened. A lot of parents could happily kill with their bare hands anyone who hurt their baby. Ask Jenna and Simon, I'm sure they'll agree.'

'I'm not a father, so I couldn't say,' he replied, glancing around, wishing someone else would come along, but they seemed to be entirely alone.

'Yes, Robert did bad things, but sometimes there was a good reason for them.'

'Most of the time there wasn't,' he retorted.

'Everyone's very hard on him but if you read Jane's account about him then you'd feel differently. He couldn't have been all bad to inspire such love.'

'Maybe, but we'll never know for sure because they're all dead,' he said, trying to drill that fact into her head.

Cameron was relieved when Lucy and Shannon suddenly appeared. They were arm-in-arm and chatting happily. Kate frowned and took a few steps back from Cameron.

'There you are,' he said, rushing up to Shannon and sweeping her to him. 'I thought I'd lost you forever.'

'It'll take more than a maze to do that,' she smiled.

As the pair kissed, both Kate and Lucy appeared put out. The cousins glanced at each other, recognising they both had a crush on the two halves of that pair.

'Hello, is anyone there?' called a tremulous voice.

Harmony stumbled into the centre from the opposite side of the maze. Her hair was in disarray, leaves stuck in it.

'What happened to you?' frowned Kate.

'I tripped over a loose flag and fell into a hedge.'

Kate's eyes widened. 'Did you damage it?'

'No, but it tore out a few strands of my hair,' she replied, taking no offence to the question.

They all jumped at the sound of a blood-curdling cry and Simon tore into the centre of the maze, wild-eyed.

'What's wrong?' Lucy asked him as he came to a sudden halt and glanced back over his shoulder at the direction he'd come.

'Someone was following me,' he exclaimed.

'It was probably Harry playing a trick on you.'

'No, it wasn't him. It wasn't anyone.'

'Then how could someone have been following you?'

'I heard them breathing on the other side of the hedge. When I peered through it, no one was there.'

'It was just the breeze,' said Kate.

'They were inhaling and exhaling, like a person, I swear.' He frowned when they all smiled. 'I'm not making it up.'

'We don't think you are,' replied Kate. 'You just let your imagination get the better of you. The acoustics are strange in this place.' She hooked her arm through his. 'Let's get out of here. There's so much more to see.'

'I'd like that,' he replied with a dopey smile, feeling better already.

'He has got it bad,' commented Lucy to the others as the two of them left together. 'I feel sorry for Jenna,' she added before following.

Harmony went too, leaving Cameron and Shannon alone together.

'Aren't you coming?' she asked him when he refused to move.

'Kate was telling me how much like Robert I am and I don't like it. He was a murderer, for God's sake.'

'Did you tell her you don't like it?'

'Aye, but she didn't listen.'

'Want me to have a word with her?'

'No, thanks. Maybe we should leave, just get away from this place. It has such a bad history.'

'We can if you want but it's so beautiful and all that was over a century ago. You were excited yesterday about being around your cousins again.'

'I know but Harry's more sarcastic than ever, Jenna's bitter and Kate's just weird.'

'Lucy's nice. We had a lovely chat going through the maze.'

'She's the only one who reminds me of the person I used to know. The others have changed so much.'

'Which is even more reason why you should get to know them all over again. Just give it a bit longer. We've been here barely twelve hours.'

'Maybe you're right. I could just do without all the comparisons to Robert.'

'I get that. It must be creepy for you.'

'It is but it's not just that. Terrible things have happened here. What if they start happening again now an Alardyce is back in residence?'

'I think you're being a bit superstitious. All that was over decades ago.'

'I suppose,' he mumbled reluctantly.

'Come on, let's carry on with the tour of the estate. We've not had a break in ages, so let's make the most of it.'

The twinkle in her green eyes made him feel better and he kissed her. 'All right, I'll do it, for you.'

As they left together, Cameron's arm slung around her shoulders, he couldn't help but look back over his shoulder at the fountain, imagining he saw a widening patch of blood on the cracked flags. He blinked and the impression vanished. It must have just been the shadows.

* * *

After the party had regrouped, the tour continued further down the rear gardens, which were vaster than everyone had initially thought. Kate continued to lead the way, Jenna, Simon and Harry falling behind the more athletic members of the group.

'And here we are,' said Kate with an eager smile, turning to address them all when they reached the boundary wall marking the end of Alardyce territory. 'The family crypt.'

'I might have known,' sighed Harry. 'Is there no cheerful Alardyce summerhouse or rose garden?'

'There were but they were destroyed ages ago,' she replied dismissively.

'This crypt was built with the house in 1867 and housed every Alardyce up to 1897, when it ceased to be used and all Alardyces were instead buried in the family plot in the village cemetery. Even Alardyces who didn't live in Edinburgh were brought here for burial, so there are quite a lot of bodies in the crypt.'

'Wow, a whole thirty years,' said Harry sarcastically.

'Why did it stop being used?' enquired Harmony.

'Because Henry had his brother Edward interred here,' replied Kate. 'No one else wanted to be buried alongside him.'

'Why not?'

Kate frowned at Harry. 'Have you told her nothing of our history?'

'I've given her a vague outline,' he replied with a dismissive wave.

'Edward was a rapist and serial killer,' Kate told her. 'He was hanged for his crimes. His older brother Henry, who inherited the estate on their father's death, had his body brought back here for burial. He told no one else but it came out later and the family decided they didn't want to lie next to him for eternity, so they bought the plot at the church. Besides, there's two murder victims in here too,' she added, nodding at the crypt.

'What?' her relatives exclaimed as one.

'Oh,' she said, a little shocked by their reaction. 'Didn't you know?'

'No, we did not,' retorted Jenna. 'Who are they?'

'A man called Hobbs and Robert's paternal grandmother.'

'You mean the footman's mother?' said Harry.

'Yes. Robert killed them both. Henry helped him cover up the crimes by stashing the bodies in here.'

'More victims of Robert's?' sighed Cameron, shaking his head. 'Jesus Christ.'

'Have the police been notified?' said Lucy.

'I did have a word with a certain chief constable friend of mine,' replied Kate. 'He's a big fan and he said to leave them where they were. It's not as if the killer can be prosecuted and it would just waste police resources which could be put to much better use.'

'Surely something has to be done?' spluttered Jenna. 'You can't just leave them in there.'

'What do you want the police to do? Dig up Robert and stick his body in a prison cell?'

'I suppose not, but it does seem wrong.'

'I agree they're best left where they are,' said Lucy. 'No good can come from disturbing the dead, and who the hell would want to go in there and rummage through all those dead bodies to find the right ones?'

Jenna shivered. 'Good point.'

Kate's smile was sunny. 'Does anyone want a look inside the crypt? I have the key.'

They all shook their heads.

'In that case, we'll move on. I thought we could take a walk into the village and visit our relatives in the churchyard. It's not far.'

'God, this is like the Addams Family's day out,' sighed Harry.

'There's a lovely café in the village,' she added cheerfully. 'They do home-made cakes and scones. We can stop there after the church.'

This cheered them all a little and they obediently tramped along the path that cut through the grounds of Alardyce House to the village, Kate continuing to lead the way.

'The boundary of the village starts a lot closer to the house than it did in the Victorian era,' she called over her shoulder as they walked, providing them with a running commentary. 'Back then, they would have had to walk a lot further, but the village is practically on our doorstep now.'

'Wasn't there a lake with the house?' Lucy asked Kate.

'Yes, but it was part of the land that was sold off,' she replied bitterly. 'The person who bought that section of land built a house next to it, so we can't visit it as it's private property, which is a shame because it really is beautiful. The good news is the current owners are having money troubles, so I hope to buy it back soon.'

'Let me guess,' said Harry. 'Someone died at the lake, didn't they?'

'Yes. Robert threw the mad housekeeper in it when she attacked his mother and she drowned.'

'Robert's racking up quite the body count,' commented Shannon. Her smile dropped when she noticed Cameron's troubled look, and she took his arm.

5

The family had to cross the new main road into the village, which was quite busy. After making a mad dash across it, they found themselves entering a surprisingly cosmopolitan village complete with a couple of trendy coffee shops, a florist's, a delicatessen and a bookshop.

'It's a long way from the quaint wee village I'd imagined,' said Lucy sadly.

'I think it's lovely,' smiled Jenna.

Simon, Jenna and Harry were lured towards the coffee shop by the delicious aroma but, to their consternation, Kate waved them on past it, heading towards the church at the far end of the street.

They all spotted the way passersby and the people sitting outside the coffee shop nudged each other and pointed at Kate. What was more astonishing was the transformation in Kate. She put on a dazzling smile and tossed back her mane of chestnut-coloured hair. When a young couple approached and asked if they could have their photograph taken with her, she kindly obliged, posing for the camera with them. This encouraged more people to step forward and Kate vanished within the horde, leaving her family outside the circle of admirers.

'Wow, that's quite a contrast,' said Lucy.

'What do you mean?' replied Jenna.

'Well, with us she's just Kate, our cousin. Now we're seeing the famous film star and her fans can't take their eyes off her.'

'She's got that mysterious something that magnetises other people,' said Harry.

'I wish I had it,' said Jenna.

'It's a double-edged sword, a blessing as well as a curse,' replied Harry. 'I've seen a few people with the same quality leave absolute carnage in their wake. They don't mean to, but they can't help it. It's all part of their curse.'

'Don't talk about curses. We've already had enough weirdness and it's only the second day.'

They decided to take a seat at one of the coffee shop's outdoor tables and enjoy a drink and a cake while they waited for Kate to finish signing autographs and posing for photos. Eventually her fans left her alone, filing off in different directions with delighted smiles. Only her family saw the light die in Kate's eyes and the smile drop from her face as she strode towards them. They all knew she wasn't sad because the admiration had stopped. She was relieved it was over.

'That really was something,' said Harmony as Kate joined them at their table. 'I've never seen anything like it.'

'I don't know how you stand it,' commented Shannon. 'All that attention would drive me crazy.'

'You get used to it,' shrugged Kate. 'And they were all really nice. Some people can be so pushy and I've had my arse and boobs grabbed too many times to count.'

They all looked at Simon when he giggled and blushed.

'Not being able to go anywhere without getting swamped seems a hefty price to pay for fame,' said Shannon.

'I pay it gladly,' replied Kate, gazing off in the direction of Alardyce House, even though it wasn't visible from the village.

'I wouldn't worry too much,' said Harry. 'They'll soon get used to your presence around here and it should calm down for you.'

'You're probably right. Anyway, are you ready to carry on to the church?'

'Let's finish our coffees first,' said Jenna. 'I'm gasping.'

At that point, a fawning waiter crept up to Kate, curling in on himself as though he wasn't worthy to be in her presence, and asked if he could fetch her anything.

'Do you have kombucha?' she asked him.

'Err, no, sorry,' he replied, clearly clueless as to what that was.

'What the hell's kombucha?' Harry asked her.

'It's sugar, tea and yeast.'

'Sounds delightful,' he grimaced.

'How about coconut water?' she asked the waiter.

'Sorry, Ms Alardyce,' replied the waiter, who was becoming increasingly distressed that he couldn't accommodate his illustrious guest.

'Pomegranate juice?'

'Yes, now that we can do,' he said with a delighted grin.

'Perfect,' she replied with her most devastating smile, revealing her perfect white teeth.

'I'll fetch it at once,' he said before rushing back inside to prepare her order.

'You should have asked him for the entire café,' said Shannon. 'I'm sure he would have given it to you.'

Kate's response was another smile before she tilted her face up to the sun, enjoying the warmth.

Once they had all finished their drinks, the waiter practically ignoring the rest of the table to tend solely to Kate's needs, the family continued on to the church. More people waved to Kate and called out her name, but thankfully she wasn't swamped again as she had been earlier and they reached the church undisturbed.

'This way,' said Kate, marching straight past the building and around the side.

'Aren't we going in?' said Lucy, pointing to the church.

'Later. There's something I want to show you first.'

'Does anyone else get the feeling she's taking us to the graveyard?' said Cameron.

Everyone nodded.

They found Kate standing at a spot towards the rear of the kirkyard gazing at the headstones. They gathered around her. None were surprised to see the surname *Alardyce* adorning each stone.

'Here they are,' she said, not taking her eyes off the graves. 'Amy, Henry, Jane.' There was a reverent pause before she added, 'And Robert.'

They all stared at the graves curiously.

'There are more with the name Alardyce,' said Lucy.

'Yes, there's John; he was Henry and Amy's oldest son. Unlike his younger brother, he managed to survive two world wars. He married and had two sons and a daughter and they're here too. Amy and Henry's only daughter Lydia is also here. Even though she married a marquess with a huge estate and his own family crypt further north, she insisted on being buried here. Robert and Jane's children are also here. Did you know their daughter Emily became a very famous concert pianist?'

'I remember Gran telling me about that,' said Jenna, smiling about her family's history for the first time. 'She had an amazing career, travelling all over the world. She had affairs with an Italian count and a Danish prince but she allowed no man to become her master and remained single right up to her death aged eighty-three in her extravagant apartment in Paris. She was also very rich and left every penny to her brother James and his children. She was a real trailblazer.'

'She was,' smiled Kate. 'Emily certainly had her father's ambition and determination to succeed.'

'I'd say it was her talent that made all that happen.'

Kate shrugged. 'That was part of it too.'

Jenna rolled her eyes.

'Isn't it amazing being so close to them,' continued Kate.

'I don't think it is,' muttered Harry, shoving his hands into his jeans pockets. 'I've always found graveyards creepy.'

'Personally, I find them restful,' Kate replied, her gaze on the headstones.

'I like them too,' said Lucy. 'I love studying the inscriptions, wondering what their lives were like.'

'I understand what you mean,' said Harmony. 'The veil between the living and the dead is so thin. Visiting graveyards is one of the ways in which we can break through it.'

Harry regarded his girlfriend with a raised eyebrow but didn't comment, mainly because he had no idea what to say.

'We should have brought flowers,' said Kate, gesturing to the graves. 'We walked right past the florist's. I meant to call in on the way, but all the autograph signing made me forget.'

'We can always pop back for some,' said Lucy.

'Yes. I think they'd like that,' she murmured thoughtfully, staring at the graves.

Cameron, Simon and Harry glanced at each other with identical cynical expressions. The women were feeling the reverence of the occasion, even Shannon and Harmony, who weren't related to the dead, but the men were finding it a lot harder.

'I'll show you the church now,' said Kate when she eventually managed to tear her gaze off the graves. 'Amy and Henry got married here and all the Alardyce children were christened here too.'

The church dated back to the seventeenth century, a beautiful little stone-built building that had been very well preserved and had survived the passage of time mainly thanks to the Alardyce fortune.

'I'm not at all religious,' said Kate. 'But the church needs a new roof and I've already said I'll pay for the repairs. It would be terrible to see somewhere so full of history destroyed.'

'And it'll earn you a lot of brownie points with the locals,' replied Harry.

'Still the same old Harry, always looking out for the main chance,' she replied with a fond smile. 'But I'm doing it because I want to, not to curry favour.'

'Is Magda's cottage still here?' Lucy asked her.

'Unfortunately, no. It was burnt down not long after she died.'

'Who's Magda?' said Shannon.

'The village witch,' replied Lucy with relish. 'Everyone was scared of her, except our family. She was a really clever woman who could cure illnesses the doctors at the time couldn't. She was also psychic. She became very good friends with Amy and saved her life more than once.'

'The locals were all suspicious of her,' added Kate. 'Especially the men but they were also frightened of her. She had a pet wolf called Fenrir.'

'She was really awesome and no one knew how old she was when she died,' continued Lucy. 'Some people said she was in her sixties, some over a hundred. In that time, her intelligence meant she was called a witch, so when she died, the locals burnt down her home out of fear, thinking they could destroy the "evil".'

'It was left a ruin for years,' said Kate. 'They wouldn't even take any of the stone that was left to put into other buildings, afraid it would carry the witch's curse. It was only demolished entirely in the 1940s and even then the land was left barren for ages, until a housing developer bought it in the eighties and put an ugly house on it.'

'She sounds interesting,' smiled Shannon. 'Where is she buried?'

'In there at her own request,' replied Kate, gesturing to the woodland that lay on the other side of the village. 'The local vicar said he would never bury a witch in consecrated ground. There was a headstone to mark the spot, but it kept getting stolen. The villagers always replaced it, worried they'd anger her spirit if they didn't. That only stopped in the 1950s. Instead, they dumped a big slab of stone on the spot that was too heavy to lift.'

'Let's go and see it,' said Shannon, eyes sparkling.

'I don't think that's a good idea,' replied Cameron.

'Why not? Don't tell me you're scared,' she grinned before breaking into a long-legged stride in that direction.

'I'll come,' said Lucy, hurrying after her.

'I'll go too,' said Harmony. 'I want to feel the energy. It will probably be powerful,' she added before heading off into the woods.

'Shan, wait,' called Cameron before breaking into a jog to catch up with her. For some reason, he didn't want to let her out of his sight. He couldn't explain this vague feeling of unease, it was just the general sense that something unpleasant was heading their way, something they had no chance of stopping.

'Anyone else coming?' Kate asked the others, already walking off in that direction. She was a little annoyed that her talk of the witch hadn't had the big impact she'd hoped for. Of course, her family members had already heard about Magda many times from their grandmother, so it was nothing new to them. However, Simon, Harmony and Shannon hadn't and they were treating it like it was just another tourist spot.

'I'll come,' grinned Simon. 'I've never seen a witch's grave before.'

'What about your mother's?' muttered Jenna, scowling as he hurried after Kate.

'It looks like we've been left behind again,' said Harry as they watched the others vanish into the trees. He wrapped an arm around Jenna when she stared after her husband as he walked alongside Kate. 'How do you fancy going back to that café?'

'I'd prefer to go to the pub and get pissed,' she replied.

'Let's go.'

* * *

Cameron quickly caught up with Shannon and grasped her hand.

'What's wrong?' she said when she caught the look in his eyes.

'I don't like this,' he replied.

'Don't tell me you're scared of the witch like all those superstitious idiots back in the day?'

'No, but I do have a bad feeling.'

'Why?'

'I don't know, I just get the sense something bad is going to happen.'

'Like what?'

'I wish I knew.'

'You're being silly. These woods are beautiful.'

'I don't think you should go running off on your own like that.'

'What is this?' she frowned. 'You've never spoken to me like this before.'

'Oh dear, Cam,' said Lucy as she passed them by. 'You're not the jealous type, are you?'

'You don't know my family's history,' he told Shannon, deciding to ignore his cousin. 'Bad things happen to Alardyces around here.'

'From what I've heard your family lived here for decades and the majority of your relatives lived long, happy lives.'

'Some of them did, not all. This place just makes me uneasy.'

'You're still shook up after seeing that portrait of Robert.'

'Shannon,' called Lucy. 'It's over here.'

'You need to relax more,' she told her boyfriend before jogging over to Lucy, who stood before a large stone slab on the ground.

'Is something wrong?' Kate asked Cameron as she and Simon caught up with him.

'Just stubborn girlfriends,' he sighed.

'Don't let her walk all over you.'

'I don't,' he muttered, wishing she'd stay out of it.

'It doesn't look that way to us,' smiled Simon before he and Kate continued on their way, leaving him to frown after them.

When Kate stumbled on a tree root, Simon offered her his arm and, to his obvious delight, she took it and bestowed upon him another smile.

Cameron joined them in gathering around the stone and stared down at it solemnly. The name Magda Magrath was etched on it along with the year 1926. The grave was untended, weeds snaking up around the stone.

'Not much of a dedication, is it?' said Simon.

'She doesn't need anything more,' said Kate. 'Her personal power will long outlive this marker.'

'I can feel her energy,' breathed Harmony, crouching down and placing her hand upon the slab. 'It's so strong, like she's still alive under there.'

Simon and Cameron both took a step back from the grave.

'She was a good woman,' said Kate. 'She helped people and saved a lot of lives. She wasn't evil. Jane speaks very highly of her in her journal. After Amy died, the two became best friends and Magda spent a lot of time at Alardyce House. She was practically a member of the family.'

'We should try contacting her,' said Harmony.

'Why would we want to do that?' said an alarmed Simon.

'To communicate with her. I bet you'd love to talk to her,' she told Kate. 'Don't worry, I've held loads of séances in my time. I know what I'm doing.'

'I don't care. A witch's grave should not be tampered with,' Simon replied.

'What do you say, Kate?' said Harmony, deciding to ignore him. 'It'll be fun.'

Kate smiled darkly. 'I think it's a wonderful idea.'

'I agree with Simon,' said Lucy. 'Some things shouldn't be meddled with.'

They all looked up at the sky when it suddenly darkened and thick grey cloud moved in, obscuring the sun. The temperature suddenly shot up, increasing the humidity, causing them all to break out in a sweat.

'The witch doesn't like us talking about this,' rasped Simon. 'She's getting angry.'

'Don't be ridiculous,' Cameron told him. 'The weather report said it might thunder today. That's all.'

'No, it's her. We're annoying her. I don't want a witch's curse,' Simon cried before turning and running back the way they'd come.

'Maybe now's not the right time for a séance,' said Harmony, getting to her feet.

'Why?' said a wide-eyed Lucy. 'Because Magda's angry?'

'No,' she chuckled. 'Because it's going to rain.'

'Oh, of course,' she replied, recalling that she was supposed to be a logical, down-to-earth professional. There was just something about this woodland that felt other-worldly and she wasn't sure she liked it.

'We'd better start heading back,' said Cameron.

They left the woods together. Realising they were missing someone, Cameron glanced back over his shoulder and saw Kate still standing by the grave. Her lips were moving, as though she was talking to it.

'Kate, are you coming?' he called.

She murmured something else to the grave before turning to him. 'Yep, right behind you.'

'Not if I can help it,' he said before rushing after the others. Seeing her talk to a witch's grave had been a little unsettling and made him wonder just how far her obsession with the family history had gone.

'Where are they?' said Harmony when they returned to the spot where they'd left Jenna and Harry.

'They've probably gone back to the coffee shop,' said Simon.

'Let's head over there then before it starts chucking it down,' said Shannon.

They reached the coffee shop just as the heavens opened.

'I don't see them,' said Simon, scanning the faces of everyone inside. The coffee shop was full, everyone having hurried in to escape the rain. Concerned, he took out his phone and made a call. 'Jenna, where are you?' His face creased. 'Why are you slurring? Seriously, we've only been gone ten minutes.' He hung up. 'They're in the pub. Jenna sounds drunk and it's not even dinnertime. It's Harry's fault, he's leading her astray,' he growled before turning on his heel and storming out.

'Oh, please,' said Kate. 'You know no one can make Jenna do anything she doesn't want to do.'

The pub was a pretty stone building, colourful flower boxes adorning the window ledges, a sign proudly displaying the name The Cauldron swinging in the breeze, which was starting to pick up.

'The owners are obviously capitalising on Magda's memory,' said Lucy, disapproval in her tone.

They all ducked inside the cosy pub, which was a bit quieter than the café. The large room was divided into smaller, more intimate areas. Harry and Jenna were sitting together in a booth by a window, giggling.

'What the bloody hell is this?' demanded Simon, storming up to them. 'How dare you get my wife drunk?' he demanded of Harry.

'I didn't get her drunk,' he replied indignantly. 'She did it to herself by ordering two double whiskies and downing them one after the other.'

Simon turned his attention to Jenna. 'Double whiskies? That's not like you, sweetheart.'

'What do you care?' she retorted. 'You've abandoned me every chance you've had.'

'That's not true.'

'Yes, it is. Well, do you know what, Simon? I don't care. Now sod off, me and Harry are talking.'

When Simon turned puce with anger, Harry decided some diplomacy was in order. 'Perhaps we should be getting back to the house?' he said.

'I think that's a very good idea,' retorted Simon with a hard look his way.

Jenna casually shrugged, drained her glass of the remaining whisky and got to her feet. When Simon held his hand out to her, she gave him an indignant look before flouncing past him towards the door.

'What's her problem?' he exclaimed, watching his wife leave, the rest of the family following her.

'You've only yourself to blame,' Harry whispered in his ear. 'The way you've been fawning over Kate.'

'I have not,' he retorted, his face turning crimson.

'Aye, you have. The fact that your entire face as well as your ears have turned pink tells me you know exactly what you've done.'

With that, Harry left, Simon scowling after him.

6

The atmosphere on the family's return to the house was subdued. Jenna was resolutely ignoring Simon, who was being driven rather frantic by her inattention. She'd never treated him like this before. He kept trying to encourage her to talk to him in private, but she just smiled serenely and said she wanted to spend time with the family she hadn't seen in years. Deciding to give up, he stormed into the billiard room and slammed the door shut.

Everyone was relieved when the doorbell rang, breaking the awkwardness. The heavy rain cast the house in gloom and made them all consider their earlier conversation about ghosts.

'Here's another guest,' smiled Kate while Marcus went to answer the door.

'I didn't know there was another guest,' said Harry. 'Please don't tell me it's Aunty Carol,' he added, referring to Jenna's mother.

'God, no. It's a good friend of mine.'

'I wonder if it's a famous actor,' said Jenna excitedly. 'I read she's very good friends with Gerard Butler and Tom Hiddleston.'

'That's all we need,' muttered Harry. 'That pair turning up.'

'I wouldn't mind,' smiled Harmony.

Kate escorted in neither actor but a tall man with dark brown hair and a chiselled jaw. He wore light grey trousers and a white shirt, the matching grey jacket folded over one arm.

'Everyone,' said Kate, 'this is my good friend, Chris Mountebank. He's a director.'

'I've heard of you,' said Harmony excitedly. 'You directed *A Cold Winter* and *March of the Hares*.'

'I've seen those films too,' gasped Jenna. 'They were amazing. *March of the Hares* made me cry and I never cry at films.'

'Well, I've never heard of either of them,' said Harry.

'That's because you only watch films about aliens,' Harmony told him.

Harry smiled. 'She's got me there.'

'We didn't know we were going to have a famous director in our midst,' said Jenna, looking Kate's way.

'Chris is my surprise,' she replied. 'Why don't you all take a seat and I'll explain. Marcus, could we have some fresh coffee, please?'

They settled together in the drawing room and Marcus furnished them with more coffee, Harry encouraging him to slip some brandy into his mug again.

'What about Simon?' Cameron asked Jenna. 'He's still in the billiard room.'

She waved a dismissive hand. 'Leave him. He'll be happy playing with his balls.'

Harry sniggered into his coffee.

'So, what's this about?' said Cameron, getting the feeling Kate was about to spring something big on them.

'Chris is here because I want to make a film about our family's history.'

They all stared at her in surprise.

'Seriously?' said Cameron, arching an eyebrow.

'Yes,' she replied breezily. 'It will be centred around Robert.'

'Why the hell would you want to do that?' spluttered Harry. 'It's a horrible story full of torture and death.'

'I think it's got a lot of potential,' said Chris in his clipped English accent. 'Kate will play Amy herself, so you can guarantee full justice will be done to your family.'

'Amy came to live here when she was seventeen,' Cameron told her pointedly.

'So?' she replied defensively.

'You're thirty-two.'

'I can play young and innocent.'

'From what I've heard, she wasn't very innocent,' chuckled Harry.

'And I'll be playing her right through her life to her death,' continued Kate. 'It's not uncommon to have an actress at the midway point between the two ages of a character's life.'

'That's true,' said Chris. 'You never have a seventeen-year-old playing a seventeen-year-old, that would be a nightmare. Usually, they're in their early twenties or even older if they'll be playing the character in their later life. Besides, Kate's such a wonderful actress she can pull anything off.'

'Thank you, Chris,' she smiled, tilting her body towards his and giving him the full effect of her huge blue eyes. His answering look said he was already smitten.

'I think it's exciting,' enthused Lucy. 'Have you got any other actors lined up?'

'Yes,' said Kate, once again appreciating her eagerness. 'Tom Drake for Henry.'

'Doesn't he do those action films where he's leaping from skyscrapers and shooting bad guys with machine guns?' said Harry.

'Yes, but he's very versatile. He's already proved he can do this.'

'Oh, yes?' said Harry, the mischievous smile returning. 'And how did he do that?'

'By reading for the part. Get your mind out of the gutter, for once in your life.'

Harry's smile broadened. 'Why start now?'

'Wait,' said Jenna. 'You mean there's already a script?'

'Yes,' replied Kate. 'I wrote it myself.'

They all stared at her in surprise.

'How long have you been working on this?' Cameron asked her.

'Two years,' replied Kate. 'That's how long it took me to write the script anyway. I had some help from a historical researcher.'

'You could have come to me for that,' frowned Lucy.

'Sorry, I didn't know if you'd approve and I didn't want anything to get in the way of this project. If you like, you can be the historical adviser on set. I know you're more than qualified. You'll be paid, of course.'

'Oh my God, I would love that,' she enthused.

'Fantastic.' Kate smiled. 'And what do the rest of you think?'

'It's a mad bloody idea,' retorted Harry. 'We don't want all the skeletons pulling out of the family closet in such a public way.'

'I agree,' said Jenna. 'I hate the idea. This is our family we're talking about.'

'I hate to break it to you,' said Kate, 'but the skeletons were pulled out of the closet decades ago. It's not like any of this is a secret. It was reported in all the newspapers at the time.'

'Correction, some of it was,' said Harry. 'I'm guessing you've used Jane's journals to write your film, which include a lot of things the public never knew about, like all the murders Robert committed.'

'That is true but what's the harm?'

'I don't want everyone knowing I have a murderer's blood in my veins.'

'I thought you'd enjoy all the attention. It could lead to magazine and newspaper deals and they'd pay you a lot of money for a juicy interview.'

Harry hesitated at this statement. 'Money?'

The corner of Kate's mouth lifted at the greed that filled his eyes. Before inviting them all here, she'd paid a private investigator to look into her cousins' lives, anticipating resistance to her project; consequently, she knew Harry was perpetually short of money. He'd set up numerous businesses, all of which had failed, usually due to his terrible mismanagement of funds. She knew all their weak spots and how to play on them. Already she had Lucy on side simply by telling her she could be the historical advisor. The promise of a big payday would win Harry over. Cameron and Jenna would be harder to convince but she was confident she could manage it.

'Yes, Harry,' she pressed. 'Lots of it.'

'Well, I don't approve at all,' said Jenna, eyes flashing with her inner fire.

'Now don't be so hasty,' Harry told her. 'Maybe it wouldn't be so bad, and we must support Kate in her career.'

'I agree,' said Lucy. 'And this could be the perfect way to exorcise our family's demons.'

'By putting them all into a major film?' said Jenna. 'It would be so humiliating. I couldn't stand the shame.'

'It would get everyone interested in our family,' said Kate. 'Just think about your holiday park – people will be queuing up to stay once they know you're one of The Infamous Alardyces, which is the working title of the script, by the way.'

The corner of Kate's mouth lifted again when Jenna hesitated. The private investigator had told her that Jenna's business was in fact struggling. She and Simon had overreached themselves financially with all the fancy new additions to their site and so far, the bookings hadn't reflected all the money they'd poured into it. There was a real danger they could lose it all within the year.

'You really think so?' said Jenna.

'Oh yes,' said Chris. 'After all, there's no such thing as bad publicity.'

'Well, perhaps we should at least read the script? It's not fair to Kate to dismiss it so quickly.'

'Thank you, Jenna,' said Kate graciously. She turned to the last obstacle, knowing this one would be the toughest of all. 'And what do you think, Cam?'

He sighed when all eyes turned his way. 'I'm not sure,' he began slowly. 'You've blindsided me with this. I'm assuming it will be filmed here?'

'Of course.'

'I have to say, I don't really like it. You'll be putting so much new information out there about unsolved crimes. Have you thought that the police might take Jane's journals from you? What if they charge you with concealing evidence?'

'My chief constable friend has assured me that won't happen. I've already gone into the legal ramifications and it won't be a problem.'

'Can he guarantee that?'

'Yes,' she said so forcefully he was a little thrown.

'Come on, Cam,' said Harry. 'What harm can it do?'

'It will be embarrassing, for one.'

'So what? It was over a century ago. It's not like you were there.'

'Aye,' said Jenna. 'Take the pole out of your arse, Cam. This could be a good opportunity for our whole family.'

'I don't suppose my objection will stop it from happening?' he sighed. 'Seeing how I've been outvoted.' He glanced accusingly at Jenna, who looked away from his black-eyed gaze.

'No, it won't,' replied Kate. 'But I would feel much better if I had your approval.'

Cameron glanced at Shannon, wondering what her thoughts were on the matter.

'I don't think it could do much harm,' she said gently, placing her hand on his knee.

He nodded and looked back at Kate. 'I want to read the script first. Then I'll decide.'

'No problem,' she said. 'I've already prepared scripts for you all. Marcus,' she called.

The butler nodded, turned to the antique sideboard he was standing beside and opened the doors. From it he produced several bundles of papers, which he proceeded to hand out to everyone, including Chris and Kate.

'You should all read the script,' said Kate. 'Let me know what you think about it this evening.'

With that, the family got to their feet and filed out of the room, all heading in different directions, wanting to be alone with their thoughts.

'Well,' said Kate with a satisfied smile once they'd all gone. 'I think that went well.'

'They did take it better than I'd expected,' replied Chris. 'After all, no one wants their family secrets spilling out for the world to see.'

'I knew Jenna, Harry and Lucy would get into line. Cameron was my worry. He's always been a bit of a dark horse. If anyone will throw a spanner in the works, it's him.'

'You didn't make him your offer.'

'I want to see what he makes of the script first. If he still objects, then I'll drop that particular bombshell on him,' she added with a devious smile.

* * *

Three hours later, Cameron had finished reading the script about The Infamous Alardyces. With a sigh, he dumped it on the bed beside him and leaned back against the ornate headboard. He was in the bedroom that Kate had informed them had belonged to John, Amy and Henry's eldest son. This hadn't meant that much to Cameron. However, after reading the script, which he knew was full of meticulous historical detail, he did feel a little closer to his Victorian ancestors. His gran had scared him with her stories about them, but he'd been a little boy, relentlessly bullied at school for his weight, miserable and lonely. The last thing he'd wanted to hear about was how his great-great-grandmother had almost died after being tortured by her own cousin, had her fingernails torn out with such savagery the bones had snapped and left her fingers deformed and painful for the rest of her life. When their gran had tried to take him aside to tell him more of her 'stories', he'd run to his mother, who hated all that, and stuck to her like a limpet until his gran had given up and gone to hunt out another of his cousins. Now he was a grown man and much stronger mentally as well as physically. He could handle all the trauma. Reading through the script, he'd seen another side to the story, one of incredible love that couldn't be destroyed, and perhaps that did deserve to be told.

The door opened and Shannon walked in. Cameron smiled at how her eyes sparkled.

'I've just had a lovely walk with Harmony,' she said.

'I hope she didn't threaten to resurrect any dead witches again?'

'No,' she laughed. 'She's really knowledgeable about plants and herbs. She was teaching me about them.'

'She sounds to be a bit of a witch herself.'

'I think you're right,' she said, perching on the edge of the bed beside him. She picked up the script. 'Have you finished reading it?'

Cameron nodded.

'And what's the verdict?'

'It's pretty good. It seems Kate has another talent.'

'Because being a beautiful, successful actress isn't enough for her,' she said wryly.

'She's managed to get across the good sides of the family. Gran only concentrated on the bad. To be honest, it's made me come round to the idea a bit.'

'Really? I didn't think you'd change your mind.'

'There was such a strong love between them and if that can come across on the screen then it might actually redeem my ancestors.'

'That's nice. So, you're going to give your permission?'

'I don't see why not, and I don't want to get in the way of Kate's career. She's worked so hard to get to where she is.'

'I think that's very generous of you,' she smiled, leaning into him. 'You deserve a treat.'

Cameron pulled her into his arms and kissed her, Shannon giggling when he rolled her onto her back, crumpling the script beneath her.

* * *

The family gathered in the dining room that evening before the forbidding portraits of their ancestors. Chris joined them at the table, sitting to Kate's left, while Cameron sat on her right. Cameron didn't want to be there but that was where the place card said he was supposed to sit. He was facing the portrait of Robert and he wondered if that had been done on purpose. Shannon was seated further down the table between Simon and Harry. Kate looked impossibly glamorous in a floor-length red dress, her hair piled atop her head.

As Marcus went around the table filling their wine glasses, Kate said, 'So, have you all had a chance to read the script?'

'I have,' said Harry. 'And I think it's masterful.'

'Me too,' chimed in Jenna. 'It's excellent and is sure to be a hit.'

Simon said, 'Yes, excellent,' when his wife threw him a warning look.

Kate's smile was sweet, even though inwardly she experienced a contemptuous pleasure. How predictable of them to be so supportive now they thought they'd get something out of it.

'Thank you. I really appreciate that,' she said.

'I enjoyed it too,' replied Lucy. 'The historical detail was wonderful.'

Kate smiled and nodded before looking to Cameron. She leaned into him. 'And what did you think, Cam?'

'I enjoyed it,' he smiled.

Kate was so surprised she allowed the shock to slip into her eyes just for a moment before she wiped it out, replacing it with confidence. 'Really?'

'Aye, really. I saw another side to our family, one of great love, and I liked it.'

'Well, this is a turn up for the books. I admit if there was going to be a roadblock, I thought you'd be the one to put it there.'

'I don't want to stand in your way, Kate.'

'That means a lot to me,' she said softly, covering his hand with her own.

He shifted uncomfortably at the way she gazed at him and slowly pulled his hand out from under hers.

'I'm glad you've accepted,' she continued. 'Because I have an offer to put to you – I want you to play Robert in the film.'

He gaped at her. 'What?'

'It makes sense with your resemblance to the character,' said Chris.

'He's not a character, he was a real-life person,' Cam told him, surprised by how defensive he suddenly felt.

'I do apologise, it was just a turn of phrase,' Chris said, sounding genuinely contrite. 'I would never dream of denigrating any of your relatives.'

'I'm not an actor. The closest I've ever got was the school nativity.'

'He was the stable,' Harry told Chris with a grin.

Chris, who didn't know about Cameron's weight issues when he was a child, merely smiled politely while not understanding the joke.

'That doesn't matter,' Kate told Cameron. 'We can hire an acting coach.'

'But... I don't want to act,' he replied. 'I'm happy running my gyms.' He already owned two successful gyms, wanting to help people lose weight and get fit just as he had, and he was in negotiations to purchase a third. He also owned two shops selling sports equipment and clothing.

'Are you kidding?' said Harry. 'Have you any idea how much money there is to be made in that industry? Just look at Kate.'

'She has talent, I don't.'

'We don't know that yet,' said Kate. 'Let's see what the acting coach says.'

'I really don't think this is a good idea.'

'Beauden will be arriving tomorrow morning, so we'll know more then.'

'Beauden?'

'The acting coach. He's a giant in the industry. If anyone can teach you, he can.'

'I don't want an acting coach,' he exclaimed.

'Why don't you just talk to Beauden,' said Chris reasonably. 'See what he says.'

'Why are you pushing for this? Surely you want a professional playing Robert rather than a complete amateur?'

'Your resemblance to Robert Alardyce seems too good an opportunity to pass up and it would be amazing to have two members of the Alardyce family in the film.'

'I really don't like this idea...'

'Just talk to Beauden,' said Chris. 'And take it from there.'

Cameron looked from him to Kate and back again, feeling like he was being railroaded into this, but determined to stand his ground. He wasn't a pushover, far from it, but there was something surreal about Alardyce House that made him feel like this wasn't reality, that he'd wake up back in his bed at home in Glasgow and his normal life. The sensation was disorientating and sapped his strength a little. He got the feeling he would soon find out whether he took after Robert in more than just physical appearance. He glanced at the portrait on the wall, his own black eyes connecting with those of his ancestor's, which seemed to contain a knowing look.

* * *

After dinner, when they'd all retired to the drawing room, the doorbell rang again and Marcus escorted in a tall, slender man with pale skin and dark eyes. His face looked like it had been carved from marble. His cheekbones were very chiselled, nose aquiline and mouth full and sensuous. He smiled, making his hazel eyes twinkle, and ran a hand through his thick dark hair, which immediately sprang back into place. This smile made Jenna, Harmony and Shannon blush while Lucy remained unmoved.

'Tom,' smiled Kate, getting to her feet to greet him with a hug and a kiss on the cheek. 'How wonderful to see you. Thanks for coming.'

'It's great to be here. This place is amazing,' he grinned, his accent pure south London. 'I can practically feel Henry's presence. I can't wait to get stuck into this film.'

'Tom loves the history,' she explained to her guests. 'He's been so enthusiastic about this project from the beginning and has really done his research. It's why I know he'll do Henry so much justice. Have you noticed that he looks like him too? He has the same build and skin and eye colour.'

'Aye, there is a resemblance,' said Lucy.

'I'm a huge fan of your films, Mr Drake,' said Simon excitedly, getting to his feet and extending his hand to him. 'Especially your latest one – *When the Sky Falls*. That scene where you drove the car off the bridge was amazing.'

'Thanks,' smiled Tom, shaking his hand heartily. 'That was done on the first take too.'

'Awesome,' he replied, gazing at him.

'So you did that and not a stuntman?' said Cameron, raising an eyebrow.

'Well, yeah, it was a stuntman, but I helped arrange the stunt,' replied Tom, with a flicker of defensiveness.

'Aye, course.'

The sarcasm in Cameron's tone was lost on no one, and Shannon gave her boyfriend a questioning look. Normally he was the epitome of politeness. After all the bullying he'd endured as a child, he couldn't bear the thought of hurting anyone's feelings as he'd been hurt, so he went out of his way to avoid doing anything that might make someone feel ill at ease. Cameron just shrugged back at her. He was aware that wasn't like him, but he couldn't help it; he was annoyed. He felt he was being pushed into something he didn't want to do and he was pushing back against it.

'Stuntman or not, it was a great film,' said Simon. 'And *you* made it a great film.'

Tom's easy smile returned. 'Thanks so much, it's always good to meet a fan.' He cast Cameron a glower, irritated by his smirk.

Kate's sharp gaze took all of this in and inwardly she smiled. She'd had a feeling Cameron's likeness to Robert wasn't just skin deep. Hopefully she could prod him in subtle ways and ensure his true nature soon came out.

7

Shannon was woken by the sound of a zip being unfastened. With a yawn, she sat up and squinted in the gloom. Only the lamp was on and she could see Cameron throwing things into a suitcase.

'What are you doing?' she frowned.

'Leaving,' he replied.

'Why?'

'No way am I going to be in a film.'

'Why does that mean you have to go?'

'You heard them last night, they're trying to force me into it. Well, sod that. No one makes me do anything I don't want to do.'

'You're telling me. So you're going to let them drive you out, are you?'

'They're not driving me out. I'm choosing to leave.'

'We've only been here a day and a half. Perhaps you should give it longer?'

'I've given it long enough.'

'You haven't seen your cousins in years. If you leave now, you'll regret it.'

Cameron stopped tossing clothes into the suitcase and sighed. 'You might be right but let's face it, this place is weird and so is Kate.'

'She's not weird, she's just passionate about this house and her family history.'

'I saw her talking to the witch's grave.'

'So? Plenty of people talk to graves.'

'I don't like the way she looks at me either. It makes me uncomfortable.'

'I have noticed that but you're a good-looking man, Cam. Lots of women look at you. It's a permanent cross I have to bear.'

A slow grin spread across his face. 'Men look at you too because you're gorgeous.'

'I wouldn't go that far. In fact, only you seem to think so.'

He let the T-shirt he was holding drop into the suitcase, clambered onto the bed and crawled across it on all fours towards her, a wicked grin on his face. Shannon couldn't help but smile back.

'You're the most beautiful woman I ever saw,' he whispered in her ear, making her tingle. 'Kate thinks she's all that, but you're so much more.'

'I like being at Alardyce,' she breathed as he kissed her neck. 'You never say things like that at home.'

'Then I should because I love you so much,' he said before kissing her hard on the mouth.

With a moan, Shannon slid her fingers through his thick dark hair and they fell back onto the bed together.

'This place really is having an effect on you,' she said as he pushed up her thin silk nightie.

Cameron raised his head to look at her. 'What do you mean?'

'I just mean that it's making you more romantic.' Her smile faltered at the troubled look in his eyes. 'What's wrong? It's a good thing.'

'Aye, I know but...'

'But what?' she said when he sighed and sat up.

'I'm afraid it'll bring out something unpleasant in me.'

'Is this to do with Robert?'

He nodded. 'There's always been something bad in the Alardyce blood.'

'Not for a long time. You told me that everyone who came after Robert was normal, no obvious psychotic tendencies.'

'We can't be 100 per cent certain about that. My family's good at covering things up.'

'You are nothing like him. We've been together for four years now and I know that you're one of the gentlest, kindest men I've ever met. You're not in the slightest bit violent and you certainly don't hurt women like he did.'

'Aye, but I can be devious when I want to be. How I bought my first gym—'

'Was perfectly legal and above board.'

'Technically it was but I told Gregor that if he tried to buy it, I'd tell his wife about his affair. I blackmailed someone to get what I wanted. That sounds like something Robert would do.'

'Gregor deserved it, he's an arsehole who got too used to getting his own way.'

'I suppose but it made me feel really shitty. All I could think about at the time was getting what I wanted. Nothing else mattered.'

Shannon got the feeling Kate shared the exact same drive – it was why she was a famous actress as well as the owner of Alardyce House – but she didn't think telling Cameron that would help. 'There's nothing wrong with having ambition, and now look at you – you own two very successful gyms and two sports shops. Why haven't you told your family about how successful you are?'

'I didn't want to seem like I was rubbing their noses in it. Harry's clearly skint and I overheard Simon on the phone last night. His and Jenna's business is struggling. I think part of the reason why they're here is to tap Kate for money.'

'Well, that was very thoughtful of you. Does that sound like something Robert Alardyce would do?'

'No. He'd enjoy rubbing his wealth in their faces.'

'Exactly. You're not him, so stop worrying.'

'I won't be able to relax until we're away from this place.'

'Do you really want to go?'

Cameron hesitated before replying. He really wanted to spend time with his cousins but he was afraid Kate's project would bring out the Alardyce darkness in him. 'Yes.'

'Fine, we can leave if it's worrying you that much, but we're only here for a few days, I'm sure you can make it. Just be firm and say no when Kate presses you to be in the film. You can be stubborn when you want to be.'

'So can she.'

'Are you sure you don't want to be in the film? I think you'd be great.'

'I'd be awful and I hate being in front of a camera, even to have my photo taken.'

'Having a major role would give you a lot of control. You'd be able to veto anything you didn't like. If you pass up the chance, then you'll have no say whatsoever.'

'I don't want a say,' he replied, not liking the project now he knew Kate wanted him to be a part of it. 'The past is gone. I don't know why Kate keeps trying to drag it into the present.'

'Have you thought that a lot of your bias might belong to your parents and not you?'

Cameron's brow creased. 'What do you mean?'

'You told me your parents didn't like to talk about your family's past and always shut down your gran when she tried. That would have had an effect on you at such a young age. I'm just saying that you might be surprised by the results if you approach it with an open mind.'

He pondered on this before nodding. 'Maybe you're right and I do have some childhood bias. Plus, I've hardly spent any time with Lucy. She's the one I want to catch up with the most. Okay,' he continued. 'I'll give it a bit more time and I'll stand up to Kate more.'

'Good. I just know you'd regret it if you left too early.'

'You're probably right.'

Shannon couldn't help but smile when mischief crept into his gaze again.

'We've got some time before Lurch serves breakfast,' he said. 'So let's make the most of it,' he added before pressing his lips to hers.

* * *

Shannon strode into the dining room for breakfast, feeling fabulous. Alardyce was really doing something to Cameron and whatever that was, she liked it. He'd always been a good lover, but this morning had been on another level. Kate, Lucy, Harmony and Harry all regarded her with smiles. Only Jenna looked a bit down.

'Well, someone's got a sparkle in her eye,' smiled Kate. 'Did you and Cameron have a good night?'

'No, we had a good morning,' she smiled back, taking her seat at the dining table.

'I can't remember the last time I had a good night or a good morning,' muttered Jenna, who sat with her shoulders slumped. Simon was still in their room, so he missed this comment.

'There is something about the air here,' said Harry, who also looked surprisingly bright. His eyes weren't bloodshot as they normally were, indicating he hadn't drunk as much the previous evening. 'I haven't felt so good in ages. And I only had two glasses of wine, a port and some brandy last night.'

'Only?' said Jenna.

'That's not much for him,' replied Harmony, who was sitting beside him at the table.

'Alardyce's magic doesn't look to be having much of an effect on you,' Harry told Jenna. 'Your bottom lip's nearly touching the table.'

'Me and Simon haven't been getting on very well since we arrived. Truth be told, we haven't been getting on very well for the last six months.'

'Oh, I'm sorry to hear that. Why's that then?'

'Things turn stale after ten years of marriage. It's only natural I suppose.'

'Then this is the perfect opportunity to find each other again,' said Harmony. 'You don't have the bairns and you're in a beautiful, peaceful place among friends.'

Jenna's expression was positively hostile. 'I know you mean well but we barely know each other.'

'You should listen to her,' said Harry. 'She's a sex therapist too.'

'Really?' smiled Kate. 'That's fascinating. Why didn't you tell us?'

'I like to get to know people a bit more first,' replied Harmony modestly. 'It makes some people uncomfortable.'

'Wow,' said Jenna. She hesitated before adding, 'Could we talk later, in private?'

'Of course.'

'Thanks.' Jenna glanced at Kate and frowned. 'What are you smiling at?'

'Nothing,' she said before turning her attention to spreading margarine on her toast.

'More visitors?' said Harry when the doorbell rang, pealing through the house.

'That will be Beauden,' replied Kate.

'Oh aye. I remember you talking about him last night.'

Marcus entered the room, his po-face putting an instant dampener on any good mood. 'Mr Beauden Argentuil,' he announced grandly.

'Sounds like a shade of paint in B&Q,' grinned Harry.

In flounced a small, thin, middle-aged man in an all-white safari suit, a light blue scarf tied around his neck. His pale brown hair sat atop a thin, ferrety face but his eyes were large and expressive, softening the look.

'Beauden,' smiled Kate, rising to greet him. 'How wonderful to see you.'

Gently he took her by the shoulders and bestowed a warm kiss on each cheek.

'And it's wonderful to be here,' he beamed. 'I love this place already. Such beauty and tranquillity. It's hard to believe so many bad things happened here.' His voice was soft but a lot deeper than his slight frame suggested. He turned to study Harry. 'Is this my new pupil? There is some resemblance,' he continued, looking from him to the portrait on the wall. 'But he's older and more bloated than our Robert.'

'I am not bloated,' spluttered Harry.

'And he hasn't as much hair,' continued Beauden as though he hadn't spoken.

'You're a second away from getting punched right in your rat face,' growled Harry, shooting to his feet.

Kate waved a hand, indicating for him to retake his seat. 'This isn't Cameron,' she said. 'This is my other cousin, Harry.'

'Thank goodness for that,' said Beauden. 'I'm very good at what I do but I can't sculpt new masterpieces from dried up clay.'

'Say one more word,' said Harry, snatching up the fish slice Marcus had been using to serve the kippers, 'and those white safari pants will be down and this will be up.'

'That's nothing,' sniffed Beauden. 'I went to Eton.'

Harry gaped at him before looking from Jenna to Harmony, both of whom were having to stifle their laughter.

'Why don't you join us for breakfast?' Kate asked Beauden.

'I will have a little toast and jam, thank you. I caught a flight from Heathrow to Edinburgh, which landed last night. I would have been here sooner, but I had one of my heads, so I checked into a delightful little hotel and had a hearty dinner, restoring my equilibrium. A quaint little man drove me here in his taxi. He had the most extraordinary accent, but he was a friendly, chatty chap. So far, it's all been very pleasant.'

'There's time yet,' glowered Harry, retaking his seat.

'So, where is my new project?' said Beauden, sitting beside Kate.

'He should be down soon,' she replied. 'A word of warning – he's very reluctant.'

'He doesn't want to be an actor,' Shannon told the new arrival. 'And he won't be pushed into it.'

'I don't push people,' said Beauden. 'I encourage, I support, I animate and inspire,' he said, waving his hands theatrically.

'That's all well and good but he's dead against it.'

'I've faced tougher prospects in my time. If there is real talent, I will sniff it out and make it bloom and when that blossoming happens, they fall in love with the art and become an addict. Kate herself here will tell you.'

'It's true,' she smiled. 'All I wanted to do my entire life was act but at one point I had such awful self-doubt it almost crippled me. Beauden helped me get over that. A couple of weeks later, I landed my first major role.'

'Where you shone like the sun,' he smiled, patting her hand. 'You eclipsed every other actor in that film.'

'And I've you to thank for it. I know that if Cam does have any latent talent, then Beauden's the one to bring it out in him,' Kate told the table.

'You'll have a tough fight on your hands,' said Shannon.

'I love a good battle,' replied Beauden with satisfaction. 'Are Chris and Tom here?' he asked Kate.

'They are.'

He clapped his hands together in a delicate way. 'Oh, how exciting. Chris is an old friend and Tom is a protégé of mine, one of my best.' He winked at Kate. 'But not *the* best.'

Cameron stalked into the room, ready to defend himself against any pressure to become something he didn't want to be. That determination was reflected in his eyes, making him appear hard and a little dangerous.

Beauden's jaw dropped and he got to his feet, eyes flicking from the portrait of Robert and back to Cameron. 'Good gracious, it's like the man himself stepped out of the picture frame. Now this is much more like it. No bloating or hair loss here.'

'Have you forgotten about the fish slice?' snapped Harry.

'Oh, don't get upset, darling,' Beauden told him. 'That anger is doing your receding hairline no favours.'

'That's it, you little worm,' he yelled, leaping to his feet again.

Harmony clamped her hand down on Harry's arm. 'Don't let him wind you up. You're always handing over control of your emotions to other people.'

'He keeps insulting me,' he spluttered.

'Does his good opinion of you really mean that much?'

'I...' He trailed off as he considered her words. 'Actually, you're right, sweetheart. He's not important enough for me to bother with.'

With a satisfied smile, he retook his seat.

Beauden hadn't heard any of this as he was too busy studying Cameron, who stared back at him with hard black eyes. 'Now this really is wonderful fresh clay.'

'Clay?' frowned Cameron.

'It means I see endless possibilities in you, my dear.'

'Dear?' he said, frown deepening.

'You should think yourself lucky,' replied Harry. 'He called me darling.'

'Is this the acting coach?' Cameron asked Kate.

'Yes,' she smiled. 'Beauden's a genius.'

'He's wasting his time. I want nothing to do with this film.'

With that pronouncement, he took a seat beside Shannon.

'You must be off your bloody rocker,' Harry told him. 'If someone asked me to be in a major film, I'd jump at the chance.'

'I'm sure we could fit you in somewhere,' replied Kate. 'But it won't be a leading role.'

'That doesn't matter, just as long as the camera gets a good look at me. And I don't want to be a servant. Make me someone rich and noble, in keeping with my lineage.'

'We'll do our best, Lord Harry,' smiled Kate.

'That's all I can ask,' he smiled back.

Kate turned her attention to Cameron. 'I understand you're reluctant but why don't you just talk to Beauden?'

'Because I get the feeling Beauden is very persuasive,' he replied, casting a suspicious glance at the acting coach, who merely smiled back at him and raised his teacup to him in a toast.

'Have you thought that this could turn out to be the best thing that's ever happened to you?' pressed Kate.

'Not possible,' said Cameron, smiling at Shannon. 'Because that's already happened.'

'Aww, that's so sweet,' said Jenna. 'I wish someone would say that to me,' she added wistfully before her expression hardened. 'Fat chance being married to that useless lump of a husband of mine.'

There was an awkward moment of silence before Kate continued.

'Acting is extremely satisfying,' she said, determined to bring Cameron round to her way of thinking. 'It also pays very well.'

'I have enough money,' he replied.

'No one can have enough money,' said Harry.

'I can.' Cameron looked back at Kate. 'Hasn't it occurred to you that I might not have your talent? I could be completely useless.'

'So that's the real reason why you're so against it?' she said, a corner of her mouth lifting in that sly way he was coming to know so well. 'You're afraid of making a fool of yourself.'

'No, I'm not.'

'Oh yes you are.' Kate knew she'd hit the mark when his eyes flickered. 'I know you went through a lot at school,' she said more gently. 'You were embarrassed, humiliated, but that won't happen now, I promise. Only Beauden will see what you can do initially and if you really have no talent then no one else need know and he will keep it to himself. He hasn't got where he is today by being indiscreet but if you can do it, think what it would mean for your future.'

'I'm not like you, Kate. I don't like being in the spotlight, I never have.'

'It's not like that when you're actually in the middle of it. You lose yourself in the character,' she said, eyes shining with passion for her art. 'You become them and in that moment, nothing else matters.'

'That's just it – I don't want to become Robert Alardyce.'

The passion vanished from Kate's eyes, that hard understanding returning as she once again plucked another secret from his soul. She knew that he was afraid of the role bringing out something in him that was better left dormant.

'You'll only be pretending to be him,' she said. 'You're old enough to know reality from fantasy.'

'I'm not doing it, so you can give up trying to persuade me.' Cameron looked to Beauden. 'I'm sorry you had a wasted journey.'

'Oh, I've not,' he smiled. 'Kate is a dear friend who I enjoy spending time with. Although it is such a shame,' he sighed, eyes flicking to the portrait of Robert. 'The resemblance is uncanny. It would have been wonderful for people to see Robert himself in the flesh on screen.'

'Sorry, but it's not happening,' he said, a note of irritation creeping into his tone, black eyes flashing.

'That's fine,' he smiled. 'I completely understand. In fact, I believe I have just the person to play Robert – Clay Wilson. He's an up-and-coming young actor who's had several roles in some very big productions. He's got some wonderful ideas for playing Robert. First and foremost, he wants to play him with a Spanish accent.'

Cameron almost choked on the tea he'd just taken a sip of. 'Spanish?' he gasped.

'Oh yes. He thinks it will bring an exotic touch to the character.'

'But he wasn't Spanish. He was born to English and Scottish parents. He never even went to Spain.'

'True but he did spend some time in Argentina, where they speak Spanish,' he smiled.

'Only for a few months. Not long enough to develop an accent.'

'Clay believes he can make it work and I agree.'

'Kate,' said Cameron, turning to her. 'Surely you see that's an insane plan?'

'Not really,' she replied. 'I had a friend who spent a year in Australia and she came back with the accent.'

'But Robert spent years in South Africa. Surely it would make more sense for him to have a South African accent, even though he didn't?'

'But a Spanish accent is so sexy,' she replied with a twinkle in her eye. 'Anyway, what do you care? You want nothing to do with it.'

'That doesn't mean I'm happy with you changing our family's history for dramatic effect. It belongs to us all, not just you.'

'Sorry, but that's just the way it is.'

He gaped at her before turning to his relatives for help. 'Lucy, as a historian, surely you see this is madness?'

'I agree, it is,' she scowled. 'It seems these days all films change history, replacing what really happened with dull clichés that we've seen a million times and I'm buggered if you're going to do the same to our own family's history. If that's how it's going to be then I refuse to work on it.'

'What do you want me to do?' said Kate casually. 'Clay bears a strong resemblance to Robert; he was in fact my first choice, until I saw Cameron yesterday. There's no one else I can think of. Clay's also the only other man I know with eyes so dark they look black. That's pretty hard to find and for me, it's all about the eyes,' she purred.

'I thought you of all people would want to shield our ancestors from disloyal interpretations of their characters,' Lucy told her. 'Tell this Clay idiot that he can't use a Spanish accent.'

'If I do, he won't agree to be in the film.'

'Good. Then you can get someone who isn't a complete twat.'

'Excuse me, dear,' Beauden told Lucy. 'It's far too early for twats, especially at the breakfast table.'

'Sorry, but I can't help how I feel. It's absolutely out of the question.'

'I understand your feelings, really I do. Thank you,' added Beauden when Marcus placed two slices of brown toast and a pot of jam before him. He took in Marcus's sturdy build and good looks, even if they were rather sombre, and he smiled. 'Very much,' he added with a wink.

Marcus's countenance didn't change and he turned his attention to removing the used crockery from the table.

'What was I saying?' said Beauden. 'Oh yes, of course. You've got to understand that a lot of what you see in a film is interpretive. And if an actor thinks doing something differently will help them represent the character more faithfully then it's best to let them do it.'

'What Beauden's trying to say is that this is the best we've got, so we have to run with it,' said Kate.

'And you're happy with that, are you?' Lucy demanded of her. 'I know what these people mean to you, which is why I can't believe you'd sanction this.'

'I see what this is,' chimed in a voice.

Everyone turned to look at Cameron.

'You're trying to get me to agree to do it by coming up with this ludicrous suggestion,' he told Kate. 'No way would you allow Robert to be portrayed as something he wasn't. Lucy's right, he means far too much to you. Well, your trick has failed. I'm still not doing it.'

'Then Clay will play him with a Spanish accent,' she replied.

'No he won't,' said Cameron knowingly. 'You'd get in another actor rather than see that happen. Sorry, Kate, but you've lost this one.' He smiled victoriously when her eyes narrowed. 'Could I have some porridge, please, Marcus?' he added with an air of satisfaction. 'I've suddenly got an appetite.'

'Certainly, sir.'

'Is that true, Kate?' demanded Lucy. 'Was that a ploy to get Cameron to play Robert?'

'Yes,' she replied in a hard tone, gaze locked on a smug Cameron.

'Thank God for that,' she breathed. 'I thought you were serious.'

'It was true about Clay playing him though,' said Beauden, who was carefully spreading jam on his toast, ensuring he went right up to the edge of the crust with it. 'Although he will emulate Robert's genuine accent.'

'You're much better sticking with him,' Cameron told Kate. 'At least he'll know what he's doing.'

The door opened and Tom entered, bestowing upon them all a white-toothed smile. 'Good morning, everyone.'

Jenna finally came to life and beamed back at him, the sadness vanishing from her eyes. 'Morning,' she replied cheerfully. 'I hope you slept well?'

'Like a log. The bed was so comfortable. Just a bit lonely.'

When he winked at her, she blushed and giggled.

Tom greeted Beauden with a hearty handshake before taking the empty chair beside him.

Chris entered the room, looking pale and washed out.

'Oh dear,' said Beauden. 'Someone's been burning the candle at both ends.'

'I didn't sleep very well,' he yawned. 'I was out like a light, but I kept getting woken up.'

'By what?'

'It's hard to say,' he replied, a shadow passing across his face. 'Bad dreams, I suppose, although I'm not really prone to nightmares. This will sound ridiculous, but it felt like someone was standing over me, watching me, and they resented my presence in their room.'

'You mean a ghost?' said Harmony.

'I wouldn't go that far. Like I said, it was just a bad dream but sometimes it felt like their face was just inches from my own.'

There was a beat of silence as they all pondered this.

'Which room are you in?' Lucy asked him.

'It looks out over the rear gardens, the third door on the left.'

'That's not Edward's old room, is it?'

'Edward?' he frowned. Chris's eyes widened. After reading Kate's script, he knew exactly who she was referring to.

'Do you know, I think you might be right, Lucy,' said Kate. 'I felt something odd about that room the very first time I went in there. It made me so uncomfortable I never went back. The decorators made a bad job of it and it took a threatening letter from my lawyer to make them redo their shoddy work. They wouldn't say what was wrong, only that they felt they weren't welcome in there and they did a wonderful job of the rest of the house.'

'I'm sure it's nothing like that,' said Chris, covering how uneasy Kate's words had made him with a nervous laugh. 'I'm more inclined to believe I just had a nightmare.'

'In that case, will you spend another night in that room?' said Harry with a knowing smile.

'Errr...' he began.

'I'll swap rooms with you,' said Tom. 'I've always wanted to stay in a haunted house and it looks like I'm about to fulfil that ambition.'

'What if you wake up and find someone standing over you?' Harry asked him.

'It doesn't worry me. I trained for three months with the SAS in the desert preparing for my last film.'

'And they taught you how to handle ghosts?' smiled Harry.

'No, but they did train me to deal with any unexpected situation, and if Edward Alardyce is haunting that room, he's in for a shock,' he said with a confident smile.

'We could always hold a séance,' said Harmony. 'Find out exactly who's still in residence here.'

'That could be interesting,' replied Shannon.

'You shouldn't mess with things like that,' said Jenna. 'God knows what you could unleash.'

'It would be perfectly safe,' said Harmony. 'I've done it plenty of times before and not had any trouble.'

'I like it,' beamed Beauden. He looked to Kate. 'We could get your ancestors' opinions about your film straight from the horse's mouth.'

'That's a great idea,' smiled Kate. She looked to Harmony. 'Do you think you could really contact my relatives?'

'Absolutely,' she replied. 'But only if they want to be contacted, of course.'

'Let's do it. Tonight.'

'Don't tell me you believe in all this rubbish?' Jenna demanded of Kate.

'I don't know if I do but I'm willing to keep an open mind.'

'Do you agree this is a waste of time, Harry?' said Jenna, thinking out of them all he would be the most likely to agree with her.

'I've been to Harmony's séances,' he began slowly. 'And I can't explain what I experienced.'

'You'd probably had too much brandy,' she said flatly.

'Possibly.'

'What do you think, Cam?' she said, hoping he would speak some sense.

'I don't know, I've never been to a séance before,' he replied. 'And I can't see what harm it can do. Nothing will happen.'

'That's because you've never seen my Harmony in action,' said Harry, smiling at his girlfriend and sliding an arm around her shoulders. 'She's a multi-talented woman.'

'Please don't call me "my Harmony",' she retorted. 'You know I hate it when you objectify me.'

'Sorry,' he replied, removing his arm.

Beauden smiled at how uneasy the majority of the people gathered around the table obviously were about the séance. 'I can see my stay here is going to be very interesting.'

8

After breakfast, Kate headed into the study so she could be alone with her thoughts. There was so much to consider, such as how to remove the current obstacles blocking her latest ambition. This film was the icing on the cake. She had Alardyce House and it would be a stage on which to tell her family's story, and Cameron had to be a part of it. He *was* Robert, whether he knew it or not. It had occurred to her that he could be a terrible actor but whatever force that had guided her through life so far was telling her that he would be perfect and she was determined to get her own way.

Kate turned to the window and gazed out at the grounds, just as Henry had done countless times and his son John after him, along with so many other Alardyces. This had always been the study where the family's business was conducted and now it was up to her to steer the ship.

There was a knock at the door.

'Come in,' she called.

The door opened and in walked Shannon. Kate turned to face her, neither woman speaking until she'd closed the door behind her.

'We need to talk about Cam,' said Shannon.

'You're right, we do, especially as to why you've not managed to convince him to be in my film yet.'

Kate was an organised woman and never went into anything without doing a lot of preparation first. The private investigator she'd hired to look into her cousins had been given very specific instructions, and those included looking into not just her cousins but their partners too. When she'd seen the images of Cameron on social media, she'd known he had to play Robert, but her biggest dilemma had been how to make that happen. She'd soon seen the path she must take when the investigator had told her all about Shannon's financial troubles, which Cameron was blissfully unaware of.

'You should be thanking me,' replied Shannon stonily. 'If it wasn't for me, he would have left already. I woke up to find him packing.'

Kate arched an eyebrow. 'Really?'

'Yes. I managed to convince him that he'd regret leaving so soon; he really was excited about getting to know you all again. He can be very sentimental.'

'Then at least you've done something to justify the money I'm paying you.'

'You can't keep pushing him so hard, and that crap about the Spanish accent was the wrong thing to do. Cam's a very honest man and lying to him will only make him dig his heels in harder. You need to play on his emotions. He has a deep love for his family. Make him feel like he'll be protecting your history. That's the way to get around him.'

'Even though he hates our history?'

'I don't think he does. He's just been brainwashed by his parents. They really didn't want him to come here but he was determined to meet up with you all.'

'My mother was against it too and I'm not sure why. At least we haven't lost our ability to defy them,' Kate said with a wry smile. 'What else are you going to do to convince Cam to be in the film?'

'That's not up to me. My job was to get him here and make sure he stays. It's up to you to persuade him.'

'Would another ten grand convince you to press the issue?'

Shannon's lips pursed but her eyes lit up with indecision and greed. 'I hate deceiving him.'

'I sympathise but I can't help but wonder what he would say if he knew you've been stealing from his businesses.'

'It's not stealing,' she snapped back. 'I was just moving some money around.'

'To support your own failing restaurant.'

'I'm going to pay it back, every penny.'

'But we're not talking pennies, are we? We're talking fifty thousand pounds. Another ten grand would ensure your debt to him is entirely paid off and he need never know.' Kate's eyes narrowed when Shannon looked down at the floor. 'You haven't put the forty grand I've already given you back into his accounts, have you? You've put it into your own.'

'I'm nearly solvent again,' she said desperately. 'And when I am I can replace it and he'll never find out.'

'I don't understand why you didn't just confide in him in the first place. He's so in love with you he would have happily given you the money.'

Tears filled Shannon's eyes and she bit her lower lip.

'I haven't seen Cam in sixteen years, but I do know that loyalty and trust are very important to him. He'll never be able to forgive you if he found out that you'd stolen from him.'

'He can't find out.' Steel filled Shannon's eyes. 'Ever.'

'And he won't hear it from me, as long as I get what I want.'

'What do you expect me to do?' exclaimed Shannon. 'I can't force him, and that idiot of an acting coach of yours has probably scuppered your chances for good.'

Kate paused to mull over her options before replying. 'I'll tell you what I'll do – forget the extra ten grand. Make it another fifty, only this payment will go straight into Cam's account and not yours. Not only will you be able to cover up your crime, but your own business will be afloat once more. All your problems solved at once by doing me one little favour.'

'And if I fail?'

'I won't tell him what you've done because I won't need to; he'll find out for himself. He's not a stupid man. All you could do then is pray he doesn't go to the police.'

Shannon sighed and nodded, wiping away the tears that were forming in her eyes with the back of her hand. 'Fine, I'll do it but for God's sake, stop trying to force him. This must be done gently.'

'I understand.'

Shannon nodded and turned to leave. The moment her back was turned, Kate's expression hardened, her eyes shooting daggers. This woman had betrayed a member of her family. She wasn't fit to be in this house – it felt like she was polluting it – but unfortunately Kate needed her. Once Shannon had fulfilled her duty, Kate would ensure she never saw Cameron again. It wouldn't be easy, the man was smitten, but she would find a way to come between them. He deserved far better.

Kate turned back to the window to continue her perusal of the garden, attempting to conjure her family's presence here, wondering what thoughts had passed through Henry's mind as he'd stood in this very spot, attempting to work out how he could control his errant stepson and lure him away from the dark side. Had he known early on it would be useless or had he hoped Robert could be saved? Kate knew she possessed this dark side herself. Jane had written in her journal that Robert had broken the Alardyce curse, that not another member of their family would be doomed to carry his evil in their veins, but she'd been wrong; it had only been lying dormant. Kate felt it inside herself. She hadn't the urge to physically hurt people as Robert and Edward had done. Rather, she preferred to injure them in more subtle ways, such as the actresses whose careers she'd ruined just so she could get the part she wanted, often by using the services of the private investigator who'd so successfully dug up the dirt on Shannon. Blackmail was her weapon of choice and it worked every time. She had considered using it on Cameron to get him to cooperate, but her sniffer dog of an investigator had been unable to come up with anything on Mr Squeaky Clean. Even if he had, she wanted Cameron to be a willing part of this project, not coerced into it. She knew she had Robert's ruthlessness, as well as his determination to succeed. His blood in her veins had given her an enormous gift and enabled her to achieve all her ambitions before she was thirty-five. The film was the final one. It wouldn't matter what happened after that, she would be happy to turn into a recluse like the previous owner and live here quietly amongst the ghosts for the rest of her life. All that mattered was getting this film completed.

The Alardyce curse was very much alive and well and living inside her. Something told her it was also inside Cameron, coiled up and sleeping, waiting for a single event to wake it up. She could see it in his black eyes. The prospect excited her. When he finally realised who he truly was, nothing would be capable of stopping either of them.

Everyone would fear the Alardyce name once again.

* * *

Shannon headed into the conservatory, needing time alone to think. For some reason, everyone seemed to avoid this room and she wasn't sure why. It was beautiful, looking out over the gardens, the maze in the distance. It was full of plants, all lush and green, as well as colourful blooms that released their perfume into the air. The plants and furniture had been arranged in a way that provided private little nooks. She took a seat on a rattan couch that was hidden from view of the door leading into the house by a huge majesty palm tree and buried her face in her hands.

How the hell had she got herself into this mess? At first, she'd only stolen small amounts of money from Cameron's businesses. It had been easy for her, telling herself she'd pay it back the following month, but she'd never made enough profit from her restaurant to do that and the situation had snowballed, Shannon taking more and more while always telling herself she could pay it back. When it started to become clear that wouldn't happen, she'd turned to the bank, hoping to get a loan to hide her crime, but the bank had refused because her credit history was so bad. Kate's offer had seemed like a godsend and all she had to do was persuade Cameron to take part in a film. She'd known it wouldn't be a simple task, aware of his hatred of the limelight, but she was also aware of the sway she had over him. It made her feel bad that her influence came not from her powers of persuasion but because he loved her so much. Even so, her task had turned out to be harder than she'd thought. At least he'd decided to stay at Alardyce House. What she had to do was make Cameron think that being in his bitch of a cousin's film would be to his advantage or, even better, that he would be helping her personally.

Shannon whipped round in her seat, sensing someone was standing right behind her, but no one was there. The feeling, however, didn't go away.

'Who's there?' she called.

There was no answer.

'Harry, is that you?' she said, thinking that if anyone would play a practical joke on her it would be him.

Unease gripped Shannon when there was no response. There wasn't a flicker of movement.

Getting to her feet, she peered around the leaves of the palm tree and saw nothing. It was possible someone was concealed among the greenery at the other side of the room, but the stillness in the air was such that it felt like no one else was there.

No one living, anyway, said the voice in her head.

Shannon got to her feet and hurried towards the door, head held high, doing her best to maintain her dignity while fighting the urge to break into a run, eyes feeling to bore into her back. She left the conservatory and breathed a sigh of relief. No wonder everyone avoided that room. Putting the incident behind her, she headed into the drawing room where she'd last seen Cameron, but he wasn't there.

'Have you seen Cam?' she asked Harry and Harmony, who were the only ones there, ruling out the possibility of Harry playing a practical joke on her in the conservatory.

'He went for a walk in the garden with Lucy,' replied the latter.

'Thanks.'

Shannon hurried into the hallway and paused to shove her feet into her trainers before rushing outside. The light rain that had started yesterday evening had dried up and the sun had returned with a vengeance, beating down on her head. She couldn't see Cameron and Lucy in the grounds in front of the house, so she headed around the back. Shannon spotted them not far from the maze, walking together and talking. Their conversation looked to be rather intense. Was now the right time to approach him? Failure to pick her moment properly could be devastating to her plan.

While she was dithering about what to do, Cameron spotted her and waved. Left with no choice, Shannon jogged over to them.

'I hope I'm not interrupting,' she said. 'I can leave you to it if you're catching up.'

'There's no need for that,' he smiled, slinging an arm around her shoulders.

'I have to phone work anyway,' said Lucy. 'I've had a text message from my boss saying he needs to talk to me urgently.'

'I hope you don't have to go back to work,' replied Cameron with concern. 'We've not even started catching up yet.'

'Not a chance. I haven't taken a holiday in two years, so he knows I'm owed this. He's a bit dithery. He's probably lost the key to his desk or locked his lunch in the safe again. He's always doing stupid stuff like that. I'll catch up with you later,' she said before wandering off, already taking out her phone and dialling her boss's number.

'Fancy taking a walk back into the village?' Cameron asked Shannon. 'I want to explore it properly. All we concentrated on last time were the graves.'

'Sounds good,' she replied, taking his hand. 'Listen, Cam, there's something I need to tell you.'

'What's that?'

He looked so happy she felt dreadful for what she was about to say. 'I'm in trouble.'

Concern filled his eyes. 'What sort of trouble? If it's that ex of yours again I'll kill him.'

'No, it's not him. I haven't heard from Steve since you had a word with him.' If she was honest with herself, Shannon had been very doubtful about what effect Cameron would have on her vicious ex-boyfriend. Although Cameron was well-built and muscular, he was so gentle, but he'd successfully scared off Steve. He'd never gone into detail about what he'd said or done. Shannon had often wondered but never dared ask. 'I'm in financial trouble,' she continued. 'My business is failing and I don't know what to do.'

'But I thought your restaurant was really successful?'

'It was, then Covid hit and I couldn't recover. I kept hanging in there, hoping things would get better but they never did. I'm in so deep and I'm scared.' She closed her eyes and sucked in a breath. 'God, it feels good to finally get that off my chest.'

'Why didn't you tell me before?'

'Because I was embarrassed and ashamed. You know what my parents are like, they're so pushy. Can you imagine the grief I'd get if they found out I'd failed? I thought I could pull it back and no one need know, but it's gone too far.' The tears that filled Shannon's eyes were genuine, not part of the act, and she let them roll unchecked down her face.

Cameron pulled her into his arms and she clung on to him.

'I wish you'd told me sooner,' he said. 'It must have been a nightmare coping with this alone.'

'It's been bloody awful,' she rasped into his strong shoulder.

'I can only imagine. How much are you in debt by?'

'Ninety grand,' she replied. That was a lie, it was actually fifty grand, but she wanted to give him a figure he couldn't possibly match. The last thing she wanted was for him to say he'd give her the money from his own business. That might lead to him figuring out what she'd done.

'Jesus,' he breathed, pulling back slightly so he could look into her eyes. 'I would give you the money, but I don't have that amount to spare.' He had feared lockdown would kill off his own businesses, but he'd got through it by giving fitness and nutritional classes online, the money from these side businesses keeping him afloat. In fact, so many people hadn't wanted to get behind on their fitness schedule that they'd signed up to his online classes in droves and he'd made a profit.

'I know and it's fine,' she replied, forcing a smile. 'I would never expect you to give me so much. I just had to confide in someone. It was eating me alive.'

'How long do you have to get the money together?'

'A month before I lose the restaurant and my creditors seize all the equipment, leaving me with nothing.'

'Would you be able to pull back the business if you did get the cash?'

'Aye, definitely. It would let me get over the damage lockdown caused and clear my debts. The restaurant's still busy, I've just been unable to get ahead. I haven't paid my suppliers in weeks and they're threatening to cut me off. If that happens, I really will be finished.'

Cameron nodded, expression serious. Shannon held her breath as she gazed up at him, the way his black eyes flickered telling her he was considering doing something he really didn't want to do.

'Why don't you go into the village and I'll catch you up?' he said, already striding back towards the house.

'Where are you going?' she called.

'I need to speak to someone,' he replied.

Shannon watched him go, praying he was going to talk to Kate. She hated the thought of him being pushed into something he was against but there was no choice. Plus this project would be good for him too. It would make even more people flock to his gyms and shops.

The thought did nothing to ease her guilt.

* * *

Cameron entered the house and was immediately met by Marcus.

'Where's Kate?' he asked the butler.

'Ms Alardyce is in the study, sir.'

'Thanks,' he replied before striding past him, turning right at the end of the hall onto another corridor. Raising his hand, he knocked on the study door.

'Come in,' called a voice.

He entered to find Kate sitting in an old armchair reading her damn script.

'Cameron,' she smiled. 'This is a pleasant surprise. How can I help you?'

'How much will I get paid to play Robert?'

Kate placed the script on the small table beside the chair and regarded him seriously. 'That's a bit of a difficult question to answer. You see, I've just taken a phone call from an executive at a major streaming channel. They want another period drama and me and Chris are in talks with them to make nine hour-long episodes instead of a film.'

Cameron swallowed hard. 'Nine?'

'Yes, which is amazing because we can get in our entire family history now.'

'So you wouldn't need me for a bit?' he said, not knowing whether to feel pleased or not about that. 'Because Robert doesn't come into the story until later.'

'Nope. This series will start and end with Robert. Amy's story prior to his birth and when he was a child will be told in flashbacks. He really will be the star of the show.'

'I would have thought you'd want the starring role.'

'This isn't about me, it's about the best way to tell our family's history.'

'Does that mean I'd get paid more than if it was a film?'

'Yes, quite a bit more.'

'How much?'

'Why are you suddenly so concerned about money? I thought you were doing okay.'

'I am, but something's come up and I need cash fast.'

'How fast?'

'In the next month.'

'Wow, this is a surprise. You wouldn't get paid that quickly. It'll take months just for filming to begin.'

'Bugger,' he sighed.

'But I'd be willing to advance you the money.'

'You would?'

Kate nodded. 'I don't want to do this project without you and I'm willing to do anything to get you involved.'

'Even though you'll lose out if it turns out I'm a shite actor?'

'Yes, although I would expect you to work with Beauden first. He'll know immediately if you're up to the job.'

'Fine. Where is he? Let's get it over with.'

'You can't do it now. He's in his room doing his morning exercises.'

'Then we'll do it later. I said I'd meet Shannon in the village anyway.'

'Why have you changed your tune so quickly? You were adamant barely an hour ago that you weren't doing it.'

'I have my reasons. So, can you estimate how much I'll get paid?'

'No, it's impossible. I don't even know what the budget will be yet. You're best telling me how much you want to do it.'

'A hundred grand,' he replied. As the lion's share would go to Shannon, he might as well get something out of it.

'That shouldn't be a problem, I could even get you more. I'll have the money in your account in a few days.'

Cameron blinked at her. 'That's it?'

'Yes. Why, is there something else you want?'

'No, I just can't believe you're giving in so easily. What if this programme's never made?'

Kate's smile could only be described as amused. 'Cam, I always get what I want. This is happening; there's already too many interested parties involved and I have a lot of influence. Has something happened? If you're having money trouble, I want to help.'

'You're already helping. You can't know how grateful I am, especially as we haven't seen each other in years.'

'You're family and I always help family, Cam,' she said softly.

He nodded. 'We're lucky to have you in our lives.'

Kate's eyes glistened with emotion. 'That means so much to me. Thank you.'

Cameron was rather touched by that look, even if he wasn't happy about being forced into something he didn't want to do. 'Well, I'll leave you to it. Shannon will be wondering what's happened to me.'

'I'll call my accountant first thing Monday morning and we can arrange the transfer of the money.'

'Thanks. You can't know how much I mean that.'

Cameron gave her hand a gentle squeeze before leaving, quietly closing the door behind him.

The wistfulness vanished from Kate's eyes. She smiled and leaned back in her chair. Once again, she'd got her own way.

* * *

Shannon anxiously watched Cameron stride along the main street of the village towards her, his face set. Did that look mean Kate had told him the truth or had he finally agreed to do something he didn't want to do? It was impossible to tell. In a way, it would be a relief if he finally did know what she'd done. She wouldn't have to lie to him any more, but she would lose him and he was undoubtedly the best thing in her life. On the other hand, if he did do the film then the money could be paid back, her business would be saved and all would be well. After all, it was just a film, a few months out of his life. It would soon be over and he wouldn't have to do it again. Surely that wasn't so bad?

It was difficult for her not to squirm with anticipation as he stormed up to her. It felt as though she was standing at a crossroads with no idea what direction her life was about to take. Her very future hinged on the conversation he'd just had with Kate because she knew that was who he'd spoken to. Women turned to look at him as he passed them by but as usual he paid them no attention. Shannon knew he could have had his pick and she still couldn't understand why he'd chosen her. Granted, she was pretty, in an ordinary way, but she was nothing compared to the women who went to his gyms and regularly hit on him. But then again, he really had no idea how handsome he was. Not even the portrait of Robert Alardyce had made him see. Before this mess she could console herself with the fact that they were soulmates, but that consolation had vanished the moment she'd stolen from him. If they really were soulmates, how had she betrayed him so easily?

'Everything okay?' she asked nervously as he approached her.

Cameron nodded, his eyes flashing in that way she'd only really seen since they'd been at Alardyce.

'I've agreed to do Kate's sodding TV programme.'

'TV programme?' she frowned. 'I thought it was a film.'

'She's had an offer from a streaming channel who want to make it into a TV programme instead. Kate's accepted because she'll be able to tell more of the story. It'll be nine episodes in total.'

'Why did you agree? I thought you were dead against it.'

'She's going to pay me enough money to save your business. She even said she'll pay me in advance and transfer it into my account on Monday. As soon as I have it, we can pay off all your debts and get your restaurant back on its feet.' He didn't add that first he had to convince Beauden that he could act because that would only worry her.

Emotion welled up deep inside Shannon, like oil bursting from a vein in the earth, and she thought it might drown her. 'Cam,' she rasped, burying her face in her hands.

'Hey, it's okay,' he said, pulling her to him and kissing the top of her head. 'I really don't mind. I'll do anything to help you.'

'But you'll hate it.'

'I don't know that I will, I've never done it before. I might love it. This could be the start of a brand-new career for me.'

The enthusiasm in his voice didn't match the look in his eyes. Shannon wasn't fooled but she desperately wanted to believe. 'That's true,' she said, forcing a smile. 'You could end up being as big a star as Kate.'

'You never know.'

'I hate it that you've been pushed into this because of me.'

'I don't.' He cupped her face in his hands. 'I'd do anything for you, Shan.'

'God, I love you.'

'I love you too,' he said before kissing her.

They embraced in the middle of the pavement, forcing passersby to go around them.

Shannon began to calm down. Her business and her relationship were saved. Yes, Cameron would have to do the television programme, but as he said, he might actually enjoy the work. Then, for the very first time in her life, everything would be perfect.

9

Cameron and Shannon had lunch in the village pub before returning to the house together. While Shannon sat out in the back garden with Lucy and Harry, Cameron went in search of Beauden. He found him playing billiards with Chris and Tom.

'Can I have a word?' Cameron asked him.

'Yes, of course,' he smiled pleasantly.

Beauden replaced his cue in the rack and the two men left together.

'How can I help?' Beauden asked Cameron.

'I've agreed to do this TV programme for Kate.'

'You have? How wonderful. And you want me to analyse your abilities?'

'Aye, please, if it's convenient?'

'Any time for you, dear Cameron. Let's go into the dining room. I believe it's all clear now,' he replied before turning and hurrying off in that direction. He moved with small, quick movements, like a mouse scurrying across the floor.

Cameron followed him into the dining room and stared up at the portrait of Robert, who seemed to glare back down at him with even more disapproval. His expression said there would be consequences if Cameron made a bad job of representing him. It was hard for Cameron to think of this man as his great-grandfather. Grandfathers were supposed to be sweet elderly men with white hair and frail limbs. Robert had died in his thirties, so he hadn't reached old age.

Beauden closed the door behind him and studied Cameron as he in turn studied the portrait.

'You shouldn't be afraid of him, you know,' he said.

Cameron turned to him with a frown. 'Why would I be afraid of a dead man?'

'Because you're frightened you'll turn out just like him.'

'I bloody well won't,' he retorted.

'That's the spirit. Don't let him intimidate you. That's no insult to you; he intimidates us all when we're eating. I've never seen such a fearsome portrait. It really looks alive.'

'You're not helping.'

'The fact is, he's not alive. It's just the skill of the artist giving that illusion. But you are, meaning you automatically have more power than him.'

'I suppose,' he replied, although he didn't feel this sentiment.

'Right, go on then.'

'Go on what?'

'Be Robert.'

'How?'

'You tell me, he's your grandfather.'

'Is that what you tell all the actors you train, *go on then?*'

'No, but this is a rare case. I've never worked with someone playing their own relative before.'

Cameron shifted uncomfortably. 'I'll feel stupid.'

'Ah ha, so you do have an idea of how to do it then?'

'I've pictured him in my mind since I was a wee boy.'

'That's great. Do that then.'

'But I don't know how.'

'That's a lie, you've already told me you do.'

'Do you always have an answer to every question?' Cam snapped.

'If you're serious about this project then you'll have to do this in front of a lot more people than me. There'll be the director, assistant directors, other actors, cameramen, lighting technicians; the list is endless. Sets are busy places, you know.'

'You're not making me feel better. What should I say?'

'I'll tell you what, I'll fetch the script. Just give me a minute.'

Beauden left and Cameron stared up at the picture, attempting to mimic Robert's haughty pose. He felt an idiot even when he was alone, so how could he hope to do it in front of other people? He had the horrible feeling he had absolutely no talent for being someone else. His one attempt at acting would fail and Shannon would lose her restaurant.

Beauden returned with the script. 'I've found the perfect place for you to start,' he said, holding it out to him at a certain page. 'I think the most important thing we need to work on is Robert's strength. One thing I gleaned from this script is his absolute faith in himself. What he wants he always gets and he knows no one is capable of stopping him. It's this part when he's in South Africa and dealing with some little worm called Peter Anderson. This scene shows Robert's cool head under pressure, as well as his aggression. If you can pull off this scene then you can manage the rest, I'm sure of it. I'll play the role of Peter,' he added before tilting his head from side to side and jogging up and down on the spot.

'What are you doing?' frowned Cameron.

'Just getting into character.' Beauden closed his eyes and took a deep breath. He opened his eyes and regarded Cameron gravely. 'I heard you were attacked last night.'

'Eh? No, I wasn't.'

'That's a line in the script.'

'Oh, right, sorry. That was very convincing.'

'I'm not the top acting coach in the country for no reason. Now it's your turn.'

'Okay,' said Cameron, looking down at the script in his hand. 'I was?' he replied.

'Don't say it so flatly. Put a little life into it. Remember, you're a rich, powerful man completely confident in his own abilities. Peter is just a little tick you can easily squash and you'll enjoy it too.'

'It's hard to feel like that. I'm really not an aggressive person.'

'That doesn't matter. All you need to do is act aggressive. Look to your grandfather for inspiration,' he added, gesturing to the portrait. 'Imagine what he'd look like angry. His blood is in your veins. You can do this, Cameron, I have faith in you and so does Kate.'

'How can you when you don't even know me?'

'Because I get a feeling deep in my gut when I get a new student and I feel it with you, Cam. May I call you Cam?'

He nodded.

'If this talent runs in the family, then, judging by Kate's performances, you have it in bucketloads. Now, let's continue.' Beauden looked back down at the script. 'Who was it, robbers?' he said.

Cameron kept Shannon firmly in his mind. He was doing this for her. If he failed, the consequences would fall on her, not him. He had to give this his all, despite how ridiculous he felt. 'No, it wasn't robbers,' he said, putting a little more depth and determination into his voice. 'You know exactly who it was.'

'That was better,' smiled Beauden. 'See, we've started on the path already. Whatever's driving you, use it. It will help you.'

Cameron nodded in understanding, keeping his girlfriend firmly in mind.

'Right, where were we?' said Beauden, eyes scanning the script. 'Ah, yes. Barnaby?' he said, widening his eyes.

'You must think me quite the fool,' said Cameron.

'You're supposed to grab me by the front of the shirt and shove me up against the wall there,' Beauden told him.

'I might hurt you,' he said, taking in Beauden's slight frame.

'Do you think Robert would have cared about hurting the real Peter? Of course not. Now I'm aware that there is a certain size difference. Those broad shoulders of yours are making me a little nervous but I'm perfectly willing to suffer for my art. It certainly won't be the first time.'

'Well, okay, but I'll only do it gently.'

'As you wish.'

With one hand, Cameron grasped the front of Beauden's shirt and very carefully tilted him back towards the wall. 'You must think me quite the fool.'

'You're so concerned with not hurting me that you've lost all the aggression. It says a lot for your own good character but what we need for this project is the bad and we all have bad inside us, Cam.'

'I just feel so self-conscious,' he replied, releasing Beauden. 'I'm afraid you'll laugh at me.'

'I would never do that. I'm a professional and I see nothing remotely amusing about acting. You know I taught Tom?'

Cameron nodded.

'He was terrible when he first came to me. A piece of wood would have put on a more convincing performance, but the man was just so damn magnetic I knew he was born to perform. He too was held back by self-consciousness, but we managed to move past it and unlock all his wonderful talent. Now look at him – one of the top actors in not just this country but all over the world. If he can do it, then so can you.'

'I really appreciate your faith in me but there's something else holding me back.'

'What's that?'

'I was bullied all through primary school and for the majority of high school too. When I was sixteen, I had a growth spurt. I shot up, the weight fell off, and I got into sports and working out. Only then did it all stop. Even now, all these years later, I can remember all the jokes and name-calling but most of all, I remember the laughter.' These last few words were reduced to a whisper as shame and embarrassment overtook Cameron. But he was doing this for the woman he loved and bravery was required.

Beauden's face softened with sympathy and he patted his shoulder. 'I can sympathise. I too was tormented at school for being the opposite – small and skinny – but that only made me more determined to succeed and show the world and all those pathetic bullies what I could do. I was very satisfied to discover that not one of the fools who picked on me made anything of their own lives. I understand your experiences left a deep wound inside you.'

Cameron nodded sadly.

'You must have felt angry about what those bullies did to you.'

'Aye, I did. I used to fantasise about how I would punish the bastards.'

Beauden smiled when Cameron's voice came out in a deep growl. 'And how would you do that?' he asked him.

'I wanted to batter the living shite out of them. I used to imagine punching and kicking them all until they begged me to stop. But I wouldn't listen and I would keep going until they stopped moving and I knew they could never hurt me again. It would make me feel better for a wee bit, then I'd go into school and all that bravery would leave me when I saw them again.'

'But you still have all that anger and now you keep a tight rein on yourself because you're afraid of it finally breaking free and hurting someone.' He smiled when Cameron's eyes widened. 'I've been through what you've been through, so I understand. I managed to exorcise my own anger when I discovered two of my own bullies were homeless drug addicts and another was in prison for fraud. My anger turned to pity before I dismissed them entirely from my mind and finally turned my full attention to my own wonderful life.'

'I'd like that. To finally forget about them.'

'This is how you can rid yourself of the anger – channel it into playing Robert. Acting can be very cathartic; it allows you to express things you can't normally. You daren't display your anger in your normal life, so let Robert get rid of it for you.' Beauden knew he'd got through to Cameron when his eyes lit up with hope. 'Shall we try again from the beginning?'

'Aye, just give me a minute.'

Cameron looked to the portrait of his great-grandfather before reading what was coming up next in the script.

Beauden patiently waited as he closed his eyes and lowered his head, breathing deeply. He was a little startled when Cameron's head suddenly snapped up and in those black eyes of his, rather than kindness and openness, he saw a mocking derision.

'Err,' said Beauden, so thrown he had to look down at the script again. He knew the first line, but he wanted to escape that gaze. 'I heard you were attacked last night,' he said.

Cameron arched a disdainful eyebrow. 'I was?'

'Who was it, robbers?'

Cameron paused before replying, the way his assessing gaze drilled right through Beauden making him distinctly uncomfortable.

'No, it wasn't robbers.' Cameron tilted his head down slightly in a threatening manner. 'You know exactly who it was.'

'Barnaby?'

Beauden couldn't help but gasp with surprise when Cameron grabbed him by the front of the shirt with one hand and slammed him rather painfully back against the wall.

'You must think me quite the fool,' he growled, black eyes full of wrath.

Beauden could feel the raw strength in Cameron's limbs and knew he could easily crush him should he so choose. It was a disturbing feeling. He glanced at the script. 'What do you mean?' he said, voice coming out in an effortless shriek.

'You arranged that attack on me,' said Cameron, banging him against the wall again, all his previous concerns for Beauden's well-being apparently gone.

The anger and contempt in Cameron's face was joined by slyness, broken only by the fact that he was forced to look at the script again. 'All this time you've been working against me for your family and don't even think of lying. I've just returned from your uncle's office.'

It took Beauden a moment to remember this wasn't real and that his frantic brain didn't actually need to come up with an excuse. It was all just make-believe. He also knew this scene grew increasingly violent and he had no desire to be slammed against a wall again.

'Well done, Cameron,' he said. 'I knew you could do it.'

Cameron blinked a few times, as though waking from a dream. 'I did?'

'Oh, yes. I've no doubt you can play Robert Alardyce,' he replied, feeling like he needed to catch his breath. 'Right, I need to tell Kate the good news. I suggest you read the script in depth. It will have to change as it's being made into a television series, but I do believe she's going to use this script as the spine of the new one, so it would be a good idea for you to familiarise yourself with it.'

Beauden glanced at the portrait of Robert as he left. He could have sworn it was smirking.

* * *

Kate had joined Harry, Lucy, Shannon, Chris and Tom in the garden. Harmony was with Jenna and Simon in their room giving them some counselling at the former's request with the latter's reluctant agreement.

They were all startled when Beauden burst out of the patio doors.

'I'm pleased to tell you that Cameron will have no problem playing Robert,' he said breathlessly.

'You're certain?' replied Kate.

'No doubt about it. For a disconcerting moment back there, your great-grandfather was reborn. Now if you'll excuse me, I need to go and count my bruises.'

'Bruises? What did he do?'

'Let's just say he really threw himself into the role. I pity whoever you choose to play Peter Anderson,' he added before heading back into the house.

'This is great news,' said Chris with an easy smile. 'Once again, Kate, your instincts were spot on.'

'It looks like acting is a family talent,' said Tom, picking up a green olive from the dish Marcus had placed on the table and tossing it into his mouth. After one chew he grimaced but was left with no choice but to swallow it.

Kate glanced at Shannon, who looked very relieved, before turning back to Chris. 'Why are you so surprised?'

'I'm not,' he replied. 'I've already learnt that it's never wise to doubt Kate Alardyce.'

* * *

The guests at Alardyce House once again gathered together in the dining room for dinner. Cameron took his usual place at the table opposite the portrait of his doppelganger. This time he paid it more attention. He took in how the man held himself proudly, the tinge of arrogance in his eyes. Most of all, he saw how he folded his large white hands. Cameron looked down at his own hands and for the first time saw they were the same. Were they capable of causing as much harm as Robert's had? God, he hoped he didn't lose himself playing this role as he had earlier in the day. He glanced at Shannon sitting across the table from him. No, he would not let her down. She'd backed him to the hilt when he'd been setting up his gyms, been there for him through all the worry and stress; she even did his accounts for him, and he refused to let her down the first time she needed him. The only way he would be able to help her was by really delving into the personality of his ancestor, no matter how much he didn't want to.

Kate noticed Cameron was staring at the painting and once again felt triumphant. Everything was coming together as she'd planned. It was amazing what an iron will could achieve. Failing simply wasn't an option for her, hence she'd never once failed at anything. Now all she needed to do was get Shannon out of the way. She felt that as long as she was around, Cameron would never really be able to sink his teeth into the role of Robert. His love for her would act like a shield. Kate intended to take him on a journey back into the past to draw out his own darkness, which was just like the shadow she carried in her own soul, Robert's legacy to them both. Only then would her project work properly and her ancestors live again through the screen. The problem was how to get Shannon out of the way. She couldn't tell Cameron that his girlfriend had been stealing from him because her own plot to get him to play Robert would be revealed and he'd change his mind. Paying him the money in advance would ensure something tied him to the project, but his heart wouldn't be in it and it would only work if he committed himself body and soul. Shannon had to be the sacrifice to make the past live again, to make Kate feel she was truly connected to her ancestors, to the people she really wanted to be with. Cameron was the key to all that. It wouldn't be easy separating him from Shannon; he was clearly in love. It was vital something shatter that love. She had toyed with the idea of asking Tom to seduce Shannon and ensuring Cameron caught them together in a compromising position. Tom would have no qualms about that, he had very few morals and would see it as a challenge, but she didn't think Shannon would fall for his superficial charm. Shannon didn't trust her and would therefore be on her guard. Whatever Kate came up with would have to completely blindside Shannon, leaving her no time to react. Kate was certain her sharp brain would very soon come up with the solution.

Lucy looked from Cameron studying the painting of Robert to Kate, who was in turn studying Cameron, and she understood his agreeing to play Robert had changed something. She could feel a change in the air, like the power dynamics had shifted. Looking around the table, it seemed only she sensed this. Everyone else was behaving normally. Jenna and Simon sat on opposing sides of the table, casting each other sullen glances. It seemed Harmony's counselling had had little effect. Everyone else was listening to Tom holding court, telling funny anecdotes about various stars he'd worked with. Out of all her cousins, Lucy liked Cameron the best. He'd always been sweet and kind. When they'd been children, he'd gone out of his way to try and help others even when he was dealing with so much shit of his own. Neither had he ever denigrated or mocked anyone, as Kate and Harry liked to do. Jenna had her vicious moments too. She didn't like the thought of Cameron being sucked into something he didn't want to be a part of and understood that something had happened to persuade him otherwise. What that was she couldn't think but she swore she would do all in her power to stop Kate from taking advantage of him.

10

After dinner, they all retired to the drawing room. Jenna scrambled to take the empty spot on the couch beside Tom and sat so close to him she was almost on his lap.

'Tell us more of your stories, Tom,' she smiled, ignoring Harry's loud sigh.

'I think Tom's monopolised the conversation for long enough,' said Kate. 'He'd talk all night, given the opportunity.'

'I don't mind,' said Jenna, fluttering her eyelashes at him.

'I really think we should give someone else the floor,' said Kate kindly but firmly.

'Why don't we have that séance?' said Harmony.

'I love it,' smiled Kate.

'Err, I'm not so sure about that,' replied Lucy. 'You're messing with forces you don't understand.'

'But I do understand them,' said Harmony. 'I've held loads of séances.'

'And what if something nasty comes through?'

'So what if it does? I'll kick it out like I've done plenty of times before.'

'This place has such a tragic history. God knows what you'll be inviting in.'

'I've held séances in worse places than this – abandoned mental hospitals, prisons. This will be easy and especially powerful as this house has a lot of personal meaning to some of you and a lot of love was shared here.'

'As well as a lot of evil,' added Lucy.

'Relax, it'll be fine with Harmony in control,' said Harry. 'She really does have a gift. It runs in the family. Her mother and grandmother are talented mediums too.'

'I never thought you'd be a believer.'

'I wasn't, until I met Harmony.'

'I'm up for it,' said Shannon. 'I've always wanted to take part in a séance.'

'I must confess, I'm curious,' chimed in Beauden.

'What do you think, Chris?' said Kate.

'No offence, Harmony, but I think it's a lot of claptrap,' he replied. 'However, I am willing to sit in and watch you all jump at shadows,' he smiled.

'No offence taken,' said Harmony. 'I've met plenty of sceptics before, none of whom remained sceptics after attending one of my séances.'

'She's right, you know,' Harry told him with a wicked grin.

'What do you think, Cam?' said Lucy.

He shrugged. 'I don't believe in it, but I won't object if you want to do it.'

Kate turned to Jenna, but she was too busy throwing Simon triumphant glances about her close proximity to a Hollywood heartthrob while he sat in the armchair in the corner, glaring back at her.

'Let's do it,' said Kate, eyes sparkling with excitement.

'Great,' smiled Harmony. 'We need a circular table and candles.'

Kate rang for Marcus and put her request to him. He said there was a round table in the conservatory that could be used. Cameron offered to give him a hand with it and the two men returned a few minutes later carrying the table between them and placed it in the centre of the room. Marcus then left again and returned with the candles, which were placed in a silver candelabra in the middle of the table. Chairs were arranged and those wanting to take part took their seats. Cameron, Lucy, Tom, Simon and Jenna remained where they were while the others took their places.

'Don't tell us you're not joining in,' Kate told Tom. 'The man who's usually up for any adventure.'

'You're all wasting your time,' he replied. 'And I want to sit here and laugh.'

'Is that really the reason, or are you scared?'

Just as she'd known it would, this slight to his courage had the desired effect and he leapt up. 'Well, it could be interesting.'

'I agree,' said Jenna, jumping up too. 'It'll be fun.'

More chairs were added to the table, Jenna ensuring her chair was placed right beside Tom's.

'You're not leaving me out,' said Simon, grabbing one of the spare chairs and dragging it noisily across the floor before shoving it between Tom and his wife.

'What are you doing?' scowled Jenna. 'There's no room here. Go to the other side.'

'You must be frigging joking.'

Simon was not to be swayed. He'd had a few glasses of wine and felt very fortified against the handsomest and most talented Hollywood had to offer. He glared at Tom until he shifted his chair to the left, forcing everyone else to do the same to make space for him. Simon placed his chair in the ensuing gap with all the pride of Neil Armstrong planting the flag on the moon. Jenna pouted and folded her arms across her chest.

While all this was going on, Harmony had lit the candles. Marcus had already gone, leaving them to it.

Harmony retook her seat to address the table. 'I want you all to think of who you'd like to contact and what questions you want to ask.'

'I think we should leave that to the family,' said Chris. 'Us interlopers should just observe.'

'That's fair,' replied Beauden.

'We need to think very carefully about who we want to contact,' said Harry. 'Some very forceful personalities have lived in this house.'

'And that force won't leave them just because they've crossed over,' said Harmony. 'They will be the person they were while alive, so it's wise to bear that in mind.'

Kate nodded in understanding. 'Perhaps Jane or Amy would be the best bet?'

'Oh, good,' said Harry. 'For a moment there, I felt sure you'd suggest Robert.'

'I don't think that would be very wise,' said Harmony.

'Let's try Jane,' said Kate. 'I feel so close to her after reading her journals.'

'All right. Do you have an item she owned or a picture of her, one small enough to sit on the table?' she added before Kate suggested bringing through the enormous portrait from the dining room.

'I have a picture we could use. Just a sec.'

She rose and hurried from the room.

'Are you sure about this, Harmony?' said Lucy.

'Absolutely,' she replied with a serene smile. 'There's really nothing to worry about.'

'I hope you're right.'

Kate returned with a small black and white photograph of Jane in her younger days, looking beautiful with her blonde hair coiled into a bun, softened by a few curls left down around her face. She wore a jacquard dinner dress, the bodice underneath pulling her in at the waist.

'Beautiful girl,' said Tom. 'Hey, she's the woman in the picture in the dining room.'

'I see you're still the proverbial lightning bolt,' smiled Beauden.

'Could one of you record the session?' said Harmony, turning to those not sitting at the table. 'Often noises or interactions that can't be heard during the séance may be picked up on a recording.'

'I'll do that,' said Cameron, taking out his phone, as always anxious to help whenever he could.

'Thank you. Everyone else turn off your mobile phones. Don't just put them on silent, turn them off completely.'

They all pulled their phones from their pockets and switched them off before replacing them, apart from Cameron, who held his phone ready to record.

'Aren't we using a Ouija board?' said Chris.

'No, because we don't have one,' replied Harmony with a cheerful smile, in her element. 'We'll do table rapping instead but we can only ask yes-no questions for that. After a question is asked, listen carefully and give it a bit of time. It takes a spirit a tremendous amount of energy to respond, so be patient. It's also vital that you're relaxed. That makes it much easier for the spirits to connect. The dark is much more conducive to contact. Could someone close all the curtains please?'

Lucy rose and began pulling them shut. The curtains were thick blackout ones, so they plunged the room into gloom.

'Just put on one lamp,' said Harmony.

Lucy switched on the one closest to the table, leaving the rest of the room in shadow.

'Now,' said Harmony. 'We'll take a few minutes to relax first. If you're really not comfortable, it's fine to sit out. It's important that only those who are ready to take part in the séance remain at the table.'

No one moved and all regarded her expectantly.

'Take long, deep breaths,' said Harmony in a soft, soothing voice. 'Feel yourselves relaxing, sinking into your seats, your muscles unwinding.'

She gave them a couple of minutes to compose themselves before telling everyone to join hands.

'All of you think about Jane.' Harmony turned her attention to the ceiling. 'We are here to contact Jane Alardyce,' she called to the air. 'We require her guidance. Only spirits of love and light are welcome in this space. I call upon my spirit guides to keep away all negative energies and entities. Jane Alardyce, if you are here, please join us.'

With that, she lapsed into silence, eyes closed. The others looked at each other across the table, unsure what to do. The room was deathly quiet, the only sound the soughing of the wind through the trees outside, but it was soft and soothing.

'Maybe she's busy?' offered Tom when nothing happened.

'There is someone here, standing close to us,' said Harmony. 'I can feel them.'

The others glanced around uneasily but saw nothing.

'Jane,' called Harmony. 'If you're here, please make your presence known. Your relatives are anxious to connect with you.'

'Not all of us are,' muttered Jenna.

Simon encouraged her with a single look to be quiet. Her response was a haughty sneer worthy of Robert himself.

'Jane Alardyce, are you here?' called Harmony. 'If you are, please let us know.'

They all jumped when there was a loud knock.

'That was one of you, wasn't it?' Jenna hissed at the others sitting out at the side of the room.

'Course it wasn't them,' replied Simon. 'That knock sounded to come from the middle of the table.'

'Then it was Harry playing a joke.'

'Excuse me,' he said. 'I may be the proverbial rebel but I'm not a philistine.'

'No one made the noise,' said Kate. 'We're all holding hands.'

'Someone could have kicked the underside of the table,' rasped Jenna, eyes wide.

'Jane, is that you?' said Harmony, ignoring the bickering. 'Knock once for yes, twice for no and three times for don't know or if the answer requires more clarification.'

'Why wouldn't she know who she is?' frowned Tom.

'Be quiet,' Kate told him.

They all waited in anxious silence, Jenna gripping on tightly to Simon and Chris's hands, making them wince.

There was a single loud knock that sounded to come from the very centre of the table, making them all jump again.

'Someone's kicking the table,' said Jenna. 'They have to be.'

'They're not,' said Cameron. 'I can clearly see under the table and no one moved.'

'Please stop talking,' said Harmony. 'It's interfering with the connection.'

When Kate gave her a warning look, Jenna decided to remain silent although she was sure someone was taking the mickey out of them all. The recording Cameron was making would soon prove the truth.

'You are Jane Alardyce?' said Harmony for clarification.

Another loud knock burst from the middle of the table.

'Do you have a message for Kate, your granddaughter?'

One knock.

'Can she ask you a question?'

The next knock was clear but slightly quieter.

Harmony nodded at Kate. 'Go ahead.'

She nodded back. 'Do you approve of the script I've written about the family's lives?'

One knock.

'That's great. Thank you,' she smiled to the air. 'I really want to do justice to you all. Are you happy that this house is back in our family?'

This next knock was louder, a firm affirmation.

'This is ridiculous,' sighed Jenna.

Everyone ignored her.

'I want to thank you for writing your journal,' Kate told the air. 'It's wonderful reading the truth about our family and it's made me feel so much closer to you all.'

'You said you have a message for Kate?' said Harmony.

Another knock.

'Is it about the film Kate wants to make?'

Two knocks.

'No,' said Harmony. 'Do you have good news?'

Two knocks.

'Bad news?'

One knock.

'She has bad news for you,' Harmony told Kate as all the faces around the table grew pale and drawn.

'Is it a warning of danger?' Harmony asked the air.

One knock.

'Is the danger to us all?'

One knock.

'It's always one knock,' said Tom with a nervous laugh. 'Maybe she's got stuck?'

'Shut up,' Beauden told him.

'Is the danger in this house?' pressed Harmony.

Three knocks.

'At last, a bit of variety,' said Tom. 'Ow,' he added when Simon squeezed his hand hard.

'You don't know?' said Harmony.

One knock.

'Is the danger to one of us?'

One knock.

'Is it physical danger?'

One knock.

'This is ridiculous,' said Tom. 'We could be at this all night.' He raised his face to the ceiling. 'Who is the person posing the danger?'

'It's yes or no questions only, you idiot,' said a contemptuous Simon, all respect he had for the man gone the moment he'd started flirting with his wife.

'Are you watching over us?' Harmony asked the air.

One knock.

'And Robert,' said Kate eagerly. 'Is he here too?'

One knock.

'Are you all here – Amy, Henry, John, the whole family?'

One knock.

'Full house,' smiled Tom. He glared at Simon when he jabbed him with his elbow.

Kate hesitated before adding, 'Matthew?'

Two knocks.

'Thank God,' she breathed. 'Edward?'

One knock. This rang out loud and solemn and was of a deeper tone than all the others.

'Is he the one who poses the danger?'

Three knocks.

'Does that mean a living person poses a danger as well as him?'

One knock, a lot softer this time.

'Oh no,' breathed Jenna, looking around nervously.

'The connection's fading,' said Harmony. 'She's used up all her energy.'

'Is there anyone else who wants to talk to us?' cried Kate. 'Robert, are you here?'

There was no answering knock and she slumped back in her seat with disappointment.

Everyone jumped again when there was another loud knock and the door opened.

'I wondered if anyone would like some coffee?' said Marcus solemnly.

'Jesus Christ, you nearly gave me a heart attack,' cried Harry, a hand pressed to his chest. 'What are you trying to do, kill us all?'

'I'm sorry, sir. Did I disturb at an inopportune moment?'

'Aye, you did, you arsehole,' he barked.

'It's my fault,' said Kate. 'I never told him we didn't want to be disturbed.'

'May I switch on a light, madam?' said Marcus. 'It's very dark in here.'

'Yes, thank you.'

Marcus switched on the lamps, illuminating the shadowy corners of the room, and everyone breathed a sigh of relief.

'Are you okay?' Harry asked Harmony, who was sagging in her seat.

'Just tired,' she murmured.

'Marcus, could you fetch her some hot sweet tea and toast and jam?'

'Of course, sir.' He bowed, seemingly holding no grudge against him for the insult. 'Can I get anyone else anything?'

They all gave him orders for various fortifying alcoholic drinks, which he left to prepare without a flicker of concern.

'Was that all real?' said Chris. 'I'm still not sure someone was having us on, like Jenna said.'

'It was real enough,' murmured Harmony. 'I'm drained of energy.'

'Let's take a look at the footage you recorded, Cam,' said Lucy. 'That should prove it.'

They all rushed over to where Cameron sat, gathering behind the couch to peer over his shoulder as he pressed play on the video he'd taken. Only Harmony remained where she was, lacking the strength to rise.

'Look,' said Kate excitedly. 'No one knocks with their hands or feet.'

'The camera wasn't on them,' said Jenna, nodding at those who had sat out of the séance.

'It wasn't us,' retorted Lucy. 'I'd never do anything like that.'

'I didn't mean you, sweetheart,' replied Jenna. 'I know you wouldn't.'

'And neither would I,' said Shannon.

'That just leaves me and I had my hands full,' said Cameron, nodding at the phone.

'There was someone else,' said Beauden. 'Marcus.'

'He's cracked it,' said Jenna, pointing at Beauden. 'Marcus was behind it.'

'Are you forgetting that he wasn't even in the room?' Kate demanded of her cousin.

'He could have used some trick, like a ventriloquist throwing his voice.'

'Impossible. That noise came from inside the room. Besides, he didn't even know what we were doing.'

Chris, who hadn't taken his eyes off the footage on Cameron's phone, suddenly exclaimed, 'There, look.'

'At what?' said Tom, frantically glancing around the room.

'On the screen. Wind it back to where Marcus opens the door.'

'So he did do it after all,' said Jenna triumphantly.

'No, I don't think he did. Pause, Cam,' he said excitedly.

'What are we looking at?' said Kate as they all leaned in to look at the still frame.

'Marcus has two shadows.'

'How can you tell?' said Beauden, squinting at the screen.

'It was dark inside the room and the light was on in the hall, meaning his shadow was cast in front of him. So why is there a second shadow standing next to him?'

'Oh my God, you're right,' exclaimed Shannon. 'He has two shadows.'

'Impossible, no one has two shadows,' said Beauden.

'Meaning one didn't belong to him. It was someone else.'

Shivers ran down all their spines. Only Kate looked around the room excitedly.

'I don't think we can rule out a trick of the light or perhaps some fault on the phone,' said Simon.

'You're right,' said Jenna. 'It must be a mistake.'

'If only we could enlarge the image,' said Chris.

'We can watch it through the television,' suggested Kate, gesturing to the one hanging from the wall.

'While you do that, we can recreate the moment,' said Chris, getting into director mode. 'Cameron, you're closest to Marcus in size and height. Go out into the hall and close the door and make sure you leave the hall light on. When you hear my call, open the door and stand in the same exact spot Marcus did.'

He nodded, handed his phone to Kate and left the room.

'Tom, turn out the light,' said Chris, to the dismay of some of the party.

'Right, we're ready,' called Chris once the room had been plunged into darkness again.

Cameron opened the door and remained on the threshold.

'There,' said Chris. 'His shadow is in front of him, just as Marcus's was.'

'And there's no shadow beside him,' said Beauden.

'Exactly.'

Everyone's eyes widened when a shadow formed on Cameron's left, growing larger. They sagged with relief when Marcus appeared beside him carrying a tray of drinks.

'He did it again,' cried Harry.

'Marcus,' said Chris. 'Is anyone else in the house?'

'No, sir. Do you still require your drinks?' he added when they all stared at him.

'Yes, please, Marcus,' said Kate, who had connected the phone to the television and was bringing up the footage. 'Just leave the tray on the table and we'll sort them out.'

'Very well, madam.'

No one spoke as he entered the room and put down the tray. If he thought there was anything strange going on, he didn't show it. When he'd left, Cameron stepped into the room and closed the door behind him. After collecting their drinks from the tray, they all gathered around the television to watch the replay.

'It's definitely a shadow,' said Beauden. 'No doubt about it. They look to be of similar height to Marcus but more slender, not as stocky.'

'What does it mean?' said Shannon.

'It means there was someone else present at the séance tonight,' said a voice.

They all turned to Harmony, who was still slumped in her chair at the table cradling a brandy.

'Who?' said Kate.

'I don't know but it was definitely a spirit. I could look at the footage, see if I get any impressions,' she replied, hauling herself to her feet.

To the surprise of his cousins, Harry hurried to her side and wrapped an arm around her waist to support her. It seemed his feelings for her ran deeper than he'd let on.

Harmony practically fell into the armchair closest to the television and peered at the screen. 'It's male, I'm sure of it,' she said after a moment's consideration.

'Who is it?' said Kate, gripping onto the back of the chair she was sitting in, nails digging into the soft fabric.

'I can't tell,' she sighed, pressing a hand to her head. 'Sorry.'

'Okay,' said a disappointed Kate, patting her shoulder.

'I'm not convinced about that footage,' said Jenna. 'There are so many possible explanations. We need an expert to look at it.'

'I know a couple of videographers who'd be able to give their verdict,' said Kate. 'I'll email them the footage in the morning.'

'Sounds like a plan. Can we turn the lights back on, please?'

All the lights were switched on although the curtains were left closed as it was getting dark outside. No one wanted to open the curtains for fear of seeing a shadowy face peering in at them. Whether that face would be human or more ethereal, they had no idea.

11

Everyone retired to bed reluctantly that night, particularly those who were sleeping alone, apart from Kate, who seemed energised by the evening's events. Tom hesitated outside the door to Edward's old bedroom, suddenly regretting his decision to swap with Chris.

'Aren't you going in?' Chris asked him.

'I don't feel tired,' he replied, throwing up a front of bravado. 'I thought I might go for a walk instead.'

'Out there, in the pitch black? You're forgetting, you're not in the city now. The village is a good walk away and there's not a single light until you reach the road.' He smiled when Tom swallowed nervously. He might be a tough guy on the big screen, but Chris knew he was really a coward, despite all his boasting.

'You're right,' said Tom, feigning nonchalance. 'I don't want to fall over and hurt myself, not with this new project starting soon.'

'Quite right,' said Chris with a knowing smile. 'Night then.'

'Wait,' called Tom when he started to walk away.

Chris stopped and turned to face him with a questioning look.

'Fancy a nightcap? I've got a nice bottle of Scotch in my room.'

'No thanks, I'm really tired.' He raised an eyebrow when Tom shuffled awkwardly. 'Are you scared of going in there alone?'

'Course not. I'm afraid of nothing. I'm Tom fucking Drake.'

'That's all right then. Goodnight, Tom fucking Drake.'

Chris opened the door to his new room and disappeared inside. Tom was left alone on the landing, feeling forlorn.

'Pull yourself together,' he told himself.

Taking a deep breath, he grasped the door handle, palm sweating, and slowly turned it. The door swung open with an eerie creak that almost caused him to race back downstairs. Tom held his breath, terrified of seeing the same shadowy figure that he'd seen on the television screen standing in his room. However, the light cast from the hallway showed him the room was empty.

Tilting his head and throwing back his shoulders, Tom stepped inside and closed the door.

* * *

'What did you make of tonight?' said Shannon as she climbed into bed.

'I don't know,' replied Cameron, stripping off down to his boxer shorts. 'I watched everyone really carefully and I swear no one made that knocking sound.'

'And I know I didn't make the noise and you didn't, which leaves Lucy and Marcus.'

'I'm certain Lucy didn't do it. She hates practical jokes and she's too scientific-minded. She saw the séance as an experiment and would do nothing to mess with it.'

'After only knowing her a short time I can well believe it. That leaves Marcus but he seems too straightlaced to mess about like that.'

'But we don't know him,' he replied, climbing into bed beside her.

'We should check out the rooms either side of the drawing room to see if there's any way he could have been messing with us.'

'Good idea,' said Cameron, sliding his arm around her waist.

Guilt filled Shannon once again as he kissed her. She wasn't sure she could live with what she'd done. Perhaps if she explained, he could forgive her. She would keep Kate's name out of it. Pissing off that woman wouldn't help.

'Cam,' she said. 'There's something I need to tell you.'

'What?' he replied, kissing her neck.

Shannon moaned and tilted back her head, the thoughts momentarily vanishing from her mind when his hand slid up her thigh. 'It's about... about...'

He raised his head to look into her eyes. 'Is it something serious, like what we were discussing earlier?'

She gazed into his black eyes, wrestling with herself. Telling him might unburden her conscience but she was certain it would lose her this man who was gorgeous not just on the outside but the inside too. She would never find another like him. 'It doesn't matter,' she said.

'You sure?'

Shannon smiled and nodded. She wrapped her thighs around his waist, running her hands up his muscular back. She would just have to learn to live with the guilt.

* * *

Kate couldn't sleep. She was too wired after the séance, which had filled her head with questions. Had that mysterious shadow been real or just a trick of the light? Had the knocks really been caused by Jane or someone else? Were her ancestors still resident in the house?

Unable to sleep, she pulled on her robe and slippers and silently slipped downstairs. The moon was bright and full, it's pale light slanting through the windows, illuminating her path, making Alardyce House look even more magical.

She wondered if she was flogging a dead horse with this house and would end up going as peculiar as the last owner, floating about like Miss Havisham from *Great Expectations*, although she wouldn't be mourning the loss of a lover but her ancestors. She'd recently been offered the role of Miss Havisham in a new TV adaptation, and it had been tempting to believe it was an omen, but the truth was the present didn't really interest her. It never had. Her mother had blamed her gran for this quirk in her daughter's nature. What her mother failed to understand was that Kate had adored listening to her grandmother's tales because they reminded her of what she loved the most. She was a woman born too late and the consequences of this had left her feeling disconnected from the world around her and all those who dwelt within it, constantly longing for people and a place she could never have. On the surface, she had everything anyone could want – money, fame, looks – but it meant nothing other than a way to bring her to this very place. The problem was, it was the right place but in the wrong time, meaning she could never be truly happy, and that thought was very depressing. The séance had given her hope. If those she longed to be with the most still lingered here, then perhaps all was not lost. Happiness may one day be hers, even if she only caught fleeting glimpses of those people and could only talk to them through a medium. As she walked, she let her fingertips slide along the walls, which held so many memories.

'If only you could talk,' she whispered.

Kate moved into the drawing room and pulled open the curtains which everyone had been too afraid to open earlier. She smiled up at the moon shining full and radiant upon the house. Her ancestors had stood here in this very spot gazing up at the same sight, the thought bringing peace to her heart. She could imagine them moving around her, taking a seat in the armchair, reading on the couch, standing by the fireplace to talk, the echoes of their voices hanging in the air. Her mother would tell her it was just her imagination, that these things weren't real. Kate had constantly been told that her imagination was a bad thing, that it made her walk around with her head in the clouds, ignoring the real world, that she would never amount to anything. Her blue eyes narrowed and filled with malice. Her mother was now very careful never to say or do anything to upset her, afraid the money her daughter paid her each month would stop. Now no one dared contradict her or tell her she was a fool. The power of her new position was heady indeed.

The feeling that someone was standing right behind her suddenly became very strong. Rather than be afraid, Kate was filled with joy. She spun round on her heel, hoping to catch a glimpse of them before they had the chance to vanish. No one was visible but she could still feel them. It was a heaviness in the air, of something extraordinary disrupting the ordinary.

'Who are you?' she said. When nothing happened, she added, 'Why won't you answer? Are you afraid of me? You should know that I'm not afraid of you.'

'Who are you talking to?' said a voice.

Kate was annoyed with herself when she jumped. She whirled round to see a shadowy figure standing in the doorway. It took her a moment to realise it was Cameron wearing black jogging bottoms and a black T-shirt.

'Just going over some lines I need to learn for an upcoming production,' she murmured, the lie easily tripping off her tongue.

He stepped into the room, and thanks to the moonlight, she could see his hair was mussed up. This irritated her because she knew it was from sex and not sleep. She had no idea what he saw in Shannon; he really could do better than a plain-looking thief. His arrival had also scared off whatever presence had been hovering around her, if it had even been there at all. Now it was gone, she was starting to doubt herself.

'What are you doing up?' Kate asked him.

'I could ask you the same question.'

'I asked first,' she replied, a twinkle in her eye.

'I was thirsty and needed some water, but I couldn't find the kitchen. Your turn.'

'I couldn't sleep.'

'So you decided to stand around in the dark?'

'I wanted to look at the moon. It's magnificent.'

Cameron stood right beside her, and Kate couldn't help but glance up at him as he gazed out of the window. God, he was handsome. Even if he hadn't resembled Robert, she would still have found him very attractive.

'You're right, it is,' he smiled.

Kate enjoyed watching him gazing at the moonlight, its beams reflected in his eyes, turning them from black to silver.

'This place is special,' he added. 'Almost otherworldly.'

'I'm glad you realise that,' she replied. 'I was beginning to think it was just me.'

'Definitely not. You did a good thing getting it back. It should be with our family.'

'It's a relief to hear that. No one else seems to agree.'

'Lucy definitely does, I know that for a fact. Jenna's too caught up in her marital problems and Harry's, well, Harry.'

'True,' she smiled. 'It's a shame about Simon and Jenna. Despite what they're going through, I do think they love each other.'

'You're probably right. Let's hope they work it out.' He tore his gaze away from the moon. 'So, how do I get to the kitchen?'

'I'll show you. I could use a cup of chamomile tea. It might help me sleep.'

They left the drawing room and made their way down the hallway.

'I was surprised to find you down here after the séance,' said Cameron.

'I don't scare easily.'

'So it seems. Do you think what happened was real or a joke?'

'I can't be certain, but I'm inclined to think it was real. We'll soon find out when I email that footage to a couple of friends tomorrow. It was brave of you to come down here alone too.'

'When I heard whispering, I did wonder what I'd find when I looked inside the drawing room.'

'Yet still you looked,' she said, giving him a sideways smile.

'Because I'm nosy,' he grinned back.

'I can't imagine Tom doing the same. He's probably hiding under his bed right now, regretting agreeing to swap rooms with Chris.'

'So, he is a big wuss then?'

'Oh, yes. In his last film he had to work with an Alsatian. He screamed when it barked at him.'

Cameron's deep chuckle made her smile. It was a sexy, masculine sound.

'Here we are,' said Kate as they entered the kitchen.

She hit the switch to the left of the door and the room was flooded with light. The sight grated on Kate. It was just too damn modern. She'd decided to leave it as it was because it was a good quality kitchen and had everything she needed but she was regretting that decision now because it felt to be out of sync with the rest of the house. She made a mental note to contact her interior designer once her house guests had left.

'That was easy,' said Cameron. 'I feel stupid for not being able to find it.'

Cameron poured a glass of water from the jug in the fridge before downing the lot and refilling it.

'Someone's thirsty,' she said with a raised eyebrow.

'It's so warm,' he replied.

Kate knew that wasn't the real reason. He was dehydrated because he'd just had hot sex with a woman who was completely unworthy of him. The impulse to tell him what his sainted girlfriend had done almost overcame Kate, but she controlled it. When she did manage to separate him from Shannon, she would not destroy her own chances with him in the process.

'Shannon seems nice,' she said instead, annoyed by the way his eyes lit up.

'Isn't she?' he replied. 'I'm so lucky to have met her.'

'At the gym?'

'Aye. She knocked me off my feet the second I saw her.'

'She is very pretty.'

'She's more than that, she's beautiful. I'm thinking of asking her to marry me.'

Kate almost wanted to cry for the man. There was something so innocent about him, and that would be destroyed the moment he found out about Shannon's betrayal. But that would be a good thing. Only then would he finally come into his true inheritance and realise his full potential. He already had the looks and brains. He just needed to bring out the ruthlessness and Kate would have her companion in this world.

'Wow, that's brilliant,' she said so sweetly no one would ever have guessed her true emotions. 'When are you going to pop the question?'

'I was thinking of doing it here. It seems appropriate and it's such a romantic place.'

'Sounds perfect. Have you got a ring?'

'No. I haven't planned it, but I spotted a jewellers in the village.'

'You'll easily find something there. They have beautiful jewellery at fair prices too. I can help you choose something, if you like. I know my diamonds.'

'Thanks, that would be great.'

'I'm sure she'll say yes.'

'I hope so. I don't know what I'll do if she says no. She's my soulmate.' He smiled self-deprecatingly. 'God, listen to me talking about soulmates.'

'I think it's lovely. Too many men are afraid to put themselves out there, but not you.'

'Are you seeing anyone?'

'No. Men seem to get fed up with me pretty quickly,' she replied with an awkward smile. 'And it's difficult maintaining a relationship in my line of work. I've dated a few actors, but they've been filming in one part of the world while I've been in another and you soon grow apart. Now I've bought this house, I want to settle down a bit. I'm tired of travelling all the time. I might confine myself to projects that are based in the UK, finally put down some roots.'

'Do you want kids?'

'I don't know, I've not really thought about it until recently. This house can feel lonely with just me rattling around inside it. The laughter of children would be nice.'

Cameron smiled, surprised Kate was showing such a gentle, vulnerable side. Even as a child there'd always been something hard and impervious about her, but it seemed age was mellowing her.

'It would be a great place to raise kids,' he said. 'Loads of space for them to run about, lovely gardens, peaceful.'

Kate sighed wistfully. 'The sad thing is, I don't think I'll ever find a man to share that with.'

'You're beautiful and successful, you'll find someone.' Cameron's heart went out to Kate when her huge blue eyes filled with tears. 'Don't cry,' he said, wrapping her in his arms.

'I'm sorry,' she rasped, clinging on to him, enjoying how strong and firm he was. 'I try not to let it get to me, but I can't help it. I suppose it's seeing how happy you and Shannon are. I'm even jealous of Jenna and Simon, despite their problems. They've shared a home together for years, enjoyed that closeness, had two lovely daughters, and that jealousy makes me feel so guilty. I mean, I'm so happy for you all but I also want what you have.' She raised her head to look into his face. 'Does that make me bad?'

Cameron swallowed hard as he gazed into those eyes that had captured countless people through a screen. They were even more powerful in real life. He'd never noticed before how red her lips were and even though she wore no make-up, her skin was still flawless and creamy. He also became very conscious of the fact that her large breasts were pressed against his chest. A spot of colour rose in both her cheeks and her luscious red lips parted slightly as they continued to stare at each other.

He cleared his throat before replying. 'No, it doesn't make you bad.'

'I want to love powerfully and be loved like that in return and to feel like a real woman.'

Cameron thought there wasn't a more real woman in the world; she oozed femininity with her soft skin and curves and that mass of gorgeous chestnut hair. The mad urge to run his thumb across her lips almost overcame him and he felt her grip on his waist tighten.

Shannon popped into his mind and he hastily released Kate. It was like waking from a spell. He'd never once considered cheating on his girlfriend before. All day at his gyms he was confronted by ultra-fit women in tight clothes and they didn't move him at all, but Kate had woven some sort of enchantment over him. No, it wasn't fair to blame her. She couldn't have known the treacherous thoughts that were running through his mind. It was the curse of all beautiful women for men to blame their own weakness and attraction on them instead of themselves. He was the only one to blame. He'd been right about Alardyce's magic, which seemed to live inside Kate herself. No wonder she felt such a special connection to the place.

'I'd better get back to Shannon,' he said, picking up the glass of water. 'She'll be wondering where I am.'

'And I'll make my tea and head back to bed. Thanks for listening, Cam. I appreciate it.'

'Anytime,' he replied, being careful to maintain a distance between them.

'What time do you want to go to the jewellers in the morning?'

Cameron wasn't sure that trip would be wise now in case the same compulsion overcame him again, but he reasoned it would be safe in the middle of a village in the cold light of day. Plus he didn't want to upset her by rejecting her kind offer; it was clear she was emotionally fragile. 'How about nine? That won't be too early, will it?'

'Nine's perfect. You'd better get to bed then,' she said before picking up the kettle and walking over to the sink to fill it up.

'Right, see you tomorrow then.' He glanced at the clock on the wall and saw it was just after midnight. 'Or rather, later today.'

'Yep. Night,' she replied without turning round. Kate smiled, sensing his confusion. They'd gone from that intimate moment to her dismissing him, and he was wondering if he'd imagined it all. Good. It would be much easier for her to catch him in her web if he wasn't sure which way was up and which was down.

* * *

Shannon was sitting up in bed, reading. 'There you are,' she smiled when Cameron entered carrying a glass of water. She put down the book. 'Did you get lost?'

'I couldn't find the kitchen, but Kate showed me.'

Shannon's smile faltered. 'Kate?'

'Aye. She was in the drawing room, she couldn't sleep.'

Cameron remained standing by the door, clutching his glass of water. The sight of Shannon only heightened the guilt he felt about his close encounter with Kate, and he was reluctant to get closer to her.

Shannon for her part thought that meant Kate had told him about what she'd done and hot, raw panic rose up inside her. 'Aren't you coming back to bed?' she said.

Cameron was so consumed by his own thoughts that he didn't notice how agitated Shannon was, and he nodded.

He placed the glass on the beside cabinet, stripped off his T-shirt and jogging bottoms and got into bed. They remained sitting up awkwardly beside each other.

'Can I have some water, please?' she said.

'Aye, sorry,' he replied, handing her the glass.

She took it from him and sipped the cool liquid, finding it hard to swallow because she was so nervous. As she studied him, she realised he didn't seem angry or even hurt. Just a bit fretful.

Shannon decided to take a chance. 'Are you all right?' she said, putting the glass down on the bedside cabinet. 'You seem distracted.'

He forced a smile and turned to look at her. 'Sorry, I'm just tired.'

She was relieved when he held his arm out to her and she nestled into his chest. 'I thought for a moment you'd seen a ghost down there.'

'No,' he said, his warm laugh reassuring her even more. 'Although Kate did look a bit ghostly in her white robe and slippers.'

'So she was just wandering around the house?'

'Yep.'

'That's weird. I know she's your cousin, but don't you think she's a bit strange?' Shannon hated being under Kate's thumb and couldn't help the vindictiveness that rose inside her.

'There is an… unearthliness about her.'

'That's an odd choice of word.'

'I know but it's the only one that fits. It's like she doesn't quite belong in our world.'

'She seems to be doing just fine for someone who doesn't belong with this big house and her millions in the bank,' she said a little bitterly.

'But there is a vulnerability about her too.'

Shannon wanted to both laugh and cry at his naivety. 'Really?' she said doubtfully.

'Aye. She got a bit upset when we were in the kitchen saying how she wants to settle down only she can't find the right man. She even wants kids.'

Anger gripped Shannon. She'd seen the way Kate looked at Cameron, her own cousin, the sick, twisted cow. She'd set her sights on him and now she had a hold over Shannon she probably intended to use it to get her out of the way, leaving the road free and clear for her to make a move on him. That bitch didn't want children running around her posh house, making a mess and lots of noise. Shannon could imagine Kate putting on the waterworks, using her baby blues to powerful effect on sweet, compassionate Cameron. 'How would she manage that with her lifestyle?' she said instead, knowing a direct attack on Kate's character wouldn't be the right way to go.

'She said she's only going to take on projects in the UK from now on. She seemed really serious. I think it's this place. It used to be a family home and she wants to bring that back.'

'Kate seems a little too obsessed with this house, if you ask me.'

'You're right, she is, ever since she was a little girl. It's amazing that she's actually achieved her dream and bought it.'

The admiration was clear in his voice and Shannon's guts clenched with loathing. She didn't think she'd hated anyone more than Kate Alardyce. Part of Shannon thought it was her own fault that she was under the awful woman's thumb but another part of her wanted to blame the bitch for the whole thing. Kate acted sweet and kind when that's all it was – an act. Underneath she was a ruthless bitch who always got what she wanted. Now she wanted Cameron, and Shannon was terrified she would get him.

She nestled into him closer, making the most of the feel of his skin against hers, of the sound of his heartbeat beneath her ear, wondering if soon he would be taken from her.

12

Kate and Cameron strolled towards Alardyce village at nine o'clock the next morning. The weather was a little cooler, a gentle breeze agitating the limbs of the row of beech trees. There were a few clouds in the sky, but they were light and fluffy and didn't threaten any rain.

'I wish it would rain properly,' sighed Kate. 'I'm sick of all this sunshine.'

'I thought you loved this sort of weather,' replied Cameron.

'Personally, I prefer grey rainy days. A good storm is even better with thunder and lightning.'

'Give me the sun any day,' he smiled, tilting his face skywards.

'Are you ready to do more work with Beauden today?'

His smile vanished and his eyes flickered. 'I suppose.'

'You really don't have to do it if you don't want to. I hate the thought of pushing you into it.'

'It's not a case of that. I *have* to do it.'

'Why?' she frowned.

Cameron sighed. Perhaps it would be better if he took her into his confidence. The worry was starting to get to him. 'You can't tell anyone else what I'm about to say.'

'I won't say a word, I swear. I'm not the type to blab people's secrets about,' she said, injecting the right amount of hurt into her tone.

'Aye, I know. Sorry. It's just... Shannon's restaurant is struggling, so we really need the money.'

'God, I'm sorry to hear that. I thought things were going so well.'

'So did I until yesterday.'

'And that's why you want to work on this project?'

'Aye, and I'm going to be honest – the money is the only reason.'

'I appreciate you being so candid with me. I just hope you do enjoy it. Filming can be slow and boring, involving hanging around for hours on end, but when you're in that moment and you just gel with the character, it's so exciting. A real rush,' she breathed. 'There's nothing else like it.'

'You never know, I might get bitten by the acting bug like you did.'

'Beauden's certain you can do it and there's no one's judgement I trust more.'

'I hope I don't let you down. To be honest, it's a lot of pressure on my shoulders. If I'm crap, then the whole thing will be too.'

Kate smiled and linked her arm through his. 'You won't be crap. I have faith in you.'

Cameron's smile failed to reach his eyes. He couldn't quite believe that he was going to be the star of a television programme. He kept thinking it was a joke on Kate's part and at any moment she'd burst out laughing at his gullibility. Once again, he was very aware of how close she was to him as they walked arm-in-arm, but there wasn't the intimacy of the previous night. Perhaps he'd imagined it, overcome with the moonlight and the enchantment of Alardyce House? God, he hoped so.

* * *

Kate helped Cameron select a beautiful platinum ring with a pear-shaped centre stone. It cost him two grand but he wanted to show Shannon how serious he was about them spending the rest of their lives together.

'She'll love it,' smiled Kate as they left the shop together, Cameron's purchase tucked safely into the pocket of his jeans in a small black box.

'I hope so. I'm so nervous about asking her.'

'Don't be. No way will she say no. How will you do it?'

'I was thinking candles and champagne.'

'No problem. I have a few bottles of Bollinger in the wine cellar, you can have one of those, and we've got plenty of candles. Ask Marcus, he'll set you up.'

'Thanks, that's really kind of you. I thought I'd ask Shannon in the conservatory.'

'Really?' she said slowly, thinking of the uncomfortable atmosphere in that room. 'Any particular reason why?'

'I just thought it looked nice. I've not been in there myself, other than on the tour you gave us. Why, do you think it's a bad idea?'

Kate's lips spread into a slow smile. 'Not at all. You're right, it is a lovely room and it'll look so romantic in the candlelight. If you let me know what time I can ensure you're not disturbed by the others.'

'That would be great. The last thing I want is a half-cut Harry bursting in when I'm down on one knee. I thought I'd do it straight after dinner.'

'I'll make sure they're all kept busy.'

Kate wouldn't disturb his proposal to the thief. In fact, she'd go out of her way to ensure it all went smoothly. For now, it was important she played the helpful, caring cousin. That way, Cameron would turn to her when it inevitably went wrong.

* * *

On arrival back at Alardyce House, Cameron remained outside in the garden while Kate headed inside. Taking out his phone, he wandered down to the very edge of the garden where the beech trees grew. Here the atmosphere was definitely different, not as potent, lacking the ethereal feel of the rest of the grounds and the house. That was fine by him, he didn't need ethereal for this conversation.

'Hi, Guy,' he said when his best friend answered the phone. 'Can you do me a favour? I need to free up some capital from the gyms. Can you go through the accounts and let me know my options? Aye, Shannon does do them, but I need the money for her. It's a surprise, so don't let on. Yeah, on the laptop in the office. Cheers, pal, I owe you one.'

Cameron hung up, hoping his friend would come through for him. Guy had recently qualified as a chartered accountant and was very good at his job. Already he had a full client list. He would have used his services himself if Shannon hadn't already been doing his books for him; he hadn't wanted to offend her by giving the job to someone else. She too was very capable and had a great head for figures. Maybe if her business couldn't be saved, she could retrain and become an accountant? It wasn't as glamorous as being a restauranteur, but it was much more reliable work and it paid well. It would be good for her to have a back-up plan. Hopefully she would soon be his wife, so what was his would be hers anyway, but it was sensible to know how he stood financially.

The future was golden and bright. With Shannon by his side, he could do anything.

* * *

That afternoon, Shannon took a walk with Harmony. The two of them got along very well and she found Harmony interesting company. They had similar senses of humour and together they could laugh at the smallest thing.

'Look, there's Tom,' said Harmony, gesturing to the man himself who was in the treeline marking the far boundary of the rear gardens. 'What the hell is he doing?'

'I think it's tai chi,' frowned Shannon, squinting in his direction.

'He looks a proper dick,' chuckled Harmony. 'Mine and Harry's room is next to the one he stayed in last night. We heard him squeal like a girl at about two o'clock in the morning.'

'Really? I wonder if he met Edward Alardyce's unquiet spirit?'

'If he did, he'd never admit it. Anyway, that's not the best part. Just as I was thinking of knocking and making sure he was okay, I heard him run out of his room. I got up and saw the door to Jenna's room was open. As it was pitch black, I couldn't make out what was going on, but it sounded like there was a fight happening. The light went on in their room and Tom was on the floor, being punched by Simon.'

'Really? I'd no idea Simon had it in him.'

'Simon stopped when he realised who it was. He told Tom he hadn't known it was him, he thought it was an intruder. Tom was practically crying,' chuckled Harmony.

'He's not such a tough guy then?'

'Not in the slightest.'

'It'll be interesting to see if he'll stay in that room again tonight or if he insists on switching back with Chris.'

'He might not, he has his pride.'

'But it's also clear that he's a coward.'

'That's true. I thought he was going to burst into tears during the séance.'

Shannon looked to Harmony curiously. 'I still don't know what to make of all that.'

'You and me both,' she replied. 'All I know is there's some very peculiar energy in this place, and not just the house but the grounds too.'

The women laughed when Tom overexerted himself and toppled backwards with a startled cry, vanishing into the undergrowth.

'We should check he's okay,' said Harmony.

'No need,' replied Shannon when Tom staggered out of a bush, leaves tangled in his hair.

'I can't believe I used to think he was hot. Now he's just disappointing.'

'What do you think of Kate?' said Shannon, eyes narrowing. 'Do you think she's disappointing too?'

'No, I don't. She's a very impressive woman and a brilliant actress.'

'Oh yes, she certainly is,' she sighed. 'She's perfect at everything.'

'You don't like her?'

'I don't like the way she looks at Cam. Do you agree that she shouldn't look at her cousin that way?'

'You can hardly blame her, your boyfriend's gorgeous. I've seen Jenna giving him a few saucy glances too,' said Harmony, eyes twinkling. 'Besides, they're only second cousins.'

'It's more than that with Kate. It's not because he's gorgeous, it's because he looks like Robert Alardyce and that's what's bothering me – it's not that Kate fancies her cousin, it's that she fancies her great-grandfather.'

'When you put it like that, it is weird.'

'Too right it is,' said Shannon, eyes flashing.

'I don't think it's anything to worry about. Besides, it's not like Kate lives on your doorstep, is it?'

'No, thank God, although I'm starting to wonder if there's not enough miles between here and Glasgow.'

'You know, it could one day come in useful being on good terms with a rich, connected woman.'

'I see what you're saying, but I just get the feeling that if we're around her too much then she might twist Cam.'

'Twist him?'

'Make him like her.'

'I don't think you need to worry. She's always jet-setting about the world, filming.'

'She told Cam she wants to stay put in the UK from now on. This might sound selfish, but after this week is over, I don't want them to see each other again for another sixteen years.'

'They might not. People always say they'll stay in touch, but life gets in the way and good intentions fall by the wayside.'

'I hope that happens with Cam and Kate.'

Harmony was a little surprised by the vehemence in Shannon's voice but then again, she wasn't the jealous type. It never bothered her when anyone flirted with her man. The way she saw it, everyone was free to do as they pleased. What right did she have to make a claim on someone else's emotions? But she knew her beliefs weren't the norm. It might seem strange to the majority of the world but to Shannon it made a lot of sense.

The two women came around the side of the house to see a large black SUV parked on the drive.

'It looks like more guests have arrived,' said Shannon.

They headed inside the house to find Kate greeting a middle-aged man and woman in her grand hallway. The woman was very smartly dressed, neat as a pin in her knee-length black skirt and light-blue blouse. A man stood beside her with thick steel-grey hair but his trousers and shirt were obviously expensive, as was the huge watch that dangled from his muscular wrist.

'Harmony, Shannon,' said Kate with a smile so radiant it grated on Shannon's nerves. 'I want you to meet my friends, Gail and Eric Fairchild. Gail's a costume designer, the best in the industry, and Eric's a producer and casting director. They're both going to work on the project about the family. I invited them here because they couldn't wait to see the house.'

'And because they want to meet Cam,' said Shannon coolly.

Kate's smile didn't falter. In fact, Shannon's snippy tone only broadened it. 'That too.' She turned back to the newcomers. 'Gail, Eric, this is Harmony, my cousin Harry's partner, and Shannon, Cameron's partner.'

'Lovely to meet you both,' said Gail, shaking their hands while Eric gave them polite nods.

'Why don't you come on through?' Kate told the newcomers. 'Marcus will fetch you tea and sandwiches.'

'How Victorian,' smiled Gail. 'Will the sandwiches be cucumber ones?'

'I can ask him if you like,' replied Kate. She paused to look at Harmony and Shannon. 'Feel free to join us.'

'No thanks,' said Shannon. 'We'll give you some privacy to talk.'

'As you wish,' replied Kate before she and the Fairchilds vanished into the drawing room.

'They're here to make sure Cam doesn't back out of this stupid TV programme,' hissed Shannon.

'Or they could be good friends of Kate's who want to see her new home,' said Harmony reasonably.

Personally, Harmony thought Shannon was being a bit paranoid, but it wasn't for her to interfere. 'Right, I need a bath before dinner. I'll see you later.'

'Yeah, see you,' said Shannon distractedly, glaring at the door into the drawing room, which had been closed.

Harmony was such a sunny presence that without her, Shannon felt a bit bereft, especially as her own mood was so low. She was just wondering what to do with herself when Cameron came bounding through the front door like a big, beautiful puppy, Harry by his side. The two cousins were laughing and joking together.

'I take it you two have been having fun?' she asked them.

'Oh yes,' replied Harry with that naughty glint in his eyes. 'We've just seen Tom slinking through the back door covered in leaves and grass stains.'

'That's because he fell into a bush doing tai chi.'

The two men looked at each other and laughed.

'I wish I'd seen that,' chuckled Harry. 'What an arsehole.' He turned back to Cameron. 'You ready for me to thrash you at billiards now?'

'Aye – if you don't mind?' he asked Shannon.

'I don't mind at all,' she replied. 'Go and have fun.'

'What will you do?'

'I'll grab my book and do some reading in the garden.'

'Okay, see you later,' he said, pecking her on the lips.

'For God's sake,' said Harry. 'You're not going to war.'

'I know but I'll still miss her,' said Cameron with an adoring smile Shannon's way.

'Get in that billiard room before I vomit all over Kate's lovely restored floor,' he said, playfully nudging him in the shoulder.

Shannon watched the two men go. She used to love the way Cameron smiled at her. Now it made her feel guilty and unworthy.

Rather than head up to her bedroom, some impulse drew Shannon into the dining room. She looked to the portrait of Amy first, who was so like Kate with her auburn hair, voluptuous mouth and large bosom. She turned from it with a sneer to Robert's portrait, which looked even more arrogant and smug.

'You're not having him,' she told his image. 'He's mine, not yours, and I won't let you take him.'

Robert's eyes seemed to narrow and his brow creased, the power in those black eyes becoming even more compelling. Was the overwhelming guilt she was experiencing loosening her grip on reality? Still, that arrogance infuriated her.

'You won't win,' she told the image. 'I won't let you.'

'Who are you talking to?' said a voice.

Shannon gasped and whirled round to see Kate standing in the doorway.

'What are you doing there?' said Shannon, her heart thumping from the fright she'd got. 'I thought you were in the drawing room with your guests.'

'I was but Gail wants some iced water, so I was on my way to the kitchen to tell Marcus when I heard talking in here.'

To Shannon's dismay, Kate stepped inside and closed the door. She moved to stand right beside Shannon and stared up at Robert's portrait.

'I often talk to him myself,' she said. 'He looks so alive, doesn't he? He's got more life about him than most living people I know.'

'What's that supposed to mean?'

'Everyone today is so caught up in the petty things, all the stuff that doesn't matter, and it's made them forget how to really live. Not Robert. He never once forgot and he lived his life to the fullest, but that one life wasn't enough. He wants more.'

An icy hand gripped Shannon's heart. 'What do you mean?'

'I mean his life was cut tragically short. He still has so much left to do and he wants to come back.'

Kate's eyes filled with a mania that turned Shannon's throat dry. 'That's why you want Cam to play him in the TV programme, isn't it? You really think Robert can somehow come back through him?'

'I don't just think it, I know it. There's a reason why they're so identical.'

Shannon frantically shook her head. 'You're off your bloody head. They look alike because they're relatives, that's all.'

'There's more to it than that. Look at me and Amy,' she said, gesturing to the portrait behind them. 'There's undoubtedly a resemblance but there are also a lot of differences too. No one has ever gasped at her portrait as they have Robert's and said I'm the very image of her, and that's the difference.'

'It's just a coincidence.'

'Coincidence is a word people use when they don't understand the full facts and I do understand the facts, Shannon.'

Kate's eyes were wide and unblinking. It struck Shannon that she wasn't just obsessed or strange; Kate was actually mad. Whether she'd always been that way and no one had noticed or if this house had done it to her, she didn't know. She backed away from her, wanting to escape those wild, staring eyes, but Kate was standing between herself and the door, so Shannon was forced to retreat to the far wall.

'You need to set Cam free,' said Kate, slowly advancing on her. 'Only then will he be able to realise his full potential.'

'What do you mean, set him free?'

'Break up with him then leave this house and never see him again.'

'Piss off.'

Kate took another step towards her, so sudden and aggressive Shannon backed up again, wincing when she bumped into the wall.

'I mean it,' she hissed. 'If you stay with him, you'll only drag him down and ruin his life. You've already put a big dent in his finances. What will you do next, cheat on him?'

'I could never hurt him like that. You're mad, do you know that? From what I've heard, you weren't very stable to begin with, but this place has made you lose it completely, especially that thing,' she added, nodding at the portrait of Robert.

Kate's expression darkened. 'Do not call him a thing. He's far more than you could ever hope to be.'

'You talk about him as though he's still alive but he's just dust and bones.

The only place he lives is in your diseased mind.' Shannon was almost breathless with rage and a little fear, which made talking difficult. Her voice came out weak and timid when inside she wanted to put her fist right through Kate's lovely face.

Kate smiled. 'You really know nothing. You're just as blinkered and ignorant as the rest of humanity, putting all your faith in the tangible. There's far more to this world than you think but you're too stupid to ever see it. Cam's different though and I will show him the real truth.'

'You need help. Can't you see this isn't normal?'

'You only think that because you're so ignorant. If you'd had my experiences...' Kate trailed off and turned to look at the portrait of Robert.

While she was distracted, Shannon took the opportunity to run towards the door, being careful to keep the dining table between them.

'I'm going to tell Cam what you said and take him far from here,' Shannon told her.

'No, you won't,' replied Kate calmly, not bothering to even look her way. 'Because if you do, I'll tell him what you've done. Neither will I give you the rest of the money to pay off your debts.'

Shannon hesitated, her hand on the door handle. 'We had a deal.'

'True, and I'm perfectly willing to follow through, but if you take Cameron away from me then it's off.'

Shannon sighed, her shoulders slumping, hating the hold this mad bitch had over her.

'What you can do is go to Cameron and tell him it's over between you and then leave,' continued Kate, turning to face her. 'If you do that, I'll give you an extra hundred grand.'

Shannon was almost tempted by such a huge sum, but she shook her head. 'He means far more to me than money.'

'Two hundred,' pressed Kate, eyes shining with determination.

'No. Your money can't buy you everything you want.'

With that, she flung open the door and hurried out. As it swung closed behind her, Kate turned to Robert's portrait.

'Don't worry, I'll find a way to get rid of the thief,' she told his image with a venomous smile.

13

As Shannon hurried past the billiard room, she heard Cameron and Harry's laughter emanating from within. She hesitated outside the door, tempted to go in and tell them everything. The desire to unburden herself was almost overwhelming and it would automatically take away Kate's power over her, but she would lose Cameron and her restaurant. All she could do was play Kate at her own game until she'd got the money and repaid it back into his account. Only then would she be able to deny Kate's claims, and with how fragile her sanity was it would be easy to make her look delusional. Neither would Cameron have to do that ridiculous TV programme. He would be free. No, she had to play it smarter. Despite her madness, Kate was very clever and manipulative.

Instead, Shannon decided to stick to her plan and pretend everything was normal. Kate was banking on her breaking down, confessing everything to Cameron and doing her dirty work for her, but she would not give her the satisfaction.

After retrieving her book from her bedroom, she hurried outside, rushing through the conservatory to the back door so she wouldn't have to go past the dining room again. As she moved through the conservatory, she kept her head down, sensing that angry, intimidating presence even though no one else was there. God, this place was creepy.

Once outside, Shannon breathed a sigh of relief. The sound of chatter drifted towards her on the gentle breeze. Looking up, she saw more clouds had amassed in the sky, thick and pregnant with threat. It appeared they were soon in for a downpour, although it was still very warm. In fact, the temperature only seemed to have increased, the humidity causing sweat to break out between her shoulder blades.

Following the sound of chatter around the side of the house, she found Lucy, Jenna, Simon and Chris sitting together around a table, drinking wine.

'Shannon,' smiled Jenna, who was clearly a little tipsy. 'Park yer arse and have a glass of pinot.'

Thinking that was just what she needed, she took the spare chair between Lucy and Chris. Jenna and her husband appeared to be getting on much better. They'd pulled up their chairs close to each other and both were smiling.

'I thought you'd be inside with your friends,' Shannon told Chris while Simon poured her a glass of wine.

'Friends?' he replied.

'A couple called the Fairchilds. They've just arrived.'

'Really?' he smiled, getting to his feet. 'I didn't know. Kate told me they were coming but she wasn't sure when they were going to arrive.'

'Who's this?' said Lucy.

'They're both in the business,' he replied. 'Gail's a costume designer and Eric's a producer and casting director. They're both really excited about Kate's new project. I know Gail can't wait to get stuck into the costumes; the Victorian era's her speciality.'

With that he headed back inside the house carrying his glass of wine.

'You two look happier,' Shannon told Jenna and Simon.

'That's because he's my hero,' replied the former, gazing adoringly at her husband.

'Really?' said Shannon, thinking she'd never seen anyone less heroic-looking in her life.

'Aye. There was an incident last night and he came to my rescue.'

'Incident?' said Shannon, glancing at Lucy, wondering if she already knew the story. Judging by her lack of surprise, she did. Shannon didn't like to say that Harmony had already told her because they might not know she'd been a witness.

'Yes,' continued Jenna. 'Someone came into our room last night and

Simon saw them off. It turned out it was just Tom, but Simon launched himself at him and punched him to the floor. It was amazing,' she beamed at her husband, who smiled proudly.

'Why would you think Tom was an intruder?'

'Because he burst into our room, waking us up. It was dark, so we couldn't see who it was. Simon didn't hesitate, he just went for him.'

Shannon caught the malicious gleam in Simon's eyes. She got the feeling he'd known exactly who he was attacking. 'Why did Tom burst into your room?'

'He said there was someone in his room. Simon went with him to check – he was brave twice in one night – but no one was there. The idiot probably dreamt it.'

Shannon thought that was quite a change in Jenna's attitude towards her screen idol.

'I knew Tom was a big wuss,' said Lucy. 'There's nothing heroic about him, he's just a good actor.'

'You're so right,' replied Jenna. 'He was shaking and crying like a big girl. It was so embarrassing. He's nothing compared to my Simon.'

Simon looked incredibly pleased with himself and wrapped an arm around her shoulders.

'Is Tom okay?' said Shannon.

'He has some bruises,' replied Jenna. 'He was lucky Simon realised who he was otherwise he'd be in hospital now.'

'It's always the quiet ones you've got to watch,' said Lucy, casting Simon a sideways look.

'That incident really brought us back together,' continued Jenna. 'It feels like when we were first married.'

'There's nothing like beating the shite out of someone to get your relationship back on track,' smiled Lucy. 'Have you seen Harmony?' she asked Shannon.

Shannon wasn't fooled by how casually Lucy spoke. She knew she had a crush on Harmony. 'She said she was going for a bath.'

'Oh,' she replied, the corner of her mouth lifting into a smile as this statement conjured up certain mental pictures. 'She's really nice, isn't she?'

'She is. I get on really well with her.'

'Me too. It's hard for me to feel comfortable with people I don't know well but I can talk to her about anything.' Lucy blushed. 'That's so rare for me.'

'I know what you mean,' said Jenna. 'I find it difficult making small talk with the tourists we get staying at the camp.' Her eyes took on a dark look. 'Sometimes I find myself wishing they'd just drive into the sea so I won't have to deal with them again.' When they all stared at her, she shook herself out of it and smiled. 'Sorry, I know that sounded weird but I'm so bloody tired of it.'

'So am I,' said Simon. 'And do you know what we're going to do?'

'What?' replied Jenna.

'We're going to sell the place. I'm sick to death of it.'

'Oh, Simon,' breathed Jenna, eyes filling with tears. 'You don't know how happy I am to hear you say that. I wonder how much we'd get for it?'

'I've already had a good offer.'

'You have? How much?'

He whispered a figure in her ear that made her eyes light up. 'Really?' she shrieked. 'That's wonderful.' Jenna's enthusiasm dampened slightly. 'But what will we do instead?'

'We're going to move to Perth like we've always wanted to and buy that house we were looking at online. I've already checked and it's still available. It means we'll be mortgage-free and still have some left over.'

'But we have to work. The money from the sale of the site won't last forever.'

'We'll find something, don't worry. For once in our lives, let's take a risk.'

'Okay,' she smiled.

'That's my girl,' he smiled back before kissing her.

They became so passionate it made the others uncomfortable.

'Do you fancy going for a walk?' Shannon asked Lucy.

'You read my mind,' she replied.

The two women got to their feet and strode off, heading deeper into the gardens.

'I can't believe how much better Simon and Jenna are getting on,' said Shannon. 'And all because Simon punched Tom.'

'I'll never understand relationships,' replied Lucy.

'I wanted to ask you something about Kate.'

'Oh, yes?'

'Did she ever have any strange tendencies when she was younger?'

Lucy frowned. 'What do you mean?'

'She told me she thinks Robert's portrait is alive.'

'Well, it certainly gives that impression. The artist did an amazing job.'

'I don't mean like that. She actually thinks he lives through it and that he can come back to life one day.'

Lucy came to a startled halt. 'She told you that?'

Shannon nodded. Her eyes were full of concern, but she had a plan. If she could convince Kate's family that she was mad then it didn't matter what she told them; they wouldn't believe her. She could replace the money in Cameron's accounts and she would ensure no trace of the theft was left, making Kate's accusations seem the result of a disturbed mind.

'She always was obsessed with him,' said Lucy. 'I get the feeling that if he hadn't been so handsome then she would have fixated on another of our ancestors.'

'I thought I should mention it to someone because it was so weird,' said Shannon, filling her voice and eyes with false sympathy. 'I don't like speaking badly about her after how kind she's been inviting us all to stay in her house, but I just had to tell someone.'

'You haven't mentioned it to Cam then?'

'I didn't like to. He was having a good laugh with Harry and I didn't want to spoil his fun. You were the only other person I felt comfortable enough with to tell.' Shannon had taken onboard Lucy's statement about finding it difficult to connect to people and knew this would resonate with her. She realised she was right when Lucy smiled and her eyes flared with happiness.

'I appreciate your confidence in me, but I don't know what to do with this information.'

'You don't need to do anything. Just keep an eye on Kate and hope this obsession of hers doesn't go too far. I don't want to tell Cam because he might be playing Robert in this new project of hers and he could be put off if he understood the depth of Kate's obsession.'

'That's a good point.' Lucy chewed her lower lip thoughtfully. 'Should we tell anyone else?'

'Let's keep it between us, for now,' replied Shannon, knowing a shared secret would only appeal to Lucy's desire for human connection even more. 'I could be wrong, in which case no one else needs to know but if I'm right then we can tell the others. I really don't want to worry Cam right now, he's got enough on his shoulders what with this TV programme.'

'I just hope her obsession will settle down now she's finally achieved her dream of owning Alardyce House.'

'Or it could make it worse. What about her parents? Could they help?'

'Her dad died years ago and her mother won't dare say anything against her, not with Kate funding her lifestyle.'

'Is there any other family?'

'There's her aunts and uncles, my parents and Harry's, Cam's and Jenna's. They all used to be close just like we were, but they won't want to get involved, especially now Kate's bought this house. They all hate the place. If there is anything to be done about her mental state, then it will be down to us four.'

'That's a lot of weight on your shoulders.'

She shrugged. 'We're all adults now. Hopefully making this TV programme will get it out of her system.'

'I doubt it. She did seem rather fanatical.' Shannon cast her eyes shamefully to the ground. 'I hate talking about a member of your family like this, but I had to confide in someone. It felt wrong keeping quiet about it.'

Lucy patted her shoulder. 'You did the right thing. If Kate is struggling, then it's better we know.'

Shannon smiled and linked arms with Lucy, who beamed at her for this show of friendship. Shannon knew she had a strong ally in this woman. Satisfaction rolled around inside her. Kate might be a manipulative bitch, but it turned out she was too.

* * *

When Cameron entered the drawing room after his game of billiards with Harry, he saw Kate had company and immediately excused himself. Harry had gone into the kitchen to make himself a sandwich. Cameron had left him bickering with Mrs Clapperton, the cook, who guarded the contents of the fridge with a jealous aggression.

'No, don't go, Cam,' said Kate. 'I want you to meet my friends.'

Introductions were made and Cameron greeted Gail and Eric with his usual friendliness. Chris and Beauden were also present and watched with interest.

'They'll be working on the TV programme with us,' Kate told Cameron, gesturing to the Fairchilds.

The new arrivals were quick to spot the way Cameron's smile faltered.

'Oh,' he said. 'That's good. Well, I'll leave you to it. I have things to do,' he added with a meaningful look Kate's way.

His cousin understood that meant he was going to prepare his surprise for Shannon and her guts twisted with loathing. 'Don't let me keep you then,' she said sweetly.

'Nice to meet you,' he told Gail and Eric before hurrying from the room.

'He doesn't seem very enthusiastic about this production,' commented Eric.

'He'll soon come round,' replied Kate. 'It's just all so new to him.'

'Although he's very easy on the eye, he does seem too sweet to play a character like Robert,' said Gail. 'He reminds me of a contented labrador.'

'Beauden's already worked with him and has assured me he can do it.'

'You're certain?' Eric asked him with a raised eyebrow.

'Yes,' replied Beauden, steepling his fingers together. 'There's absolutely no doubt. He scared me a bit when we were reading through the script. The man can be extremely intimidating when he wants to be.'

Eric's sceptical eyebrow was raised even further. 'Really?'

'Yes, really,' said Beauden, a little annoyed by the doubt in his voice. He was not accustomed to people mistrusting his judgement.

'Let's arrange another read through for tomorrow morning,' said Eric. 'I want to see this for myself.'

'And you will, have no fear about that,' retorted Beauden, although he was a little worried about Cameron becoming self-conscious in front of another spectator.

'I also want to see how he interacts with you playing his mother,' Eric told Kate.

'Won't you find that strange?' Gail asked her.

'Kate can handle it,' said Eric confidently. 'It's Cameron I'm worried about.'

The door opened and Tom swanned in. 'Here I am,' he announced.

'Wonderful,' muttered Eric, while Gail greeted him with a kiss on the cheek and a gentle squeeze of both hands. She frowned at the bruises to Tom's face. 'What happened to you?'

'Ah, that,' he mumbled. 'It was a little misunderstanding last night. I got lost returning to my room after nipping to the bathroom and I went into the wrong bedroom. Simon leapt on me like a frigging lunatic and began hitting me.' Tom threw back his shoulders and resumed his usual swagger. 'He's lucky I didn't throw him through the window with all the martial arts training I've had but I didn't want to hurt him, he's such a string bean.'

'That eye does look painful,' said Gail, showing a lot more concern for his welfare than her husband, who was trying not to laugh.

'It's nothing. I've had much worse.'

'Like when that Alsatian barked at you on the set of *The Big Blue*?' said Eric.

Tom's cheeks coloured. Embarrassment turned to anger when Eric smiled with amusement. The bastard had always hated him, although he'd never been able to work out why. 'Oh, that? I'd forgotten about it,' he said with a dismissive wave. But he hadn't. The memory of his girlish scream and the ensuing humiliation would never leave him.

'We were discussing Cameron's suitability for playing Robert Alardyce,' Gail told Tom kindly.

'I think he'll be terrific,' he replied.

'Really?' said Gail, who had never heard Tom praise another actor before. He always saw other male actors as competition and never missed an opportunity to denigrate them. The female ones, however, he was happy to praise, for a price.

'Yep, I've no doubt and not just because of his creepy resemblance to Robert Alardyce. There's something in his black eyes that says he has a very dark side.'

'We saw none of that,' said Eric.

'To be fair,' Chris told him, 'you were only in his company for about thirty seconds.'

'That's a good point,' said Gail, narrowing her eyes at her husband.

Eric held up his hands. 'All right, I'll give him a chance.'

'How big of you,' said Gail sarcastically.

Kate smiled. Gail was the only person in the world who could get away with talking to the great Eric Fairchild like that. Everyone else was too busy licking his boots, hoping he'd throw them a scrap from his table. Gail, however, held her husband in no such awe. In fact, it was the other way around. He was absolutely devoted to her. Before he met Gail, it was rumoured he often used the casting couch to decide which actress got which role, but that fell by the wayside when Gail came into his life. She made it very clear that she wouldn't put up with that sort of nonsense and would divorce him the second she got wind of any such shenanigans. She wanted to be the only woman in his life. Everyone in the industry had given the marriage six months but seven years later they were still going strong. Whether Eric had kept his promise of fidelity to his wife or had just got better at hiding his affairs, no one was sure.

There was a loud knock at the front door, followed by the sound of the bell ringing.

'Are you expecting more guests?' Beauden asked Kate.

'No,' she replied.

'It sounds like it's urgent,' said Chris when the knocking became more frantic.

'Marcus will handle it.'

They heard the door open and Marcus's dour voice enquire the caller's name.

'Where is she?' shrieked a male voice with an American accent. 'I have to see her.'

'See whom, sir?'

'Kate. Get out of my way, you asshole.'

There was the sound of a scuffle followed by a bang.

'Christ, they're attacking Marcus,' exclaimed Tom.

'Why don't you go and rescue him with your considerable martial arts skills?' said Eric sarcastically.

'I will,' he replied, rushing to the drawing room door. Tom hesitated when he realised no one was following. 'Well, aren't you coming?'

'We don't need to when we've got someone so capable to handle the situation for us,' replied Beauden. 'We'll only get in your way.'

'Oh, right,' he mumbled before reluctantly turning back to the door.

'Kate, where are you?' cried the same deep voice. 'I need you... Ow.'

'I'd better get out there,' said Kate, getting to her feet.

Tom's bravado returned now someone else was going. 'Stay behind me,' he told her. 'I don't want you to get hurt.'

Cautiously he opened the door and peered out. Marcus had pinned the intruder against a wall, an arm across his throat. The intruder was big and strapping with light brown hair and startling blue eyes. His shoulders were almost as wide as he was tall and he stood a couple of inches above Marcus. Despite his superior size, he flailed uselessly against the butler.

'Kate,' rasped the newcomer when he saw her standing in the doorway. 'I need you.'

His words trailed off when Marcus pushed down harder on his throat.

'What are you doing here, Noah?' she sighed in a bored tone. Kate had hoped never to see her ex-boyfriend again but she should have known he wouldn't give up so easily. She'd dumped him because he was boring and clingy and all his appearance here now generated inside her was mild irritation.

Noah tried to reply but Marcus's arm across his neck prevented further speech.

'You can let him go, Marcus,' she said.

The butler nodded and released Noah, although he remained ready to intervene should the need arise.

'I had to see you,' he breathed. 'I've been going out of my mind. I have to be with you.'

'Why?' she said coolly.

'Because I love you,' he cried. 'And I can't be apart from you a second longer.'

'I told you I don't want to see you again.'

'I know you didn't mean that, honey. We're meant to be together.'

The noise drew the attention of the other guests and Cameron and Harry appeared, the latter holding a sandwich on a plate, having triumphed over the redoubtable cook.

'Who's this walloper?' said Harry.

'Walloper?' exclaimed the newcomer. 'I'm Noah Gantry, star of the Max Beechman series,' he added, his pride reasserting itself.

Beauden and the others had followed Kate and Tom out of the drawing room and had gathered to watch the show.

'Oh.' Harry looked back at Noah. 'I've never heard of Max Beecher.'

'Beechman,' he growled. 'It's the most streamed series of the year.'

'Oh. Well done,' he said with a sardonic smile.

Noah grunted with annoyance before turning his attention back to Kate. 'I've booked us two tickets to Vegas. Let's go and get married.'

'No,' she replied. 'I don't want to marry anyone.'

'But... we belong together. I want you to be my wife.'

'Tough because I don't want you.'

'You can't do this to me, Kate,' he cried. 'I want you, I need you.'

'Well, I don't want you. You're boring. All you talk about is your stupid series and how many weights you lifted in the gym. I need intellectual stimulation as well as physical and, sweetheart, you just don't do it for me.'

His face contorted with rage and, before Marcus could stop him, he ran at Kate, arms extended.

Tom threw himself back out of the way as the enormous tank steamed towards Kate, who stood there confidently with one hand on her hip.

Before Noah could reach her, Cameron grasped him by the shoulders and threw him back against the wall. While Noah was momentarily stunned, Marcus leapt on him, shoved him to the floor and twisted both arms up his back.

'Wow, Cam,' said Harry. 'I didn't know you had it in you.'

'I've had to deal with several arseholes getting heavy with women in my gyms,' he replied.

'You were amazing,' Kate told Cameron, filling her eyes with gratitude and just the right amount of fear, although Noah didn't worry her in the slightest. 'I don't know what I would have done without you.'

'I really didn't do anything,' he replied modestly.

'You saved me,' she breathed, taking his hand. 'Thank you.'

At that moment, Shannon and Lucy came through the front door. The former was furious to see her nemesis holding her boyfriend's hand. Lucy's attention, however, was drawn to the big man pinned to the floor by Marcus.

'What the hell's going on?' demanded Shannon.

Kate released Cameron's hand, and the smugness in her eyes as she looked back at her irritated Shannon even more.

'It seems we have an obsessed idiot,' said Harry, nodding at Noah.

'Is that Max Beechman?' replied Lucy.

'He wants me to go to Las Vegas with him to get married,' said Kate. 'He didn't take it very well when I said no.'

'You're making a fool of yourself, Noah,' Eric told him. 'You should leave before you make it worse for yourself.'

'I'm going nowhere without Kate,' he growled, grimacing when Marcus's grip on his arm tightened.

'I should mention that I'm very good friends with the producer of Max Beechman and he would take it badly if he heard about this, he's very fond of Kate. I also know that Liam Hemsworth is desperate to take on the role. If you were kicked out, then…'

'No way am I letting that dickhead take my spot.'

'Then I suggest you pull yourself together and leave quietly. You've humiliated yourself enough for one day.'

Noah sighed and nodded. 'You're right.'

'Let him go, Marcus,' said Kate.

The butler released him and everyone watched as Noah slowly climbed to his feet. He turned to look at Kate.

'You won't come with me to Vegas then? We don't have to get married, we could just have fun.'

'No. It's over. Accept it.'

'Just go,' said Eric when Noah opened his mouth to yell back at her. 'Or I will call your producer.'

Noah closed his mouth again, eyes glittering with anger before he stormed out, Shannon and Lucy hastily stepping aside to allow him to pass. Marcus closed and locked the door behind him.

'You need to be careful,' Gail told Kate. 'The man's obsessed.'

'He's harmless,' she replied.

'Harmless?' said Beauden. 'He's built like the proverbial brick outhouse.'

'I'm fine. Besides, I have Cam and Marcus to protect me.'

'But I don't live here,' replied Cameron. 'And Marcus can't be around all the time. At least improve your security, you're vulnerable out here.'

'I think that's a very good idea,' Eric told Kate.

'Fine, I'll consult a security expert. Now, shall we get back to our meeting?'

While Beauden, Chris, Gail, Eric and Tom filed back inside the drawing room, Kate turned to Cameron and gave his arm a gentle squeeze. 'Thank you,' she told him.

'Anytime,' he smiled back.

Shannon's hands curled into fists as their eyes locked before Kate released his arm and followed her friends into the drawing room.

'Were you in the army, Marcus?' said Harry.

'No sir, I was in the navy. Eight years in the Royal Marines.'

'I knew it, you have a military bearing.'

Marcus nodded in acknowledgement.

'Why was Kate thanking you?' Shannon demanded of Cameron. 'Marcus was the one who pinned down that psycho.'

'Cameron was the one who threw him against a wall,' said Harry.

'You did?' smiled Lucy. 'You bad ass, Cam.'

'Thanks,' he said coyly. He caught the anger in his girlfriend's eyes. 'What's wrong?'

'Nothing,' she muttered before rushing for the stairs.

'What did I do?' Cameron asked Harry.

'You really know nothing about women, do you?' he replied.

'What do you mean?'

'God, it's just sad,' he sighed, rolling his eyes. 'She's jealous of seeing the beautiful, famous actress holding your hand.'

'Why? That's ridiculous. There's nothing between me and Kate.'

'Shannon obviously doesn't see it that way.'

Cameron's eyes tick-tocked from side to side as he considered Harry's words. Realisation finally began to dawn. It had never occurred to him that Shannon could be jealous because he wasn't the jealous type. 'Christ,' he said before rushing upstairs after her.

'He's lucky I'm here,' Harry told Lucy.

'That was all very odd with Kate's ex-boyfriend,' she replied.

'Women like her attract obsessed freaks like moths to a flame. She's probably used to it.'

'I suppose.' Lucy lowered her voice. 'Have you noticed anything strange about Kate?'

'In what way?'

'She's really obsessed with this house and Robert Alardyce,' she whispered.

'Aye, you're right, but I'm sure it's harmless.'

'What if it's not?'

'What are you suggesting?'

'That Kate might be losing herself. You saw her at the graves. I think we should keep an eye on her. We don't want her getting lost down the rabbit hole like Gran did and ending her days in a care home, ranting and raving about our relatives. Did you know that in her final days Gran said they were haunting her?'

'Aye, but she did have dementia, so it's only to be expected.'

'Or maybe the past drove her mad?'

Lucy thought she should have gone to Jenna instead. She at least might have taken her seriously. Harry had always been so laid-back, he never let anything bother him.

'Stop worrying. You need to relax and enjoy yourself.'

'I find it hard relaxing.'

'That's always been your trouble. How about I thrash you at billiards like I did Cameron?'

'Well, okay.'

'That's the spirit,' he grinned, slinging an arm around her shoulders and leading her towards the billiard room. 'You'll feel much better if you let loose a wee bit.'

Lucy wasn't sure she could let loose. What Shannon said had worried her; she'd seen the mania in Kate's eyes. What if the Alardyce curse was still alive and well?

14

'Honestly, babe, it didn't mean anything,' Cameron told Shannon for the tenth time. 'She was only thanking me for helping her.'

'It looked a lot more than that,' she snapped back. They were in the privacy of their bedroom and Cameron was a little stunned by Shannon's extreme reaction to something he considered to be completely innocent.

'Well, it wasn't. She's my cousin, for God's sake.'

'Like that matters to her,' she retorted, eyes flashing.

'What's that supposed to mean?'

'Oh, come on, Cam. You must have seen how she looks at you. She wants you.'

The intimate moment he and Kate had shared in the kitchen returned but he hastily brushed aside the memory. 'That's ridiculous. She only wants me to be in her TV programme.'

'And how she'll love working so closely with you.'

'You're totally wrong about this, Shan. I'm just a cousin to her and even if she did fancy me, which she doesn't, it wouldn't matter because I'm with you.'

'How can I compete with her? She's gorgeous and rich and has everything I don't.'

'That's not the way I see it. In fact, I love you so much I was going to ask you to marry me tonight.'

Her eyes widened. 'What?'

Cameron went down on one knee before her and produced the ring box from his jeans pocket. He'd been carrying it around with him for fear of her finding it before he was ready to pop the question. 'This wasn't how I wanted to ask you, I had arranged a much more romantic setting, but it'll have to do.' He opened the box and she gasped at the glittering ring inside. 'Will you marry me?'

Shannon was speechless. She'd allowed Kate's poison to infiltrate her mind and had started to persuade herself that her rival would steal him from her when all the time Cameron had wanted to marry her. Tears filled her eyes. It was true, he really did love her. She wasn't going to lose him.

'Yes, I'll marry you,' she cried.

With a smile, Cameron plucked the ring from the box and slid it onto her finger.

Shannon's face creased. 'I've made such an idiot of myself,' she said, allowing the tears to spill down her cheeks.

'It doesn't matter,' he replied before kissing her.

They fell back onto the bed together, frantically tearing off each other's clothes. Shannon clung on to him as he made love to her, revelling in the knowledge that he was all hers. They made quite a lot of noise but neither cared.

'Have you any idea how happy you've made me?' he smiled down at her as they caught their breath.

'I do because I feel it too,' she beamed up at him, stroking his face with her fingers.

Cameron kissed her fingertips. 'When do you want to get married?'

'As soon as possible.'

'I was hoping you'd say that. I was thinking we could go to Egypt for our honeymoon. I know you've always wanted to go.'

'That would be amazing. We could take a cruise down the Nile.'

'Perfect, although I can't promise that I'll let you out of the bedroom very much.'

'I don't care, just as long as we're together. We could go to Blackpool and I'd still be happy because I'd be Mrs Alardyce.'

'What is it?' he frowned when her eyes flickered.

'Nothing,' she said, forcing the smile back on her face. It had only just occurred to her that she'd have that bloody surname, but she was happy to pay the price if it meant Cameron would be her husband; she'd dreamed of him popping the question ever since they'd got together.

'Good,' he said, pleased nothing could spoil this perfect moment.

* * *

The dining table at Alardyce House was becoming increasingly full but it was so large there was still plenty of room for all the guests, even with the new arrivals.

Cameron couldn't help but roll his eyes when Gail and Eric gawped at the portrait of Robert on the wall before turning to himself.

'Aye, I know,' he mumbled.

'Well,' said Eric, who felt his doubts about casting Kate's inexperienced cousin in the leading role ease slightly. 'That really is something.'

'Isn't it?' said Kate with a breezy smile. 'Now you'll understand why I'm so keen to involve Cam in this project.'

'Yes,' he replied, giving the portrait an odd frown before taking his seat. His back was turned to the picture and he glanced over his shoulder at it, feeling like it was staring at him. It was one of those creepy pictures where the eyes followed you around the room and they felt to be boring into the back of his skull.

'I have to ask though,' said Gail, turning her attention to the rest of the Alardyce family. 'What do you all think about this production?'

'I think it's exciting,' smiled Harry. 'And Kate has promised me a minor if gallant role. You don't need to worry about my acting skills. I'll just be in the background, brightening up the scene for you.'

'That's very generous of you.'

Harry picked up on the irony in her voice, but hers was a sense of humour he could appreciate, so he smiled.

Gail couldn't help but be charmed by that smile and returned it.

'By the way,' Kate told the table as Marcus brought in the soup. 'One of my videographer friends got back to me about that footage and he said he couldn't find any explanation for the shadow.'

'What's this?' said Eric.

'We had a séance last night and a strange shadow showed up on camera.'

While Eric's lip curled with cynicism, Gail's eyes widened with interest. 'Really?' she said.

'Yes. Harmony's quite the psychic.'

'Do you tell fortunes?' Gail asked Harmony.

'No,' she replied. 'I just contact the dead.'

'Would you be willing to hold another séance here tonight?'

'Is there someone in particular you wish to contact?' she replied.

'No, I just think it would be interesting in this house with its history.'

'We can have another séance tonight, if you like,' Kate told Gail.

'I really don't think that's a good idea,' babbled Tom nervously.

They all turned to look at him.

He cleared his throat before continuing, realising he'd sounded a little hysterical. 'I mean,' he continued in a calmer tone, 'that Chris has already had one shock. He felt a presence in his room, so naturally I said I'd sleep in there instead, to make him feel better.'

'And you came running into our room crying that someone was standing over you,' Simon told him.

Tom scowled at Simon. God, he hated that bastard. And to think when they'd first met he'd claimed to be a fan. 'I was not crying,' he said firmly. 'I was merely concerned that we had an intruder and I was trying to warn you. Then you lost control of yourself.'

'So you're the one who did that to his face,' Gail told Simon, her eyes dancing.

'Aye, I did,' he replied, tilting back his head, daring her to make something of it.

'He was so brave,' said Jenna with an adoring gaze at her husband. 'I went to pieces. I thought it was a burglar and we were both going to be murdered, but Simon didn't hesitate. He sprang straight into action.'

'It was assault, pure and simple,' glowered Tom. 'I make my living with my face. You're lucky I don't sue you,' he told Simon who, to his irritation, merely grinned.

'No one's suing anyone,' Chris told him. 'Do you want it all over social media that you burst into a married couple's bedroom in the middle of the night because you thought you'd seen a ghost then got beaten up? That is not the sort of publicity we want before beginning this production.'

'I know and that's why I haven't made a big deal of it,' shrugged Tom. 'He hits like a girl anyway.'

'And you scream like one,' retorted Simon.

Tom slammed down his spoon and glared at him.

'That's enough, you two,' said Kate. 'You're behaving like children. Now concentrate on this lovely soup Mrs Clapperton's made.'

Her chiding had the desired effect and they both dropped the subject.

'So,' said Lucy, breaking the awkward silence. 'If there's no scientific explanation for that shadow, then what's left?'

'It's a spirit,' said Harmony.

'That's ridiculous,' said Tom.

'Why?' she replied, her gaze so intense he was forced to look away from it.

'Ghosts don't exist,' he mumbled.

'How do you know?'

'Because I've never seen one.'

'Yes, you have,' she said, casually dipping her spoon into her soup. 'You saw Edward Alardyce's spirit last night.'

An incoherent splutter emanated from the back of Tom's throat before he recovered himself and said, 'I didn't see anything, it was just a dream.'

'Edward's in that room. I've seen him,' said Harmony as though it was the most natural thing in the world.

'You've been in my room?' he frowned.

'You left the door open. I was passing and I saw him standing there, looking out of the window. He turned to face me and smiled. I've never seen such evil or madness in one smile before.'

It was Eric's turn to choke on his soup. He coughed, Gail patting him on the back, and he took a sip of water from the glass on the table. 'Are you serious?' he rasped, eyes watering.

'Yes,' she replied so calmly it was impossible for him to argue.

'Perhaps we should leave talk of ghosts while we eat?' said Gail tactfully. 'We don't want anyone else choking.'

Harmony shrugged and serenely returned her attention to her soup, apparently oblivious to the tension she'd caused.

Shannon saw the perfect way to break that tension. She looked across the table at Cameron, who smiled and nodded.

'We've got an announcement to make,' she said, drawing everyone's attention to herself. 'This afternoon, Cam asked me to marry him and I said yes,' she beamed, holding out her hand so everyone could see the ring.

The table broke into noisy applause, those who didn't know the happy couple joining in just as rapturously as the conversation had been beautifully drawn away from the awkward subject of ghosts.

'Congratulations,' Harry's voice boomed above all the others. 'I hope you'll be very happy together.'

'We will,' smiled Cameron confidently.

'That's a beautiful ring,' said Jenna.

'Isn't it?' beamed Shannon.

'I'm so glad you like it,' said Kate. 'Poor Cam was agonising over which one to get you.'

Shannon's smile fell. 'You knew about this?'

'He asked for my help. He wanted to arrange a romantic surprise for you in the conservatory with candles and champagne.'

'The conservatory?' she said, recalling the awful atmosphere in that room.

'Yes. Why didn't you stick to the plan, Cam?' Kate asked him.

'It just seemed the right time earlier,' he replied.

'Well, we can still have the champagne. Marcus, bring in six bottles of the Bolly, will you?' she said, to Harry's delight.

The butler bowed and left to carry out his instructions.

'Did anyone else know about this?' Shannon asked the table.

'No,' said Kate. 'Just me.'

All the good feelings inside Shannon died. That sweet, innocent look didn't fool her for a moment. Kate wanted her to know that she'd been part of Cameron's plan from the beginning, had even helped him choose the ring, knowing that every time she looked at it, Shannon would think of her. Already everything was ruined, tainted by Kate and her poison.

'This is certainly turning into a holiday to remember,' smiled Harry.

'It is,' murmured Shannon.

She glanced down the table at Kate, who sat there like a queen on her throne. Kate smiled back at her, triumph written all over her face. It seemed the bitch was determined to dog her future. Shannon knew that as long as she was with Cameron, she'd never be rid of Kate bloody Alardyce. Rebellion rose inside her. She'd see her dead before she allowed her to ruin her life.

* * *

As had become the routine at Alardyce House, the party retired to the drawing room after dinner to be served coffee and brandy by Marcus. Eric had even brought cigars but as Kate had a strict no-smoking policy, he was forced to smoke outside with the rest of the men. Cameron was too health-conscious to join them.

'You really do make a lovely couple,' Gail told Shannon and Cameron.

'Thanks,' said Cameron, turning to smile at his fiancée sitting beside him on the couch and taking her hand.

'I wish you many long, happy years together,' she added, raising her brandy glass in a toast.

The happy couple beamed and nodded in acknowledgement.

'I can't wait to get you fitted up for your costume,' Gail told Cameron. 'I've already got the perfect design in mind, aided by all the images Kate sent me of the style of clothes Robert wore.' She was quick to spot Cameron's down-cast look. 'Am I right in assuming you don't have much enthusiasm for this production?'

'It's not that,' he sighed. 'I've absolutely no acting experience and I'm afraid of making an arse of myself.' The troubling memories of the taunts he'd endured as a child returned, making him feel even more uncomfortable. However, he recognised another feeling among the memories, something new, something potent. It was anger. The past that had haunted him for so long was helping him tap into a dark part of himself he hadn't even realised existed until now. All the rage that had built up through all those years of bullying would help him bring Robert Alardyce to life.

The rest of the men returned to the room, bringing with them the vague smell of cigar smoke.

'Everyone's got to start somewhere,' Gail kindly told Cameron as they retook their seats. 'Even Tom and Kate began with no experience. I'm sure you'll soon pick it up.'

'I'm worried about letting so many people down.'

'Don't worry about what other people think so much,' Harry told him. 'I don't care what anyone thinks of me and it's so liberating.'

'I wish I could be like you.'

'Why don't you give us a little demonstration of what you can do?' suggested Eric, guile in his eyes.

'Now?' frowned Cameron. 'In front of everyone?' he added, appalled.

Eric nodded. 'As Beauden's no doubt explained, if you take on the role, you'll have to perform in front of lots of people. I also believe Kate's written a couple of steamy sex scenes for Robert, not just with whoever will play Jane but with prostitutes too. She told me her grandfather was very fond of the brothels in his younger days.'

'No one mentioned sex scenes to me,' glowered Shannon.

'They didn't mention them to me either,' said Cameron, frowning at his cousin.

'Don't worry about it,' replied Kate. 'They're very tasteful and you'll only have to show your chest and bottom.'

Harry chuckled into his brandy.

'I am not doing that,' exclaimed Cameron.

'You'll get paid extra.'

This gave him pause. 'Really?' He turned to Shannon. 'What do you think?'

'I hate it,' she said vehemently. 'I can't watch you kiss other women.'

'It's nothing to worry about,' said Gail. 'Actors do it regularly and it never interferes with their relationships; well, at least not all the time. Everyone's very professional. It's just a job to them and we employ intimacy coordinators to make sure everyone's comfortable with what they have to do.'

'There has to be at least one sex scene,' said Eric. 'The audience will expect it.'

'I don't remember anyone getting their arse out in *Downton Abbey*,' said Shannon.

Harry chuckled again, louder this time.

'This production will be far darker than *Downton Abbey*,' said Eric wryly.

'All this can be discussed later, when we've got the final script,' said Chris. 'We might even be able to use a body double if you object so much.'

'That would be good,' said Cameron, feeling slightly better.

Eric settled back in his chair and fixed Cameron with a steady gaze. 'Well, we're waiting.'

'For what?' he replied.

'For you to show us what you can do.' He smiled with satisfaction at the panic that lit up his eyes.

'I have a copy of the script here,' said Kate. She rose and produced a bundle of papers from a drawer in the sideboard.

'I'll fetch mine from my room,' said Beauden before leaving.

Kate tossed the script she held into Cameron's lap. 'There you go.'

'Thanks,' he muttered, picking it up.

'I'll sit right here, so I can give you some tips.'

Kate sat on the other side of Cameron, smiling at Shannon when she glared at her.

Beauden quickly returned with his own copy of the script.

'I'll take that, if you don't mind,' Eric told him. 'I'd like to test Cameron personally.'

'As you wish,' he replied, handing him the script, thinking it would serve him right if he ended up with his own bruises.

Eric skimmed through the script, looking for something suitable. 'Here's the perfect scene – the confrontation between Robert and Inspector Murphy in the restaurant. Page 142.'

With a sense of foreboding, Cameron flicked through the script and found the relevant page.

'Ready?' Eric asked him.

Cameron hated the way his eyes twinkled. Eric expected him to fail. In fact, he was so confident he was no doubt already planning which professional actor he could bring in to replace him. Fuck him and his smugness. He glanced at Shannon and sadness swept over him. He was doing this for her, to save her restaurant and for their future as husband and wife. Defiance washed away the embarrassment. He could do this.

'Give me a sec,' he said before getting to his feet and rushing from the room.

'Is he coming back?' said Eric, already victorious.

'Of course he is,' replied Kate. 'Cameron never gives up.'

Shannon wanted to ask her how the hell she knew that. She felt like she didn't know Cameron any more but she had to own that Kate was right. Whatever Cameron put his mind to, he succeeded at. A little voice nagged at the back of her mind that he was slowly slipping away from her and she didn't know how to bring him back to her.

15

Cameron stood before the painting of Robert in the dining room, once again taking in every detail, attempting to mimic his poise and confidence. He jumped when the door opened and Marcus entered.

'Do excuse me, sir,' said the butler. 'I didn't realise anyone was in here.'

'Could you give me a moment? I need to do something.'

A puzzled frown creased Marcus's forehead, but he nodded and left. Cameron turned his attention back to the portrait.

'Help me, please,' he whispered to it.

The arrogance in Robert's hard black gaze intensified and Cameron drank in that expression, allowing it to fill him up. He closed his eyes and thought back to the taunts and bullying he'd endured as a child. He imagined punching all those bullies right in their bastard faces, knocking them off their feet, staring down at them coldly, pitiless in victory...

Cameron opened his eyes and his lips curled back into a smile as he regarded the portrait, his grip on the script tightening, creasing the pages.

'Thank you,' he told the picture before confidently stalking from the room.

* * *

Eric's smile fell when Cameron returned looking very different to the uncertain man who'd left. Somehow, he looked even taller and broader and he swaggered in rather than walked. When those black eyes fixed on him, a tingle of unease ran down his spine. Beauden smiled, knowing exactly what was coming.

'I thought we could do the scene at this table,' said Eric, getting to his feet and gesturing to the small rectangular one at the side of the room.

Cameron shrugged as though it didn't matter in the slightest to him. He took a seat at the table and turned in the chair to regard him expectantly. Eric stood before him, shifted awkwardly and cleared his throat before looking down at the script to avoid that intimidating gaze. The members of the Alardyce family all glanced at each other, surprised by the change in Cameron, all except Kate, who smiled knowingly.

'Mr Alardyce,' said Eric, taking the chair opposite Cameron. 'Long time no see.'

They read through the first page, Cameron's demeanour growing increasingly colder. He didn't stumble over a single word, only needing to briefly glance at the script for his next line.

'I'm not speaking to you,' said Cameron, rising to his feet in accordance with the directions in the script. 'I'm going to a real restaurant for something to eat and if you know what's good for you, you'll stay well away from me.'

'Is that a threat?' said Eric.

Cameron planted his hands on the table and loomed over Eric, who stared up at him nervously. He'd never felt more powerless in front of an actor before, as though Cameron's black eyes were draining him of all his strength.

'Try me and see,' growled Cameron.

There wasn't another line in this scene for Eric, to his consternation as it would have been nice to have something to break the awkward moment, especially as Cameron was still glaring at him.

The room erupted into applause, breaking the spell. Cameron shook himself out of it and smiled. 'Was that okay?' he said, his uncertain manner so at odds with how he'd been a moment ago.

'Okay?' exclaimed Lucy. 'That was amazing.'

'She's right,' said Harry. 'I'd no idea you had it in you.'

'You were actually scary,' said Jenna. 'I bet that's just how Robert was in real life.'

Cameron's questioning gaze found Shannon's and she nodded.

'They're right,' she told him. 'It was incredible.'

'It seems acting is a family talent,' smiled Gail.

Eric hastily resumed his place in the armchair beside Beauden.

'Do you believe me now?' Beauden whispered in his ear.

Eric nodded, still feeling a little shaken.

'I think that performance clinches it,' Chris told Cameron. 'You can easily do this and Beauden will coach you through it.'

'Just as long as I don't end up with more bruises,' smiled Beauden.

An astonished Cameron retook his seat between his fiancée and cousin. Kate placed her hand on his arm and leaned into him. 'I always believed in you,' she whispered in his ear.

'Thanks,' he smiled.

Shannon took his hand, drawing his attention away from her rival. 'It really was amazing, Cam. You're so talented.'

'Thanks,' he repeated, bewildered by all the praise. He knew they weren't just making it up because if he'd been crap, Harry would have been the first to point it out, but he hadn't.

'Maybe we should give Harry a more prominent role seeing how his cousins have so much talent,' said Gail. 'He could be another amazing find.'

Harry smiled, shot to his feet and launched into a speech from *Richard III*.

'Now is the winter of our discontent,' he pronounced, throwing his arms wide.

They all listened in amused surprise as he hammed it up, although his gaze said he thought he was taking his audience to rapturous heights with his performance. When he'd finished, he awaited the applause he felt he was owed but all he got was an astonished silence.

'Or I could be wrong,' said Gail.

'What do you mean?' demanded Harry, lowering his arms. 'That was wonderful, better than Olivier himself.'

'Sit down, babe,' Harmony told him, patting the seat beside her. 'You've entertained us enough for one night, you must be so exhausted.'

'Can you hear that noise?' said Simon.

'I don't hear anything,' replied Jenna.

'There it is again – listen. It's the sound of Shakespeare turning in his grave.'

'You cheeky bastard,' snapped Harry. He retook his seat, seeing his glorious film career already crumbling before his eyes.

'Don't worry, Harry, we'll find you something to do in the production,' Kate told him.

'So,' said Gail. 'Are we having this séance or not?'

'Another one?' sighed Beauden.

'We should do it tomorrow,' said Harmony. 'The moon will be full then.'

'Does that make a difference?' replied Gail.

'My intuitive powers will be at their height, making it easier for me to establish a connection.' She noted the cynical look in Eric's eyes but she couldn't care less what he thought about anything. The man obviously had a very closed mind. Cameron had proved him wrong and so would she.

'Maybe we could contact Robert?' said Gail. 'Then you could learn from the man first hand, Cameron.'

Cameron didn't like this idea at all. Just looking at Robert's portrait affected him strongly enough.

'You shouldn't make jokes like that,' Beauden told her.

'Don't tell me you believe in all this guff?' Eric asked him.

'I believe there is more out there than we can possibly imagine and it shouldn't be mocked.'

'I never thought I'd hear those words from you.'

'You might be saying the same after spending some time in this house. There's something very different about it.'

'That's because it's been built on a strong energy vortex,' said Harmony. 'A weakening between our world and the other world.'

'Jesus, this is turning into *Stranger Things*,' sighed Eric. 'I bet the previous occupants of this house never reported anything weird.'

'Actually, they did,' said Kate. 'Do you want to hear about it?'

'No, I do not.'

'There are several people here who probably have fascinating stories to tell.' Harry looked to Chris. 'Who's the biggest twat you've ever worked with?' he eagerly asked.

'I am not going to answer that,' smiled Chris. 'But I do have other interesting stories.'

As everyone settled back to listen to Chris's anecdotes, Shannon excused herself and left the room. She was still annoyed that Kate had been in on Cameron's proposal and wanted some peace and quiet to mull things over.

She sneaked out a side door into the garden and walked around to the rear of the house, enjoying the night air, which was significantly cooler than it had been. The stars weren't visible tonight, obscured by cloud. Bad weather was definitely closing in. It would be nice to have this run of uncomfortably hot weather broken.

'Shannon,' said a voice.

'Bloody hell,' she cried, visibly jumping. Shannon squinted into the gathering gloom. 'Cam?'

'Aye, it's me,' he said, jogging up to her. 'Sorry for startling you. Are you okay?'

'Yeah, I just needed some fresh air.'

'I think there's more to it than that. Why were you so annoyed when you found out Kate knew I intended to propose?'

'She always seems to be sticking her nose into our business.'

'But we've only been here three days.'

'She thinks she has the right to lord it over us lesser mortals because she's so rich.'

'I don't think it's like that, she just wants to help. She was really supportive when I told her.'

'Only because she's trying to stay on your good side so you'll be in her stupid TV programme.'

'You really don't like her, do you?'

'No. I'm sorry, I know she's your cousin, but I can't help how I feel.'

'I suppose it's not fair of me to expect you to like every member of my family. After all, I don't like your brother.'

'Yeah, that's true... Wait, you don't like Adam?'

'Nope. He's a leech.'

'I've never heard you talk about a member of my family like that before,' she said, shocked. He'd been nothing but polite and charming to her family. Once again, another side of Cameron she hadn't known existed was revealing itself.

'I felt it was time you knew,' he replied with no apology in his tone.

'This is because of Robert Alardyce. Playing him is changing you.'

'What do you mean?' he laughed.

'You're becoming more like him.'

'You're imagining it,' he said, wrapping his arms around her waist and pulling her closer.

'No, I'm not...'

Shannon's words were cut off when he kissed her. Gently he pushed her up against the wall, already unzipping her jeans.

'What are you doing?' she whispered.

'I can't keep my hands off you,' he breathed.

'Cameron, stop. Anyone could come out here.'

'I know. Exciting, isn't it?'

The clouds parted, allowing the moon to peek out. The light illuminated Cameron's face and what Shannon saw made her gasp and recoil. It wasn't her Cam, it was Robert Alardyce staring back at her out of those cold black eyes.

'What's wrong?' he said when she stumbled away from him.

'You're not yourself, Cam. It's this place, it's twisting you,' she said, backing up to the door while fastening her jeans.

'No, it's not,' he frowned in confusion, following her. 'Where's this coming from?'

Shannon's gaze was drawn by movement down the garden towards that awful crypt, the moonlight hitting the stone. Why hadn't she realised it was there when she'd first come outside?

'Something's over there,' she rasped.

'Where?' he said, turning to look.

'There, to the left of the crypt. I can see something moving. It's stopped and it's staring at us,' she gasped before racing towards the door.

'Shannon,' he called.

She ignored him and rushed inside, almost bowling over Harry. She didn't apologise and ran for the stairs.

'What's wrong with her?' Harry asked Cameron.

'She said she saw something down by the crypt and freaked out. Should I go after her?'

'In my experience, it's better to give a woman time to cool off before trying to talk to her.'

'Suppose.' Cameron watched Harry produce a cigar and light it. 'She said playing Robert is twisting me.'

Harry laughed, puffing smoke out of his mouth. 'If you ask me, she's more worried about this new opportunity changing things between you.'

'You think?'

'Of course. What if you're a success and wind up with legions of female fans all clamouring for your body? Shannon's just feeling a bit insecure.'

'Even though I've asked her to marry me?'

'As a man who's been married several times, a ring doesn't guarantee a long, happy future together and she's worried she'll lose you to something she's powerless against.'

'Maybe I shouldn't do this TV programme. I don't want to risk my relationship with Shannon.' There might be another way to come up with the money; he could get a bank loan or remortgage his house.

'It's up to you but you might end up resenting her for taking the chance away from you, especially if it's a huge hit and you've missed out on the opportunity of a lifetime.'

'Or it could flop and the only thing I'd miss out on is humiliation.'

'It won't flop. Kate doesn't do flops. That's why those studio bigwigs rushed to come here. They know it'll be a massive hit and they want to make sure they're on board the gravy train.'

'Since we've been here, I've seen a side to Shannon I didn't know existed with all the jealousy and paranoia.' Cameron looked back at the crypt. 'This place seems to be getting to her. I'm hoping it'll stop when we leave. Perhaps we should go?'

'You can't leave yet, we're still catching up. We've not even had the chance to do some male bonding yet.'

'I don't want to go but I've got think of what's best for Shannon.'

'Take my advice, Cam, and don't give in. What you do now will set the tone for the rest of your married life. Do you want her to rule the roost?'

'She won't do that, we're a team.'

'Aye, right,' he laughed.

'It's true.'

'I've got an idea – Harmony's going into Edinburgh tomorrow. There's a crystal shop she wants to visit. Why don't you send Shannon with her? Getting away from Alardyce for a bit will do her good and us cousins can spend some quality time together.'

'That's a great idea. It'll cheer her right up.'

'There you go then,' said Harry with satisfaction, puffing on his cigar.

'Can I ask you something, Harry?'

'Fire away.'

'Why did you come here? I mean, I've been able to work out why the others turned up. Lucy's fascination for history brought her here and Jenna was hoping a holiday away from the kids could save her marriage, but I didn't think you'd come.'

'To be perfectly honest, I was hoping to recapture my youth. The times we played together were the happiest of my life. Everything went downhill once our parents fell out and we weren't allowed to see each other again. I was hoping to get some of that old happiness back.' Harry's smile was for once sheepish. 'Pathetic, eh?'

'No, not at all,' replied Cameron. 'I loved our childhoods too. I'm lucky, my life's gone well, but I really wanted to reconnect with you all.'

'I hope you're not regretting that decision now?'

'No, even though things haven't gone as I'd expected. Right, I'd better go and find Shannon.'

While Cameron headed back inside the house, Harry remained in the garden, enjoying his cigar. Kate emerged a couple of minutes later.

'Have you seen Cam?' she asked him.

'He's somewhere inside.'

'Do you have any plans for tomorrow? I was thinking we could all have lunch at the village pub.'

'I don't but Harmony's going into Edinburgh and she's going to ask Shannon to go with her.'

'Why?' she replied, her interest piqued.

'Cameron thinks Shannon's getting a bit of cabin fever.'

'Why would he think that?'

'You're full of curiosity, aren't you?' he said, the corner of his mouth lifting.

'Shannon has been acting strange, don't you think? She's very jumpy.'

'A bit,' he shrugged.

'I think she's unhinged. Don't tell Cam I said that, he obviously adores her; why, I can't imagine. She is a bit of a shrew.'

'Careful, Kate. Anyone would think you were jealous.'

'I'm not jealous, just concerned. Cameron could have a bright future and she'll only hold him back. I've seen her type many times.'

'And you've seen them all off, I suppose.'

'I'm not interested in Cam romantically. I just want to be a cousin to him and to work with him on this production.'

Harry blew out a stream of smoke, dropped the cigar and ground it out under foot. 'I don't believe you, Kate. You have that same look in your eye as you always got whenever you talked about this house. You already have the house, so now you need a new target, and that's Cameron.'

'He's my cousin.'

'Second cousin. What Kate Alardyce wants, she always gets, right?'

Kate didn't respond; she merely smiled as he returned to the house. It was only to be expected, Harry always was sharp and he was a man of the world, much more so than Cameron. She also knew that he wouldn't interfere with her plans; he was the live and let live type, which was good. She really liked Harry and didn't want to crush him under her boot heel.

16

'I'm not sure I should go to Edinburgh today,' Shannon told Cameron for the second time.

'Why not?' he replied. 'It's one of your favourite cities and you don't get the chance to visit very often.'

'What will you do without me?'

'Me, Lucy and Harry are going into the village to have a proper look around and have some lunch at the pub.'

'That sounds nice. Aren't Jenna and Kate going with you?' she added, trying to keep her tone light and failing.

'No. Jenna and Simon want to spend some time together to reconnect; those are Jenna's words by the way, not mine. Kate's staying here with her thespian friends to discuss the production.'

'Won't they want you for that?' she said suspiciously.

'No, it's all the pre-production stuff.'

'Listen to you, you sound like an expert already.'

'I wouldn't go that far.' He slid his arms around her waist. 'Have a look in any bridal shops you might pass, get some ideas.' He produced some notes from his pocket. 'And take this, enjoy yourself.'

'You don't need to give me money,' she sighed.

'I know but I want to. We're going to be married and what's mine will be yours anyway, so you may as well start now.'

Shannon's eyes gleamed. Perhaps that could be another way out of the mess she'd got herself into? She couldn't be accused of stealing something that belonged to her. 'That's really kind,' she said, taking the money. 'I want to marry you as soon as possible.'

'Me too. Now go and have fun with Harmony.'

'I'll do my best,' she smiled, slipping the cash into her handbag.

They headed downstairs together, arms around each other. Harmony was already waiting at the front door.

'Ready?' she smiled at Shannon.

'Yep,' she replied. She turned to Cameron and they kissed goodbye.

Before leaving, Shannon paused to look back at her fiancé, expecting to see Kate standing beside him with that insufferable smirk on her face, but there was no sign of her.

'I'll miss you,' she said, not wanting to leave him alone here, getting the feeling the awful place would infect him even more without her to ward it off.

'I'll miss you too,' he smiled back.

After taking one last lingering look at her fiancé, she finally left with Harmony.

Cameron remained in the hallway, wondering what he should do with himself while he waited for Harry and Lucy to finish breakfast. Just as he'd decided to head into the billiard room, he turned and almost walked into Kate, who had appeared out of nowhere. She looked beautiful. Her hair was for once held back in a high ponytail, which only showed off those delicious red lips and big blue eyes even more. She was dressed more casually in black pedal pusher leggings and a sleeveless white blouse, but the outfit only made her look even more feminine.

'So Shannon's finally let you off the leash, has she?' she purred.

'What leash?' frowned Cameron.

'She does like to keep you close.'

'We're a close couple.'

Kate tilted her head to one side. 'Are you sure that's all it is?'

'What do you mean?'

'Oh, nothing. I hear you're going into the village with Harry and Lucy. Have fun,' she smiled before sashaying across the hall and into the drawing room.

Cameron frowned. What had she meant about a leash? Had she been trying to say that Shannon controlled him? He and Shannon were a team, equals. Still, he hadn't liked Kate's words at all.

'What's up with you?' said Lucy as she and Harry emerged from the direction of the dining room.

'Why does everyone keep sneaking up on me today?' demanded Cameron.

'Careful, Lucy,' grinned Harry. 'If we piss him off his dark side will come out again. We saw it up close and personal yesterday when you were doing that reading with Eric. You proper shit him up,' he chuckled.

Cameron's eyes narrowed. 'That was just acting. After listening to your *Richard III* speech it's clear why you wouldn't understand that.'

Lucy felt a little sad. The Cameron she'd known as a child would never have said anything like that for fear of hurting Harry's feelings. When Harry just chuckled, she reasoned Cameron knew it was pretty hard to insult him but still, it was a shame.

'Right,' grinned Harry, clapping his hands together. 'Let's go and terrorise the village of Alardyce.'

'As our great-great-grandfather did before us,' smiled Cameron.

'Precisely,' said Harry. He linked his arm through Lucy's. 'Let's get there before it starts chucking it down.'

The day was a lot duller and greyer but it was still very warm, the threat of a storm hanging in the air. Lucy felt the weather reflected what was going on inside the house. Tensions were rising and it was only a matter of time before someone snapped.

* * *

After touring all the shops in the village, of which there were quite a few, they headed into a bookshop from which it was very difficult to extract Lucy.

'Shall we come back for you tomorrow?' Harry asked her.

'Give me a minute, will you? It's not like we're in a hurry. The history selection here is brilliant.'

Ten minutes later Lucy had finally chosen her books and paid and they could leave.

'Why don't we buy some flowers and visit the family graves?' she asked the men.

'Not you as well,' said Harry. 'Why are all the women in our family obsessed with the dead?'

'I'm not obsessed. I just think it would be a nice thing to do and it could be good research for Cameron. He might find being near Robert's mortal remains inspiring.'

'You really do have a ghoulish streak.'

'I agree that it would be a nice gesture,' said Cameron. 'They are our family after all.'

'Fine,' sighed Harry. 'Let's get it over and done with. The pub will be open by now.'

After purchasing several roses from the florist, they wandered into the kirkyard. No one else was there. A new graveyard had been opened on the edge of the village in the 1950s when Alardyce had quickly expanded, the old cemetery being too small to cope with the new influx of residents, so most of the dead in this graveyard had been long forgotten with no one to tend their graves or remember who they were.

They placed a rose on all of the Alardyce graves, but they were drawn back to Amy's, Henry's, Jane's and Robert's headstones, standing before them in revered silence.

'How does it feel knowing the man you're going to play is just under your feet?' Harry asked Cameron.

'I wish you wouldn't say things like that,' he replied.

'I'm not creeping you out, am I?' he said with a wicked smile. 'Why don't you lie down next to them, get a feel for it?'

'Do you want a smack in the mouth?'

'There, you're getting into the spirit of the role already.'

'What if they are still at the house?' said Lucy.

'I beg your pardon?' said Harry, eyebrows shooting up his forehead.

'I mean, what if Kate's right and they never left? They could be watching us, judging us.'

'I hope they weren't watching last night. What me and Harmony got up to is banned even in Thailand.'

'Aye, right. I heard you snoring through the wall.'

'They're dead and gone,' said Cameron firmly. 'This time is ours, not theirs.'

'Well said, Cam,' replied Harry, deciding to ignore Lucy's comment.

'That shadow on the video you took had to come from somewhere,' said Lucy.

The breeze suddenly picked up, whistling through the gravestones, scattering the petals of the roses they'd so reverently placed.

'It's a sign,' added Lucy.

'What's wrong with you?' Harry asked her. 'I thought you were a logical archaeologist.'

'I'm a historian, not an archaeologist, and being here in Alardyce has changed my outlook a bit.'

He regarded her with one of his shark-like smiles. 'You've had an experience that you've kept to yourself, haven't you?'

'No,' she replied uneasily. 'I've not seen anything, it's just the atmosphere. I remember what Harmony said about the veil being thinner here and I think she's right. What do you reckon, Cam?'

'I think we've all let our imaginations get the better of us,' he replied.

There was an enormous thunderclap that made Harry jump.

'Jesus, this place is going to give me a heart attack,' he gasped, pressing a hand to his chest.

'Let's get inside the church,' cried Lucy when the breeze whipped up to a gale, hurling cool, fat droplets of rain into their faces.

As they rushed to the church, the droplets turned into a downpour and they were drenched by the time they burst through the door. The interior of the church was peaceful, quiet and cool. No one else was about.

'Great,' said Harry. 'How long are we going to be stuck in here?'

'Until the rain stops,' replied Cameron.

'God knows how long that will be.' Harry cringed. 'Sorry,' he told the air.

'What a beautiful building,' said Lucy, studying it with an expert eye. 'The T-shape tells me it was expanded from a typical medieval rectangle. The pulpit's in the middle of the south wall, meaning it was probably moved during the reformation. And just look at those eighteenth-century box pews.'

'Aye, they're great,' said Harry flatly. When Lucy continued to witter on about the architecture, he added, 'I'm tempted to go back outside and stand in the rain.' This statement was greeted with a loud clap of thunder. 'Maybe not.'

'We may as well make ourselves comfortable,' said Cameron, taking a seat in a pew.

Harry sat beside him and grimaced. 'Comfortable is not the word I'd use. These seats are like medieval instruments of torture. We're going to end up with piles.' He sighed heavily. 'This is hardly the fun day out I'd envisaged, trapped in a draughty church in a storm with Indiana Jones,' he said, gesturing to Lucy.

'I told you, I'm a historian, not an archaeologist,' she snapped.

'What have you got against archaeologists?' Harry chuckled.

She sighed at his raised eyebrow. 'I dated an archaeologist once and she was a cow. She stole from me too.'

'Ah, the embittered ex. Now I understand. What about you, Cam? Have you had any partners who stole from you?'

'No,' he replied. 'At least, I don't think so and I know Shan would never do anything like that. She's so lovely.'

'True. She'll make you a wonderful wife.'

'I know,' he smiled happily. 'But it's good to hear that from an expert,' he added wryly.

'I'm no expert. In fact, I'm a terrible judge of women, that's why I've been married so many times.' His smile for once was sheepish rather than blasé. 'I'm lucky Harmony puts up with me, but she's so laid back my faults don't seem to bother her.'

There was another flash of light that illuminated the stained-glass windows, followed by a massive growl of thunder.

'The storm sounds to be right above us,' said Lucy, looking up at the vaulted ceiling.

'Good,' replied Harry. 'Hopefully it'll soon move on and then we can go to the pub. I'm starving after all the walking about we've done.'

Another flash of lightning and Cameron saw that one of the windows depicted Salome holding the severed head of John the Baptist, blood dripping from the neck, and he shivered. 'Maybe we could make a run for it to the pub?' he suggested. 'It's only up the road.'

'Are you mad?' said Lucy. 'Do you want to get struck by lightning?'

'And I don't run,' announced Harry.

The wind picked up, howling around the church, searching for a way in through the old, stalwart stone. The rain attacked the roof with renewed vigour, hammering off it.

'This storm has been building for a while,' said Harry. 'The air's felt electric the past couple of days. It's a good thing though, it'll clear out that awful humidity. I'm tired of my underwear sticking to my arse.'

'Language,' Lucy told him, gesturing to the building, reminding him of where they were.

'Oh, aye. Sorry.'

Cameron got to his feet to look out of one of the windows, avoiding the one with John the Baptist's severed head. Instead, he peered out around the side of Archangel Michael holding aloft his flaming sword. The gravestones of his family stood out in stark relief, but his attention was particularly drawn to Robert's. He recalled Lucy's words about being so physically close to the man he was going to play.

There was another flash of lightning and Cameron's eyes widened when he saw a dark figure standing right beside Robert's grave.

'Christ,' he gasped, taking a step back. 'Someone's out there,' he said, pointing to the window.

Harry and Lucy rushed to stand either side of him.

'I don't see anything,' said Harry, squinting through the glass.

'They're there, standing by Robert's grave.'

Harry's look was knowing. 'Is someone's imagination getting the better of him?'

'It's not my imagination. I saw them as clearly as I'm seeing you.'

'Wait,' said Lucy. 'Someone is out there.'

Another brilliant flash of lightning and a clap of thunder accompanied this statement.

'They're coming to the door,' said Lucy.

The three of them turned to look at the heavy oak door, waiting for it to slam open and that dark, intimidating figure to be revealed. A loud bang on the door made Lucy gasp and grab hold of Cameron's hand.

'It was just the thunder,' rasped Harry.

'Thunder doesn't knock on doors,' she retorted.

The storm continued to rage and the wind to rush around the building. Cameron swore he could hear the sound of whispering, only it didn't resemble a breeze trying to find its way in. It sounded more like voices. The room suddenly felt to be full of people and the thought that they were in the middle of a funeral made him shudder. He turned, expecting to see dozens of outraged faces staring back at him, but all he saw was the empty room.

There was a louder knock and Lucy's grip on his hand tightened.

Cameron's jaw set. 'I'm going to open it.'

'Are you mad?' said Harry. 'God only knows what's on the other side of it.'

'Ghosts don't knock.'

'One was knocking at Alardyce House just a couple of nights ago,' he exclaimed.

'I'm still going to open it.'

'Wait, Cam...'

He released Lucy's hand and strode towards the door, determined to face down whatever was on the other side. His rational mind told him nothing was there, that the figure he'd seen had been a trick of the light and the only thing banging at the door was a bench that had been blown over and was being rocked against the door by the wind.

Grasping the heavy iron handle, he glanced over his shoulder at his cousins before gritting his teeth, turning the handle and pulling open the door.

To his astonishment, he was greeted by a tall, black figure. It took his startled brain a moment to comprehend that it wasn't the spectre of Robert Alardyce.

'Thank you so much,' said the vicar, rushing inside, shaking the raindrops from his hair. 'I got caught between the vicarage and here when the storm began. At least I wasn't carrying my umbrella,' he added before closing the door behind him, blocking out the tempest. He blinked at Cameron. 'Are you all right? Did I give you a wee fright?'

'Just a bit.'

The vicar was an amiable man in his forties with a long, pleasant face and cheerful smile.

'Storms always do play on our imagination; they bring out our primal instincts. Hello,' he smiled at Lucy and Harry over Cameron's shoulder.

'Hello,' they replied in unison.

'I saw you standing outside by one of the graves,' said Cameron.

'Aye, that was me. I tripped over a tree root and almost fell over. My shoe came off and I was trying to shove my foot back in it. I take it you've come inside for shelter?'

'Yes, if that's okay?'

'Of course it is. The House of God is open to anyone who needs it.'

'Thanks,' he mumbled, a little embarrassed as he wasn't at all religious.

'I'm Paul Reynolds,' he said, extending his hand for him to shake. 'I've been the vicar here for the last fourteen years.'

'Nice to meet you,' replied Cameron, shaking his hand. 'I'm Cameron Alardyce and these are my cousins, Lucy and Harry.'

'Alardyce? I take it you're staying at Alardyce House? I heard the lords of the manor were back in residence,' he smiled.

'I wouldn't call us that and Kate's the one who owns the house. We're just visiting.'

'Ah, yes, the actress. The village is thrilled to have her here. Have you seen your family's graves in our little kirkyard?'

'We were visiting them when the storm broke.'

'That is bad luck, especially after all the lovely weather we've had recently. Actually, I was hoping you would pop by as I've something to show you that I think you'll find of great interest. Come through to the vestry and I'll make you a cup of tea.'

'That would be great, thanks.'

'You have a beautiful church,' Lucy told Paul as they followed him down the aisle to the rear of the building. The vicar's sunny presence had put all three Alardyces at their ease.

'Thank you,' he smiled, full of enthusiasm. 'I love it here. The people are so friendly and I've always wanted such an idyllic-looking parish. Here we are,' he added, pushing open a side door.

They entered what appeared to be a cosy study with a desk, filing cabinet and lamp.

'Drat,' sighed Paul when he saw the leak coming through the ceiling to the right of the desk. 'The roof needs repairing and Kate has very kindly offered to pay for the whole thing, which is wonderfully generous of her. Work's due to start next week and I can't wait.'

He took the plastic bin from the corner of the room, placed it under the drip then took the seat behind the desk with a smile.

'I'm afraid I can only offer you one chair,' he told them.

The two men gallantly allowed Lucy to take the seat and Cameron stood by her side while Harry elected to lean against the wall.

After filling the kettle and switching it on to boil, Paul sat behind the desk and opened one of the drawers.

'Kate asked me to go through the old parish records to see if I could find anything connected with her family,' he told them. 'And I had a bit of luck. I found the usual marriage and death certificates and there were no surprises there. However, I did find an exhumation licence.'

'Exhumation?' said Harry. 'You mean someone was dug up?'

'Yes, Robert Alardyce to be precise, in 1953. The request was made by his grandson, Thomas Alardyce, when he inherited the title. Thomas's father James, Robert's son, died tragically young fighting in the Second World War, so he inherited from his Uncle John instead.'

'Do you know why he wanted Robert exhumed?' said Cameron.

'This is where it gets delicate. He wanted to make sure his grandfather was really dead.'

'What?' exclaimed all three cousins.

Paul placed the document on the desk. 'You can see for yourself.'

They all peered down at the application for an exhumation licence and the reason given – there was doubt the deceased was dead.

'And they actually dug him up?' Harry asked the vicar.

'Oh yes and sure enough, there was his body, although of course he was little more than bones by then.'

'How could they be sure it was Robert? There were no DNA tests back then.'

'He was identified by all the items his wife had said he was buried with – clothes, wedding ring and a pocket watch that had belonged to his biological father. It had an inscription inside. His thick black hair hadn't deteriorated at all and witnesses said it was just as it had been when he'd been alive. A couple of elderly residents who'd known Robert were present to assist with the identification.'

'Did none of the family object?' said Lucy.

'Robert's wife had passed away by then, as had his parents, half-siblings and son.'

'What about his daughter, Emily?'

'She was in Paris at the time, so she wasn't even consulted. I don't believe she even knew about it.'

'But… why would Thomas think he wasn't dead?'

'Apparently, he'd seen him a lot about the house. Never full on, just glimpses from the corner of his eye. Thomas was convinced Robert was watching him and judging how he was running the estate. When I found this order, I spoke to my oldest parishioner. She's in her late eighties now and her mother worked in Alardyce House for years as a housekeeper. Her mother told her Thomas was rather unstable. Not only was he reckless with money but he had a few mental health issues that would probably be recognised now and easily treated but were a stigma back in those days.'

'What sort of mental health issues?' said Cameron.

'Aggression, a certain, err, tendency to visit ladies of the night but to the point of addiction. He was also paranoid; he thought everyone was conspiring against him, including his own family. He made all the servants uneasy, especially the female ones.'

'Did he ever attack any of them?'

'No, I don't believe it ever got that far. Things settled down when he married a lovely lady called Maria. She brought him a lot of stability and he adored the son and daughter they had together. But he couldn't let go of the thought that his grandfather was haunting him.'

'Did the exhumation convince him Robert was dead?'

'For a few years, then the paranoia started again but he died shortly after of pneumonia aged just forty-five. Maria found him wandering in the garden after spending all night outside in the rain in his underwear, babbling like a lunatic, and he never recovered. He kept saying he had to escape Robert, that he couldn't bear him watching him any more. There was a portrait of him in the dining room that had been commissioned by his father, James, but Thomas destroyed it personally. He said Robert could come through the painting.'

Cameron swallowed hard at this statement, thinking of the portrait back at the house Kate had commissioned.

'That is so tragic,' said Lucy. 'But why have we never heard this story before? Our gran knew everything about our family and she never mentioned Thomas.'

'Perhaps she didn't want to upset you?'

'I don't think it was that. She told us all the other gruesome details.'

'She couldn't have known,' said Cameron. 'Meaning the family hushed it up.'

'Mental illness was looked down on back then. It was seen as shameful.'

'According to my parishioner, the family did what they could to ensure

Thomas rarely left the house,' said Paul. 'So that explanation would make sense.'

The three cousins sat in shocked silence while Paul prepared them a cup of tea each and handed them around.

'It looks like the storm's easing up,' said Paul, peering out of the window. 'There's a break in the clouds.' He turned back to the Alardyces and sighed. 'I'm sorry if I've put a dampener on your day.'

'Not at all,' replied Lucy. 'We appreciate you telling us something we had no idea about.'

'I just wish it was a more cheerful story.'

'Our family history doesn't have many cheerful moments,' she replied with a sad smile.

'I'm sure there must be plenty. They just get overshadowed by the bad.'

The cousins glanced at each other, thinking the vicar had no idea how bad the dark side of the Alardyce family could get.

17

After they'd finished their tea, the cousins excused themselves and left the church. As they passed through the kirkyard they noted the petals of the roses they'd placed on the graves had been scattered across the ground by the storm, looking like drops of blood.

They walked to the pub in silence, enjoying how much lighter and fresher the weather was while mulling over what Paul had told them. Lucy had the exhumation licence safely stowed in her handbag.

They found a quiet table at the back of the pub.

'This is on me,' said Harry. 'What do you want?'

Lucy and Cameron gave him their food and drink orders and he strolled up to the bar, lacking his usual sparkle.

'Well,' said Lucy. 'What did you make of what the vicar said?'

'I don't know,' Cameron slowly replied. 'I'm still taking it in.'

'Kate told me that Jane said in her journal Robert had broken the Alardyce curse. What if he didn't? What if it's still alive and well?'

'Thomas wasn't a well man. It happens sometimes. In everyone's family history there'll be at least one instance of mental illness. Like the vicar said, if it had been today, he would have been properly diagnosed, probably paranoid schizophrenia, and been treated. He wasn't haunted or cursed, he was just ill.'

Lucy nodded. 'You're right. I'm being a daftie, aren't I? It's probably after being stuck in an old church in a storm,' she said with a self-deprecating smile.

'Most likely.'

'Do you think we should tell Kate about this?'

'Aye, course. She'll find it fascinating.'

'I'm not so sure we should.'

'Why not?'

Lucy sighed heavily and looked out of the window. Cameron recognised the way she bit her lower lip, indicating she was deep in thought, and wanted to make sure she got what she was about to say absolutely right. It was a habit she'd had when she was a child.

'I think Kate's a bit too fanatical about our family's history and this might make it worse. I worry about her mental health and this news could tip her over the edge. The way she looks at Robert's portrait is a little worrying, then she pushed for the séance because she wanted to contact our dead relatives. What do you think she'll do if she discovers Thomas thought Robert was haunting the house?'

'I understand what you're saying but I don't think it'll upset her. She'll realise Thomas was mentally ill.' Doubt crept into his gaze. 'Won't she?'

Lucy shrugged.

They discussed the matter with Harry when he returned to the table carrying their drinks. He laughed when they'd finished explaining their fears to him.

'Kate's an intelligent woman,' he told them. 'She's not going to suddenly have a mental breakdown because of something some doolally relative did years ago.'

Harry had a way of making your worst fears seem silly, and both Cameron and Lucy began to wonder if they were worrying unnecessarily.

'Maybe not,' said Cameron. 'But it could make her own obsession worse.'

'She didn't get where she is today without having a cool, level head,' replied Harry. 'I read in an article that she's one of the most influential actresses in the film industry today.'

'Perhaps you're right, and she'd be furious if she found out we'd kept this from her. The vicar will probably discuss it directly with her and she'll find out anyway.'

'Exactly. Kate will be fine,' said Harry with a dismissive wave before sipping his red wine.

'I don't like the way she looks at Robert's portrait, though,' pressed Lucy.

'I'm sure Robert himself would have loved it. From what I've heard, he was an egotistical bastard.'

Harry's face lit up with that wicked grin, which both Cameron and Lucy were now both very familiar with.

'What if that shadow from the séance was Thomas's unhappy spectre?' continued Harry. 'I bet it's never occurred to Kate that the house could be haunted by relatives she doesn't give a shite about. That would be hilarious.'

'I don't find it funny,' frowned Lucy.

'Lighten up a bit. I'm only pulling your leg. You always were far too serious.'

'I don't think there's anything amusing about this situation. Not only do we carry the blood of murderers in our veins but lunatics too.'

They glanced at each other as they digested this statement.

'I don't think you should use the word *lunatic* any more,' said Cameron. 'It could be classed as offensive.'

'Jesus Christ,' sighed Harry, rolling his eyes. 'You'll be trying to get seventy-five-year-old Christmas songs banned next because they might offend some over-sensitive idiot with nothing better to do. I hate all this PC crap. It's one step off fascism only no one can bloody see it coming.'

'I'm just saying it's not fair to call someone who is mentally unwell a lunatic.'

'If digging up dead grandfathers and running about all night half-naked in the rain aren't the actions of a lunatic then I don't know what is. Anyway, you know we have to tell Kate about Thomas. It's the least we can do after she's had us in her house for days, gobbling up all her food and drink like locusts. I'm sure we can rely on her to behave like a grown-up about it. She might even know already only she chose not to share it with us because she's not interested in anyone who came after Robert.'

Cameron nodded in agreement while Lucy looked doubtful, but she decided not to object.

* * *

After enjoying a subdued lunch together, Harry, Cameron and Lucy returned to Alardyce House. They'd agreed that the first thing they'd do was tell Kate about what they'd learnt from the vicar.

They found her in the drawing room with Gail and Beauden. She smiled at her cousins when they entered.

'Did you enjoy your trip into the village?'

They all nodded.

'I hope you didn't get caught in the storm. At least it's cleared the air a bit. It's nowhere near as stuffy as it was, although the sun's already back out.' Her smile faltered when they just stared at her in response. 'Is everything okay?'

'Can we talk to you in private?' replied Lucy.

'Of course.'

'We'll leave you to it,' said Gail, getting to her feet and tactfully leaving the room with Beauden.

'Well, what is it?' said Kate, who was getting worried.

'We ended up taking shelter in the church during the storm,' began Cameron. 'And we had an interesting talk with the vicar. He gave us this.'

Cameron nodded at Lucy, who produced the exhumation licence from her handbag and held it out to Kate.

She took it from Lucy and frowned as she studied it. 'Exhumation for Robert Alardyce.' The surprise in her eyes said she'd had no idea about this. 'There was doubt the deceased was actually dead,' she murmured.

Cameron relayed everything the vicar had told them, leaving nothing out.

As he spoke, Lucy anxiously studied Kate's expression, hoping this news wouldn't exacerbate her obsession. She appeared attentive and absorbed but there was nothing to indicate that she was taking an unhealthy interest in what he was saying.

'Wow,' breathed Kate once Cameron had finished. 'I don't know what to make of that.'

'You really didn't know?' Harry asked her.

'No, I've never heard of this before and Gran never mentioned it either.'

'We think it must have been covered up,' said Cameron. 'The family wouldn't want rumours of mental illness circulating.'

'I know that Thomas married into a very well-to-do family with connections to the Royal Family. That would be even more incentive to hush it up.

Maria's father would have hated it being known that his only daughter had married a lunatic.'

'You shouldn't use the term lunatic,' Harry told her with an amused smile. 'Cameron thinks it's insensitive.'

'I can't believe they actually dug up Robert to satisfy Thomas's delusions,' said Kate, lip curling with disgust. 'It's obscene.'

'Perhaps they were at their wits' end and it was the only way they could think of to snap him out of it?'

Kate just nodded as she continued to study the slip of paper she held. 'I'll keep this safe with the rest of the Alardyce documents. I must remember to thank Paul for going to all that trouble.'

'If you ask me, he's a little smitten with you.' Harry winked at her. 'And who could blame him?'

'He's not smitten,' she replied with a modest smile. 'He's just very kind.'

'He might be a vicar but he's still a man.'

'Why does everything have to link back to sex with you?'

'Because it's the way of the world. If sex isn't at the root of something, then money is.'

'I'd love to talk to this parishioner whose mother worked here. Did Paul give you their name?'

They shook their heads.

'Not to worry, I'll speak to him about it at some point. I don't have time at the moment, me and Chris are really getting stuck into the new script with Tom, Eric and Gail's help.'

Lucy smiled. It seemed Kate had already put the new information about Thomas Alardyce on the back burner. Perhaps she had been worrying needlessly after all. 'That's great.'

'It's coming along really nicely. We've definitely got a winner on our hands.'

'Wonderful.' Lucy was already wondering if Shannon had jumped to conclusions; her cousin looked so relaxed and happy. 'I bet you'll do really well out of this TV programme, Cam,' she said, nudging him with her elbow.

'Aye, that would be good,' he replied, thinking how great it would be to come out of this with not only enough money to save Shannon's business but to plough into the wedding too. They could have a really grand ceremony as well as an exotic honeymoon, but that would mean postponing getting married until he'd been paid. Still, he didn't think Shannon would mind too much.

'Why don't you look through what we've put together?' Kate asked him. 'I'd love to get your take on it.'

Kate placed the exhumation licence safely in a drawer in the sideboard before taking a seat on the couch.

'Come, sit,' she said, patting the space beside her.

'Oh, right,' he replied, not having realised she meant right at that moment.

'I'll leave you to it,' said Harry. 'I'm going for a lie down.'

'I'll go to my room and study my new books,' Lucy said, clutching the carrier bag she held excitedly.

'Could you lend me one? It'll help me fall asleep faster.'

'Very funny.'

Cameron watched them go with a sinking feeling. He wasn't keen on being alone with Kate after the way she'd kept looking at him, but she appeared to be all innocence as she produced her notes, so he sat beside her on the couch.

'We've got the outline of the first episode already,' she told him, eyes shining with excitement. 'The plot is the same, we've just expanded on it and put in more detail.'

As she went through her copious notes, Cameron found himself becoming infected with her enthusiasm. He had to admit, it was a very interesting script and he got caught up in the story. It was the first time he'd taken pleasure in his family history.

'It'll be weird you playing my mum,' he told Kate.

'Only if we let it be weird. I'm sure we can be professional enough to rise above it.'

'You will but I'm not so sure about me.'

'You really have no idea what a raw talent you have. We're all thrilled by it. Beauden was just saying he can't wait to work with you and I've never seen anyone change Eric's mind so quickly. He's all for you playing Robert now, he's no doubt you'll be great.' She placed her hand over his and looked deep into his eyes in a way that had captivated audiences her entire career. 'I hope you understand what an opportunity this is for you. It's lifechanging.'

'I don't want my life to change,' he replied, fighting against the feeling of being sucked into that beautiful gaze. 'I love it the way it is.'

'Everything changes, Cam. It's the one thing you can rely on in life and this will only enhance it. You'll never have to worry about money again and think of what you and Shannon could do with your earnings. You could buy a beautiful big house together, fill it with children, if that's what you want.'

'It is.'

'And you'll be able to give those children everything they could ever want. There'll be nothing to stop you from sharing the perfect life together.'

'I like the sound of that,' he smiled.

Shannon entered the drawing room, her good mood after her trip to Edinburgh evaporating when she found her fiancé holding hands with and gazing into the eyes of one of the most beautiful women in the country.

'What's going on?' she demanded.

Cameron turned in his seat and smiled. 'Shan, I didn't know you were back.'

'Obviously,' she replied in a cold voice.

'Did you have a nice time?' he said, getting to his feet and walking over to her.

'Yes. What were you two doing?'

'Going through the notes Kate made about the production.'

Shannon studied him carefully. His gaze was open and honest, as it usually was. No sign of deception. She knew it was hard for Cameron to lie; he normally displayed some indication. Kate, however, was her usual smug self.

'I thought you were going into the village with Harry and Lucy?' Shannon asked him.

'We got back an hour ago.'

'Did you have a nice time?' It was difficult for Shannon to talk as all her muscles had gone rigid with anger.

'Aye, apart from getting caught in a thunderstorm. Was there any thunder in Edinburgh?'

'No.'

'Did you have lunch at The Witchery as you planned?'

'Yes, and it was lovely,' she hissed, gaze flicking back to Kate while her mind frantically imagined all the things they could have got up to together in her absence.

'Great,' smiled Cameron. 'Kate says they reckon this production will be a huge hit and I'll earn a lot of money from it. We can buy that big house together we've always dreamed of and have an amazing honeymoon.'

'Wonderful,' she muttered while still staring suspiciously at Kate. The logical part of herself didn't believe they'd got up to anything together – Cameron was a loyal man – but she couldn't help but feel jealous.

Taking a deep breath, she forced a smile. 'I got you a present,' she told him. Taking his hand, she led him to the door.

'You didn't need to get me anything,' he replied.

'Yes I did although I can't show you here. It's for us to enjoy alone,' she whispered with a mischievous smile before leading him out of the room.

Kate was irritated by the way Cameron didn't even look back at her as he left with Shannon. No matter, he'd soon discover the thieving cow's true nature and dump her.

Now she was alone, she produced the exhumation licence from the drawer she'd placed it in and stared down at it. Were her cousins right and Thomas had merely been a madman, or had there been some truth to his wild claims?

She was determined to find out.

* * *

After dinner, Harmony announced that she was willing to hold another séance, if everyone was in agreement.

'I don't want to sit through that again,' Tom hastily replied. 'I'd much rather play billiards. I've got a taste for the game since I've been here.'

'I'll come with you,' Jenna told him. 'I don't want to go through that again either.'

This caused Simon to shoot to his feet and glower at Tom. 'Me too.'

'Why?' retorted Tom. 'Do you want to attack me again?'

'Don't worry,' smiled Eric. 'I'm sure you can use some of the moves the SAS taught you.'

'Yeah,' Tom told Simon. 'You're lucky I didn't pull any of those on you.'

'I'll come with you,' said Harry. 'Just in case a fight needs to be broken up.'

'Me too,' replied Eric. 'I want no part of this charade.'

'Sorry about him,' Gail told Harmony as her husband left with the others. 'He can't deal with anything remotely spiritual.'

'No need to apologise,' she replied. 'I've met plenty of people like him.'

The table and candles were once again brought in. The curtains were drawn and all the lamps turned out apart from one.

'Are you sure you want to stay for this?' Shannon whispered to Cameron.

'I'm really curious to see if the same thing happens again,' he replied. 'Harmony,' he called. 'Do you want me to film it?'

'Yes please,' she said.

'Are you joining in?' he asked Shannon.

'No,' she replied. 'I'll just watch again.'

The participants sat around the table, only Shannon and Cameron electing to watch from the couch.

'Everyone, join hands,' said Harmony.

The same ritual was followed. Gail was the only one at the table who hadn't been present for the last séance and she remained quiet, although her eyes sparkled with excitement.

'Who do you wish to contact?' Harmony asked Kate.

'Thomas Alardyce,' she replied.

'Who's that?' Shannon whispered to Cameron when she noticed his eyes widen with surprise.

'I'll tell you later,' he whispered back, not wanting to disturb the others.

Shannon took this to mean there was some secret he and Kate were in on together and she hated it. The poison continued to do its work inside her.

Harmony repeatedly asked for Thomas, but nothing happened. At Kate's request, she tried calling for Jane again, then Robert, Amy and Henry, but they got no response.

'Well, that's disappointing,' commented Beauden. 'I was hoping for at least a little knocking.'

'The dead don't obey the whims of the living,' said Harmony. 'They only come through when they want to, or maybe they have nothing else to say to us.'

Kate leaned back in her chair, chewing her lip thoughtfully. 'We could try asking for Edward?'

'No,' said Lucy. 'I absolutely forbid it.'

'The serial killer?' said Gail excitedly.

'Yes. He's the last person we want to hear from.'

'What harm could it do? I mean, he's dead.'

'His personality will remain unchanged,' said Harmony. 'And I strongly advise against calling on such an evil soul.'

'Perhaps it's for the best,' said Chris. 'There could be consequences we've never even considered.'

'Good point,' said Beauden. 'I suggest we turn on the lights and have a whisky.'

Everyone seemed keen on this idea and while the curtains were opened, Kate poured everyone a whisky. Cameron went to tell the others that it was over.

When he was down the corridor, halfway between the drawing room and the billiard room, he happened to glance to his left, down another darkened corridor, the light failing to penetrate its depths, and saw a figure standing there.

'Hi Marcus,' he called. 'Don't worry, the séance is over.'

The figure didn't reply. Cameron couldn't see the man's face, but he knew he was staring at him. The arms dangled loosely at his sides and his shoulders were hunched forward slightly. Marcus wasn't standing tall and proud as he normally did.

'Are you okay?' Cameron asked him, wondering if he was ill.

Without a word, Marcus slowly turned and walked back the way he'd come, limping on his right foot. A little spooked, Cameron rushed towards the door of the billiard room and flung it open.

'The séance is over,' he announced.

His sudden arrival made Harry jump, who had been in the middle of taking a shot. Instead of hitting the ball, his cue went straight up into the air, narrowly missing the overhead light. He huffed and turned to face Cameron. 'Never interrupt a man's shot,' he told him.

'Did anything happen?' Jenna asked Cameron.

'Nothing at all,' he replied.

'Oh, good,' she smiled.

'Kate's handing round the whiskies.'

'Then what are we waiting for?' said Harry.

Cameron hung back and let his cousin scurry past him, not wanting to head down that corridor alone. He waited for the others and as they passed by that dark passage, he failed to see anyone standing there, to his relief.

They returned to the drawing room to find Marcus was there, clearing away the candles.

'What were you doing in the corridor outside the study?' Cameron quietly asked him.

'Excuse me, sir?' he said, turning to face him. 'When was this?'

'Just now.'

'It wasn't me, sir. I've just come from the kitchen in the other wing.'

'But I saw someone standing there.'

'Perhaps it was one of the other guests?'

'No, they were all in here or the billiard room. Is there another member of staff in the house?'

'No. Mrs Clapperton's gone home.'

A cold, slithery feeling came over Cameron.

'What's going on?' He whipped round to be confronted by Shannon.

'Nothing,' he told her. 'I just thought I saw Marcus in the hall when I went to get the others from the billiard room but it wasn't him.'

This excuse sounded so lame to Shannon that she thought he must be making it up. Her gaze automatically leapt to Kate and back again, wondering what he was trying to hide.

Cameron frowned at his fiancée when the skin around her face seemed to tighten and her eyes narrowed, highlighting the dark shadows circling them that he'd only just realised were there. She looked angry and he couldn't figure out why.

'What's wrong?' he said.

She glared at him for another second before shaking herself out of it. The muscles in her face relaxed, meaning the skin was no longer taut around her skull, dispelling the uncomfortable impression.

'Nothing,' she said before wandering to the other side of the room and splashing some whisky into a glass.

Cameron wondered if he should get her to tell him what was wrong, but he lacked the energy. He seemed to be doing that a lot lately and he was getting tired of it. Resentment, something he'd never felt about Shannon before, rose inside him. This was supposed to be about him reconnecting with his family and she was making it all about her.

Gail asked Cameron if anything had shown up on the footage and he was glad of the distraction. They sat on the couch together to study it. Shannon, who had expected Cameron to ask her what was wrong and to make her feel better with his gentle, coaxing words, was shocked to find him staring at his phone with Gail. This wasn't like him at all. Her eyes narrowed and she turned to look at Kate, who was chatting animatedly with Beauden and Chris, her eyes sparkling, looking impossibly beautiful. She wasn't looking at her, but Shannon got the feeling the bitch knew exactly what had happened. Kate was turning Cameron against her, slowly taking him from her. He would probably never leave this house; he would want to stay with her. Shannon would see her dead first.

A hand on her arm and a voice in her ear plucked at Shannon's taut nerves.

'What?' she yelled at the figure standing beside her.

The room went silent, everyone turning to look. Harmony stood beside Shannon, appearing a little hurt.

'Sorry,' mumbled Harmony. 'I didn't mean to disturb you.'

Despite herself, Shannon managed to force a smile. 'I'm the one who should apologise. You made me jump, that's all.'

The smile returned to Harmony's face. 'No problem. I should know better than to sneak up on people just after a séance, even if nothing did happen. They can affect people in strange ways.'

As she continued to talk, Shannon glanced at Cameron, who was frowning back at her with confusion in his eyes. She then looked to Kate, who once again appeared triumphant, which made Shannon want to put her fist right through her perfectly veneered teeth.

18

'Something's wrong, isn't it?' Cameron asked Shannon once they were alone in their room together. 'I've never seen you like this before.'

Shannon pouted and folded her arms across her chest. She was already in her nightie and sitting up in bed, the duvet across her lap. Cameron was in the middle of changing, stripping off his clothes down to his boxer shorts. For once the sight of his gorgeous body failed to move Shannon as she was so pissed off. In fact, she was so angry she was finding it hard to even look at him.

'Please, talk to me,' he pressed when she failed to respond, sitting on the bed beside her. 'We've just got engaged, we should be happier than ever.'

'Why wouldn't you tell me who Thomas Alardyce is?' she demanded, finally meeting his gaze.

'You mean earlier?'

Shannon nodded firmly.

Cameron paused before replying, puzzled as to why that would annoy her. 'Because the séance had started and I didn't want to interrupt.'

'So it's not because it's some delicious secret between you and Kate then?'

His frown deepened. 'What are you talking about?'

'I've never even heard you mention Thomas before. Only you and Kate know about him and you don't want anyone else intruding on a secret between the two of you.'

'Thomas isn't a secret. He's Robert's grandson. When me, Harry and Lucy sheltered in the church during the storm, we spoke to the vicar who told us he'd found an exhumation licence filled out by Thomas requesting Robert be exhumed because he was convinced he wasn't dead and was still living here, at the house.'

'What? But that's insane.'

'Thomas was mad but the family at the time did a good job of covering it up. Not even our gran knew about it. The vicar only found out because he spoke to one of his parishioners whose mother worked here as a servant and saw it all. So you see, it's not a secret. Harry and Lucy know too, as does the vicar and at least one other person in the village.'

Shannon bit her lower lip, feeling incredibly foolish. She'd allowed herself to get worked up over nothing. 'I'm sorry, Cam.'

'Where did you get this idea about a secret from?'

'My overactive imagination. I feel so stupid.'

'Good. You should.'

He'd never spoken so coldly to her before and her eyes widened. 'I'm really sorry. Please forgive me.'

Rather than open his arms to her so she could fall into them, he regarded her coolly.

'Something's happened to you since we've been here, Shan. You're letting petty jealousy get the better of you when you don't need to. You're the woman I love, you're the one I asked to marry me, not Kate. She's just a cousin to me.'

'I know and I'm sorry, but she really winds me up. Sometimes she looks at me so smugly I can't stand it.'

'Why would she look at you like that? She's no reason to. You're imagining it.'

Shannon couldn't tell him about the hold Kate had over her but if he knew then he'd understand where she was coming from. However, her hands were tied and the intense emotion her predicament was causing her was only making her look crazy. 'Maybe,' she mumbled. She took his hand. 'We need to get away from this place. It's toxic and I don't like it.'

To her surprise, he tugged his hand free, another thing he'd never done before.

'I don't believe this,' he said. 'I'm expected to put up with your loser brother intruding on our lives whenever he feels like it for weeks at a time, but you can't give me a few days with my family. Have you any idea how selfish you sound?'

Shannon stared at him in surprise. His black eyes flashed and his jaw was clenched. He looked more like the portrait in the dining room than the man she knew and loved.

'You look so angry,' she said. 'Where's my sweet, amiable Cameron gone?'

'Don't you mean the gullible and pliable Cameron? That's the man you really want, isn't it? You've got too used to having everything your own way while giving me nothing in return. Well, I'm sick of it. You can leave if you want to but I'm staying here with my family.'

'And with Kate,' she muttered.

'Yes, with Kate,' he retorted. 'And Lucy and Harry and Jenna because they're my family and I love them. What's next? Do you want me to stop seeing my parents and sister too?'

'I would never ask that of you. I like all your family, except Kate.'

'Well, you'll just have to deal with it because, for once, you are not getting your own way.'

With that, he lay down and presented her with his bare back, pulling the duvet up to his chin.

Shannon was momentarily lost for words. Cameron had never spoken to her like this before. She'd only ever known him to be sweet and loving. It was Kate's fault; she was corrupting him. She shook herself out of her surprise. It was vital she fight for him and save him from his mad cousin or he would be truly lost.

'Don't do this, Cam,' she said. 'We always swore we'd never go to sleep on an argument. I can't stand it when we fall out.'

He whipped back round to face her with such fury she recoiled.

'Deal with it because I'm so angry I can't even look at you.'

With that, he turned back over, closed his eyes and feigned sleep. Shannon remained sitting up in bed, staring at his back, silent tears running down her face.

* * *

There was a muted atmosphere in Alardyce House the following morning. The rain had returned, heavier than ever, the rear gardens invisible because of the sheet of rain that pounded down on the house. The guests knew they were going to spend the day trapped inside together as the weather forecast had said the rain would only get worse over the next couple of days and there was a risk of flooding.

'This weather doesn't worry me,' Tom told them all at breakfast that morning. 'I've had adverse weather driving training.'

Everyone just gave him a withering look that made him stare sheepishly at his bowl of porridge.

'At least we've got plenty of space to spread out in this huge house,' said Chris cheerfully.

'We could play some games,' offered Gail. 'I've got Trivial Pursuit in the car.'

This statement was greeted with a chorus of groans.

'We can continue working on the script,' said Kate.

Shannon scowled at her cereal, which she was running her spoon through listlessly, her appetite gone. Cameron still hadn't spoken to her since their fight the previous night. She'd lain awake for hours, frantically thinking about how she could make it up to him before falling into a fitful sleep. When she'd woken at seven thirty that morning, she'd found his side of the bed empty. Even now, sitting across from her at the table, he avoided her eyes and it broke her heart.

'And we could work together, Cameron,' Beauden told him. 'I'm itching to put you through your paces.'

'Aye, sounds good,' he replied in his usual amiable tone.

This soothed Shannon a bit. If he was working with Beauden, then he couldn't be around the man-eating slag.

'I'm going to do some yoga, if anyone wants to join me?' said Harmony. 'I teach it too, so I could run a class.'

'That sounds lovely,' smiled Gail. 'I've just started yoga and I'm really enjoying it.'

'I'll have a go too,' said Lucy.

'Do you want to join our yoga class?' Harmony sweetly asked Shannon.

For the first time that day, Cameron actually looked at Shannon, his gaze sweeping up to meet hers, awaiting her reply with that same coolness which was becoming a part of his nature.

'Why not?' she smiled, feeling confident now she knew he'd be tucked away with Beauden. 'It sounds fun and I could use the exercise.'

'Brilliant. We'll meet in an hour in the conservatory.'

Shannon's smile fell. 'The conservatory?'

'Yes. Why, what's wrong?'

Everyone regarded Shannon curiously and she felt her cheeks heat. Obviously they hadn't felt what she had in there. 'Will there be enough room with all the plants?'

'There's enough for our purposes.'

'Okay.' Shannon decided not to fret about it. If Harmony was truly psychic, then she'd pick up on the presence in there. She might even be able to get rid of it. Or maybe nothing was in there and she'd imagined the whole thing? The way she was feeling she wouldn't be surprised. It was hard knowing what was real any more.

After breakfast, the party broke up. Shannon hurried after Cameron as he strode with Beauden down the hall to the parlour where they'd agreed to work together.

'Cam, can I have a word?' she said.

He turned to her with a look of irritation. 'I'll meet you in there,' he told Beauden.

'As you like,' he replied, picking up on the atmosphere between the couple.

Shannon waited until he was out of earshot before continuing. 'We have to get this sorted out, babe. We can't go on like this.'

'And are you going to try and get along with Kate?' replied Cameron.

'I'll do my best,' she said in a meek, resigned voice. 'We won't ever be best friends but I'm sure we can get along better.'

It was a huge relief to her when the warmth returned to his eyes, making him look like her Cam again.

'Good. Thanks, sweetheart. I appreciate it,' he said before kissing her.

Shannon revelled in the kiss, holding on to him tightly.

'I've got to go,' he said softly. 'I don't want to keep Beauden waiting. Enjoy your yoga.'

Shannon watched until he'd vanished inside the parlour, feeling warm and safe now everything was okay between them.

She turned and almost walked smack into Kate, whose expression was severe.

'I see everything's harmonious between you and Cam again,' she said, voice sounding tight in her throat.

'Yes. Why wouldn't it be?'

'He wouldn't even look at you at breakfast,' she said, lip curling with disgust. 'Not that I can blame him, but what made him react like that?' Kate leaned in closer to Shannon, who in response leaned away from her. 'What did you do to him?'

'I didn't do anything.' It was tempting to snap back something nasty at her, but she'd told Cameron she would make friends with Kate and she was determined to do it. Shannon's smile was forced but she was amazed that she'd managed to produce it at all. 'Right, I'm off to get ready for yoga. Have a nice morning,' she said happily before walking away, not even bothering to glance back at her rival, leaving Kate to stare after her. Perhaps this was the right way to go rather than rising to Kate's catty comments all the time. She felt so much better.

* * *

'Excellent, Cameron,' said Beauden. 'Really well done.'

'Thanks,' he replied with a modest smile.

'You're a natural actor. It really is effortless for you.'

'I wouldn't go that far but it's starting to feel a little easier. There's just one thing that worries me – the sex scenes.'

'We've talked and agreed you can use a body double for the most intense scenes. Of course, you'll be required for close-ups, but you won't need to show your naked body.'

'But I will have to kiss other women?'

'Yes. I'm afraid there's no getting round that, although I do know of one actor who refuses to kiss anyone but his wife. She acts as a stand-in for the actresses he's working with.'

'That's really nice. Maybe Shannon could do the same?'

'The awkward thing is the actor in question is very established and can make such demands.'

'But I'm a newbie, so I won't be able to?'

'Precisely. Kate's influence might be enough but I'm not sure. You should know that sets are very unromantic places. Nothing kills the mood like a burly lighting man looming over you while you're working. If it would make you feel better, Shannon could be on set.'

'I don't think I'd be comfortable with that. It would be even harder to kiss another woman with her watching me.'

'I have to say, I really do think your consideration for her feelings is commendable. Keep that up and you'll have a wonderful life together.'

'I hope so,' he mumbled.

Beauden raised an eyebrow. 'Trouble in paradise?'

'Shannon's changed since she's been here. She's become paranoid and she hates Kate.'

'Most women do.'

'Shannon doesn't need to worry though. Kate's my cousin.'

'Second cousin. It's not enough to negate the threat.'

Cameron thought it ironic that Beauden, who was gay, knew a lot more about women than he did. 'I suppose I could do more to reassure Shannon, but why should I?'

'Because you're going to be working closely with Kate. If you reassure her before that starts then trust me, it will make your life a lot easier in the future.'

'I suppose, and I do want my cousins back in my life permanently. I don't want to lose touch with them again.'

'Then you need to stop the rot now. Talk to her but most of all listen to her.'

'You're right, I do need to do that.' He glanced at the clock on the fireplace. 'We've been working for two hours. It didn't feel that long.'

'Which shows that you've been enjoying yourself.'

Cameron smiled. 'I have actually.'

'See, it won't be so bad, will it, Robert?'

Cameron's smile fell. 'You called me Robert.'

'Sorry, it's because we've been reading through the script. And you're very convincing.'

Cameron didn't like being referred to as Robert when he wasn't acting but decided not to make a big deal of a slip of the tongue. 'Right, I'll go and find Shannon and talk to her.'

'Good for you.'

Cameron left Beauden and headed into the conservatory to see if the yoga lesson was still going on, but no one was there. He hovered in the doorway, unwilling to go in any further, feeling like the room didn't want him.

Next, he checked their room, but she wasn't there either. He encountered Harry at the top of the stairs.

'Have you seen Shannon?' he asked him.

'Yes, she's in the billiard room with Harmony forming a battle plan.'

'Battle plan?'

'There was an incident in the conservatory while they were doing yoga. Harmony's planning to exorcise a malevolent spirit.'

'Really?' said Cameron, half-laughing, thinking it was one of Harry's jokes.

'You need to wipe that look off your face. Harmony takes these things very seriously.'

'Where are you going?' he said as Harry continued on past him towards the bedrooms.

'To fetch her bottle of holy water.'

Cameron blinked at him. 'She has holy water?'

'She always carries it in case of an emergency.'

Cameron watched with his mouth hanging open as Harry hurried into his and Harmony's bedroom.

'Has everyone gone mad?' he murmured.

He wandered into the drawing room but that was also empty. Instead, he headed to the study and knocked on the door.

'Come in,' called Kate's voice.

He entered to find her sitting at her desk, Eric and Chris on either side of her, the three of them going over the script.

'Have you heard Harmony's going to be doing an exorcism?'

'Are you serious?' she replied.

'That's what Harry told me. Apparently, she's going to get rid of the presence in the conservatory.'

'What presence?'

'You'd need to ask Harmony that.'

'No one's performing an exorcism in my home,' she said, getting to her feet. 'A séance is one thing, but this is crossing a line.'

'Harry said they're in the billiard room.'

'Right,' she frowned, determination etched across her face.

'I've got to see this,' Eric smiled at Chris before the two men got to their feet and followed her out of the room.

The three men walked behind Kate as she stalked through the house, the tension in her gait telling them she was not happy. They checked the billiard room, but no one was there.

No one spoke as they continued on down the corridor, the men sensing Kate was not in the mood for mindless chatter. They entered the conservatory to find Harmony walking around the room with a small silver bottle, sprinkling water about the place while chanting something to herself. Harry, Gail, Shannon and Lucy looked on.

'What's going on?' demanded Kate.

They all looked round at the sound of her voice.

'Just a little exorcism,' said Harmony.

'Oh no, that is not happening in my house. You can stop it immediately.'

'But I've already started.'

'Then you can unstart.'

'You were fine with the séances,' replied Harmony. Her tone wasn't at all adversarial, just curious.

'I don't trust exorcisms. I've heard too many horror stories and I won't have it going on under my own roof. Neither did you ask permission.'

'You're right, I'm sorry,' said Harmony. 'I thought I was doing you a favour.'

She looked so contrite Kate immediately softened. 'I appreciate that but it's really not necessary.'

'Okay, I'll stop.'

'Thank you.' Kate felt a little guilty about how harshly she'd spoken when she realised Harmony was upset. Kate liked Harmony. Although kooky, she was sweet with a good heart. 'I'll tell you what – why don't you run one of your meditation classes for us instead?'

This brought the smile back to Harmony's face. 'I'd love to.'

'Great. Let's go into the drawing room.'

'Okay, I'll just close this down here.'

They watched Harmony mutter a few more words to herself, none of which they could hear, and wave her arms around a little before she turned to them with a smile. 'All done.'

She and Kate left the room together, walking arm-in-arm, all animosity gone.

'You went telling tales, didn't you?' Harry quietly asked Cameron.

'I thought she had a right to know. It was a dangerous idea.'

'Harmony knows what she's doing.'

'It's not her house.'

Harry couldn't reply to that, so he just shook his head and stalked out of the room, the others following. Only Shannon remained behind.

'Why did you tell Kate?' she demanded.

Cameron inwardly sighed. He could see the paranoia had returned to her eyes, which were looking increasingly haunted.

'Because it was the right thing to do. How would you feel if someone started performing random exorcisms in our house?'

'I wouldn't mind if they were casting out something nasty.'

'You would mind and you'd be the first to kick off. Kate's right, they are dangerous.'

'It's typical of you to take her side.'

'Aye, I am taking her side in this because she's right. I hope you're not going to start all that again after you promised you'd make an effort to get along with her.'

As Cameron had just been working with Beauden, he failed to realise that the personality of Robert Alardyce, which he was so good at imitating, was very close to the surface and it showed in his black eyes, turning them cool and hard, like hot molten lava setting into rough pumice. Shannon decided to backtrack, not wanting him to be angry with her again. 'You're right, of course, babe. There was nothing else you could have done. This is her house, after all.'

He studied her suspiciously before his gaze softened. 'Aye, it is. Some of us are forgetting that we're only guests here.'

'Yes, and we've done precious little to thank her for her trouble.'

'Exactly.' He smiled and held out his hand to her. 'Come on.'

She smiled back and took his hand, allowing him to lead her out of the conservatory while refusing to look back at that invisible presence, feeling angry eyes burning into her.

* * *

Lunch was a long, lazy affair. As the rain continued to pelt down, they saw little reason to rush their meal as they couldn't go outside. They even took their coffee at the table rather than go into the drawing room, enjoying casually chatting while ranged around the table together. The atmosphere between them all was more relaxed than it had been so far as they were starting to get to know each other and were becoming comfortable in one another's company.

Beauden was a natural orator and was entertaining them all with ghost stories. A few of those gathered around the table had protested that they didn't want to listen to ghost stories, particularly Tom and Jenna, but they'd soon realised that all his stories were funny and he soon had everyone chuckling.

Just as Beauden was beginning another story, Cameron's phone rang. Taking it out, he saw it was Guy.

'Excuse me,' he told the table. Cameron got to his feet and left the room, closing the door behind him. He could hear the murmur of Beauden's voice followed by the sound of laughter.

'Okay, I can talk,' he said into the handset.

As he listened to his friend speak, Cameron's stomach plummeted and he turned cold.

'It must be a mistake. I can't have lost that much money,' he rasped, feeling like his throat was closing up.

'You haven't lost it,' replied Guy. 'Your businesses are doing really well. This money's been stolen. It's been transferred out of your accounts into someone else's.'

'You mean I've been hacked?'

'No. The transfer was made from your own computer. I hate to say this, Cam, but it went into Shannon's business account.'

'No, she wouldn't do that. Maybe she meant to put it into my account and got it wrong.'

'There's no error, pal,' Guy said as gently as he could in his harsh Glaswegian brogue. 'There were three withdrawals – one for twenty-five grand, one for ten and one for fifteen, all within a few weeks of each other.'

Cameron sighed and pressed a hand to his forehead, lightheaded with shock. 'She told me her restaurant's in trouble, that she's in danger of bankruptcy.'

'It looks like she's been trying to use your money to stay afloat. Unfortunately, the loss of the fifty grand means you can't buy that third gym.'

'Actually, I can. My cousin Kate's paying me a hundred grand.'

'For what?' replied Guy with surprise.

'To play my own great-great-grandfather in her new TV programme. She said she'll advance me the money.'

'That's a relief because if you'd pulled out of that purchase it would have been a big black mark against you. Listen, I'm really sorry about this, pal. I'm as shocked as you are. What do you want me to do?'

'I don't know, I can't think. I need to talk to Shannon first. I'll get back to you.'

'No problem.'

Cameron hung up and frantically tried to think what to do. He knew he could rely on Guy to keep what he'd learnt to himself; he was the soul of discretion. There must be some error. No way would Shannon steal from him; she was the one person in the world he trusted absolutely. If she hadn't told him about her restaurant failing, then he wouldn't have believed it at all, but he'd seen how desperate she'd looked. She'd also been behaving very oddly lately. Was guilt really at the heart of her paranoia rather than jealousy? Did she hate Kate for her success and money? Could guilt make her see things that weren't there, such as something moving around the crypt that night? It would explain everything.

Anger started to overtake the shock. How could she do this to him? It wasn't just the fact that she'd stolen so much money from him that hurt, it was that she was willing to put his own businesses at risk that he'd spent years building up to bail herself out. That wasn't the act of someone who loved him.

He stalked back to the dining room and flung open the door.

Beauden trailed off and they all turned to look when Cameron just stood there, making no move to sit down.

Shannon swallowed hard when he glared at her with that frightening look in his black eyes, the one he used when portraying Robert.

'Cam,' said Kate softly, the only person at the table who dared address him as he looked so fierce. 'Is something wrong?'

'I've just had some shocking news,' he replied, eyes never leaving Shannon, who squirmed uncomfortably in her seat. 'Shan, I need a word.' There was no *please*, none of his usual manners, telling everyone, even those who hadn't known him long, that something was very wrong.

'I hope no one's ill,' said Kate sympathetically.

'No, it's nothing like that,' he replied, attention still fixed on his fiancée. 'Well,' he said to Shannon. 'Aren't you coming?'

This was uttered in a way that indicated a refusal would not be accepted. There was a new force to his personality that it was impossible to ignore, and Shannon felt compelled to obey.

As soon as she rose, he turned and stalked off down the corridor, vanishing out of sight. Shannon regarded the rest of the table with large worried eyes, wishing she could stay with them. Even Kate's company would be preferable to Cameron's at that moment, but she knew she had no choice. Her secret was out and it was time to face the consequences.

19

The moment Shannon closed the dining room door behind her, she heard excited chatter start up inside as they all wondered what she could have done. Humiliated, she hurried down the hall with her head bowed to where Cameron waited for her at the door to the parlour. She just managed to glimpse him before he stalked inside.

Taking a deep breath, she followed and entered to find him standing at the window, staring out into the sodden gardens, the rain streaking the glass. Quietly, she closed the door behind her.

'What's this about, Cam?' she said, trying to sound carefree and innocent.

He turned to look at her with that awful dark look in his eyes.

'You know very well what it's about – fifty thousand pounds.'

Even though she'd known it was coming, Shannon's heart still skipped a beat. Her palms started to sweat and she swallowed nervously.

'What, no denial?' he said sarcastically. 'No blaming it on a mistake or someone else?'

'I'm so sorry,' she whispered, a tear sliding down her cheek.

Shannon tilted her face to the floor, missing the distress that filled Cameron's eyes.

'So you did steal from me?' he said, voice tight.

She nodded. 'I didn't mean for it to go as far as it did. I thought I could just take a bit to get my business back on its feet. I'd replace it and you never needed to know but it wasn't enough, so I took more and more and the next thing I knew I'd taken fifty grand. I'm so sorry, babe, I hate myself for it. I'll do anything to make it up to you and I swear I'll pay back every penny.'

She stared at him expectantly, the tears continuing to roll down her face, hoping for some measure of sympathy, but he was impervious to her plight.

'Do you know the worst part of what you've just said?' he asked her.

'What?' she replied.

'The fact that you said I never needed to know. If you'd just asked me, I would have happily given you the money. I would have done anything for you.'

Shannon was quick to pick up on his use of the past tense, as though everything he felt for her had already gone. 'I hated lying to you, it's been tearing me apart.'

He folded his arms across his chest. 'I suppose that's why you've been acting so paranoid lately. You've been having a go at me just for spending time with my cousin when all the time it was your own guilt talking.'

'You're right, I've no excuse but we can get through this, I know it.'

When she reached out for his hand, he took a step back.

'Don't touch me,' he growled. 'I don't want you anywhere near me. We're through.'

'No, Cam, please,' she cried. 'We can work it out, let's just talk some more. You're still upset. Once you've had time to calm down...'

'I won't change my mind. You're not the woman I thought you were. All this time I was in love with an illusion. My Shannon would not have betrayed me like this.'

'I didn't betray you,' she exclaimed. 'It was just a temporary solution...'

'It wasn't a temporary solution,' he thundered. 'You stole from me and covered it up. If I hadn't asked Guy to go through my accounts, then I would have married you blissfully unaware and I would never have found out. I bet you laughed at me behind my back – good old naïve, trusting Cameron. What a fucking idiot.'

Cameron rarely used the 'f' word and it shocked her. 'I never once thought that about you. It wasn't like that.'

'I don't believe you. In fact, I can't believe a word you say ever again.'

'I've never lied to you about anything before and I never will again, I promise.'

'Liar,' he hissed, eyes narrowing.

'Why did you ask Guy to go through the accounts anyway?' she demanded.

'Because I wanted to see where I stood financially before we married and to help save your business. I didn't want to ask you because I thought, in my stupidity, that you'd protest and say you wouldn't take a penny. No wonder you were so quick to agree to marry me because then you'd have access to all my money. All I can say is, thank Christ for Guy. He stopped me from making the biggest mistake of my life.'

Shannon visibly winced. 'We're not a mistake. You're the best thing that ever happened to me. We're great together.'

'You've betrayed me and I can never trust you again. What was the plan, Shannon? Keep stealing from me until I had nothing left and then leave me?'

'I would never do that to you. I agreed to marry you because I love you, nothing else.'

He held out his hand and for one happy moment, Shannon thought he wanted to take her own hand.

'Ring,' he said.

'Excuse me?'

'I want the ring back.'

'But you gave it to me.'

'As a promise of marriage but that's not happening now.'

'You're breaking it off?' she said incredulously.

'Yes. We're over.'

Frantically she shook her head, her heart breaking. 'No, it can't be.'

'It is,' he said, still being hard and impervious.

Shannon took his face in her hands. 'This can't be happening. We're so happy.'

'Correction – we were. You ruined it.'

'Why are you giving up on us so easily? What about all the plans we made?'

'That was when I thought I was marrying someone else.'

'Don't do this to me, Cam. Please,' she sobbed. 'I've already called my family to tell them we're engaged. What will I say now?'

'Tell them the truth – that you're a thieving bitch.'

'Cam!' she exclaimed.

'We've nothing else to say to each other. Give me the ring.' He wanted that back; it had cost him two grand and he begrudged her conning him out of any more money.

Shannon sighed, knowing he was right. 'Fine,' she said, removing the ring from her finger and dumping it in his hand.

He slipped the ring into his pocket and stared at her coldly. 'I won't keep you any longer, you'll need to go and pack.'

'You want me to leave?'

'Yes. When you get back to Glasgow, you can start moving your things out of my flat. I don't want you to be there when I return. I'll give you a couple of weeks to find a new place.'

'You're throwing me out of our home?' she exclaimed.

'It's my home. I own it and pay for everything,' he said flatly. 'Goodbye, Shannon.'

'Cam, wait,' she cried, following him. 'We need to talk more. This can't be the end.'

He stopped so suddenly she almost walked into the back of him, and he whipped round to face her, his icy imperiousness driving all the words from her mind.

'I don't want to see or speak to you again, Shannon. We're over. Accept it and move on. I already have.'

'Cam,' she rasped, voice cracking as he strode out of the room, slamming the door shut behind him.

Once outside the parlour, Cameron's hard demeanour cracked and tears welled in his eyes. He couldn't go up to his room, so he rushed towards the back of the house and through the rear door, wanting to escape before anyone found him and asked what was wrong.

The moment he was outside, Cameron broke into a run, not caring that the rain was still pouring down, saturating him immediately as he shot across the lawn and into the trees.

He turned to look back at Alardyce House, out of breath from the turbulent emotion rather than the exercise. Everything had changed in the space of a few minutes. It was so shocking it was surreal, as though he could wake up at any moment. He simply couldn't believe that Shannon had not only stolen from him but that their relationship was over. They wouldn't get married, buy a house and have children. The future he'd envisaged had fallen away, leaving him with absolutely nothing. For four years she'd been the very centre of his world, they'd done everything together and he'd taken it for granted that they would live out the rest of their lives together. They could never get back what they'd once had. He felt stupid, like he'd been tricked into loving someone who'd never existed. At least he'd found out before he'd married her. If they'd already been wed, the grasping bitch could have taken everything from him.

Although he knew he'd had a lucky escape, Cameron still mourned the loss of the life he'd thought he was going to have, as well as the Shannon he loved.

His tears mingled with the rain. He stared back at the house, which seemed to watch him in a strange, sympathetic way, the only observer to the crumbling of his life. Its walls, which had turned a deep grey in the dreich weather, suddenly appeared to be a place of warmth and refuge. Hopefully his ancestral home could bring him the comfort and healing he needed. He didn't think Kate would mind him staying on after what she'd said about being lonely. If she said no, he didn't know what he would do.

Cameron remained under the birch trees, which couldn't shelter him entirely from the rain. Even when he started to shiver with cold and he was saturated right through to his underwear, he remained where he was, wanting nothing but the sound of the rain and the sight of the house.

The conservatory door opened and a figure hurried out, sheltered by a large green golf umbrella. He could hear the squelching of their shoes in the sodden grass as they rushed over to him. From their hair and the elegant way they moved, he knew it was Kate.

'Cameron, what are you doing?' she called. 'You're soaking.'

'It's over, Kate,' he murmured.

'You and Shannon?' she said, holding the umbrella so it was covering them both.

He nodded dumbly, his gaze on the house.

'I knew something was wrong. We could hear Shannon crying.'

'Has she told you anything?' he continued in that strange, soft voice.

'No, she refused to talk to anyone. She's in your room.'

'Good. Hopefully she's packing.'

'Packing? What's going on?'

'She stole fifty thousand pounds from me.'

It was fortunate Kate was such a gifted actress. It enabled her to look completely surprised. 'Oh my God, that's terrible. Are you sure?'

'There's no doubt. An accountant pal of mine discovered the theft. Shannon admitted it when I confronted her about it.'

'I can't believe it. I take it she took it to support her failing restaurant?'

'Aye. The irony is, I would have given her the money if she'd just asked. She didn't need to steal it.' His hands curled into fists. 'I hate thieves.'

'Why don't you come inside, you're shaking with cold. You're going to make yourself ill.'

'What does it matter?'

'It matters a lot. Your life's not over.' She linked her arm through his. 'Now come on in and get warm before you die of pneumonia like Thomas did.'

At first, Cameron wouldn't move but she tugged at his arm so insistently he relented and obediently allowed her to lead him back to the house through the conservatory. She opened the door to find the others standing there. All were shocked by his appearance.

'Cam,' exclaimed Lucy. 'What's happened?'

'Let him get warm and dry first,' said Kate, immediately taking charge. 'Harry, ask Marcus to run him a warm bath.'

'Will do,' he nodded before rushing off to carry out his assignment.

'Simon, fetch the throw from the back of that couch over there. Jenna, brandy.'

They obeyed without question and quickly returned with the requested items. Simon draped the throw around Cameron's shoulders and Jenna shoved the brandy glass into his trembling hands.

'Come on, upstairs,' said Kate, steering him down the hall to the stairs. 'You need to get those wet clothes off.' She didn't want anyone else intruding on this moment; she wanted to be his rock while he recovered from what that silly bitch had done.

'I don't want to go in my room,' he told her. 'Shannon will be there.'

'Then you can go straight into the bathroom. I can hear Marcus running the water.'

She steered Cameron upstairs and into one of the bathrooms, leaving him in her butler's capable hands before heading into the room Cameron and Shannon had been sharing. She found Shannon shoving her things into a suitcase, eyes bloodshot and nose bright red. The woman looked a mess.

'I hear Cameron finally knows the truth,' she said, closing the door behind her.

'And how you're enjoying it,' replied Shannon in a tired, flat voice.

'I'm glad he's finally realised what you are.'

'Maybe I should tell him that you knew all along, so he knows what you are too?'

'You could but then you wouldn't get another penny out of me.'

'I probably won't anyway.'

'I'll transfer the full hundred grand to you right now, just as long as you leave and stay away from him.'

Shannon sighed, screwed up the pair of jeans she was holding and tossed them into the suitcase. 'I'm going to tell him you already knew. It's the least I can do after how much I've hurt him.'

'Do that and your little restaurant will fold. What will your precious family think of you then? Not only will you have lost your fiancé but your business too. We both know how much your parents loathe failures. No doubt you'd lose them too, then you'd really be left with nothing.'

Shannon glared at her so ferociously Kate prepared herself for an attack. She was almost disappointed when Shannon returned to her packing.

'I'll go without an argument,' she said. 'Cam's suffered enough at my hands, but I get the feeling he'll suffer more at yours.'

'I'll give him all the healing he needs,' replied Kate with a satisfied smile. That smile broadened when distressed tears filled Shannon's eyes.

'I don't need to tell him what you are,' croaked Shannon. 'He'll find out for himself. I just hate to think of what he'll have to go through first to discover it.'

'I'll never steal from him like you have.'

'No, you won't, but at least I never loved him just because he reminded me of my dead grandfather, you sick bitch.'

'Your opinion really means nothing,' said Kate, picking up a blouse off the bed that was waiting to be put into the suitcase. She grimaced at the ugly garment and let it drop. 'And I want you to know that you can't take my money and then go behind my back and tell Cam everything. I have a few friends who are well known restaurant critics. I'll ensure your crappy little place will be destroyed in their reviews. You'll also be harassed with visits from environmental health.'

Shannon didn't reply until she'd tossed the rest of her clothes into the suitcase and zipped it up.

'I won't say anything. We made a deal. You've kept your part and I'll do the same.' Shannon picked up the suitcase by the handle. 'I made the mistake of thinking Cameron was innocent and naïve. I was wrong and you're wrong too. He will see you for what you really are – ugly.'

Kate smiled as Shannon stalked to the door on this parting shot. She followed her out of the room and down the stairs, wanting to ensure she didn't encounter Cameron and perhaps persuade him to take her back. As he was still in the bathroom, he was kept out of her way. At the bottom of the stairs, Shannon's eyes darted about everyone assembled there and filled with disappointment when she realised Cameron was absent. All the other guests were hanging about in the grand entryway, realising something big had happened and hoping for a clue as to what that was.

'Are you leaving?' Harmony asked Shannon, noting the suitcase in her hand.

Shannon nodded, so choked with emotion she couldn't speak.

'Why? What's happened?'

'It's probably best not to ask,' Harry gently told his girlfriend when fresh tears spilled down Shannon's face.

There was a beep outside and Chris glanced out of the window. 'A taxi's just pulled up.'

'That'll be for me,' said Shannon.

'Here, let me take that for you,' said Tom, indicating her suitcase.

'Thanks,' she replied, handing it to him.

'I'll miss you,' Harmony told Shannon.

'I'll miss you too,' she croaked.

The two women hugged.

'Keep in touch, won't you?' said Harmony. 'You've got my phone number?'

Shannon nodded again, appreciating her kindness but wanting to escape before the emotion overwhelmed her completely.

Jenna, Harry and Lucy were a little standoffish as they'd already worked out that she'd hurt Cameron. Gail politely said goodbye, as did Beauden, Eric and Chris. Kate just stood at the foot of the stairs, arms folded across her chest and a look in her eyes that said *get the hell out of my house.*

Shannon was glad that she'd never have to clap eyes on the bitch again but hated the thought of leaving Cameron in her clutches. What choice did she have though? She'd already lost her fiancé, and she was damned if she was going to lose her restaurant too.

With an indignant toss of the head, Shannon followed Tom outside to the taxi, the others watching in silence. Tom handed the case to the driver, and Shannon climbed into the taxi and closed the door, staring up at the house with loathing, as though the very building was responsible for ruining her life.

The driver climbed in and the car headed back down the drive. Kate breathed a sigh of relief when it turned onto the road and vanished. As always, she'd got what she'd wanted.

'Are you going to tell us what that was all about?' Jenna asked her.

'It's up to Cameron to tell you, it's his business. Just know that he and Shannon are over.'

'Why?' said Harmony. 'What's she done?'

'Again, you'll have to ask Cam. Just know that she deserved it.'

With that pronouncement, she stalked into the drawing room, leaving her guests to regard each other with confusion.

* * *

The rest of the afternoon was spent gossiping about what could have occurred to bring about the drama. None of them guessed correctly.

Cameron didn't make an appearance until nine o'clock that evening, having hidden away in his room after his bath. He looked pale and his eyes were heavy and bloodshot. He took a seat in the corner of the room closest to the door. Realising he didn't want to talk, everyone returned to whatever they were doing.

Kate wandered over to Cameron and crouched before him. 'How are you holding up?' she whispered.

'I've never felt worse in my life,' he mumbled back.

'It's bad now but it will get better.'

'Please don't give me any cheesy platitudes. You'll be telling me to live, laugh and love next.'

Kate couldn't help but smile. 'I wouldn't dream of it. I'll fetch you a whisky,' she added, patting his shoulder and rising to her feet.

'I don't want one.'

'But you're getting one. It's the best thing in a crisis.'

She headed over to the drinks trolley and splashed a generous amount of single malt into a glass before returning to him. Everyone watched curiously from the corners of their eyes, still wondering what had occurred to split up such a close couple so suddenly.

Kate held the glass out to Cameron. 'Drink.'

When he looked up at her, Kate was shocked by the turbulence in those dark eyes. They seethed and raged and looked like they hated the whole world. Most people would have been intimidated but Kate was delighted. Cameron was finally realising his true heritage now the simpering, thieving cow was out of his life. Yes, he was full of painful emotion but one day that emotion would cool and harden inside him and destroy his innocence, turning him into the thing he was always meant to be.

Cameron took the drink from her and turned those brooding black eyes onto the unlit fireplace, dismissing her. Kate wasn't offended; it was the reaction she wanted. Inwardly she was grinning while her face was filled with sympathy as she made her way back to the card table.

'Is he okay?' said Gail as she retook her seat.

'No, but he will be. We need to take his mind off his break-up.'

'How do we do that?'

'Beauden. You can keep going through the script with him. Work will take his mind off it.'

'He doesn't look like he'd appreciate that,' he replied, glancing at Cameron, who was lost in his own thoughts.

'I don't mean right now. Try tomorrow after breakfast.'

Beauden wasn't happy with his assignment, but he didn't object as he knew arguing with Kate Alardyce was futile.

Cameron's dour, silent presence put a dampener on the evening. Harry tried to cheer him up by telling him about some of the amusing events of his life over the past sixteen years. Cameron firmly but politely said that he wanted to be alone. Harry took the hint and left him to it, wondering why he didn't bugger off upstairs and let them enjoy themselves.

Jenna and Simon were the first to sneak up to their bedroom, holding hands and giggling like teenagers. Their departure started the exodus, everyone else too polite to leave first.

Kate was the last to go up, wanting to be alone with Cameron.

'Nightcap?' she said, holding out another whisky to him.

'Why not?' he sighed, taking the glass from her. 'I won't sleep tonight anyway.'

Kate settled into the armchair closest to him, a whisky cradled in one hand. 'If you ask me, you've had a lucky escape.'

'I don't feel very lucky. Can I ask you a favour?'

'Anything.'

'Could I stay here for a couple of weeks? I told Shannon I'd give her some time to clear out of my flat.'

'That's very generous of you. It's far more than she deserves but that's a testament to your big heart. And yes, of course you can. Stay as long as you like.'

'Thanks, that's really kind.'

'Have you got someone to run your businesses?'

'Aye, Phil, my assistant manager. He's more than capable. I'll call him tomorrow and let him know that I'll be away for longer than expected. At least I can still buy that gym, thanks to you.'

'You're buying another one?'

He nodded.

'That's great. The first two must be really successful,' she said, even though she already knew this because her investigator had told her. She also knew about his impending purchase of the third gym.

'I wouldn't have been able to follow through with the sale because of Shannon stealing my money,' he said, gaze darkening. 'But thanks to you, I can still buy it.'

'We'll sort that out tomorrow and transfer the funds, so that's one less thing for you to worry about.'

Those cold eyes filled with emotion. 'I don't know what I'd do without you. If we hadn't come here, I'd be stuck trying to get Shannon out of my flat and the sale would have fallen through.'

'Don't think about what ifs, they don't do anyone any favours. I've learnt that from experience.'

'You're right but I can't help wondering what would have happened if me and Shan had married, had children.' His face crumpled and he hastily wiped away the tears. 'Sorry.'

'Don't apologise. You need to get it out. And you're in good company. I've had my heart broken too.'

'I've never felt anything like this before,' he rasped. 'How did you get over it?'

'I threw myself into my work. Combined with time, it did the trick. You just need patience and one day soon, things will get better.'

'I hope you're right. Right now, I can't imagine feeling good ever again.'

'You will, I promise. Work with Beauden tomorrow, that'll take your mind off it.'

'I'm not sure I've got the energy.'

'Trust me, it's the best antidote. In fact, it's the only one.'

When Cameron returned his attention to the fireplace, Kate knew the conversation was over. She didn't want to push him in his fragile state. Already he'd recognised how necessary she was to him, which was plenty for now.

'I'm off to bed,' she said, getting to her feet.

'I'll stay up for a while, if that's okay? I won't be able to sleep.'

'No problem. I'll let Marcus know.'

She kissed the top of his head, enjoying the feel of his soft black hair against her skin before quietly leaving the room.

Kate paused at the door to look back at him. She was startled to see a shadow standing behind his chair. When she blinked, the impression disappeared. Sometimes she scared herself as she had no idea whether these things she saw and felt were real or in her own head.

20

Kate half-expected to find Cameron still sitting in the armchair in the drawing room when she got up that morning, but it was empty, so she surmised he must have gone up to bed at some point. She wandered into the dining room to find everyone except Simon, Eric and Cameron eating breakfast at the table.

'Morning all,' she smiled before taking her seat at the head of the table. Marcus immediately swooped in to furnish her with tea, toast and jam.

'Where's Cameron?' Harry asked her.

'I assume in his room,' she replied. 'I left him last night in the drawing room.'

'We shouldn't have left him alone,' said Lucy. 'He looked so miserable. What if he does something stupid?'

'He won't.'

'You can't know that for sure. I feel so guilty. He just looked so...'

'Scary?' offered Harry.

'Exactly.'

'He wasn't in the mood to talk,' said Kate.

'You never know, they might make up,' said Jenna. 'They're such a lovely couple.'

'I think that's out of the question,' replied Kate before taking a sip of tea.

'Why? What did Shannon do?'

'As I said, that's up to Cameron to tell you.'

'It must be bad to make him dump her; he was so in love with her. Did she cheat on him?'

'No, and that's all I'm saying on the matter.'

'How come you're in on the secret?' said Harry suspiciously, having already guessed his cousin's feelings for Cameron.

'Shannon told me before she left. She thought I should know.'

'Why?' he said, knowing Shannon had disliked Kate.

'She said it was only right as I'd been such a kind hostess, and I admit I caught her at a vulnerable moment when she was packing. It all spilled out.'

Harry didn't believe that for a moment. He'd noticed that when Kate lied, her eyes narrowed slightly. It was a subtle tell but he'd become very skilled at spotting liars over the years. The only reason he could think of why Kate was in the know was because she'd already known Shannon's secret before Cameron had found out. Still, it was none of his business. Another thing his vast life experience had taught him was that it was never wise to go rummaging through other people's dirty laundry, unless you wanted a hold over them, which he suspected was exactly what Kate had done. She always got what she wanted and it was clear she wanted Cameron, who was now single and vulnerable.

'Something wrong?' Kate asked him when she realised how closely he was studying her.

Harry shrugged. 'Nope.'

'Good.' She gave him a scrutinising look before saying, 'What does everyone have planned for today?'

'The rain's finally stopped,' said Harmony. 'So it would be good to get out for a bit.' The thick grey clouds had gone, replaced by fluffy white ones, and the sun was breaking through.

'The village or somewhere further?'

'Just into the village. Lucy told me it has a great bookshop.'

'I'll come with you,' replied Lucy. 'Then I thought after we could look at the witch's grave again.'

'Why not?' she smiled. 'Sounds fun.'

Lucy beamed back at her. She wasn't bothered about seeing the grave again, but she thought the mention of it might put off anyone who was thinking of saying they'd come with them.

'It does sound fun, doesn't it?' said Harry cheerfully. 'I'll come too.'

Lucy's smile dropped. 'Really?'

'Oh, aye. I do have a ghoulish side.'

When Harry's eyes filled with knowing, Lucy looked down at her plate, blushing.

'I'll walk with you,' said Kate. 'I want to talk to Paul about the exhumation licence. I'm hoping he can give me the name of the parishioner who told him about it. She might have more invaluable knowledge about this house. Does anyone want to come?'

'I think I'll stay here,' said Jenna. 'In case Cam needs any moral support.'

'Don't give us that nonsense,' grinned Harry. 'You're wanting to hump Simon into oblivion again, aren't you?'

'I beg your pardon?' she demanded, cheeks colouring.

'I heard you going at it like the clappers when I got up to go to the toilet last night. At first, I thought it must be foxes mating, it sounded so wild, until I realised the sounds were coming from your room. I suspect that's why Simon hasn't surfaced yet. He's been worn down to a nub.'

'You're a cheeky git, do you know that?'

'So I've been told,' he smiled.

'I'll come into the village too,' said Gail. 'I've not seen it yet. I'll ask Eric if he wants to join us but he's anti-walking.'

'How can anyone be anti-walking?' frowned Harmony.

'He hates any form of exercise. If he can't get there in a vehicle then he's not interested. He refuses to go to our favourite restaurant any more after it was refurbished as he said they'd moved the toilets too far away from the dining area.'

Harry chuckled into his teacup.

The door opened and, to their surprise, Cameron walked in. He was pale and his eyes were heavy, as though he'd spent a sleepless night, but he was neatly dressed in blue jeans and a grey T-shirt. He was clean shaven and his hair was damp from the shower.

'Morning,' he said quietly as he took a seat at the table to Kate's left.

'Morning,' they replied in unison before glancing at each other, wondering what they should say.

'I hope you managed to get some sleep?' said Kate.

'Aye, a bit,' he replied. 'Could I have a strong black coffee and some porridge, please, Marcus?'

The butler nodded and began arranging his breakfast.

'We thought you'd still be resting,' said Jenna.

'You mean you thought I'd be curled up in a ball in bed, crying?'

'To be perfectly frank, yes.'

'Sod that. I need to go to the jewellers and get my money back on that ring.'

'Are you ready to tell us why you broke up?'

'I don't think...' began Kate.

'Shannon stole fifty grand from me,' he replied.

There were shocked gasps around the table.

'Bloody hell,' breathed Lucy.

'That's a hell of a lot of money,' said Harry.

'Stupidly, I let her do my accounts, so it was easy for her,' replied Cameron, eyes flashing. 'I wish I could say I was onto her, but I didn't have a clue. I only found out because I asked a friend of mine who's an accountant to have a look at the books, so I knew where I stood financially before the wedding.'

'Are you sure he didn't make a mistake?' said Harmony. 'She didn't seem the thieving type.'

'That's what I'd hoped, but Shannon admitted it. Her restaurant's failing and she stole from me to try and keep it going. Why didn't she just ask me for the money?' he muttered more to himself than anyone else. 'She didn't need to steal.'

'Sounds to me like you had a lucky escape.'

'Harry,' chided Harmony.

'It's true. Imagine if that had come out after the wedding. She could have tried to lay claim to your businesses to dig herself out of the hole.'

Cameron nodded. 'I know and that's the rock I'm clinging to in order to stop getting depressed.'

'We could see how much you loved her,' said Jenna gently.

'I still do but I'll get over it.' He frowned at the bowl of porridge Marcus placed before him. 'I've changed my mind. I'm not hungry.'

'You need to eat,' said Kate. 'You didn't have dinner last night either.'

'I'll have something for lunch.' Cameron got to his feet. 'I want to return the ring to the jewellers. I'll feel better when I've got that money back.'

With that, he left the room, not asking if anyone else was going into the village. No one offered to accompany him as it was clear he wanted to be alone.

'Shannon, a thief,' said Gail. 'I never would have thought it, although admittedly I barely knew the woman.'

'I would never have thought it about her either,' said Lucy. 'She seemed so nice.'

'From what Cameron said, she sounded to be desperate,' replied Harmony. 'She told me the restaurant means a lot to her because it was set up by her grandfather.'

'That's no excuse,' said Kate harshly. 'As Cam said, she could have just asked him for the money.'

'Maybe she didn't think so?'

'Perhaps, but stealing it was the wrong thing to do. Our family doesn't forgive. Betray us once and that's it. You're done. At least Shannon's gone. She'll never be welcomed back here either. Good riddance if you ask me.' She got to her feet with a haughty look. 'I'm going for a shower and then I'll head into the village. I'll meet you all in the hallway in one hour.'

'Her Majesty has spoken,' commented Harry when she'd gone.

* * *

Cameron successfully managed to return the ring, to the shop owner's disappointment. Knowing he had at least two thousand pounds of his money back from Shannon made Cameron feel slightly better. Rather than head back to the house and face all those pitying faces, he decided to wander around the village. He found himself back at the cemetery, staring down at the graves of his relatives, which were still scattered with the red rose petals. His life had been turned on its head since he'd come here and he felt lost and adrift. The fact that those of his bloodline lay in the soil beneath his feet was something solid and real that he could cling to. That at least couldn't be taken from him by treachery and betrayal.

'Everything changed when you came into my life,' he said, particularly addressing this comment to Robert's grave.

'I know the feeling,' replied a voice.

Cameron jumped and whirled round.

'Sorry to startle you,' smiled Kate.

'How do you move so quietly?' he gasped.

Kate shrugged. 'Just gifted, I guess. I'm going to the vicarage to speak to Paul, if you want to come.'

'Aye, I will.' He frowned. 'Where are the others?'

'They were too slow.' She linked her arm through his with a cheerful smile. 'Let's go before they get here. Paul won't appreciate all of us piling into his house bringing noise and Harry's sarcasm.'

They headed down the path that meandered through the graveyard and passed through a gate and down another short path that was secluded by trees. At the end of the path was a large Victorian villa. The house would have been grim and imposing had it not been for all the cheerful flowers in the garden and the arch of roses around the door. Even the window boxes burst with colour. It was a haven for bees and butterflies.

'Paul's a very keen gardener,' said Kate as they rang the old bell that pealed through the house.

The door was opened by a solid-looking middle-aged woman. Her features were thick and coarse and a little unpleasant.

'Yes?' snapped the woman in a way that said they were interrupting some vital work.

'Is the vicar in, please?' replied Kate. 'We'd like to speak to him.'

The woman looked Kate up and down with barely concealed disdain, which Cameron thought was rather rude but only broadened Kate's smile.

'He's in. I can ask him if he'll see you, I suppose.'

'That would be wonderful, thank you.'

Kate stared at the woman expectantly until she turned from her with a sneer and plodded back into the house.

'She's rude,' frowned Cameron.

'That's Maud,' replied Kate. 'Unfortunately, Paul inherited her with the house. She's been here so long he hasn't the heart to sack her, so he has to put up with her bad moods and awful cooking.'

'I'm starting to feel sorry for Paul.'

The housekeeper plodded back up the hallway towards them.

'He'll see you,' she muttered. 'But don't keep him long because he's busy.'

'We'll do our best,' replied Kate.

Maud scowled suspiciously at Kate's bright smile. 'This way,' she said with a jerk of the head.

Kate and Cameron stepped inside the cool, narrow hallway where little light could penetrate. They followed the grumpy housekeeper down the hall to the last door on the right and entered to find an enormous mahogany dining table that took up most of the room. Paul sat at the far end of it, papers spread out all around him.

He smiled when they entered and rose to greet his guests.

'Hello and welcome,' he said with a warm smile, dispelling the chilly reception his housekeeper had given them.

'I hope we're not interrupting,' replied Kate.

'Not at all, I've already finished writing tomorrow's sermon. I do hope learning about the exhumation didn't upset you too much?' he asked her with concern.

'No, although I was really intrigued. I'd never heard of it before; none of the family had.'

'It is interesting that it was covered up so well.'

'Our family's very good at burying its skeletons,' she said wryly.

'So it seems. I've discovered something else about your family. I hope you don't mind but I find the history so fascinating.'

Kate waved a hand graciously. 'Not at all. I appreciate your enthusiasm.'

'That is a relief. This new information isn't as dramatic as the exhumation but it's still very interesting – Thomas's only son, Mark, was also mentally unstable.'

'Don't tell us he saw ghosts too?' said Cameron.

'No, nothing like that but he was paranoid like his father. He sacked all the servants a year after he took over the title. He lost the title too because of his bad behaviour. Not only did he have affairs with the wives of several peers but there were also rumours that he blackmailed people out of their money.'

'Thanks for that, Mark,' muttered Kate. 'He was the one who lost not only the family fortune and title but the house too.'

'I'm not surprised. By the sounds of it, he was very unstable.'

'Seems to be a pattern in our family,' commented Cameron.

'Where did you get this information from?' Kate asked Paul.

'From the parishioner I mentioned.'

'The one whose mother worked at the house as a servant?'

Paul nodded.

'I'm glad you brought her up because we'd like to talk to her.'

'I'm sure she'd be delighted. The poor old soul's bedridden now, so talking is her only outlet. Be warned though, once you get her started it's hard to stop her.'

'Even better.'

'When would you like to talk to her?'

'We've some free time now, if that works for her?'

'I'll call her. She keeps a phone by her bedside.'

Cameron was a little startled when Paul produced a mobile phone from his pocket. With his old-world manners, he seemed like something out of the Victorian era himself. Such a modern object didn't look right in his hands.

'Hello, Betty. It's me, Paul. Kate Alardyce and her cousin Cameron are here and they were wondering if they could come and speak to you? Yes, I will. See you soon.' He hung up and smiled at his guests. 'She'd be delighted to talk to you. I haven't heard her sound so enthusiastic in weeks. She's free now, if you want to go. She lives just down the lane.'

'Perfect,' said Kate.

'Wonderful. I'll come with you, if you don't mind? She does like me to visit her every day.'

'What's wrong with Betty?' Cameron asked her.

'She fell and fractured her hip three months ago. Despite surgery, she's never recovered from the injury and walking causes her immense pain, so she hired a housekeeper and a private nurse.'

'That must cost her a fortune,' replied Kate.

'It does but she can afford it. Her son's something big in the tech industry. Fortunately, he loves his mother and ensures she's well cared for. He even bought her the bungalow she now lives in.'

'Children must be such a comfort,' said Kate wistfully.

Cameron gave her a look full of sympathy, understanding how much being childless hurt Kate. She gave him a gentle smile in response, grateful for that understanding. Only when he looked away did her smile turn into a malicious smirk of pleasure. She couldn't believe how perfectly everything was working out for her, although she should because somehow, it always did.

21

Betty's bungalow was a sprawling affair in its own grounds close to the vicarage, the house built around a central courtyard. In the centre of the courtyard was a sprightly fountain. Access was gained by the narrow footpath behind the vicarage.

Paul rang the doorbell and a cheerful, round woman with a ready smile opened the door, a stark contrast to the dour Maud.

'Morning, Vicar,' she beamed. 'Lovely to see you, as always.'

'Thank you, Claire. You too. How's the patient today?'

'Grumbling because she didn't like her breakfast. She says I make her scrambled eggs too often but it's one of the few things she can keep down. Come on in, she's waiting for you.'

The three of them entered, Kate and Cameron following Paul's lead and removing their shoes and leaving them in the hallway. Claire took the light jackets they wore. Even though it was warm and sunny, they were taking no chances after the previous day's weather.

'Would you like anything to drink?' Claire asked them brightly.

They all politely declined and followed her down the hall.

'You could use her at the vicarage,' Cameron told the vicar. 'She's much nicer than Maud.'

'I know, life would be much easier for me, but I can't bring myself to sack Maud. Her job is all she's got in the world. She has no family, nothing else.'

Cameron thought how being a living saint seemed an enormous burden to bear, but the vicar appeared to be contented with his lot.

Paul rapped on the door and an imperious voice commanded him to enter. The bedroom was quite gloomy and it took their eyes a few seconds to adjust.

'Betty?' squinted Paul.

'Aye, it's me,' retorted a croaky old voice. She turned her attention to Kate. 'You're finally here. I've been patiently waiting. You want to learn about your family?'

'Yes please,' replied Kate.

'Excellent. I've been waiting for this moment.' Betty looked to Cameron. 'You're an Alardyce too. I've seen plenty of pictures of Robert and you look just like him.'

'So I've heard,' he mumbled.

'The likeness makes you uneasy? Can't say I blame you. Let's hope it's just skin deep.'

'It is,' he frowned.

'You hope,' chuckled Betty. 'Does anybody want some tea?'

They all shook their heads.

'I was hoping you'd say that. At least this way we can get straight to the good stuff. Sit down,' she said, waving a hand at the couch at the side of the room.

While Kate and Cameron sat together on the couch, Paul took the small chair at the opposite side of the room.

'I knew your gran,' she told the cousins. 'We were great friends. She visited me a lot when I became too old and knackered to travel.'

Kate and Cameron looked at each other before turning back to Betty.

'Wait,' said Kate. 'Our gran came to Alardyce village?'

'Oh aye, regularly.'

'But we thought she stayed away for years.'

'No, she visited as often as she could. We knew each other from being young girls. Connie was always great fun.'

'Gran moved to Dumfries from Alardyce when she was in her twenties. I'd no idea she came back here. Why didn't she tell us?' Kate asked Cameron.

He shrugged, equally confused.

'She didn't tell anyone,' smiled Betty. 'She always told the family she was staying with a friend in Glasgow knowing they were dead against this place.'

'Because of the history?' said Kate.

'Yes.'

'That's what we never understood. Our parents and grandparents wanted nothing to do with Alardyce and it wasn't just about what Robert and Edward did. There was more to it, but they always refused to tell us.'

'And your gran never told you?'

'No. She never mentioned Thomas and the exhumation either. If you knew about that then I'm certain she did too.'

'Connie did know about it. She loved to sit at my mother's feet and listen to her tales about working at the house. My mother told Connie all the things the adults kept from her. She made your gran promise to keep it to herself though.'

'So that's why Gran never told us? Because she was keeping her promise to your mother,' said Kate, pleased there was a reasonable explanation.

'Oh no, it's not that at all. She didn't tell you because she was protecting you all.'

'From what?'

'The Alardyce curse.'

'The curse?' said Cameron, unable to hide an amused smile. 'I don't believe in curses.'

'That's what they called it back in the day. Today they'd refer to it as mental illness.'

Kate's expression darkened. 'Mental illness?'

'Yes. It's always been there in your family's blood – Edward and then Robert. Then it skipped a generation and hit Thomas and then his son. Poor Thomas. Not only was he unwell in the head but he had a club foot too. He limped heavily on his right foot. It really was a struggle for him to get around sometimes.'

Cameron's mouth suddenly went dry as he recalled that figure he'd seen in the hallway after the séance, limping on their right foot. Perhaps the séance hadn't been such a washout after all.

'The curse doesn't come out until the teenage years,' continued Betty. 'With Edward and Robert it manifested as violence. Later down the line, it came out as paranoia, which in a way is a blessing. Or maybe it was the more modern medicine that managed to get rid of the aggression? That was my mother's theory anyway but who knows for sure?'

'In her diary Jane said Robert broke the curse.'

'She was wrong. It just changed form and it only followed Robert's direct line of descent. Nothing of the sort occurred in his siblings' descendants. Just his.' Her keen eyes flicked between the cousins. 'And I believe you two are the last in his line?'

Kate and Cameron nodded, their eyes wide. 'My mother and Cam's dad descended from his line. The rest of the cousins come from Lydia's and John's.'

'Then let's hope you're lucky. It skipped Robert's son, James, so it might skip both of you.'

'It missed our parents too. None of them were mentally ill.'

'Actually, my dad suffered from depression a lot,' replied Cameron. 'But it was controlled with medication. He was never aggressive though.'

'I wonder what would have become of him without that medication?' said Betty knowingly.

'And if it does skip us both then it could affect any children we may have?' Kate asked her.

Betty shrugged. 'I'm no medical expert but I'd say there's a good chance.'

'Perhaps it would be best to discuss this with a doctor?' said Paul kindly. 'Someone who understands all the ins and outs?'

'I think that would be a good idea,' replied Cameron.

'I wouldn't worry,' said Betty, leaning back into her pillows. 'Not with all the modern drugs these days. Or there's that electric shock therapy. They dosed Thomas up good and proper with that. It made him more docile, then the effects would wear off and he'd become paranoid again.'

Neither Kate nor Cameron replied to this statement, both noting the malice in the old woman's eyes. Was she actually enjoying making them feel uncomfortable?

'Gran died of dementia,' said Cameron.

'Aye, I know,' replied Betty. 'I went to her funeral but that was the end of a long downhill journey. Do you know that she was sectioned when she was in her thirties? I see you don't,' she added when they regarded her with surprise. 'She started with the paranoia and she began talking to Robert, thinking he was haunting her, like Thomas did. She spent eighteen months in hospital, but the medication sorted her out. I remember Connie coming to see me six months after she was released. She was quite down that the medication had blocked Robert out. She saw the pills as something interfering with her connection. Good old Connie never stopped believing, even when the dementia took over.'

'Do you think it was a delusion or was it real?' Cameron asked her.

'I've asked myself that question many times and I don't know. She seemed convinced and I've always believed there's far more to this world than we know. There's a special air at Alardyce House, as though it sits on the border between two worlds. If something's going to come through, then it's going to come through there.'

Kate and Cameron glanced at each other again, not knowing what to say.

'Don't look so worried,' said Betty with a wicked chuckle. 'Hopefully neither of you will lose your marbles and start thinking you're being haunted.'

'Betty,' said Paul. His voice was heavy with warning, but he still managed to keep his tone gentle. 'That's not very nice.'

'It's the truth. I saw what the Alardyce bad blood did to their relatives. I'd hate to see it happen to this pretty pair too, or rather one of them. There's only ever one unlucky bugger in each generation. That's something at least, isn't it?' There was no sympathy in her sharp green eyes, only malicious enjoyment. 'I'm tired now,' sighed Betty. 'I need to sleep.'

Paul rose. 'We'll get out of your hair and let you rest.'

Kate and Cameron rose too. No one bid Betty goodbye as it appeared she had already drifted off. They filed outside in silence, bidding Claire goodbye on their way. No one spoke until they were heading back down the lane.

'That was... weird,' said Cameron. 'She's certainly not the sweet old lady I imagined.'

'I don't think Betty MacDonald could ever be called sweet,' replied Paul. 'She's offended a lot of residents in Alardyce over the years. Sorry, I should have warned you, but I did hope her admiration of your work, Kate, would soften her slightly. I was wrong.'

'She's a mean old cow,' scowled Kate.

'I'm not defending her rudeness, but her temperament has been made worse by her medical condition. Betty used to be a very active woman, playing tennis and golf and leading the local hiking club, so being laid up in bed all day does get to her.'

'Claire's a saint,' commented Cameron.

'She is that. No one else would put up with Betty like she does. If I were you, I wouldn't take what she had to say too much to heart. You're both smart, successful people with good lives. Concentrate on that and let the past go.'

'That's very good advice,' said Cameron with a meaningful look at Kate; however, he knew his cousin lived much more in the past than the present.

'This is where I leave you, I'm afraid,' said Paul as they reached the vicarage. 'If you ever need to talk, my door's always open.'

'Thanks,' said Cameron.

Kate was so lost in her own thoughts that she just nodded.

Paul gave them a kind smile before heading inside the vicarage. Kate and Cameron continued on through the graveyard.

'What did you think of all that?' Cameron asked his cousin. 'Kate?' he added when she failed to respond.

'Sorry,' she replied. 'I was miles away.'

'What are you thinking?'

They came to a halt before the family graves, staring down at them contemplatively.

'I don't know,' she said slowly. 'I feel a bit shellshocked.'

'Me too. I always knew our parents were keeping something from us. Perhaps this is it?'

'Maybe, but I'm sure they only did it so we wouldn't worry that we'd go mad too.'

'Perhaps.'

Kate shook herself out of her thoughts. 'Let's forget about what Betty said. It only tarnishes our relatives' memories.'

'You're probably right,' said Cameron, although he'd already decided that he would speak to his mother as soon as possible. He would keep that to himself though.

'There you are,' said a voice.

Harry led Jenna, Simon, Lucy, Harmony and Gail into the graveyard.

'Where the hell have you been?' he added.

'We've just been to see Betty,' replied Cameron.

'Who?'

'An old lady.'

'Sounds like you've had a wild time.'

'She told us some wild stuff.'

Harry's face creased with mischief. 'Did she give you her apple cobbler recipe?'

Kate was not amused. 'Let's go and discuss it.'

'Wonderful. The pub should be open.'

'I was thinking the café. It's far too early for a pub.'

'Spoilsport.'

'Have you got family matters to discuss?' said Gail. 'Because if you do, I'll take a wander around the village. I believe there are some nice shops around here.'

'I'll come with you,' said Harmony.

'Thanks. I appreciate that,' smiled Kate, glad that someone had some tact.

Gail and Harmony strolled out of the graveyard together.

'What's going on?' Jenna demanded of her cousins, sensing something wasn't right.

'Let's discuss it over a coffee,' replied Cameron reasonably.

The café was rather quiet, so they could take a table at the back of the room. Kate got the usual attention and she smiled at her adoring fans, but it was clear she was distracted. Fortunately, she was allowed to take a seat without being asked for an autograph or a selfie. The same fawning waiter took their order, treating Kate like a visiting queen and the others like baggage he had to tolerate. Once she eventually managed to get rid of him, she began to explain what Betty had told them.

'Well,' said Harry when she'd finished. 'We always knew there was a kink in the genes. Can any of us really say we're surprised?'

'I am,' replied Jenna. 'I always thought it ended with Robert. I'd no idea there was more after that. I know your dad was a bit anxious and depressed, Cam, and there was Gran's dementia, but other than that I thought our family was fine.'

'Betty could have been making it all up,' said Lucy. 'I don't know about you, but I've never heard mention of her before. Gran never talked about her.'

'I'm not so sure she is making it up,' said Harry, for once looking serious. 'You probably don't know that my own father tried to commit suicide when he was twenty-one.'

'Oh, God, that's terrible,' said Lucy sympathetically.

'He... well, he became paranoid and thought people were following him in the street. He was put on medication and it stopped and he hasn't had any episodes in years, although his moods can be up and down but he's never violent. I didn't want to say anything because my parents told me to keep it quiet, but I think I can trust you all to keep it to yourselves. I was always afraid it would happen to me too but thankfully it never has.' His charming smile returned. 'My natural sunny disposition kept anything like that at bay.'

'I've a confession to make too,' said Kate. 'One I really should have mentioned sooner. Gran always wanted to be buried here in Alardyce beside Robert and the others; it was even in her will, but my parents vetoed that and had her buried in Dumfries instead. I've arranged for her body to be moved here, in accordance with her wishes. I've checked with Paul and he said it would be fine.'

'I think that's fair,' said Lucy, to everyone's surprise. 'I thought what they did was so wrong. It was her body, she had the right to say what was done with it.'

Kate's look was grateful and she reached across the table to give Lucy's hand a gentle squeeze.

'I agree,' said Cameron. 'I never thought what they did was right either.'

'I've no objection,' said Harry when Kate looked to him. 'In my opinion when you're dead you're dead, so it makes no odds what happens to the old girl now.'

'Well, I think it's wrong,' said Jenna. 'You can't go around digging people up and moving them about.'

'It's what Gran would have wanted,' Harry told her.

'I'll have to apply for an exhumation licence just like Thomas did,' said Kate, shifting uncomfortably in her seat.

'But for very different reasons,' replied Cameron. 'You're not doing it because you think Gran's still alive. You're doing it out of respect. Thomas did it out of madness. There's a big difference.'

Lucy recalled what Shannon had said about Kate's obsession with Robert. Would she want to dig him up too?

'Are you okay?' Kate asked her when she shuddered.

'Aye,' she replied. 'Just a bit chilly.'

'So, what do you think we should do with the information Betty gave us?' Cameron asked the table.

'Forget all about it,' said Jenna.

'I think that's the best option,' replied Harry. 'If we keep going over it, we might end up driving ourselves mad. We're all fine, no paranoid or homicidal tendencies have become apparent, so it seems the faulty gene has skipped our generation. We need to stop looking at the past and concentrate on the future.' He particularly addressed this last statement to Kate.

'The problem is, I have to study the past in order to create this production,' she told him.

'By all means, do that. Just don't let it take you over. Obsession's a dangerous thing.'

Lucy's gaze met Harry's and she saw her own worries reflected in his eyes.

The waiter approached with their drinks and they decided to let the issue drop, which was a relief to them all.

* * *

Everyone noted that Kate was rather subdued that night at dinner. She picked at her food and wasn't her usual scintillating self. The only time she came alive was when anyone mentioned her precious production. Even Cameron, despite his depression over his break-up, was livelier than their hostess.

Cameron knew Betty's words had got to Kate and he managed to speak to her alone when she headed into the study after dinner rather than accompany the rest of the guests into the drawing room.

He didn't bother to knock because he had the feeling she'd just send him away, so he walked straight in and found her staring out of the window. She whipped round to face him, anger in her eyes at this intrusion into her sanctuary, the look softening when she saw who her visitor was.

'Oh, it's you,' she said.

'I wanted to make sure you're okay. You don't seem yourself.'

'I can't stop thinking about what Betty said. I thought Gran told me everything, but she hid so much. This might sound stupid and childish, but it hurts. Maybe we weren't as close as I thought? I always preferred Gran over my own mother, who did nothing but put me down and make fun of all my dreams. Gran was the only one who understood. Now I've found out that she kept a whole other life from me. Why did she never bring me to Alardyce with her? She knew how much I wanted to come.'

'Because she knew your parents would object and she didn't want to make things awkward for you.'

'Maybe.'

'There's more to it than that, isn't there?'

Kate nodded. 'What she said about the… the… craziness in the family.'

'It's getting to you?'

'People have told me my entire life that I'm obsessed with our ancestors. What if it's a symptom of mental illness?'

'I highly doubt that.'

'How can you be sure?'

'Every relative of ours who's had these issues has been struck in their teens or twenties. You're thirty-two with an extremely successful career, a busy life and friends. How could you manage all that if you were ill?'

'I don't know but it still makes me uneasy,' she said, wrapping her arms around herself, eyes filling with distress. 'What if I've got the curse?'

Tears filled her big blue eyes and the sight touched Cameron's heart. He went to her and Kate was more than happy to be enveloped in his arms.

'You're not crazy,' he said. 'You're perfectly normal and you have a life most people can only dream of. Stop worrying and enjoy it. Anyway, I could be the one carrying the curse.'

Kate tilted her face up to his. 'There's nothing wrong with you, Cam. Out of us all, you're the best. You always have been.'

'I wouldn't go that far,' he smiled.

'It's true. You've always had such a good heart. Even now, despite all your pain, you're here making sure I'm okay.'

'Because I care about you, and I want you to be happy.'

'Why though? You don't owe me anything.'

'That doesn't stop me from caring. I'm always here if you need me.'

Kate smiled. She was still in his arms and there was no sign of him letting go. Gently, she pressed her hands to his chest, which was so strong. She could feel the thud of his heart beneath her palm, which quickened at her touch.

'You've no idea how much I appreciate that,' she murmured, afraid of speaking too loudly and spoiling the moment. 'I've had to rely on myself most of my life. Now people can't do enough for me but when I was struggling to get a foothold in the industry, no one wanted to help. You've no idea how much of a comfort it is knowing there's someone who genuinely cares.'

'Your friends seem like they want the best for you too.'

'They do now but only a few years ago, Eric wouldn't give me the time of day. He said I had no talent.' Satisfaction filled her eyes. 'But I proved him wrong and now he can't wait to jump on any project of mine.'

'There you go. Can you imagine Thomas or Mark Alardyce pulling off something like that?'

Her lips twitched. 'No.'

'See, there's nothing to worry about. You're fine. Just one thing though. Don't get so caught up with the dead that you forget the living.'

'How could I ever forget you?' she breathed when she noticed his eyes slip to her lips.

Deciding to take a chance, she leaned in closer, wondering if he would pull away, but he didn't. Beneath her palm, his heart beat faster and those black eyes of his darkened even more.

Their lips met, the kiss light and gentle. They stared at each other for a moment, as though they were both startled by what had happened, but Kate wasn't. It was what she'd hoped for from the moment he'd walked through her front door.

Cameron's hand fisted in her hair as he ground his mouth against hers. Kate was a little surprised by the force of his passion, but she was more than happy to indulge it. The thought that she was being used as revenge against Shannon niggled at the back of her mind, but she pushed it away.

'You're so beautiful,' he murmured in her ear before kissing her neck. This combined with the feel of his fingers in her hair made her gasp with pleasure.

His lips found hers again and they stumbled back against the wall together, his hands sliding up and down her body, just brushing the sides of her breasts as though wanting to touch but seeking permission. With an impish smile, she took his right hand and placed it on her breast, revelling in the way his eyes darkened even more and his chest heaved. In her experience, most men's eyes brightened when they were sexually aroused, but Cameron's only got blacker and it thrilled her.

'Should we be doing this?' she murmured into his mouth when he kissed her again. 'It feels so taboo.'

Her words had been very carefully chosen and they hit their target. Cameron took her face in his hands and stared into her eyes.

'I'm so tired of being the good guy,' he growled.

Kate smiled. Finally, he'd realised who he truly was.

His head snapped round to face the door when there was a knock, anger filling his eyes at the interruption.

'Kate, are you in there?' they heard Beauden call.

'Don't reply and he'll go away,' whispered Cameron.

'The door's not locked,' she whispered back. As much as Kate didn't want this moment to be interrupted, she welcomed the intrusion. Leaving Cameron in a state of frustration would only make him want her even more.

They released each other and hastily adjusted their clothing, Kate rushing to sit behind the desk before she called, 'Come in.'

Beauden entered to a picture of innocence. Kate was sitting at the desk, her script before her and Cameron stood at her side. It was the atmosphere in the room that alerted him to the fact that he'd disturbed something. Whatever that was, it wasn't his business, so he pretended he hadn't noticed.

'I was going to ask if you'd seen Cameron but here he is,' smiled Beauden. He was a little startled by the look in the younger man's eyes. It was the same look he'd seen when Cameron had been playing Robert. It made Beauden want to retreat but he stood his ground. 'I was hoping to run through the script again, but it can wait if you're in the middle of something,' he added.

'You read our minds,' replied Kate. 'We were just looking through the script together, but we can do that later if you want to get some work done.'

'Okay,' said Beauden, wishing she'd said no. Cameron did not look happy with this arrangement. 'We could do it another time, if you like, Cam?'

The silence felt to swell and fill the room as Cameron just stared back at him coldly, obviously wishing pestilence on Beauden's inconvenient presence, but his natural manners came to the fore.

'Now's fine,' he replied.

'Wonderful. I'll fetch the script and meet you in the parlour.'

'Okay. I'll be there in a few minutes.'

Beauden nodded and hastily retreated, closing the door behind him.

Despite how much she ached for Cameron, Kate looked up at him coolly, once again toying with him. Her eyes widened with surprise when he leaned over and kissed her, all his passion still very much present.

'I wish we hadn't been interrupted,' he murmured in her ear, sending tingles shooting down her spine.

'Me too,' she replied, helplessly gazing up into those black eyes.

'Later,' he said, that single word loaded with promise.

After planting a kiss on her neck, he straightened up and left the room, pausing at the door to give her a long, intense stare before exiting.

Kate flopped back into the chair, heart thudding. A scheme of hers was, for once, going wrong. She'd intended to leave Cameron wanting more when in fact it was the other way around.

22

Beauden selected the scene he was reading with Cameron very carefully. It was a fairly mild one where Robert was talking with his younger brother and heir to the estate, John. No violence involved. Cameron once again did a good job, falling into the role effortlessly, but Beauden could tell he was distracted.

'You're thinking about Shannon, aren't you?' he said kindly.

What he wasn't expecting was the momentary confusion that filled Cameron's eyes.

'Oh, Shannon,' he replied. 'Aye.'

'I'm very sorry about your break-up.'

'The worst thing is that I feel like a bloody idiot. She was blatantly stealing from me and I had no idea. I'll never make that mistake again.'

'You mean you'll never trust another woman?'

'I wouldn't go that far but I'll make sure I pick the right one next time.'

Beauden could see another woman already occupied his thoughts, which was astonishing because he'd seen the love Cameron had for Shannon. Was it possible that love had been eradicated so quickly in light of her treachery? No, he didn't think so. What was more likely was that an infatuation with a beautiful, talented actress was providing a welcome distraction from the pain of Shannon's betrayal. The question was, should he break his cardinal rule and stick his nose into someone else's love life? It was rare anything good came of meddling, but Kate was his friend and he didn't want her to get hurt.

He had no doubt that Kate was already aware of the danger of getting involved with a man who had just gone through a painful break-up, but she obviously didn't care. However, this production had an enormous amount of promise and he didn't want to see it ruined by a falling-out between the two leads. No, something must be done.

After leaving Cameron in the parlour, he returned to the study to find Kate still working. She looked up and smiled when he entered.

'How did he get on?'

'Wonderful but I didn't come here to discuss that.'

'From that tone I'm guessing I'm about to get told off for something,' she smiled, lounging back in her chair.

'You're playing a dangerous game with Cameron.'

Kate was so shocked she'd been found out that even she was unable to conceal the surprise in her eyes. It was there just momentarily before she blinked it away. 'What do you mean?' she said, feigning innocence.

'Look, I know it's none of my business but you're my friend and I hope that one day Cameron will be too. He's on the rebound and I'm concerned about you getting hurt.'

Kate chuckled. 'When have you ever known my feelings to be hurt?'

'There's a first time for everything. What if something happens between the pair of you and then he says it meant nothing, that he was just seeking solace after what Shannon did to him? I know that would definitely hurt your pride if not your feelings.'

'You worry too much, you always have.'

'That's very true but my concerns are valid. Don't let this infatuation with Cameron ruin this project, which I know is very dear to your heart. How would you feel if he dropped out because of what went on between you?'

'He won't,' she replied, knowing the financial incentive would bond Cameron to the project. She'd already transferred the money into his account, wanting a chain to keep him tied to it. Although he no longer wanted the money to give to Shannon, he did need to replace the fifty thousand pounds she'd stolen.

Beauden was familiar with the sly look that narrowed Kate's eyes and raised the corners of her mouth. She had a hold over Cameron, no doubt one he hadn't realised the full implications of yet. 'I hope you know what you're doing,' he told her.

'I do, don't worry,' she smiled, getting to her feet. 'Let's go into the drawing room. Harmony's holding another séance. She senses a presence.'

'Not that again,' he sighed. 'You need to come up with some new parlour games.'

'Why bother when this one's so much fun?'

Cheerfully she linked her arm through his as they made their way to the door. She halted before they went through it.

'You never mentioned the fact that Cameron's my cousin,' she said.

'He's a second cousin and there's no law against it. Besides, I think that's the least of your problems. Getting romantically involved, no matter how briefly, could damage what could be a very fulfilling friendship.'

'His friendship isn't enough. I want more.'

'Have you considered that might not be what you *need*?'

Kate's eyes briefly flickered with uncertainty, telling Beauden that he'd at least made her think. That was enough interference from him. The rest was up to her.

* * *

The round table was once again brought into the drawing room and all the guests gathered around it, except Eric, who remained stubbornly put in the armchair, face buried in his newspaper, determined to ignore all the nonsense going on at the other side of the room. Tom was feeling more confident after nothing had happened the last time and he didn't want to look like a big jessie by refusing to join in again.

Beauden noted that Kate and Cameron had sat beside each other, and the way the latter suddenly jumped in his chair and the fact that Kate's hands were under the table indicated she'd just given him a surprise.

'You okay, Cam?' Lucy asked her cousin, innocent to what was really going on.

'Aye,' he replied. 'I just got… a bit of cramp but it's gone now.'

'Is everyone ready to begin?' said Harmony.

They all nodded.

'Good. The energy is at its most potent. Now's the time to start.'

Everyone turned to look when a snigger emanated from behind the newspaper.

'Ignore the narrow-minded sceptic,' said Gail with a frown her husband's way.

The usual routine was repeated while everyone held hands and Harmony asked the air if anyone had a message for them. Nothing happened, so she repeated the question.

'Oh dear,' smiled Eric, lowering the newspaper. 'It looks like no one's in.'

'Why was that first séance so strong and we've had nothing since?' frowned Harmony. 'I don't understand.'

'Maybe the message has been passed on and they don't have anything else for us?' offered Kate.

'It's possible,' murmured a puzzled Harmony.

'Well,' said a secretly relieved Tom. 'If that's it, I need to go pee.'

'It's lucky there were no knocks or Kate would have had to have that chair cleaned,' commented Simon with a spiteful smile.

Tom's look was disdainful as he got to his feet and left the room with quiet dignity.

Just as he'd closed the door behind him, there was a loud thud.

'Is that the spirits?' said Harry. 'Or did Tom fall over?'

The door burst open and the man himself tore back in. 'Did you hear that?' he cried.

'We did and we were wondering if it was you,' replied Chris.

'Me? No. I thought it came from in here.'

'It's the spirits,' breathed Harmony. 'They're trying to communicate. Quickly, reform the circle.'

Tom retook his seat and they all joined hands again.

'What is your message?' Harmony called to the air. 'Do you have a message?'

There was a ping and Eric produced his phone. 'It looks like I do,' he said cheerfully.

Gail rolled her eyes and shook her head.

'Does a member of the Alardyce family want to communicate with us?' said Harmony.

One knock.

'Are you Jane Alardyce?'

Another knock.

'This is ridiculous,' said Eric. 'It's obviously one of you lot doing it.'

'Don't interrupt,' Gail hissed at him.

He put down his phone and newspaper and went into a crouch, studying the underside of the table, convinced someone sitting at it was responsible for the noise.

'Are you here to warn us about the danger again?' Kate asked the air.

One knock.

'Is the danger still here?'

One knock.

'Is the danger from someone in this house?'

Another knock.

'Am I the one in danger?'

Eric became frustrated when there was another knock and no one's legs appeared to so much as twitch. With a grunt of annoyance, he straightened up and began studying the room instead.

Everyone sitting at the table began regarding each other suspiciously.

'We could go around the table and ask who's the dangerous person?' offered Lucy.

'No one at this table is dangerous,' replied Jenna, who was sitting beside her.

'How do you know?' retorted Lucy while glancing at Chris, Beauden and Gail, who were sitting opposite them. They really didn't know these people.

'Is Harry the dangerous one?' Harmony called to the air.

'Oh, that's charming,' he said. 'You do remember I'm your boyfriend?'

She ignored him, deep concentration etched on her face.

Two knocks were the answer to Harmony's question.

'That's you in the clear,' Simon told him. His grin dropped when Kate asked the air if he was the danger.

'I bet he is,' said Tom, frowning at Simon.

Two knocks.

This continued around the table. Then it was Cameron's turn.

'Is Cameron the danger?' said Kate.

One knock.

'Cameron, a danger?' chuckled Harry. 'Everyone knows he wouldn't hurt a fly.'

They all glanced at the man in question, who seemed as surprised as the rest of them.

'It's all nonsense,' said Eric, straightening up. He jumped when there was a loud, angry bang, as though he was being told off for his doubt.

'The spirits are pulling away,' groaned Harmony, slumping back in her chair.

Cameron realised everyone was staring at him. 'What?' he said.

'The knock said you were the danger,' Jenna told him.

'But I'm not.' His eyes flickered when they all continued to stare. 'You know I'd never hurt anyone.'

'Course we do,' said Kate, patting his hand. 'No one believes it.'

'You believed the information given to you during the last séance,' Harry told her. 'So why are you doubting this?'

'Because I think there's been a mix-up. Crossed wires.'

'I don't think spirits use wires.'

'You know what I mean.' She smiled and got to her feet. 'Who wants a drink?'

'Double whisky for me,' said Beauden, sagging back in his seat. 'No offence, Kate, but this is turning out to be the strangest holiday I've ever had.'

'Good,' she replied. 'It means you'll never forget it or this house.'

'Where's that spooky butler of yours?' Eric demanded of Kate, determined to solve the mystery.

'How should I know?' she replied.

'I'm going to find out.'

'I'll come with you,' said Tom. 'In case you need back-up.'

Eric rolled his eyes but didn't object. He'd long ago got used to Tom's hollow posturing. 'Fine. Let's go.'

As the two men exited the room, whiskies were handed round and everyone returned to the couches and armchairs, apart from Harmony, who remained slumped at the table, Harry holding a brandy glass to her lips to revive her.

'No offence,' said Lucy, 'but whatever just happened, I think it was a load of rubbish. Cameron isn't a danger to anyone. It was a terrible thing to say about him after what he's just been through.' To drive her point home, she sat beside him on the couch in solidarity.

'I agree,' replied Jenna. 'Cameron's the gentlest soul I've ever known.'

Silence filled the room.

'Did I tell you all my story about the actress and the salami?' said Beauden.

'No, but I wish you would,' smiled Harry.

As Beauden launched into his story, Kate took the seat on Cameron's other side.

'I don't believe you're a danger to me,' she whispered in his ear, giving his arm a covert squeeze.

'I'd never do anything to hurt you,' he whispered back.

Kate nodded and smiled.

'Do you want to come to my room tonight?' she added in an even quieter voice while Beauden distracted the others.

Her heart fluttered with excitement when his dark eyes felt to eat her up. He just nodded in response, but she could feel the desire radiating from him; however, it wasn't a needy longing like so many of her lovers had inflicted on her in the past. It was commanding, in control and it excited her unbearably. Shannon's actions had caused a definite shift in his personality, in her opinion for the better. Beauden's words about Cameron being on the rebound echoed in her mind. As much as she hated the thought, she was willing to take the chance to get what she wanted. She was certain she could drive all memory of the thieving shrew out of his head. It would be as though she'd never existed.

Eric and Tom returned.

'We found Marcus tidying up the kitchen,' announced the former. 'And he swore he'd been there the whole time.'

'Maybe he had?' said Gail.

'No, I don't believe it. A living person made those knocks and he's the only other person in the house, apart from us.' Eric's eyes narrowed with interest. 'Or maybe there's someone else getting into the house that we don't even know about.'

Jenna shivered. 'That's even creepier than a ghost making the knocking sounds.'

'Don't you worry,' said Simon, wrapping an arm around her. 'I'll protect you.'

'I know you will, my hero,' she smiled back at him.

Tom pulled a face.

'Maybe we'll never have an answer about those knocks,' said Chris. 'It's just one of life's mysteries.'

'It's no mystery,' said Harmony, who was starting to recover. 'It was the spirits.'

Scepticism crept into his eyes and he just nodded, not wanting to be rude.

'There's more to it and I will find out what,' said a determined Eric.

'Why can't you accept that there's not always a rational explanation?' Gail asked her husband.

'Because, in my experience, there usually is,' he replied, jaw set. 'I've had too many bastards trying to pull the wool over my eyes and none of them have succeeded, so I'm buggered if I'm going to let whoever's making those knocks win.'

'As you wish,' she sighed.

'Remind me which room is above this one?' he asked Kate.

'Cameron's,' she replied.

'Mind if I check it out?' Eric asked him.

'Go for it,' he shrugged.

With that, Eric stormed determinedly towards the door. He jumped when he flung it open to reveal Marcus.

'May I help you, sir?' the butler asked dourly.

'What are you doing lurking there?' demanded Eric. 'You've been listening in on us, haven't you?'

'I was coming to see if anyone wanted coffee. I was about to open the door when you did it yourself.'

'I don't want any coffee. I'm off to do some reconnaissance.'

'As you wish, sir,' replied Marcus with an ironic bow, stepping aside to allow him to pass. Coolly he entered the room, seemingly untouched by Eric's anger. 'Can I get anyone coffee or brandy?'

'The brandy sounds smashing, pal,' said Harry cheerfully.

The butler's look said he wasn't surprised.

'Marcus,' said Chris. 'Is it possible that someone could sneak into the house without anyone knowing?'

'I suppose so, sir,' he replied as he furnished Harry with brandy. 'But I don't see why anyone would do that.'

'Your employer is a very famous woman who doesn't take her personal security seriously enough,' he added with a frown Kate's way.

'I've already said I'll contact someone to upgrade my security here,' said Kate with a casual wave of the hand.

'I keep thinking of all those people in the village who were asking for autographs,' said Jenna. 'It's possible one of them is a loon who would want to gain access to you.'

'Or the knocking was caused by a spirit,' said Harmony, who had recovered herself. 'Which it was.'

They all looked up when there was banging and thumping from above.

'It's the spirits,' exclaimed Tom, leaping to his feet. 'They're angry that we don't believe in them and they want revenge.'

'That's just Eric attempting to mimic the sound,' said Gail.

Tom blushed. 'Oh, yeah. I knew that,' he replied, retaking his seat.

'It doesn't sound like the knocks though,' said Lucy. 'It's too muffled.'

Two minutes later, Eric burst back into the room, red-faced and sweating. 'Well?' he said.

'Well what?' replied his wife.

'Did my knocking sound like the knocks during the séance?'

'No. They were too muffled and it was obvious they were coming from upstairs.'

'Damn. Then the trick must be being pulled by some other method.'

'Or it's just the spirits,' repeated Harmony.

'No offence, but I don't believe that for a moment.'

'That's your loss.'

Eric scowled at her before he began pacing the room while mulling over the conundrum. He pondered it all evening but failed to come up with a solution.

* * *

Kate jumped when there was a knock at her bedroom door later that night. Never in her life had she felt so nervous about a man before, and it dented her pride.

'Come in,' she called softly. She was sitting up in bed, the duvet covering her legs.

The door swung open and her heart thudded harder when it revealed Cameron. His head was tilted down slightly as he regarded her, and excitement as well as a little trepidation filled Kate. The man had undoubtedly changed. Shannon had made the seed of darkness inside him sprout. Now it was time to see exactly how it had changed him.

Cameron entered and closed the door behind him. Kate allowed the duvet to slip down, revealing the emerald-green silk negligee she was wearing that left very little to the imagination.

'Are you coming to bed then?' she said, her insides twisting with desire.

Cameron nodded and stalked over to the bed. He just wore black jogging bottoms and a black vest, which seemed to be his pyjamas. Pulling back the duvet, he climbed in beside her and Kate turned onto her side, so they were facing each other. Gently she pressed her palm to his face and leaned in to kiss him. Cameron seemed hesitant but she supposed that was understandable when only recently he'd been convinced Shannon was going to be his wife.

'Are you okay?' she said.

He nodded.

Kate knew it would be up to her to make the first move. At least he was here, which proved he wanted her. She knew that kissing him would either bring out his passion or send him running from the room. Praying it wouldn't be the latter, she pressed her lips to his. At first, he remained rigid and unyielding and for a terrible moment she thought she'd lost him. He stared back at her, as though surprised, before kissing her back, arms locking around her and pulling her close. Kate pulled his vest off over his head and he was everything she'd imagined and more. As he rolled her onto her back, already parting her legs with his knee, only then did she realise the raw strength in his body, the power. Every time she'd been with a man, she'd felt to be the one in charge and that she could drop him when she pleased, as though he was nothing more than a toy to amuse her, but this man was different. She wouldn't get away with such behaviour with Cameron. It made her feel powerless but simultaneously it was the most thrilling experience of her life. Here finally was the challenge she'd been seeking, the man to stand up to her. She'd thought she'd find it in the tough action men of Hollywood, but they'd all been total washouts. Here now in her arms was the one she'd been looking for her entire life, the man to complete her.

All thought that their family members occupied the rooms just down the hall went out of their heads until it was just the two of them together and the house, that ever-present sentinel bearing witness to this new union, to the one that would keep it safe and protected.

Cameron was slow and seductive yet harsh and commanding. Even in the darkness of the room, his black eyes were visible and penetrated her just as much as that other part of his body. He claimed her entirely, Kate yielding to another person for the very first time in her life, and she revelled in it. In the past, it had always been quite difficult for her to reach a climax, but Cameron's ministrations had her soaring to heights she'd never known before and she threw back her head with an ecstatic cry, raking her nails down his back as his body moved against her own. His grip on her tightened and for a moment she thought he was going to break her bones, but the tension eased, he let out a long low groan and his body relaxed. His dark eyes met her own light blue ones. Tenderly, he brushed the hair back off her face and kissed her.

'That was wonderful,' she purred, for the first time in her life feeling completely satisfied.

'It certainly was,' he murmured into her mouth.

With one last kiss, he rolled off her. Kate lay on her side to watch him, wondering if he'd get up and return to his own room. To her delight, he held out his arm and she nestled into him, their naked bodies pressed together.

'I think the others heard us,' she said.

'I don't care.'

'Really?' she said, raising her head to look into his eyes, needing to know that he wasn't just telling her what she wanted to hear.

'Yes. All my life I've behaved how others expected me to, worried about offending or upsetting someone. I've had a gutful of it. From now on, I do what I want and to hell with everyone else.'

'My thinking exactly,' she smiled. 'If I'd cared about what others thought, I wouldn't have gone near acting. I would have become a nurse or a teacher like my mother wanted me to.'

'I can't imagine you as either of those things. No offence, but you're not the nurturing type.'

'None taken. Besides, you're right.'

'What is this between us, Kate?'

For a brief moment, she couldn't answer, too caught up in the feel of his fingertips lightly running up and down her spine.

'What do you want it to be?' she said, propping herself up on one elbow. She wanted to look into his eyes and read the truth there. Too many men had told her what she wanted to hear just to get something from her, but she knew Cameron would always tell her the truth. There may be a new dark intensity to his nature, but his innate honesty remained.

'I want to see where this goes with us,' he replied.

'Even though you just broke up with Shannon?'

'Yes. Shannon was for the old Cameron. You're perfect for the new one, unless this is just a one-time thing for you?'

The old Cameron would have said that with a wide-eyed fear of offending her, but not this man. He just wanted to know where he stood.

'I'd like to see where it goes too.' She rolled on top of him and kissed him. 'You could extend your stay here longer than a couple of weeks. Spending some time together here alone will help us see if we really are compatible.'

One hand slid up into her hair while the other gently cupped her bottom. 'Sounds like a plan to me.'

'What about your gyms and shops?'

'I'm going to sell them. I'm getting a bit bored with it all. I want a fresh challenge and I think this project of yours is that challenge. I'll get a very good price for the businesses, so that will keep me going for a while. I have investments that give me a good monthly income. I won't need to worry about money while we prepare for this production.'

Kate loved his use of the word *we*. They were now a team working together and loving each other.

She'd left the window ajar to let in some air and the cool night breeze blew in, brushing up her spine, making her shiver with delight. Cameron's eyes followed the pattern of the goosebumps and his touch only increased their number, so exquisite to her it was almost painful. The air brought with it the scent of roses from the garden and the heady perfume filled her head.

'Why is it that Shannon already seems like a distant dream?' he whispered, cupping her face in his hands. 'You're my past as well as the present. It feels like you've always been there, that you've always been my reality, that we could never escape this moment. It was always going to happen.'

'Because it's true. I felt it the second you entered this house. Everyone says I'm obsessed with Robert but it's not true. I've just been dreaming of you.'

Cameron held her tight and kissed her. Kate thought how perfect this moment was. The sweet rapturous agony of it would be forever ingrained in her mind. Everything had come together at the right time – the house, the new production and now the man. There was nothing else she wanted, no other target to strive and connive for. She had assumed this thought would be depressing. After all, what was life without a dream to chase? But instead she was overjoyed. This was everything she'd been born for, everything fate had decreed she should love united at last. The hard work was over. Now it was time to enjoy the fruits of her labour. There was no need to worry about Cameron being on the rebound because she knew he would never leave her. They were bonded in blood and love and nothing could separate them now.

23

'Where is he?' yelled a voice. 'I want to see him.'

The sound caused Kate to jump awake and she raised her head.

'What's that?' she mumbled, brushing her hair back off her face. She turned to look at Cameron, who was still asleep beside her, his pale skin making him look like a marble statue carved by a master. One hand rested on his chest, his other arm wrapped around her. Ignoring the cacophony of yelling, Kate admired the perfection of his being, his beauty. Even in repose, his inner strength shone through.

'Are they in here?' demanded the voice.

The bedroom door burst open and Shannon rushed in. She came to a startled halt when she saw Kate sitting up, naked apart from the duvet wrapped around her and Cameron splayed out on the bed beside her.

'Oh my God,' she breathed, eyes filling with tears. 'This was what you had planned all along, wasn't it?'

Kate's response was a slow, wicked smile.

'Sorry, Kate, we tried to stop her,' said Jenna, rushing in behind Shannon along with Lucy and Harry. She took in Cameron laid on the bed and her eyes widened. 'Bloody hell.'

'What is it?' said Simon, who was unable to get into the room because of the others blocking the door.

'Never mind,' said Jenna, steering him out into the hallway before he could glimpse a naked Kate.

Cameron finally woke and it took him a moment to realise what was going on. 'Shannon?' he yawned, rubbing one eye with the heel of his palm and squinting. 'What are you doing here?'

'I wanted to talk to you and resolve things but I'd no idea you were going to jump into bed with your own cousin.'

Kate watched Cameron carefully, wondering if he'd weaken now the thieving shrew was back, but his dark eyes remained cool and aloof.

'We've nothing to discuss,' he told her.

'That's not true. I know we can get past this, Cameron.'

'I've already told you it's over. Why can't you accept it?'

'Because I still love you. Please come downstairs so we can talk in private.'

'No. You should go, Shannon.'

'I'm not leaving without you.'

Lucy gently took Shannon's arm. 'I understand you're upset but this isn't helping. Come downstairs and have some breakfast, give Cameron a chance to get dressed.'

Shannon looked back at Cameron, who just regarded her with contempt. It was hard to believe this was the same man who just a couple of days ago had asked her to marry him and had told her he loved her more than anything. It was like looking back at a stranger.

'I'm too late,' she rasped, tears spilling down her face. 'She's already sunk her claws into you but I still hope to bring you back from the brink. You don't know what she's done,' she cried, pointing at Kate.

'What has she done?' replied Cameron, his expression indicating he thought Shannon was simply making up lies.

Shannon's gaze met Kate's and she saw the warning there. If she revealed her secret, then she wouldn't pay her any more money. It was a risk coming back here because Kate might decide to cut her off completely, but she had to do it. If she got Cameron back, she wouldn't care if she lost the restaurant.

'I'll wait for you downstairs,' she sighed resignedly.

Lucy and Harry followed Shannon from the room, closing the door behind them.

'Are you sure you don't want to go and talk to her?' Kate asked Cameron.

He gazed down at her, drinking in those incredible blue eyes, the alabaster skin, the magnificent breasts heaving against his chest. 'I've never been more sure of anything in my life.'

* * *

Jenna and Harmony attempted to keep Shannon company while she waited for Cameron, but she paced from room to room, unable to rest, anxiously wringing her hands. Even Harry felt bad for her and tried to distract her with his usual banter, but she ignored him, so he soon gave up. Gail and the others had already made themselves scarce, electing to enjoy the morning sunshine in the garden, knowing it was best to keep out of Kate Alardyce's dramas. Lucy was the only one without any sympathy for Shannon, hating her for taking advantage of Cameron, so she stayed out of her way.

After half an hour, Jenna also gave up her efforts, tiring of following Shannon about the house, but Harmony remained a stalwart friend, attempting to use her counselling skills to help, but she couldn't get Shannon to open up.

Shannon just happened to pass the bottom of the stairs as Cameron and Kate descended together, holding hands. He looked impossibly handsome while she was even more radiant. Bile rose in Shannon's throat as she waited for them to reach the bottom. Already they were laird and lady of the manor.

'Can we talk now?' said Shannon grudgingly, hating having to beg.

'I suppose,' replied Cameron. He turned to Kate and kissed her cheek. 'I'll meet you in the dining room.'

She smiled and winked at him, giving Shannon a dark look as she turned and strode away, her long light cream dress flowing out behind her, the matching high heels clicking across the tiles.

'Let's talk in here,' said Cameron, gesturing to the parlour door.

They both entered, Shannon desperately trying to gather her thoughts as she slowly closed the door behind them.

'Well,' he said. 'I'm waiting, and make it quick because I'm starving.'

'This isn't like you, Cam. Can't you see that she's changed you? You were never so cruel before.'

'Cruel?' he replied, arching an eyebrow. 'Cruel is stealing fifty thousand pounds from someone you claim to love. You're the last person to cast that particular stone.'

'I thought the last time we talked you seemed so different because of the shock of finding out what I'd done, but now I see it's because you're not the man I fell in love with. That's not because of what I did, it's because of what she's done to you.'

'Kate's done nothing except support me and give me the opportunity of a lifetime. I should be thanking you, Shan. What you did set me free. Before I was always so desperate to please everyone, terrified of causing offence, but you made me see that no matter how hard I try, people will always use me and hurt me, so why bother? All the old neuroses and anxiety that have plagued me since I was a child have gone. I tied myself up in knots being nice to people, hoping they wouldn't call me fat and bully me, but they did it anyway. That fear has haunted me my entire life and finally I'm rid of it. So, thanks for that, Shan.'

She was stuck as to how to reply. He looked so different to her Cam with his cold black eyes and haughty manner.

'What are you doing?' she said when he walked to the door.

'Leaving. I've nothing else to say to you.'

She ran to him and threw her arms around his neck. 'Don't go, please. I miss you so much,' she sobbed.

He pushed her back by her shoulders and held her at arm's length. 'You need to get this into your head – we're done. I don't want to see or speak to you again. I can't make it any clearer.' He thrust his face into hers and Shannon recoiled from those black eyes.

'You need to leave this place before it takes you over entirely. The Alardyce curse still lives and you're the carrier. Do yourself a favour and go back to Glasgow while there's still something good left inside you.'

With that, she hurried from the room, feeling his eyes on her. It made her nervous to turn her back on him and when she glanced over her shoulder, she saw he was watching her but there was nothing of her Cameron left. Kate and this place had stolen everything that was decent inside him and obliterated it.

With her head held high, she exited the parlour and strode towards the front door. Harmony, Harry, Jenna, Simon and Lucy were waiting there.

'Are you leaving already?' Harmony asked her.

Shannon nodded, swallowing down her tears. 'Yes. I'm wasting my time. My Cameron doesn't exist any more.'

Kate chose that moment to appear at the other end of the hall. Her painted red lips curved when she saw Shannon was leaving. The two women's eyes met and everyone watched as a silent battle was waged between them. The moment was interrupted by Cameron, who strode past Shannon without a single look and went up to Kate.

'Shall we have breakfast now?' he asked her.

'I'd love to,' she replied.

He held his hand out to her, which she accepted, and the two disappeared in the direction of the dining room without a backwards glance.

Shannon's chest heaved and fresh tears spilled down her face.

'Oh, Shannon. I'm so sorry,' said Harmony, genuinely stricken. No matter what she'd done to hurt Cameron, she didn't think she deserved such cruel treatment.

'It's okay,' she said, forcing a smile. 'Don't worry about me, I'll get over it but if I were you, I'd leave this place before it consumes you too.'

With that she departed, leaving them to glance at each other in confusion.

'Well,' said Harry as they watched Shannon climb into her car and drive away, sending up a spray of gravel. 'What do you make of that?'

'I've no idea,' replied Jenna. 'But I'm more concerned about Cameron and Kate. What the hell do they think they're doing?'

'It's none of our business.'

'Hopefully it'll fizzle out in a few days,' said Lucy. 'And it's to be expected, I suppose. Two gorgeous people stuck together in this house.'

'Aye, you're right,' said Jenna. 'It's just a lust thing. It can't last but we should still have a word.'

'Take it from me, no good will come of interfering,' said Harry. 'They're both adults, so they can do what they like.'

'Harry, you should really speak to Cam,' Jenna told him. 'He'll listen to you.'

'No, he won't and I am not getting involved. It's his life, so leave him to it. I'm going for a walk in the garden.'

With that, he strode out of the front door, refusing to look at any of them in case they tried to engage him in that conversation again.

'If he won't do it then one of us needs to tackle the situation,' said Jenna determinedly.

'I'm with Harry on this one,' said Lucy, already following her cousin out the door. 'I'm not getting involved.'

Jenna looked to Harmony. 'It's down to us then.'

'I don't feel it's my place. I'm not family.'

'But you are a counsellor and that could be useful.'

'They won't listen to us.'

'Then we'll just have to make them listen. Your skills could make all the difference.'

'I don't know about that.'

'They helped me and Simon, so they'll help Cam and Kate, and don't forget – I'm an Alardyce too, so I can be just as stubborn as them.'

'Okay, we can try, I suppose,' Harmony slowly replied.

'Good. There's no time like the present.'

The two of them headed into the dining room, Harmony reluctantly trailing behind a determined Jenna, who flung open the doors. Cameron and Kate were sitting together at the table eating and talking.

'Right, you two,' said Jenna, storming in and standing before them, hands on her hips. 'We need to talk.'

'About what?' replied Kate.

'What do you mean about what? This,' she replied, gesturing to them. 'What do you think you're doing?'

'Well, I'm having fruit and yoghurt and Cameron's having porridge.'

'Stop winding me up, Kate. I'm not in the mood. You're cousins.'

'Yes, we know. Was there anything else?'

'Aye, there is. Cameron's just come out of a very serious relationship. The last thing he should be doing is jumping straight into another one with you.'

'That's for Cameron to decide.' Kate turned to him and put on her most sultry expression. 'What do you say, Cam? I'm willing to wait if you're not ready.'

He leaned back in his chair, looking cool and impervious to Jenna's pleas. 'I'm more than ready. Shannon's already in the past for me and Kate's my future.'

'You're not thinking straight, you can't be,' replied Jenna. 'Only a couple of days ago you said you were going to marry Shannon.'

'I was wrong, she wasn't the right woman. I've found her now.'

'And what happens when you get over the trauma of the break-up and realise you're wrong about Kate, that everything you felt for her was just a way of getting over the loss of your relationship with Shannon?'

'That won't happen.'

'How can you be so sure?'

'Because I've changed. I'm no longer the old Cameron.'

'Rubbish. You've just had a shock. You'll soon be back to your normal self once you've got over it.'

'No, I'm finally my true self after years of hiding it and I'm not going back to how I used to be.'

Jenna shuffled awkwardly when Cameron continued to stare at her after making this statement, making it very clear that she was intruding and should leave.

'That's a shame,' replied Jenna, asserting herself. 'Because I really liked the old Cameron.'

'You mean the obedient doormat who always bowed down to what everyone else wanted and ignored his own needs? You might have liked him, but I didn't. He was making me miserable. This is the new me, so you'd better get used to it.'

'This isn't right. How is it that your personality's changed so much in such a short space of time?'

'Like I said, this is who I've always been but I've only just let him out, and if you don't like him then blame all the arseholes who bullied me over the years.' His eyes narrowed. 'Including Harry.'

'I'm sorry you went through all that, Cam, it must have been so distressing, but such a sudden personality shift can't be healthy. Harmony's a counsellor, so she agrees.' When Harmony didn't reply, Jenna glanced over her shoulder at her and was surprised to see the woman was staring at Robert's portrait with wide eyes. 'Hello, Harmony?'

This roused her from her stupor and she looked to Cameron and Kate. 'Sorry to disturb you,' she said before rushing out.

Now she was left alone with them, Jenna was a little unnerved by the way Cameron and Kate just stared at her, indicating her presence wasn't wanted. 'I'll go and see what's wrong with her,' she told them, glad of the excuse to leave.

Jenna exited the dining room and hurried after Harmony, who was rushing down the hall towards the front door.

'Wait,' she called, having to break into a jog to catch up. Jenna grabbed her arm, halting her in her tracks. 'What's wrong with you?'

'Didn't you see how much Cameron looks like the portrait of Robert?' demanded Harmony, eyes still wide and startled.

'That's nothing new.'

'Before it was superficial, but now he's like him in every way. He even has the same cold, calculating look in his eyes. What Simon said was a prophecy – the man in the portrait has come alive.'

'What absolute crap. You need to pull yourself together.'

'It's not crap. The message at the séance was true – Cameron is dangerous and he's going to hurt Kate.'

'I don't believe in messages delivered through séances. That man never hurt anyone in his life, he's a gentle soul.'

'He's different now, he said it himself, and it's not safe for Kate to be around him. Shannon was right, we should all leave before something bad happens. I'm going to find Harry and get the hell out of here.'

Harmony ran to the front door. She yanked it open and screamed when she saw an enormous man standing there, hand raised.

'Sorry, madam,' he said politely, lowering his hand. 'I didn't mean to startle you. I was just about to ring the bell.'

'Do yourself a favour – get back in your car and drive away as fast as you can. This place is cursed.'

The man watched with a puzzled frown as she raced past him outside.

'Don't mind her,' Jenna told the visitor. 'She's... weird.'

'Not to worry, I've met all sorts in my line of work.'

'What is your line of work?'

'Personal security. I'm here to see Kate Alardyce.'

'Come in and I'll let her know you're here.'

'Thanks,' he smiled, stepping inside.

He was very tall, standing at six and a half feet with a square jaw and a buzz cut. His suit was tailored and expensive. He removed his sunglasses to reveal lovely hazel eyes.

'And what's your name?' she said flirtatiously.

'Aaron Campbell.'

She held her hand out to him. 'I'm Jenna. It's lovely to meet you.'

'You too, madam,' he replied, shaking her hand.

'Does Kate want to hire you to protect her?'

'I'm afraid I've yet to establish that.'

'If she does, I'm sure you'll do a wonderful job,' she purred, eyes running up and down him appreciatively. 'You look so strong and capable.'

'Oh, you think so, do you?' said an angry voice.

Jenna turned to see Simon standing at the bottom of the stairs. He stomped up to them and took Jenna's hand firmly in his own.

'Listen, you,' he told Aaron, waggling his finger in his face. 'This is my wife, so keep your mitts off. Got it?'

'Yes, sir,' he replied.

'Good, because if you don't, I'll get very angry.'

'I can well imagine.'

'Right,' said Simon, frowning at him suspiciously. 'I'm glad we got that sorted. Come on, Jenna,' he told her.

'Where are we going?' she said when he led her to the stairs.

'I'm going to remind you why I'm your husband,' he retorted, jaw set.

'Oh, Simon,' she smiled.

Marcus emerged from the background and approached the visitor.

'Mr Campbell?' the butler asked him.

'Aye, that's me.'

'I'll inform Ms Alardyce that you're here. She's just at breakfast.'

Marcus vanished, leaving Aaron hanging around in the hallway, studying the impressive décor. Kate emerged a minute later with a welcoming smile accompanied by Cameron.

'Mr Campbell, thanks for coming,' she said, extending her hand to him. 'We can talk in the study.'

'I'll head into the village,' said Cameron, kissing her cheek. 'See you later.'

'Bye,' she replied, watching him go admiringly before turning to her guest. 'This way, please,' she smiled, gesturing to a door down the hall.

'Thank you.'

Aaron followed her into the study and they took their seats either side of the desk.

'My family and friends have been nagging me to up my personal security,' she began with a wry smile. 'They think I'm too isolated out here.'

'They're right but I see from your expression that you don't agree?'

'I've never had any problems before.'

'Then you've been very fortunate. I've worked for many people in your position and sometimes fans can get carried away. I noticed the only form of security you have is an alarm and I'm willing to bet that isn't set every night.'

'It is when I'm on my own but not at the moment with all the guests in the house.'

'Has anything specific occurred to make you think you need more security? Have there been any threats?'

'No but...' She sighed and shook her head. 'This is going to sound ridiculous.'

'You won't be able to shock me, madam. Believe me, I've heard it all.'

'Very well and please, call me Kate. Anyway, one of my guests is a talented medium and she suggested we hold a séance. During two of the séances, loud knocks were heard. Some of the party thought it was spirits and some thought it was someone playing a trick. As everyone was accounted for, one of my friends suggested someone had snuck in and caused those bangs. This is a large house and it would be pretty easy for someone to get in without me knowing.'

'You're right, it would. I can fully upgrade your security.'

'It would be nice to know that no one could get in unless I wanted them to.'

'That shouldn't be a problem. Is this a listed building?'

'Yes.'

'That makes things a little awkward but far from impossible. I've worked on plenty of listed buildings before.'

'You did come highly recommended,' she replied with her most charming smile. She didn't usually go for the GI Joe types but Aaron was pretty impressive, although he was certainly nothing compared to her Cameron. She smiled inwardly at the thought. *Her* Cameron. How perfect.

'That's good to hear,' said Aaron. 'Any chance I could take a look around?'

'Help yourself. You have free rein.'

'May I advise against giving strangers free rein of your home?'

'But I called you in.'

'And for all you know, I'm not Aaron Campbell. You haven't asked to see my ID or called my office to ascertain that I am who I say I am.'

'You've got me there,' she smiled.

From his pocket, he produced his professional licence. 'You need to ask for identification from everyone, apart from people you're very familiar with, of course.'

'Noted,' she said with a chastened nod. Kate certainly wasn't the type to allow herself to be told what to do; in fact, she positively bristled against it, but there was something very commanding about this man. And it would be stupid to ignore the advice of the professional that she herself had called in.

24

Cameron strolled into the village, wondering where to visit. He hadn't come here for any particular purpose, he'd just wanted to get out of the house before his cousins started to nag him about his burgeoning relationship with Kate. That was the best thing in his life right now and he didn't want that lot spoiling it.

None of the shops appealed. He wasn't one for browsing without any definite purchase in mind. Instead, he found himself drawn back to the church, or more particularly, the graveyard.

The scattered petals from the roses they'd placed on the graves were decaying, fading in colour and curling in on themselves. He felt that was what was happening to this family reunion. It had started out happily enough, but various events had occurred to contribute to its rapid decay – the séances accompanied by the odd knocks, the message saying he was a danger to Kate, the mess with Shannon followed by him and Kate getting together. He could understand why his cousins would think it odd, but it felt right to him. It wasn't a rebound relationship; there was a special, secret bond between them that he'd never felt with anyone else. Kate had helped make him stronger, fiercer, more himself while Shannon had wanted to keep him a weak child.

Once again, he was drawn to Robert's grave, the man he was emulating more and more. Would that have happened had he not been rehearsing to play him in Kate's production? Had that been the catalyst to this sudden change inside him? Whatever the reason, he was glad it had happened.

'Cameron?'

He turned to see the vicar making his way towards him.

'I thought it was you,' smiled Paul. 'I was tidying up in the church when I saw you from the window. It's very propitious that you've come as Betty has a gift for your family.'

'Really, what?'

'I don't know, she wouldn't tell me and she insists on placing it in the hands of a member of your family personally. I was going to phone Alardyce House but now you're here...'

'I can take it.'

'Wonderful, thank you. Is now convenient?'

Cameron nodded. It wasn't like he had anything better to do.

He followed the vicar down the lane to Betty's sprawling bungalow. Once again, they were shown in by the amiable Claire.

'I'm glad you've come, Vicar,' said Claire. 'She's been quite down today. A visit from you always cheers her up.'

They followed her through to Betty's room and found the old woman watching Die Hard 3 on the television that was mounted to the wall opposite her bed. Despite all the action, she looked bored and depressed. Her eyes lit up when she saw her visitors.

'Hello,' she beamed, using the remote control to pause the film. 'I'm glad you've come, I'm so bloody bored. Not even the lovely Mr Willis can cheer me up,' she added, nodding at the screen. 'Anyway, that's not your problem. Cameron, I've got something for you. Claire, go in the wardrobe, will you? On the right you'll see a walking cane,' Betty told her. 'Take it out and give it to Cameron.'

'I think you could use the walking cane more than me,' Cameron told Betty while Claire rummaged around inside the wardrobe.

'This is something your gran gave to me years ago to look after. She didn't want her own family getting their hands on it because she said they wouldn't appreciate it and would probably throw it out. I've looked after it all these years because Connie entrusted it to me but I'm nearing the end of my own life, and I don't want to pop my clogs before it's in the hands of its rightful owner. I want you to give it to Kate. It belongs to her now.'

'I will,' he replied, wondering what Kate would make of a walking cane.

'Here we go,' said Claire, producing a beautiful carved oak cane with a silver-topped handle. It was clearly antique but had been very well looked after, the silver gleaming.

'I polished it regularly,' said Betty, as if in answer to his thoughts. 'Your gran told me this cane belonged to Henry Alardyce, Robert's stepfather. He used it his entire life and after he died, his wife Amy used it to feel closer to him.'

Cameron took the cane from Claire and studied it in fascination. It was quite something holding such a personal item of his ancestors.

'I appreciate you taking such good care of it all this time,' he said.

'It's the least I could do. Connie was a good friend to me. She was the only person who didn't get offended by my big mouth.' Betty sighed and leaned back into the pillows. 'I feel better now that's done. I would have hated to die and for the vultures who constitute my family to swoop in and sell it. Now it will be cared for properly.'

'I'll go straight back to Alardyce House and give it to Kate. She'll be made up.'

'Good. Connie did say she was the rightful guardian, but she didn't dare give it to her when she was younger because she knew Kate's parents would have got rid of it.'

'I don't understand why they hate our family's past so much. Aye, parts of it are bloody and violent but it's not all terrible. There were some nice parts.'

'I think they resented the effect it had on Connie. She was obsessed by it and they were worried about that obsession taking over your generation too. Sometimes the dead never really leave, they stay in people's memories, in their very bones, and some people find that frightening.'

'Perhaps,' he murmured, recognising that was how he'd been feeling lately.

'The key is not to let them take over,' she winked. 'If you do that, you're fucked.'

'Betty,' chided Claire. 'Have you forgotten the vicar's present?'

'Don't fuss. He's heard me say much worse.'

'It's true, I have,' smiled Paul.

Cameron managed to extricate himself from Betty's, eager to hand the cane over to Kate. He smiled as he imagined the look in her eyes; she would be so happy. He used it as he walked back to the house though only when he was on the grass, not wanting to scuff the cane, but he did want to see how it felt. Henry must have been a bit shorter than himself as he had to lean over slightly to use it.

As he walked, Cameron pondered on the fickleness of his feelings. His entire life had turned around so quickly, but everything felt like it had fallen into place, as though the old had been entirely swept away and replaced by the new with very little trauma to himself.

He entered the house and found it empty, apart from Marcus, who was tidying up in the dining room.

'Where is everyone?' Cameron asked him.

'I believe some of the guests are in the garden, some are taking a walk in the woods and Mr and Mrs Fairchild have driven into the village.'

'Kate?'

'She's currently escorting Mr Campbell around the house,' he replied while continuing to efficiently clear the table. 'The last time I saw them was in the conservatory.'

Cameron headed into the conservatory but no one was there. He hastily left as that room still had the ability to make him feel uneasy. Next, he decided to try the study. He walked in and through the window saw Kate talking with Aaron outside in the garden. The conversation seemed rather furtive and jealousy immediately welled up inside him.

He rushed to the door, flung it open and strode outside. 'What's going on?' he demanded.

'Cameron,' breathed Kate, rushing up to him. 'I'm so glad you're back. Aaron found something terrible when he was surveying the house's security.'

'What?' he said with concern.

'Spy cameras in almost every room in the house.'

'Spy cameras?' He looked to Aaron with a frown. 'Are you sure?'

'Absolutely,' he replied. 'The majority are in the light fittings of the overhead lights.'

'Including my bedroom and all the bathrooms,' Kate told Cameron.

He gazed into those tear-filled blue eyes before pulling her into his arms, holding the cane in one hand. She trembled against him as she fought to keep in all her fear and emotion.

'Who the hell would plant cameras here?' said Cameron. 'Could it have been a previous owner?'

'I don't think so,' replied Aaron. 'All the equipment's brand new.'

'But...' He trailed off, thrown by this turn of events. 'I can't believe it. Who the hell would do this?'

'That's what I intend to find out. I can track the signal the cameras are emitting but I need a specific piece of equipment to do it. A colleague of mine is on his way over with it.'

'How easy is it to install these cameras? Would it take a lot of time?'

'No time at all, sir, if you know what you're doing. Whoever installed them is definitely comfortable with this technology. It would have taken a couple of minutes at the most to plant each camera.'

'Meaning anyone staying here could have done it?' Cameron realised they were both looking at him. 'It wasn't me,' he said.

'We don't think that for a moment,' said Kate, taking his hand. 'Out of them all, you're the only one I trust right now.'

'I can't imagine any of them doing anything so demented. I mean, why would they?'

'Jealousy is a powerful motivator,' said Aaron. 'It wouldn't be the first time I've seen it. Kate's a rich woman, which brings a lot of possibilities in and of itself.'

'You mean someone could be gathering information about her finances? Are these cameras listening devices too?'

Aaron nodded solemnly.

'And they're in every room, even all the bedrooms?' said Cameron, a cold, creeping feeling washing over him.

'Yes,' said an appalled Kate.

Cameron thought of everything he'd done with Kate and Shannon, things that had been witnessed by some unidentified spy, and his stomach rolled over. 'When I find out who it is,' growled Cameron, 'I'll tear their fucking head off.'

The way his eyes darkened thrilled Kate and she leaned into him. 'I know you will.'

'I strongly advise against that,' said Aaron. 'Once the culprit is identified, it would be better to hand them over to the police.'

'And have it all come out in the papers?' frowned Kate. 'I don't want a bunch of nosy journalists reporting on the fact that someone put cameras in my bathroom. I'll never live it down. No, I can't have the police involved. I'll handle it personally.'

'It might not be that easy.'

'I know whoever's responsible. They're either family or a friend.' Her voice cracked and tears filled her eyes but inside she didn't feel the fear or hurt she was displaying, only cold, hard rage, but she could never resist the opportunity to perform. 'I can't believe this,' she rasped before burying her face in Cameron's chest, loving the feel of his arms around her.

'My man should be here within the hour,' said Aaron. 'Until he arrives, I suggest you both remain outside the house. With your permission, Kate, I'll go back inside and do some more looking around.'

'Yes, go ahead,' she replied in an exhausted voice.

'Thank you,' he said before striding back inside.

'Are you sure you can trust him?' Cameron asked her.

She raised her head to look into his eyes. 'Yes, I think so. He was recommended to me by a couple of friends he's worked for. Why?'

'He could be telling you all this to scare you.'

'I don't think so, he's shown me some of the cameras.'

'Maybe he snuck in without anyone knowing and planted them himself?'

'It's possible, I suppose, but I don't see why he would bother. Besides, the man's a professional. His reputation is second-to-none and he's been in this game nearly fifteen years.'

'I don't doubt his credentials but if he is harvesting information on another client's behalf then it's the perfect cover. Maybe he wanted you to turn to him and all these cameras are just a way to get you to trust him?'

This statement gave Kate pause for thought. 'Maybe, but I really don't think it's likely. Besides, he told me the fact that there was a camera in my bathroom says this isn't just about gathering information about me. It's something worse, something perverted.' She shivered. 'It makes me feel sick.' Finally, she noticed the cane he held. 'What's that?'

'Something that will cheer you up,' he smiled. 'Henry's walking cane.'

He watched as her eyes lit up and she reached out a slightly shaky hand to take it from him.

'You're sure?' she said.

'Absolutely. I bumped into the vicar in the village and he said Betty wanted to talk to a member of our family and, seeing how I was there, would I mind going. So I went with him and she gave me this. Gran gave it to her years ago to look after. She was worried that our parents would throw it away if they got hold of it. Betty said Gran told her that after Henry died, Amy used it to feel closer to him. Gran said you were the rightful owner.'

'I know this cane,' she breathed, staring at it in wonder. 'Jane wrote about it in her diary.'

'What are you doing?' he said when she began tugging at the silver top. 'Careful, you might break it.'

'No, I won't. It's just a bit stiff because it hasn't been used in years.'

Cameron's eyes widened when she yanked off the top and out came a sword attached to the inner part of the handle. 'Jesus,' he breathed. 'I'd no idea that was in there.'

'This sword has a bloody history.'

'Why am I not surprised?' he said wryly.

'Amy killed an intruder on the estate with this,' she said, staring at the gleaming blade in fascination.

'She did?'

'Oh yes. She was attacked first; she was only defending herself. I wonder how it ended up with Gran?'

'God knows and I don't think we'll ever find out. I remember hearing about that story, but I didn't know Amy had used that to do it.'

'You were right, Cam, this has cheered me up. I'll keep it close. It could come in useful.'

'I hope you're not thinking of stabbing someone with it?' he said, raising an eyebrow.

'That all depends on the bastard who planted those cameras,' she said, eyes narrowing as she stared at the blade, seemingly hypnotised by it. Kate shook herself out of it and slid the sword back into the cane, giving the top a little twist to ensure it stayed in place. 'Don't tell anyone else about this. I want to keep it between us.'

Cameron nodded. 'If you like.' He took her face in his hands. 'Are you sure you're okay? This must have come as a hell of a shock.'

'I'll be fine, I always am,' she replied with a forced smile.

'You're so strong. Most women would have been in hysterics.'

They kissed, arms locking around each other, Kate still holding the cane in one hand.

At the sound of someone clearing their throat, they turned to see Harry standing there.

'What are you doing?' said Kate icily.

'Oh, nothing. Don't get me wrong, it doesn't matter to me if you want to get together, but it does to certain other people, especially Jenna.'

'So?'

He shrugged. 'No reason. I just thought you should know, although from what I heard when I nipped upstairs to my room, Simon's doing a great job of distracting her from her worries. Well, I'll leave you to it. Me and Harmony are going to have lunch in the village. I want to spoil her a wee bit; she's in an odd mood. Well, see you later.'

They watched him wander off with his hands in his trouser pockets, whistling a happy tune.

'How long was he standing there?' said Kate as they watched him go.

'No idea,' replied Cameron.

'You don't think he could have planted the cameras, do you?'

'As much as I hate to say it about my own cousin, he could have. He's always been a bit of a perv and we know he has money troubles. If I had to choose someone out of us all, he'd be the one I'd pick.'

'Me too,' said Kate, narrowing her eyes thoughtfully, her grip on the cane tightening.

25

Cameron and Kate had to wait another two hours for Aaron and his friend to finish checking the house, so they walked through the gardens together, hand in hand, talking and learning as much about each other as they could. Kate constantly checked Cameron for signs that he was pining for Shannon, that she was indeed just a stop gap while he recovered from the shock of their relationship ending, but he seemed relaxed and happy and he was always touching her, whether his arm was around her or he was holding her hand. They snuck into the woods to make love up against a tree after which Kate received a call from Aaron saying he needed to talk to her.

They returned to the house, their time together making Kate feel much more able to face what was to come. Aaron was waiting for them in the study with his colleague, Oliver, who was just as big and square-jawed as he was.

'Bad news, I'm afraid,' said Aaron. 'Whoever set up the cameras really knows what they're doing because they're using something that scrambles the signal so we can't track it. All we've managed to confirm is that it's definitely coming from inside the house. I recommend that you leave for a few days until we can track the signal to its source.'

'No way,' retorted Kate. 'This is my home and this creep is not chasing me out of it. You've no idea how long I've waited to live here.'

'Don't be so hasty,' Cameron told her. 'Whoever's doing this could be dangerous. You've got the rest of your life to spend in this house. A few days is a sacrifice worth making for your safety.'

'Very well put, sir,' said Aaron.

Kate stared up at Cameron, hurt in her eyes. 'I can't believe you said that. You know what this house means to me.'

'Of course I do but God knows what this prick's end game is. What if he wants to hurt you, or worse? How will you enjoy the house then?'

Cameron thought he was actually getting through to her, until anger creased her face.

'I'm going nowhere.' She looked to Aaron. 'Track him down and when you find him, rip his spleen out. I'm going for a lie down.'

With that, she stormed towards the stairs.

'I'll talk to her,' Cameron told the security consultants before rushing after Kate.

At the top of the stairs, he saw her stomp into her bedroom and slam the door shut. Before he could follow, Tom stepped out before him.

'Cameron, I need a word,' he said.

'It'll have to wait.'

'Actually, it can't.' Tom placed himself in his way, jaw gritted.

Cameron was a little puzzled by the aggression in his tone. Where was that coming from?

He looked from him to the door of Kate's room and wondered if it would be best to let her calm down a bit first before talking to her. 'All right, but make it quick.'

'It'll be as quick as I say it'll be,' growled Tom before stalking into his bedroom, Cameron following.

Once they were both inside, Tom slammed the door shut and rounded on him. 'I don't know what you think you've got going on with Kate, but you'll stop it right now.'

The steely glint in his eye and the tension in his body came as a surprise to Cameron. There was absolutely no sign of the buffoon he'd thought this man was. 'What?' he frowned.

'Now listen you,' said Tom, jabbing a digit in his face. 'The only reason I came out to this godforsaken place was for Kate and it's the only reason why I agreed to do her weird TV programme.'

'You're in love with her, aren't you?'

'Finally, the penny drops. I've been after Kate Alardyce ever since I met her five years ago and I'm going to get her. I won't let some freak of a cousin get in my way.'

Cameron stared at him in amazement. 'You really are an incredible actor, aren't you? The cowardly idiot doesn't exist, but why put on the charade? The man you really are would have appealed to her much more than that arsehole.'

'I planned to get close to her during filming. We have a couple of hot sex scenes together.'

'That still doesn't explain why you've been playing the fool with her.'

'I had no choice,' he snapped. 'I've put on this persona for so long everyone thinks it's really me.'

'Then why start it in the first place?'

'I did it so Eric would give me a part that turned out to be my breakout role. He wanted someone non-threatening, so I played the fool, only that meant I had to keep up the pretence otherwise he'd realise what I did, and Eric Fairchild can finish people in this business.'

'Wait – what about that night you freaked out and ran into Simon and Jenna's room?'

'That was all part of the ploy too.'

Cameron's smile was mocking. 'No, it wasn't. You really did see something in here and you got scared.'

'You haven't a clue what you're talking about,' he snarled back defensively. 'I'm going to let Kate see the real me and I know that when she does, she'll fall for me as hard as I fell for her.' His expression hardened again. 'So you can just fuck off.'

'I'm going nowhere.'

'You don't deserve her, you're just using her. Only recently you were going to marry another woman.'

'You know nothing about it,' he growled.

'I know enough. You're on the rebound. Soon you'll dump her and I won't let you hurt her.'

'Oh aye, and what are you going to do about it?'

Tom shoved him back against the wall. 'Don't fuck with me, Cameron. I've had training you wouldn't believe.'

Tom was knocked off his feet when Cameron headbutted him and he fell to the floor with a cry.

'That's a little something I picked up in Glasgow,' he said coolly.

Tom was far from out. He looked up with a snarl. 'Bastard,' he yelled.

He leapt to his feet and launched himself at Cameron. The two men started to grapple, Tom finding Cameron a more difficult prospect than he'd anticipated.

The door burst open to reveal Kate. 'What the hell's going on?'

Tom immediately retreated back into buffoon mood. Cameron found the way all that anger and determination was wiped from the other man's eyes a little eerie.

'He attacked me,' cried Tom, pointing at Cameron. 'And for no reason.'

'No reason?' he exclaimed. 'He's not what you think he is, Kate. All this harmless fool act is just that – an act. He's only doing it so he can get in your knickers and that's also the only reason why he's working on your production too.'

'How dare you?' said Tom, looking genuinely shocked. 'Kate is a colleague and friend and I'm part of the production because I believe in it. It's going to be huge.'

'Don't listen to him,' Cameron told her. 'He's a fraud. I don't know why he hasn't been given an Oscar because he bloody deserves one.'

'This is madness. You've got a screw loose,' Tom told Cameron. He turned imploring eyes on Kate. 'You know me, Kate, we've been friends a long time. You haven't seen this guy in years.'

She looked from one to the other in confusion, attempting to puzzle out what was going on, then she decided to stop trying.

'Idiots,' she sighed before leaving.

'Kate, wait,' called Cameron. He felt terrible. She'd just had a horrible shock, she was going through so much and here he was brawling with her friend. It was the last thing she needed. At least one person still managed to make him feel guilty.

'Leave her alone,' said Tom, grabbing his shoulder when he tried to go after her.

Cameron spun round, knocking his arm away. 'Don't you get it? She doesn't want you. If she did, she would have made it clear long ago.'

'You know nothing about it,' he hissed before driving his fist into his stomach.

Cameron dropped to the floor, panting for breath, an arm wrapped around his aching belly. All he could do was look up at Tom, who stared down at him with malice shining in his eyes.

'You're pathetic,' sneered Tom. 'And totally unworthy of her.'

Rage gripped Cameron, black and unforgiving. He hadn't felt it so strongly in a long time, not since he'd been relentlessly bullied at school and he'd fantasised about smashing in all their bastard faces. He'd lacked the courage back then because he'd been physically feeble.

But not any more.

The anger helped him overcome the ache in his stomach and he hurled himself at an unprepared Tom, who'd thought Cameron was down and out. Tom was thrown back against the wall but managed to block Cameron's fist when he attempted to punch him in the face. However, he was too slow to block the second blow, which caught him on the jaw.

There was the thunder of footsteps in the corridor outside but neither man cared, too caught up in the battle. Chris, Beauden and Eric burst in.

'What the hell do you think you're doing, you madmen?' cried Beauden.

Chris and Eric pulled the men apart while Beauden remained safely in the doorway.

'For God's sake, don't let them go,' he cried when Cameron and Tom fought to get back at each other.

'Why don't you help us then?' grimaced Chris as he struggled to keep hold of Cameron.

Jenna and Simon hurried into the room, Jenna buttoning up her blouse while Simon pulled on his T-shirt, their hair mussed up.

'Cameron, stop it,' cried Jenna.

She rushed up to her cousin and slapped him hard across the face. When those malicious black eyes were turned on her, she took a couple of steps back. Her courage reasserted itself and she tilted back her head. 'Calm down. Don't make me hit you again.'

This comment had the desired effect and the corner of his mouth lifted. 'I won't. I'd hate to endure that agony a second time.'

Jenna managed to raise a feeble smile. He'd sounded so cold and sarcastic. At least he'd calmed down though.

In response, Tom's anger also drained out of him.

'He attacked me,' he shrieked, pointing at Cameron. 'He's mad, he can't stand any other man being around Kate.'

'That's shite and you know it,' spat Cameron. 'It's all an act,' he told the others. 'He plays the fool because he wanted you to think he was harmless, Eric. It was something to do with you wanting someone non-threatening to play a certain part that turned out to be his breakout role. He's actually a vicious bastard and he acts like an idiot to put everyone off their guard.'

Eric's forehead creased as he considered these words before turning to Tom.

'It's all lies, honestly,' said Tom. 'He's making it up to get me out of the way because he thinks I want Kate when of course I don't. We're just friends.'

Tom strained his innocent look to the full when Eric continued to frown at him.

'Whatever you were arguing about, it's over now,' said Chris. 'Tom, I suggest you go and take a walk.'

'Yes, that's a good idea. I need some fresh air after being attacked.'

'You might want to get some ice for your nose while you're at it,' said Beauden. 'It's all swollen.'

'What?' he exclaimed before rushing to the mirror hanging on the wall. Tom was appalled to see his nose was indeed swollen and bright red, dried blood crusted around the left nostril. 'Bastard,' he yelled, glaring at Cameron through the glass, who smiled with satisfaction. 'I could have you done for assault.'

'No one's prosecuting anyone,' said Eric. 'Now, I suggest the two of you stay away from each other. Do you hear me?'

Tom and Cameron both nodded.

'Good.'

Cameron left the room and headed to Kate's bedroom. He knocked on the door.

'What?' she snapped.

He opened the door and entered to find her staring out of the window. She glanced at him before turning her attention back to the view.

'I take it you and Tom have finished fighting?' she said icily.

'We have,' he replied, coming up beside her. 'But he's been left with a swollen nose.'

'Good. It might bring his ego down a peg or two.'

She spoke without looking at him and this fact drove him a little crazy. 'It's true what I said – he's been putting on an act to get you to trust him.' He leaned in to whisper in her ear, conscious of the fact that the camera in this room was still in place. 'It's possible he's the one who planted the cameras.'

'I know.'

Cameron sighed with frustration. 'Why won't you look at me?'

'I'm going through so much and you're fighting with that prick.'

'He gave me no choice. I was only defending myself. He wants you, Kate. He said the two of you have a few sex scenes together in this production and he's going to take advantage of that.'

Finally, she turned to look at him, a smile in her eyes. 'You're jealous.'

'Aye, I am,' he scowled, folding his arms across his chest. 'The thought of the two of you together drives me mad.'

'You don't need to worry about that walloper.'

Cameron regarded her with surprise. It was the first time during this reunion that he'd heard her drop into her native Scottish accent or even use the lingo.

'He's perfect for playing Henry, but that's all he means to me,' she continued. 'He's just a means to an end.'

'Not according to him.'

'Tom always did have an overinflated opinion of himself. I'm only interested in him for his acting ability. Does that reassure you?'

'Not really,' he replied, scowl deepening.

Kate enjoyed his jealousy. She slid her arms around his waist. 'You've nothing to worry about, you're ten times the man he is.'

He smiled and pulled her to him. 'Good, but you should have seen him, he was a totally different man. It made me wonder if he planted those cameras.'

Her smile dropped. 'I suppose it's possible.'

'I didn't want to mention it in front of him. If he is responsible, then it's better he doesn't know he's been rumbled.'

'You're right, although I think we should tell Aaron.'

'I agree, as soon as possible. How can you stand to be in here knowing there's a camera watching you?'

'No matter where I go in this house there could be one, and I repeat – this creep is not driving me from my home.'

He kissed her. 'I understand.'

Hand in hand, they headed back downstairs together in search of Aaron. They found him and Oliver searching the conservatory.

'We found a second camera in here,' Aaron whispered to them. 'Over there, in the corner close to the door.' As he spoke, he constantly looked around.

'Are you okay?' Cameron asked him.

'Aye but…' He sighed. 'This is going to sound stupid but the entire time I've been in here, I've felt someone's been watching me. I know it's not my imagination because Oliver's felt it too and neither of us are the type to let our imaginations get the better of us.'

'It's not your imagination, we've all felt it.' Aaron and Oliver regarded her with surprise but decided it would be better not to comment.

'I've just had a run-in with Tom Drake,' Cameron told the two men and went on to relate the incident. 'What do you think?' he asked them when he'd finished.

'I'd say it sounds very strange,' replied Oliver, speaking for the first time in a voice that was surprisingly light and gentle for a man of his proportions.

'Me too,' said Aaron. 'I think we should have a word with him.'

He nodded to the door, indicating for them to step outside, which they did.

'We also need to search the guest bedrooms,' continued Aaron once they were in the garden, out of range of any camera. 'This is a very complicated system, so whoever set it up will be running it from some form of technology.'

'Like a phone?' said Kate.

'No, that sort of device wouldn't have enough memory. They would need a laptop. This is a huge house and there are cameras everywhere, each with its own individual feed.'

'I can imagine a few of the guests kicking off about having their rooms searched,' said Kate.

'And we would need their permission. We have no right to go through their things without it. The police, however…'

'No police,' said Kate firmly. 'I want you and Oliver to handle it.'

'As you wish, madam,' he said, looking not very happy with this order. 'Then there's no choice but to confide in all the guests.'

'And if anyone doesn't let you search their room then you know they're the guilty one,' said Cameron.

'I'm afraid it's not as clear cut as that, sir. People can be very protective of their personal space and property. Just because someone objects doesn't mean they're guilty.'

'Eric will object,' said Kate. 'He goes berserk if anyone touches his stuff.'

'Surely he won't when the situation is so serious?' said Cameron.

'He might but it's the only thing we can do.' She turned back to Aaron. 'Very well, you have my permission to explain the situation. How will you tackle it?'

'I think it would be best to gather everyone together in one room. That way no one can warn anyone else before I can approach them and neither can anyone slip away. I would however like to speak to Tom before the others. If he is the culprit, then it will save us some time.'

'Okay,' said Kate. 'Shall we come with you?'

'No thank you. Me and Oliver can handle it.'

'The last I saw him, he was upstairs looking at his bust nose in the mirror,' smiled Cameron.

The two men left. Cameron took Kate's hands when she let out a long, shaky breath. 'You okay?'

'Yes. I'll just be glad when this is over.'

'You could use a whisky.'

She nodded and allowed him to lead her out of the conservatory. As they passed the stairs, they heard Tom's outraged voice drifting down to them, yelling at Aaron and Oliver that they had no right to search his room.

They entered the drawing room to find all the other guests had gathered together. The door had been left open, so they'd heard every word Tom had said.

'What's going on?' Eric demanded of Kate. 'Why do those two ogres want to search Tom's room? Is it because of his fight with Cameron?'

'It's nothing to do with that,' replied Kate, running an agitated hand through her hair.

'Then what is it?'

'I can't tell you yet. Aaron and Oliver will be down shortly. They'll explain.'

'Who are they?'

'Security consultants. I asked them here to upgrade my security. Let's just say they found something that shouldn't be here.'

'What?'

'As I said, they'll explain. Thank you,' she told Cameron when he handed her a glass of whisky.

'Then I'll go and ask them myself,' said Eric, storming to the door.

Cameron placed himself before him. 'You're staying right here.'

'Get out of my way.'

'No.'

Eric was a man used to getting what he wanted at a click of his fingers, so he wasn't sure what to do when this man refused to obey. Cameron's eyes were doing that disturbing thing again where they darkened and filled with malice, and Eric knew that if he tried to push it then he'd end up with a bloodied nose too.

'Sit down, Eric,' said Gail. 'Just wait like Kate asks. I'm sure they won't be long.'

This statement allowed him to retreat from the situation with his dignity intact. 'Yes, you're right. Sorry, Kate.'

She nodded absently in response.

'The ogres must have got their way,' said Harry. 'Tom's stopped his whining.' He looked to Harmony when she shuffled from foot to foot, arms wrapped around herself. 'What's wrong?'

'The energy,' she replied. 'It's changing, getting heavier. There's danger here.'

'There's no danger,' he said, sliding an arm around her shoulders. 'You're probably picking up on how tense everyone is.' He frowned at Eric when he snorted derisively.

'No, it's more than that. There's evil in this house. Something terrible's going to happen.'

Everyone regarded each other mistrustfully. As they recalled the result of the last séance, a few eyes slipped Cameron's way.

They waited in silence for Aaron and Oliver to arrive, Cameron and Kate keeping themselves apart from the rest of the group, the former studying them all one by one, attempting to work out who the culprit was.

The two security officers arrived ten minutes later.

'Nothing in Mr Drake's room,' Aaron quietly told Kate, who nodded.

'Are we finally going to be told what's going on?' demanded Eric, rising to his feet.

Aaron looked questioningly at Kate, who nodded.

'Very well.'

They all listened in astonishment and not a little horror as the man explained the situation.

'Do you mean to say that someone's been spying on us, watching everything we do in our most private moments?' said an appalled Jenna.

'I'm afraid so,' replied Aaron.

'Oh my God.'

Everyone started talking at once. There were shrieks and tears and not a small amount of swearing.

'Shut up,' yelled Cameron.

Silence instantly filled the room and they all turned to look at him.

'This isn't about you,' he continued. 'It's about Kate. This is her home, the one she's dreamed of her entire life, and someone's invaded it in the worst way possible. We will find who's responsible and believe me when I say they will fucking pay.'

Everyone looked down at the floor to avoid his furious gaze.

Kate decided it was time she asserted herself. 'Aaron and Oliver want to search all your rooms for the source of the cameras.'

'And I dare any of you to object,' growled Cameron.

'Why would we object?' replied Beauden. 'I for one am nothing to do with this terrible event, so feel free to search my room.'

Left with no choice, everyone mumbled their assent, even Eric.

'Thank you,' said Aaron. 'I recommend you all stay here while we conduct our search.' He looked to Cameron. 'Don't let anyone leave.'

'They won't,' he replied, regarding the room with hard eyes.

Aaron and Oliver left to conduct their search.

'Kate, I'm so sorry,' said Jenna, rushing to embrace her. 'This is horrible.'

The rest of the women congregated around her, hugging her and passing on their commiserations.

'Aaron and Oliver will find who's responsible and then I'll pay some nasty sods I know to break every bone in the bastard's body,' she told them.

'Sounds like a plan to me,' said Harry, raising his whisky glass in a toast. 'Surely it can't be one of us though? We're in a large country house. That means the butler did it,' he grinned.

Cameron's eyes widened. 'Of course.'

Harry's smile fell. 'You mean you haven't considered Marcus?'

'We've been thinking about the guests.'

'Marcus wouldn't do anything like that,' said Kate. 'He's far too straight-laced. Besides, he's also my bodyguard. You saw how he handled Noah.'

'Think about it,' Cameron told her. 'He lives in this house and he has access to every area. He's even been alone here, giving him all the time in the world to plant those cameras. And he used to be a marine, meaning he probably knows how to set up all that spy equipment.'

'That is logical, but I can't believe it of him. I mean, why would he bother?'

'Maybe he's obsessed with you?'

'He's never shown any sign of it.'

'Where's his room?'

'Top floor in the converted attic.'

He kissed her cheek. 'Back soon. Harry, with me. The rest of you stay here.'

'An adventure,' smiled Harry, putting down his whisky glass. 'How exciting.'

He hurried after Cameron, the two men rushing upstairs, Harry lagging behind his more athletic cousin.

'Hang on,' panted Harry as they ascended the second flight of stairs to the attic.

'There's no time,' Cameron called back over his shoulder.

Harry paused halfway up to catch his breath while Cameron burst through the door before them. The room was large, two of the old servants' rooms having been joined together to make a single larger space. The room was clean and comfortable but entirely functional, lacking ornamentation of any kind apart from a few photographs of what appeared to be Marcus's family and another of him in military uniform.

As Cameron flung open the wardrobe doors, Harry staggered into the room, panting and sweating.

'God, I hate stairs,' he groaned.

'Check under the bed,' Cameron told him before delving into the wardrobe.

'I'd rather lie down on it,' he sighed before kneeling beside the bed and peering under it. 'Nothing, not even a speck of dust.'

'Then check the rest of it.'

Harry got to his feet and pulled back the duvet, which wasn't an easy feat as the edges had been tucked mercilessly tight into the sides. He then flipped the mattress onto the floor. 'Still nothing.'

'Put everything back and check the bedside table,' called Cameron as he thrust aside the neatly ironed clothes hanging from the rail.

'I'd no idea this adventure was going to be so exhausting,' sighed Harry.

He attempted to remake the bed so it looked undisturbed, but his bed-making skills were nowhere near as honed as Marcus's and it still looked a rumpled mess, no matter how much he tried to smooth it out.

'He'll never know,' he said wryly before turning to the bedside cabinet.

The two men completed their search and were disappointed.

'Nothing,' said Harry. 'It looks like my theory was wrong. Sorry for wasting your time.'

'Don't apologise, it was a good theory. Let's check the rest of this level just to make sure.'

They checked the old servants' rooms, but all were empty, completely bare of any furniture, so there was nothing to search. They returned to the drawing room, disappointed. Tom had joined the rest of the guests and he glowered at Cameron when he entered.

'Well?' demanded Kate the moment they entered the room.

'It seems your butler is innocent,' said Harry.

'That's a relief,' she breathed. 'I didn't think it could be him.'

'Which means it's one of us,' said Lucy, her thoughts once again slipping to the Alardyce curse. Was there a psychopath hiding among their number?

'I've been thinking about that,' said Eric. 'Could someone from the village have planted the cameras? After all, you do have your fans there, Kate.'

'It's possible I suppose, but Aaron and Oliver seemed to think whoever did it has been staying here.'

'Anyone could have snuck in and planted them. You leave all the doors unlocked most of the time.'

'I hope it is someone from outside the house,' said Gail. 'In fact, that must be it. None of us would do this to you, Kate.'

They went silent when the door opened, but it was just Marcus. 'It's eleven o'clock,' he said in his usual staid way. 'I thought you might like some tea.'

'That would be wonderful, thank you,' smiled Kate, so relieved her loyal retainer hadn't betrayed her.

'Very well, madam,' he said before leaving.

She turned back to face the room, eyes jumping from each loved face, knowing for certain that it was one of them. She didn't believe the theory about someone in the village for a moment. One of them was responsible and whoever it was, she would make them suffer.

26

It took Aaron and Oliver almost three hours to complete their search, by which time the guests confined in the drawing room were beginning to get short tempered with each other.

'Well?' Kate demanded of the two men the moment they entered the room.

'Nothing, I'm afraid,' sighed Aaron. 'We've searched the house from top to bottom, even the storage rooms. Wherever the feed from the cameras is being transmitted to, it isn't in here. We've disabled all the cameras, so you don't need to worry about being watched any more. If whoever's responsible wants to activate them again, then they'll have to physically go around each camera and I can't imagine them doing that now everyone's aware of them. I wondered if we could have the key for the crypt? We need to start searching the grounds now. It's possible an outbuilding's being used. We've called in a couple more of our people to aid in the search.'

'Certainly,' she replied. 'I'll fetch it for you. It's in the study.'

'I'll come with you,' said Cameron.

'Can we finally leave this room?' demanded Eric. 'I need to get outside before I go stir crazy.'

'You can leave the room, but you need to remain in the house until we've finished searching the grounds.'

'This is ridiculous, you can't keep us prisoners here, you're not the police.'

'You're right, we're not, but leaving will only make you look guilty.'

Kate returned with the key for the crypt and handed it to Aaron.

'Thank you,' he replied. 'Remember,' he told the others. 'You can move about the house but you must stay inside.'

The group hastily broke up, eager to escape each other's company while Aaron and Oliver headed outside to search the grounds. Soon only Cameron and Kate remained in the drawing room.

'I thought they'd never leave,' said Cameron. 'I don't want them here any more. I want it to be just the two of us getting to know each other properly.'

Kate smiled and slid her arms around his neck. 'So do I but I can hardly throw them out.'

'You won't have to. Once this is over with the cameras, they'll leave voluntarily.'

'We can but hope. Why don't we go to bed? It's safe now the cameras have been disconnected.'

'There's nothing else I'd rather do.'

They rushed upstairs together, hoping they didn't encounter anyone, which they didn't, and locked themselves in Kate's bedroom.

This time she took the lead, needing to vent some of her tempestuous emotion. She could be a very hard woman, but the discovery of the cameras had shaken her deeply. Kate practically shoved him onto his back on the bed and sat astride him, tearing down his jeans. Cameron gazed up at her, revelling in how powerful she looked.

'Oh, God, Cam,' she cried as she took him inside her.

He reached up to unfasten the front of her dress but she did the job for him, tearing it off over her head and casting it aside, her bra following suit. Grabbing his hands, she placed them on her breasts, throwing back her head as she moved.

After stroking her sleek body, he moved his hands higher, caressing her face. She looked almost ethereal, as though she wasn't really here, the result of some wild, beautiful dream that could vanish in an instant. A presentiment of dread crept over him and he pulled her down to him, kissing her and holding on to her tightly as she continued to move. Pleasure swept through him like a cleansing tide, eradicating the dread, the force of it so potent he whipped her onto her back and thrust up into her hard several times, her nails digging into his back as they both came.

'I feel so much better,' she purred as Cameron flopped onto his back, panting.

'Me too,' he smiled, holding his arms out to her.

Kate curled into him, resting her head on his chest. 'We belong here together, Cam.'

'Yes, we do,' he said, kissing the top of her head.

They dozed off in each other's arms for an hour. When they awoke, they showered together, dressed and headed back downstairs.

'Ah, there you are,' said Beauden when he encountered them at the bottom of the stairs. 'Would you like to do some more work together, Cameron? We should take every opportunity.'

'You may as well,' Kate told her lover. 'I've some work to do in the study.'

'You shouldn't be on your own,' he replied.

'He's right,' said Beauden.

'Fine. Then you can rehearse in the study with me.'

'Excellent idea. I have the scripts with me,' said Beauden, holding them up.

The three of them entered the study and Kate went to work on her laptop, making some adjustments to the script while Beauden put Cameron through his paces. Kate found herself a little distracted, smiling as her lover perfectly emulated the cold, calculated menace that Robert Alardyce had possessed. She could see that Beauden was once again a little intimidated by his performance, backing up as Cameron advanced on him while reciting his lines.

Marcus announced that lunch was ready and Beauden breathed a sigh of relief.

'You okay?' Cameron asked him.

'Yes,' he smiled back. 'It's just that you can be rather frightening.' His smile faltered as he recalled that whatever they had communicated with during the last séance had said Cameron was a danger to Kate. He glanced at his friend, who had closed the laptop and got to her feet.

'Something wrong?' she asked him as she took Cameron's hand.

'No,' he said, voice a little higher pitched than normal. 'I've just realised how hungry I am.'

'Then you'll be pleased to hear that I've ordered your favourite for lunch – rack of lamb.'

'Lovely,' he replied, following them out of the room while watching them carefully.

Cameron gazed at Kate with nothing but adoration. The man certainly didn't seem in imminent danger of attacking her, but Kate was very fickle with men and could drop them at a moment's notice. She'd left a trail of broken hearts in her wake. What if she did the same to Cameron and he didn't take it very well?

Sensing he was being watched, Cameron glanced back at him over his shoulder and Beauden found himself staring right into the hard black eyes of Robert Alardyce.

* * *

'Are they still searching the grounds?' said Jenna as she stabbed at a potato with her fork.

'They are,' replied Kate. 'Aaron assures me they'll only be another hour.'

'Then we can go out again?'

'Yes.'

'Good. Me and Simon wanted to invite you all for dinner at the village pub, on us of course. We've just confirmed that we're going to sell the holiday park for a really great price.'

Everyone congratulated them both and agreed that dinner would be very nice.

'Does anyone want to join in our billiard tournament after lunch?' said Harry.

'Why not?' smiled Eric. 'I was a demon at the game in my younger days. I'll thrash you all. To make it more interesting, how about we place bets?'

'It's a rule of mine never to bet against someone who's just told me they're really good at the thing we're going to be betting on.'

Chris grinned at Eric. 'Big mouth.'

All the guests piled into the billiard room to watch the tournament. Even though they'd been starting to grate on each other's nerves, they wanted to stick together in light of the revelation about the cameras.

The tournament ended with a tense game between Tom and Eric, which the former won, to the producer's consternation.

'Do you think Mrs Clapperton will let me get a snack from the kitchen?' Cameron asked Kate. 'Or will she try and hit me with a rolling pin?'

'Don't worry, you'll be safe,' she smiled. 'She won't be back to prepare for dinner as we're eating out tonight.'

'I'll come with you,' said Simon. 'I noticed she'd made some scones and I'm going to sneak a couple.'

'On your head be it if she finds out,' replied Kate.

'She doesn't scare me. Anyway, if she does realise, I'll just blame Tom. Let her batter that prick with her rolling pin.'

'I won't be long,' Cameron told Kate. 'Stay with the others, won't you?'

'But I need to do some more work in the study and you'll only be gone a few minutes.'

'And one of these people has been spying on you,' he whispered in her ear. 'Please, stay safe.'

'I'll ask Marcus to keep an eye on me. We know for certain that he's innocent. Does that make you feel better?'

'Yes, it does. Thank you,' he said, kissing her.

'You're a lucky bugger,' Simon told Cameron as they headed towards the kitchen. 'You're shagging Kate Alardyce.'

'Have you forgotten that you're married to Jenna?'

'No, and I love her to bits, but I can still admire other women from afar.' Simon's expression darkened. 'She was drooling over that arsehole Tom long enough.'

'You're right, he is an arsehole,' replied Cameron as they entered the spotless kitchen.

'Right,' said Simon, clapping his hands together noisily. 'Where do you think that mad cook will have stashed the scones?'

'I've no idea,' replied Cameron. 'I don't even know how to open the cupboard doors.'

'I'll start with the pantry.'

Simon wandered into the pantry while Cameron picked up a clean glass that had been left on the draining board and poured himself some water from the tap.

'Victory,' smiled Simon, emerging from the pantry holding a plate of scones covered in cling film. 'Now I just need a plate.'

They both stared at all the closed cupboard doors minus their handles helplessly.

'There's a casserole dish,' said Cameron, gesturing to the draining board. 'You could put them in that.'

'It'll have to do,' he replied, placing the scones on the counter beside the sink and carefully removing the cling film.

'I could use some fruit,' said Cameron, heading into the pantry.

'Why would you want fruit when you can have one of these bad boys?' replied Simon, gesturing to the scones.

'If I eat one of them I'll bloat up like a balloon.'

'I suppose I'm lucky being a string bean. I can eat what I like and not put on any weight.'

'Smug git,' commented Cameron, making him chuckle.

* * *

Kate was on her laptop, making some tweaks to the script. Now she'd seen Cameron playing Robert she had a much better idea of how he would have sounded, so she was making a few alterations to his lines.

So engrossed was she in her work that she barely registered the knock at the door.

'Come in,' she replied distractedly, a little annoyed by the interruption.

Marcus entered and closed the door behind him, a carrier bag dangling from one hand. 'Sorry to disturb you, madam,' he said, 'but I've got something very important to show you.'

'What is it?' she replied, leaning back in her chair, curious. Marcus looked even more serious than usual. In fact, his expression could be described as worried, something she'd never seen in him before.

'I overheard some of the guests discussing the most recent séance and apparently Cameron was named as a danger to yourself during it.'

'I wouldn't pay much attention to that.'

'I was concerned so I decided to do some investigating. I knew Mr Campbell and his associate had already checked Cameron's bedroom, so I took his car key from his room to search his vehicle.'

'You had no right to do that,' she frowned.

'I'm sorry, madam, but I've only your best interests at heart. Part of my duty is to protect you.' He produced a laptop from inside the carrier bag and placed it on her desk. 'I found this.'

'So? Everyone has a laptop these days,' she replied casually in order to hide how this news had hurt and shocked her, but she refused to condemn Cameron until she'd seen the proof.

He lifted the lid and pressed a button. The screen burst into life to reveal an image of Kate's own bedroom.

She sat bolt upright in horror. 'Impossible. He wouldn't do that to me. Anyway, the cameras have been disabled, so how is this possible?'

'This is taken from a file that was recorded yesterday while you were all at dinner. The live feed has been cut. There are more files,' he said, tapping at the computer, bringing up images of the various rooms.

'I don't believe it. Cameron's not like that.'

'With all due respect, madam, you've not seen him in sixteen years. He's a virtual stranger.'

Kate was about to yell back at him that he was wrong, until she realised that he had a point. She didn't know her cousins any more. None of them were the children they'd once been.

'Whisky, madam?' said Marcus, taking in how pale she'd gone.

'Please,' she murmured, slumping back into her chair in shock. Tears prickled her eyes but she forced them away. Kate Alardyce did not cry when she was in trouble.

'Here,' he said softly, handing her a glass.

'Thanks,' she replied, taking it from him and downing the contents.

'Another?'

'No, I need to keep a clear head. There must be some mistake. I would never have believed Cameron capable of this. I mean, why would he do it?'

'Perhaps he's obsessed with you, madam? After all, he dumped his fiancée quickly enough, a woman he claimed to love and wanted to marry, when he found out you were interested in him. It's as though she never existed. It's not my place to say this, but I did find that a little odd.'

Kate considered how the others thought that was odd too. She also thought about all the violent, unstable people there had been in their family line. Cameron was doing an excellent job of portraying Robert even though he'd never acted before in his life. Was that because he was just the same as his infamous ancestor?

She flicked through the images stored on the computer, unable to stop a tear from sliding down her cheek when she saw the footage of herself wandering about her bedroom naked and in the shower. There was footage of all the guests on there but the only images that had actually been saved into their own folder, cherry picked from the hundreds of hours of video taken, were of her.

'What do you want me to do, madam?' said Marcus, whose expression was for once soft and sympathetic. 'Should I inform Mr Campbell and his associate?'

'Yes... No.' Kate sighed and pressed a hand to her forehead. 'I need to think. Just give me a minute.'

* * *

'There,' said Simon, carefully smoothing the clingfilm back over the remaining scones. 'Mrs Clapperton will never know.'

'Do you really think she'll forget how many scones she made?' replied an amused Cameron.

'Let's hope she's got a bad memory.'

The back door opened and a very stout woman in her early sixties with greying hair tied back into a bun bustled in. 'Hello,' she said cheerfully. 'I left one of my bags. It's got my wee nephew's birthday present inside...' The woman's alert brown eyes alighted on the casserole dish containing two scones, as well as the clingfilm-covered plate, and her jovial expression turned positively murderous. 'Who's been stealing my scones?'

'I... I've no idea,' said Simon nervously. 'We came in and they were just sitting there.'

'It was you, wasn't it?' she retorted, jabbing a digit at him.

'No, honestly. We just walked in and found them like this. Cam,' he called. 'Any idea who took the scones out of the pantry?'

'How did you know they were in the pantry?' said Mrs Clapperton, eyes narrowing.

Simon flushed bright red. 'Well, it's the logical place to keep scones.'

'You stole them,' she snapped.

When she advanced on him, Simon hastily backed up past Cameron, right into the pantry, eyes widening when he stumbled over a bag of potatoes and fell onto his backside.

An idea occurred to Cameron. 'Kate said you've worked here a long time, Mrs Clapperton.'

She rounded on him. 'Aye, I've cooked here for the last three owners. What of it?'

'Do you know of any secret rooms or passages in the house?'

'What the hell do you think this is, Cluedo?'

Cameron wondered if she was related to Maud at the vicarage. 'Something's been hidden in this house and I wondered if you might know where that could be. Did you speak to Aaron?'

'I've no idea what you're talking about. Hang on – do you mean those people who are wandering about the grounds?'

'Aye.'

'No. Why would I?'

'But they spoke to everyone in the house.'

'I didn't cook lunch. That was Rosie. I was off earlier because of a doctor's appointment.'

'Take it from me, you're the picture of health,' said Simon, getting to his feet and dusting himself off.

'Who's Rosie?' Cameron asked Mrs Clapperton. 'I've never heard of her before.'

'My niece,' she replied.

'Has she worked here before?'

'No, it was just today because I had my appointment,' she snapped, still on the defensive.

'Kate never mentioned her.'

'She probably forgot, I told her about it over a week ago. She doesn't concern herself too much with lowly domestic affairs,' she added a little scathingly.

'Does Rosie know this house well?' Cameron asked Mrs Clapperton.

'No. She's a good cook for a young slip of a thing.'

'So she wouldn't know about any secret rooms in the house?'

'No, because there aren't any. Well, apart from the storage area under the garage.'

'What storage area?'

'The garage was the site of the beautiful old stables, which were knocked down and replaced with that concrete monstrosity by the idiot who bought the place with his lottery money. He put a storage area under the floor for his expensive tools; he was paranoid about burglars.'

'Does anyone else know about this storage area?'

'Marcus does because he's always in there tinkering with a classic car Kate said he could keep in it. I walked past once and saw he had the hatch open.'

'Simon, let's go,' called Cameron before racing out the back door into the garden.

'Sorry, duty calls,' Simon told a frowning Mrs Clapperton, sidling around her and rushing outside after Cameron, glad of the excuse to escape.

27

'Have you made a decision, madam?' Marcus asked Kate when she'd been silent for a few minutes.

She nodded and got to her feet. 'Yes. I'm going to ask Cameron about it myself.'

'I don't think that would be wise. Perhaps I should tackle him for you?'

'I need to see the look in his eyes when I ask him. Only then will I know for sure.'

'It could be dangerous.'

'Cam would never hurt me.'

'Trapped rats often bite when cornered.'

'Don't call him a rat,' she frowned.

'Sorry, madam, I meant no offence, but for your own safety I think either myself or Mr Campbell are better off handling this.'

'I don't agree,' she said, moving towards the door.

He placed himself in her way. 'I can't let you do this. Part of my job is to protect you.'

'I don't need you to protect me, I can look after myself. Now get out of my way.'

'No,' he said firmly but politely.

'If you don't move, you're sacked,' she spat, her temper rising. She was also confused and a little scared. This wasn't like her loyal butler. Plus, there was something in his eyes that she didn't like.

'I'm doing this for your own sake. You mustn't speak to Cameron ever again.'

'Ever again? What are you talking about?' He stared at her in a way that made her very uncomfortable. 'Move, Marcus.'

He shook his head and folded his arms across his chest.

Kate made a sudden dart for the door, but he grabbed her and pulled her to him, so her back was pressed to his front. His hand clamped down over her mouth when she tried to call for help.

'I'm sorry, Kate,' he murmured in her ear. 'I can't let you do this. He's wrong for you.'

Kate's eyes bulged as she tried to take in just what the hell was happening.

'I've loved you from the moment I first saw you on the big screen,' he continued. 'I knew that one day we'd be together. I tolerated reading about your lovers in the newspapers, knowing that they were only temporary.' His hold on her tightened. 'Then Cameron came along and, for the first time in my life, I got scared.' Marcus buried his nose in her hair, making Kate cringe. 'I was afraid he'd take you from me and I won't let anyone do that. Come with me right now so we can finally be together and I promise I won't hurt him.'

Marcus removed his hand from her mouth and Kate fought the urge to scream for help. All the security consultants were out in the grounds and Cameron and Simon were in the kitchen, which was at the opposite end of the house. If no one else was in earshot of the study then she'd lose her only chance. She had to try and talk him down instead. Cameron wouldn't be long. As soon as he was done in the kitchen he'd come here. All she had to do was stall Marcus.

'Why did you never tell me how you felt?' she said gently.

'Because I couldn't bear to be rejected, not after what I went through in my divorce. I wanted you to get to know me and fall for me naturally. I thought if I made myself indispensable to you then you would come to love me. I've been watching you for the last two years, waiting for my moment. When I found out you were returning to Scotland and buying this house, I paid someone in the village to keep me up to date on all the latest news about you.'

'Who did you pay?'

'Rosie, the girl who cooks here. She's short of money. I leapt at the chance when she said you were after a butler.'

Marcus's grip on Kate slackened slightly. It wasn't enough for her to make a break for it and she had to be very careful because this man was highly trained. But he did loosen his hold enough for her to turn in his arms to face him, and she regarded him with those eyes that had captivated so many. 'You have made yourself indispensable to me,' she said, pressing her palm to his face. Just the feel of his skin against hers filled her with revulsion but she had to do this.

'You don't love me though,' he scowled. 'You love that wanker, Cameron, and all because he looks like a dead relative of yours. I don't understand.'

'I don't love him,' she replied with a cruel laugh. 'Haven't you realised yet that I'm just using him so he'll be in my production?'

Mistrust filled Marcus's eyes. 'Really?'

'Of course. Now Shannon's left there was nothing tying him to the project. He was only doing it to get some money for her. I had to come up with another way to force him into it.'

He ran his fingertips across her lips. 'I really would love to believe that, Kate, but you're forgetting – I've seen the two of you together through the cameras, I've heard what you've said to him. You're an amazing actress but that was all genuine. You've never looked at anyone else like you look at him, not even me despite everything I've done for you.'

'Were you the one making those knocking sounds during the séances?'

'What? No. I'd never concern myself with anything so ridiculous and I was a little disappointed that you did,' he said severely. Marcus's expression softened. 'But I forgive you. Now, let's go. We can leave through this window. It opens wide enough for both of us to climb out of, I've already checked. My car isn't far.'

'But... where will we go?'

'It doesn't matter as long as we're together,' he said ardently. 'But I was thinking Gretna Green where we could be married.'

'Married?' she said, realising the man wasn't just obsessed but completely mad.

'Yes.' He cupped her face in one hand. 'We were always meant to be.'

'O... okay,' she said, thinking if she climbed out the window first she could run into the garden and find Aaron or head back into the house to the others through the side door. It was her only chance.

'We're going to have an amazing life together. I've always known it. I watch your films constantly, I can recite them all line by line.'

'That's nice,' she said, forcing another smile. Kate felt her acting skills rapidly leaving her. This was just too freaky and she was struggling with the fact that she'd been living for weeks with a complete lunatic, but it was important she keep her head.

'I'll just grab my bag and phone,' she told him.

'No. You have to leave everything behind.'

'But I need them.'

'You can get them after we're married.'

'And how can I get married without any ID?'

'We'll cross that bridge when we come to it. Now let's go before someone comes in.'

Kate glanced at the cane containing the sword, which was propped up against the wall in the corner of the room, and wondered if she could grab it before he could stop her.

'Move,' he said, pulling her towards the window by one arm.

Kate fought against the panic wanting to rise inside her but she came from strong stock and refused to give in to it. 'You're hurting me,' she moaned.

'Sorry,' he said, holding her more gently. 'I really don't want to do that.' His expression hardened. 'But I will if I have to. Do you understand?'

Kate nodded.

With his free hand, he unlocked the window, pulled it open and looked out. 'All clear,' he said. 'I'll go first.'

As he clambered out, he was forced to release her. Kate attempted to slam the window shut but he threw himself back against it, pushing it open. There was a brief contest of strength, which Kate soon lost and she ran towards the door screaming for help. When she pulled at it, she was horrified to realise it was locked and the key was absent.

Marcus climbed back inside and closed the window.

'You tricked me, you bitch,' he spat. 'You don't want to marry me at all.'

'Of course I don't want to marry you,' she shrieked back. 'You're fucking insane. Oh, God,' she breathed when he drew a large, vicious-looking knife.

'This might sound like a cliché,' he said, 'but if I can't have you then no one can, especially not that prick, Cameron.'

'Help,' she screamed, banging on the door, but there was no response.

'They're all in other parts of the house,' said Marcus. 'No one can hear you.'

Kate's eyes alighted on Henry's walking cane and she ran for it. She cried out and fell to the floor when pain shot up her left leg. She was horrified to see the knife, which he'd just thrown at her, sticking out of the side of her left thigh.

As Marcus advanced on her, Kate scrabbled forwards, straining to reach the cane...

* * *

Cameron and Simon quickly found the hatch in the garage and flipped it open to reveal a dark pit.

'I can't see anything,' said Cameron.

'Here, there's a switch,' replied Simon.

He flicked it on and the pit turned out to be a concrete hole ten feet deep and seven feet wide. Inside were several monitors with cables leading from them, indicating they'd been plugged into something.

'Holy shit,' breathed Cameron. 'Harry was right, the butler did do it. We need to warn Kate.'

Together they tore back inside the house, calling Kate's name. The first person they encountered was Jenna passing the door into the conservatory.

'Where's Marcus?' demanded Cameron.

'Why?' she frowned.

'Because he's the one who planted the cameras. Where is he?' he bellowed at her.

'I haven't seen him since he cleared away the plates after lunch,' she said, eyes bright with worry.

Cameron turned and almost ran straight into Beauden.

'You said you were looking for Marcus?' said Beauden.

'Yes,' exclaimed Cameron. 'Have you seen him?'

'I saw him go into the study about ten minutes ago.'

'Oh, hell. Kate's in there. Simon, find Aaron and Oliver and tell them what's going on,' he added before breaking into a run, the others following.

'What is going on?' said Beauden.

'Marcus is the one who planted the cameras,' Simon called back over his shoulder before running outside.

'I'll get the others,' said Jenna.

Beauden followed Cameron down the hall. When the latter tried to open the study door, he found it was locked. Frantically he began throwing himself against it, Beauden anxiously looking on. Just as Jenna returned with Harmony, Lucy, Harry and Gail, the door finally gave way with a crack and Cameron staggered inside, followed by the others. They all came to a startled halt. Kate was lying on the floor, blood pooling around her from her many stab wounds while Marcus loomed over her clutching a large knife.

'Kate,' cried Cameron in horror. Fear clutched at his heart when she didn't react to the sound of his voice, her eyes closed, skin ashen, lips blue.

Then he felt the drop.

It was as though he'd fallen inside himself and he thought he would never stop falling into the darkness, that he would be lost in it forever. The sickening sensation made his stomach lurch and his heart pound, sending adrenaline coursing through his body. The tips of his fingers twitched as the rage rose up inside him, draping itself over him like a cloak.

The others looked on in horror as his pitch-black eyes seemed to roll back in his head, just as Robert Alardyce's had.

'You're fucking dead,' he hissed at Marcus before running at him.

'Cameron, stop,' cried Beauden.

But Cameron was beyond all reason. All he could think about was tearing apart this creature who had hurt Kate.

Marcus slashed at him with the knife, but he missed, so he immediately followed it up with a punch to the face with his other hand. He was shocked when Cameron barely noticed the blow. All Cameron needed was that hesitation and he grabbed Marcus by the throat and hurled him against the wall. Marcus was a little stunned by his strength, but he managed to keep hold of the knife. Cameron brought up his arm to block the blow when Marcus attempted to stab him in the neck.

With a bellow of anger, Harry charged into the fray and grabbed hold of Marcus's arm that held the weapon, pulling it back further from Cameron, but he was sent to his knees when Marcus kicked him hard in the crotch before kicking him in the face, knocking him backwards.

Lucy rushed to Kate's side to check her pulse.

'I'll call the police and an ambulance,' exclaimed Beauden, producing his phone with shaking hands. He was trembling so much he almost dropped it, jumping when Marcus and Cameron crashed into the desk.

'She has a pulse but it's very faint,' said Lucy, eyes filled with tears. 'It looks like she's been stabbed several times. I'll try to stop the bleeding,' she said, unwinding the light scarf from around her neck and pressing it to the worst of Kate's wounds. She started to cry when Kate failed to react to what must have caused her pain.

'They're on their way,' said Beauden, hanging up. He looked to Cameron and Marcus who were still struggling and was appalled to see Marcus had forced Cameron onto his back on the desk and was attempting to stab him in the face while Cameron pushed back with all his strength.

'Time to be a man,' said Beauden determinedly.

Looking around for a weapon, he saw a heavy silver-topped cane propped up in the corner of the room. He snatched it up and sneaked up on Marcus from behind, drawing it back, ready to strike.

Sensing his approach, Marcus turned his head and Beauden found himself paralysed by the intense hatred he saw in those burning orbs. Reasserting himself, he gripped the cane harder and swung it with all his might. Marcus threw himself sideways and the cane missed his head.

'How dare you hurt that lovely woman, you animal,' cried Beauden in outrage.

His courage started to fail when Marcus advanced on him, raising the knife.

Cameron snatched the cane from Beauden's hands. When Marcus attempted to stab him, he used the cane to block it. He then tore off the top of the cane and to everyone's astonishment produced a sword with a much longer reach than Marcus's knife, ramming the point of the weapon straight into his stomach. Marcus's jaw dropped open, cheeks draining of colour. Cameron twisted the blade, enjoying the way Marcus's body went into shock and began to tremble violently.

He withdrew the blade and Marcus dropped to his knees. Cameron raised the sword above his head, gripping it with both hands as though he was going to chop off his head.

'No, Cameron, don't,' cried Beauden.

'Give me one reason why not,' he growled.

'Because I don't want to see someone be decapitated. You'll traumatise me for the rest of my life. I wish I could give you a higher reason but that's all I can think of and quite frankly, that should be enough.'

Cameron hesitated before swinging the blade. Beauden shrieked and covered his eyes. When he failed to hear a squelchy thud, he removed his hands and saw Marcus had a slash to the left side of his face. There was the glint of steel and a second longer slash opened up across his chest. With a growl, Cameron let the sword drop, grabbed Marcus by the front of the shirt, dragged him to his feet and threw him across the room. He hit the wall hard and dropped to the floor, unconscious.

'Watch him,' Cameron told Beauden before racing over to Kate.

Beauden picked up the dropped sword and held it out before him. 'I can do this,' he told himself. 'I fenced at university.'

'Kate, can you hear me?' cried Cameron, throwing himself down by her side.

She didn't respond, although her eyes flickered behind the lids.

'Kate,' he yelled louder. The amount of blood on the floor and on Lucy's hands filled him with despair.

Aaron and Oliver crashed into the room followed by Simon, Eric and Tom, all of whom froze in their tracks at the shocking scene. There were demands to know what was going on, but Cameron ignored them, gaze locked on Kate as Aaron and Oliver rushed to take over giving her first aid, Lucy gratefully moving aside to let them work.

Aaron rolled up her top to assess the wounds.

'Jesus,' he said. 'There's at least seven stab wounds. We need to stop the bleeding.'

Cameron was heartened when Kate's eyes rolled open, the blue faded and dull.

'Cam,' she breathed.

'I'm here,' he said, taking her hand in both his own. 'The ambulance is on its way, just hold on.'

Her smile was weak but serene. 'I see them.'

'Who, sweetheart?'

'The family, they're here. All of them. They're waiting for me.' She stretched out one of her hands. 'Amy, Robert, Henry and the others.' A sob rattled in her throat, but it was one of joy. 'Gran's here too.'

'Don't look at them,' said Cameron desperately. 'I want you to look at me, okay? They're the past but your future's right here.'

'I don't have one,' she said, voice growing fainter. 'I never did.'

'That's bollocks, Kate. You do have one, with me.' He clung on tighter to her hand as he felt it begin to grow limp. Aaron and Oliver fought to stop the haemorrhaging, but blood continued pooling around her.

'This is how it should be,' she said. 'In this house, so I can finally be with them.'

'They're not having you,' he said, turning to face the space in the room where her gaze was fixed.

Harmony knelt beside him and pressed a gentle hand to her forehead. 'They're waiting for you, Kate.'

'No, they're not,' yelled Cameron, knocking Harmony's hand away. 'She's staying with us.'

Harmony slowly shook her head, a tear rolling down her cheek. 'She's dying, Cam, and she wants to go. Let her.'

'No. She's not going anywhere.'

Kate managed to drag her eyes off that empty spot in the room and onto him. 'It's okay,' she said, voice just a whisper. 'This is what I want.'

'No, it's not. You have to stay here and build a life with me. I love you, Kate,' he cried.

'I've been waiting to hear that,' she smiled. 'I love…'

Her eyes widened, her body jerked and blood filled her mouth, spilling down her chin before she exhaled, the sound rattling in the back of her throat. Cameron could only watch as her pupils retreated to pinpricks and her hand went limp in his own.

No one moved or breathed. The silence was the worst thing for Cameron. It was as though the entire world had come to a standstill. He felt lightheaded and a loud whine filled his ears. It passed a few seconds later and everything started to move again. Gently he lay Kate's hand on the floor beside her, her image blurring as tears filled his eyes. Aaron and Oliver began CPR but

Cameron knew it was fruitless. She'd gone to be with the people she really wanted to be with and she wasn't coming back.

Everyone watched as Cameron rose to his feet and wiped his eyes on the backs of his hands. He looked defeated, grief-stricken, so it was a shock to them all when his eyes suddenly blazed, lips curling back over his teeth. He whipped round to face Marcus, who was starting to come round. He strode over to an alarmed Beauden and snatched the sword from his hands.

'What are you going to do?' shrieked Jenna.

'Cut his fucking head off like I should have done earlier,' he retorted. 'Cover your eyes, Beauden.'

There were appalled cries and a scramble to reach him before he could carry out his threat. Tom made an attempt, still wanting revenge for his swollen nose, but Cameron headbutted him for a second time and he fell. The sword was torn from Cameron's hand and his arms were yanked behind his back.

'Let me fucking go,' he roared.

'No,' said Aaron while Oliver continued CPR on Kate. 'He'll go to prison for what he's done.'

'That's not enough. He needs to die.'

'The police are on their way, they'll deal with him.'

'Not harshly enough,' he grunted, still struggling to free himself, but Aaron was far too efficient at his job to let go.

They all heard the wail of approaching sirens.

'Thank God,' breathed Gail. 'I'll go and meet them.'

'I'll come with you,' said Jenna, rushing out of the room with her.

Harry, his left cheek swollen, knelt beside Kate and gazed at her sadly. 'I always had the feeling she would die young,' he said. 'There was something ethereal about her, like she wasn't quite of this world.' His tearful eyes met Cameron's.

'I can't believe this,' rasped Chris, who was shaking from head to foot.

'We should all clear the room,' said Eric, the leader in him kicking in. 'This is a crime scene and we don't want to contaminate it any more than we already have.' He looked to Oliver and sighed. 'She's gone. Why can't you leave her alone?'

'I'm not stopping until the paramedics get here,' he replied determinedly while continuing the chest compressions, sweat running down his face in his efforts.

Eric, unable to stand the sight any longer, grabbed Chris by the shoulders and steered him to the door. 'Let's clear out.'

Harry got to his feet and took Harmony's hand, leading her from the room. She was the only person who looked calm and serene. Beauden followed, pale and unwell.

Tom stared at Kate with a longing that would never now be satisfied. Slowly he trailed out of the room after Beauden.

'You should go too,' Aaron told Cameron.

'I'm not leaving her.'

'The police will send you out anyway and if you don't go voluntarily, they'll force you out. The family's been through enough without seeing that too,' he added more gently.

Cameron sighed. 'All right but don't you dare let that fucker get away,' he said, pointing at Marcus.

Marcus was still laid flat on his back, staring up at the ceiling, eyes hazy, his stomach stained red with blood.

Aaron released Cameron and he slowly left the room, pausing to look down at Kate's body. Her eyes were still open, but they didn't move, locked on that spot where she said she'd seen their dead relatives. An entirely new future had opened itself up to him and it had made him tremendously happy, only for it to be immediately taken from him.

How the hell did he move on from this?

28

SIX WEEKS LATER

Cameron stared up at Alardyce House, the place that had changed the course of his entire life. He was still reeling from everything that had occurred within its walls. Without Kate, the house had returned to its slumber. Whether it would ever wake again remained to be seen. He was now its new owner. To his surprise, Kate had left almost everything to him in her will, except a generous annuity to her mother. There had also been gifts to Harry, Jenna and Lucy which meant none of them would have to worry about money again. The ragged wound that had opened up inside Cameron the day Kate had been murdered was still healing. It would take years, but he was a patient man.

'What are you going to do with it?' said Lucy, who was standing by his side with Harry, Harmony, Jenna and Simon. 'I take it you don't want to live here?'

'God no,' replied Cameron. 'But I don't want to sell it either. Kate's will stated that she wished it to remain in the hands of our family. Thankfully she left enough money to keep it in good repair for years to come.' No one had realised that Kate had been a very astute businesswoman and had invested most of her money, the dividends of which were a fortune in themselves. Then there were the royalties and residuals from all her films, which was another few million a year. 'But neither do I want it to become an attraction for murder tourists. Anyway, a television crew wants to use it for six months to film a period drama.'

'What about Kate's script?' said Lucy. 'Will that still be made?'

'Eric and Chris said they'll go ahead with it. Kate loved the script, so they see it as her legacy. I won't be a part of it. They'll have to get someone else to play Robert. They can use the house for filming, so long as they don't go in the study. I've had it sealed up anyway.'

'That's good,' said Lucy, patting his arm. 'Very respectful.'

'Alardyce House will stay with the Alardyces, I'll make damn sure of it. No changes will be made to it either. The house will remain as Kate left it.'

'Quite right.'

As they talked, they all kept their eyes on the house, afraid that if they looked away, they would miss something important, although none of them could have said what that was.

'Did you sell the gyms and shops?' Jenna asked Cameron.

'Aye, and I got the price I wanted.'

'So what will you do now?'

'I thought I'd travel for a bit. I've always wanted to see China. I leave next month.'

'You're going alone?'

He nodded. 'I want to be on my own for a while. I don't know if I'll even come back to this country. I might settle abroad. The world's my oyster,' he said with a forced smile to disguise his misery. 'This country hasn't done me much good so far.'

'I'll miss you,' said Lucy.

He wrapped an arm around her and kissed the top of her head. 'I'll miss you too. You'll have to visit me wherever I get settled.'

'I'll hold you to that.'

'Good, and that applies to you all. I don't want to lose touch with you again.'

They all nodded even though they got the feeling this could well be the last time they'd be together.

'Did you get that house in Perth?' Lucy asked Jenna and Simon.

'We did,' replied the former. 'We move in next month and we can't wait.'

'Absolutely,' smiled Simon, sliding an arm around his wife's shoulders. 'A fresh start.'

'That's something we could all use,' said Harry. 'Thanks to Kate's generosity, we're able to finally open Harmony's holistic studio. We've found the perfect place and it's got a lovely flat above it, so we're moving in together.'

'That's nice,' smiled Lucy.

'I think Harmony's the one to finally make me grow up.'

'We can but hope,' smiled Harmony, taking his hand.

'What about you, Lucy?' Jenna asked her.

'I've been offered a job as historical consultant on the period drama being filmed here,' she said. 'I'm getting tired of being stuck in a dusty old office, running around after a dippy boss. It will be hard being in this house again, but I feel one of us should be around to keep an eye on it. There's a lovely cottage for sale in the village that Paul put me onto. I'm moving in next week. Edinburgh's close enough for me to work out my notice from here.'

'Kate would have liked an Alardyce living here again.'

'That's what I thought and I can make sure the family graves are always well tended. Call me the gatekeeper.'

'I've already hired people to caretake the house,' said Cameron. 'But I'll feel better knowing you're close.'

'I'll make sure it's safe and you never know – one day you might come back.'

'I wouldn't rule it out.'

'I know Kate wanted the house preserving,' said Harry. 'But in my opinion, it should be demolished, have done with it once and for all. I reckon it's the source of the Alardyce curse.'

'No, it needs to be preserved,' said Cameron. 'Because they're all still in there.'

'Who are?' said Lucy.

'All those who've already passed on. Kate saw them. They're still in residence and now she's joined them.'

The others decided not to voice their scepticism. If that helped him cope, then there was nothing wrong with it.

'You're right,' said Harmony, the only one who agreed with him. 'They are.'

As Cameron watched the windows, he was certain he saw movement there, as though people were moving about inside. A curtain was pulled aside and he saw chestnut-coloured hair, blue eyes, the wave of a hand and a radiant smile before the curtain fell back again. He couldn't be sure he'd imagined it. Perhaps it had just been the reflection of the trees waving in the breeze, but in his heart he knew it was more.

'Those knocks at the séance were right,' he said.

'What do you mean?' replied Jenna.

'They said I was a danger to Kate. Marcus wouldn't have attacked her if she hadn't started a relationship with me. She'd still be here now...' His face creased and he looked down at his hands.

'That's not true,' she said, placing a hand on his arm. 'Marcus would have still attacked her because she would have rejected him whether she'd been with you or not.'

'She's right,' Harry told him. 'There's only one person to blame for Kate's death and that's that bastard. At least we know he'll spend the rest of his life in prison.'

'And he pleaded guilty, so we don't have to go through the trauma of a trial,' said Lucy.

'He's not doing that because he's sorry,' frowned Cameron. 'He's only doing it because the evidence was so overwhelming.'

'Still, he's going to be put away for life and that's what's important,' said Jenna.

They lapsed into thoughtful silence, all staring at the house, recalling everything they'd been through in there.

'Looks like it's going to rain,' said Lucy, glancing up at the sky.

'Why don't we go to the pub and toast Kate?' said Harry.

'That's a nice idea,' replied Jenna. 'And we can get some fresh flowers to put on her grave.'

Kate, in accordance with her will, had been buried in the Alardyce kirkyard right alongside Amy and the others. Their grandmother had also been reinterred there. Kate's grave had become a shrine to her fans, who constantly left flowers and other trinkets. Paul had presided over her funeral.

The family took one last look at Alardyce House before wandering down the drive. Only Harry hung back.

'What's wrong?' Harmony asked him.

He waited until the others were out of earshot before replying. 'I've been carrying around a secret and it's time I shared it because it's killing me.'

'What secret?' she said with concern.

'The family secret, the real reason why our parents fell out with each other. I finally got the truth out of my mum the day after Kate was killed. She knew I wouldn't stop until she gave in – Cameron and Kate were brother and sister.'

Harmony's jaw fell open. 'Seriously?'

'Yes. His dad had an affair with her mum, not a colleague at work, and got her pregnant with Kate. They all took sides and it split the family. They wanted to keep us children apart so we'd never learn the truth.'

'Are you going to tell Cameron?'

'God, no. I'm only telling you because I have to get it off my chest and I know you won't breathe a word. Let him keep his memories of her. Finding out he fell in love with his own sister would finish him once and for all.'

'You're right, it would.'

'Anyway, it's all gone and in the past. Hopefully no Alardyce will ever live in this house again and all the misery will end. Now, to the future. Will you marry me?'

'You know I will, Harry, but are you sure you want to go through it for the fifth time?'

'Absolutely, the fifth and last. Recent events have changed me. I'll love you and only you for the rest of my life, if you'll have this balding, ageing, pot-bellied idiot?'

She smiled and slid her arms around his neck. 'I certainly will and it's perfect timing because I'm pregnant.'

Harry beamed. 'You're sure?'

'I did a test this morning and then I did another one. There's no doubt.'

'You wonderful, amazing woman,' he said, kissing her. Something good had come out of this terrible tragedy. Not only had he found happiness again but it far exceeded anything he'd ever known before.

The two of them walked down the drive together hand in hand. Harry glanced over his shoulder at the house and swore he would keep his wife and child away from it. They would never set foot in the place again. It wasn't taking them too.

* * *

MORE FROM HEATHER ATKINSON

Another book from Heather Atkinson, *Pride*, is available to order now here:
https://mybook.to/PrideBackAd

ABOUT THE AUTHOR

Heather Atkinson is the author of over fifty books - predominantly in the crime fiction genre. Although Lancashire born and bred she now lives with her family, including twin teenage daughters, on the beautiful west coast of Scotland.

Download your exclusive bonus content from Heather Atkinson here:

Visit Heather's website: www.thebooksofheatheratkinson.godaddysites.com

Follow Heather on social media:

facebook.com/booksofheatheratkinson

instagram.com/heatheratkinsonauthor

ALSO BY HEATHER ATKINSON

Wicked Girls

The House of Lies

The Savage Sisters Series

Savage Sisters

A Savage Feud

A Savage Betrayal

A Savage Inheritance

Savage Blood

The Gallowburn Series

Blood Brothers

Bad Blood

Blood Ties

Blood Pact

The Alardyce Series

The Missing Girls of Alardyce House

The Cursed Heir

His Fatal Legacy

Evil at Alardyce House

The Bloody MacGregors

Fury

Pride

www.ingramcontent.com/pod-product-compliance
Ingram Content Group UK Ltd.
Pitfield, Milton Keynes, MK11 3LW, UK
UKHW041837290126
10389UKWH00009B/122

9 781806 562381